An Interlude for Love

by Émile Zola

Grand Oak Books
2013

GRAND OAK BOOKS

An Interlude for Love

Published by:
Grand Oak Books Publishing, Ltd
ISBN: 978-1-937727-51-2
Library of Congress Cataloging-in-Publication Data:

Zola, Émile (1840-1902)/An Interlude for Love

An Interlude
for Love

by Émile Zola

CHAPTER I.

The night-lamp with a bluish shade was burning on the chimney-piece, behind a book, whose shadows plunged more than half the chamber in darkness. There was a quiet gleam of light cutting across the round table and the couch, streaming over the heavy folds of the velvet curtains, and imparting an azure hue to the mirror of the rosewood wardrobe placed between the two windows. The quiet simplicity of the room, the blue tints on the hangings, furniture, and carpet, served at this hour of night to invest everything with the delightful vagueness of cloudland. Facing the windows, and within sweep of the shadow, loomed the velvet-curtained bed, a black mass, relieved only by the white of the sheets. With hands crossed on her bosom, and breathing lightly, lay Helene, asleep—mother and widow alike personified by the quiet unrestraint of her attitude.

In the midst of the silence one o'clock chimed from the timepiece. The noises of the neighborhood had died away; the dull, distant roar of the city was the only sign of life that disturbed those Trocadero heights. Helene's breathing, so light and gentle, did not ruffle the chaste repose of her bosom. She was in a beauteous sleep, peaceful yet sound, her profile perfect, her nut-brown hair twisted into a knot, and her head leaning forward somewhat, as though she had fallen asleep while eagerly listening. At the farther end of the room the open door of an adjoining closet seemed but a black square in the wall.

Still there was not a sound. The half-hour struck. The pendulum gave but a feeble tick-tack amid the general drowsiness that brooded over the whole chamber. Everything was sleeping, night-lamp and furniture alike; on the table, near an extinguished lamp, some woman's handiwork was disposed also in slumber. Helene in her sleep retained her air of gravity and kindliness.

Two o'clock struck, and the stillness was broken. A deep sigh issued from the darkness of the closet. There was a rustling of linen sheets, and then silence reigned again. Anon labored breathing broke through the gloom. Helene had not moved. Suddenly, however, she started up, for the moanings and cries of a child in pain had roused her. Dazed with sleep, she pressed her hands against her temples, but hearing a stifled sob, she leaped from her couch on to the carpet.

"Jeanne, my Jeanne, what ails you? tell me, love," she asked; and as the child remained silent, she murmured, while running towards the night-light, "Gracious Heaven! why did I go to bed when she was so ill?"

Quickly she entered the closet, where deep silence had again fallen. The feeble gleam of the lamp threw but a circular patch of light on the ceiling. Bending over the iron cot, she could at first make out nothing, but amidst the bed-clothes, tossed about in disorder, the dim light soon revealed Jeanne, with limbs quite stiff, her head flung back, the muscles of her neck swollen and rigid. Her sweet face was distorted, her eyes were open and fixed on the curtain-rod above.

"My child!" cried Helene. "My God, my God, she is dying."

Setting down the lamp, Helene touched her daughter with trembling hands. The throbbing of the pulse and the heart's action seemed to have died away. The child's puny arms and legs were stretched out convulsively, and the mother grew frantic at the sight.

"My child is dying! Help, help!" she stammered. "My child, my child!"

She wandered back to her room, brushing against the furniture, and unconscious of her movements; then, distracted, she again returned to the little bed, throwing herself on her knees, and ever appealing for help. She took Jeanne in her arms, rained kisses on her hair, and stroked her little body, begging her to answer, and seeking one word—only one word—from her silent lips. Where was the pain? Would she have some of the cooling drink she had liked the other day? Perhaps the fresh air would revive her? So she rattled on, bent on making the child speak.

"Speak to me, Jeanne, speak to me, I entreat you!"

Oh, God, and not to know what to do in this sudden terror born of the night! There was no light even. Then her ideas grew confused, though her supplications to the child continued—at one moment she was beseeching, at another answering in her own person. Thus, the pain gripped her in the stomach; no, no, it must be in the breast. It was nothing at all; she need merely keep quiet. Then Helene tried to collect her scattered senses; but as she felt her daughter stark and stiff in her embrace, her heart sickened unto death. She tried to reason with herself, and to resist the yearning to scream. But all at once, despite herself, her cry rang out

"Rosalie, Rosalie, my child is dying. Quick, hurry for the doctor."

Screaming out these words, she ran through dining-room and kitchen to a room in the rear, where the maid started up from sleep, giving vent to her surprise. Helene speeded back again. Clad only in her night-dress she moved about, seemingly not feeling the icy cold of the February night. Pah, this maid would loiter, and her child would die, Back again she hurried through the kitchen to the bedroom before a minute had elapsed. Violently, and in the dark, she slipped on a petticoat, and threw a shawl over her shoulders. The furniture in her way was overturned; the room so still and silent was filled with the echoes of her despair. Then leaving the doors open, she rushed down three flights of stairs in her slippers, consumed with the thought that she alone could bring back a doctor.

After the house-porter had opened the door Helene found herself upon the pavement, with a ringing in her ears and her mind distracted. However, she quickly ran down the Rue Vineuse and pulled the doorbell of Doctor Bodin, who had already tended Jeanne; but a servant—after an interval which seemed an eternity—informed her that the doctor was attending a woman in childbed. Helene remained stupefied on the footway; she knew no other doctor in Passy. For a few moments she rushed about the streets, gazing at the houses. A slight but keen wind was blowing, and she was walking in slippers through the light snow that had fallen during the evening. Ever before her was her daughter, with the agonizing thought that she was killing her by not finding a doctor at once. Then, as she retraced her steps along the Rue Vineuse, she rang the bell of another house. She would inquire, at all events; someone would perhaps direct her. She gave a second tug at the bell; but no one seemed to come. The wind meanwhile played with her petticoat, making it cling to her legs, and tossed her disheveled hair.

At last a servant answered her summons. "Doctor Deberle was in bed asleep." It was a doctor's house at which she had rung, so Heaven had not abandoned her, Straightway, intent upon entering, she pushed the servant aside, still repeating her prayer:

"My child, my child is dying! Oh, tell him he must come!"

The house was small and seemed full of hangings. She reached the first floor, despite the servant's opposition, always answering his protest with the words, "My child is dying!" In the apartment she entered she would have been content to wait; but the moment she heard the doctor stirring in the next room she drew near and appealed to him through the doorway:

"Oh, sir, come at once, I beseech you. My child is dying!"

When the doctor at last appeared in a short coat and without a tie, she dragged him away without allowing him to finish dressing. He at once recognized her as a resident in the next-door house, and one of his own tenants; so when he induced her to cross a garden—to shorten the way by using a side-door between the two houses —memory suddenly awoke within her.

"True, you are a doctor," she murmured, "and I knew it. But I was distracted. Oh, let us hurry!"

On the staircase she wished him to go first. She could not have admitted the Divinity to her home in a more reverent manner. Upstairs Rosalie had remained near the child, and had lit the large lamp on the table. After the doctor had entered the room he took up this lamp and cast its light upon the body of the child, which retained its painful rigidity; the head, however, had slipped forward, and nervous twitchings were ceaselessly drawing the face. For a minute he looked on in silence, his lips compressed. Helene anxiously watched him, and on noticing the mother's imploring glance, he muttered: "It will be nothing. But she must not lie here. She must have air."

Helene grasped her child in a strong embrace, and carried her away on her shoulder. She could have kissed the doctor's hand for his good tidings, and a wave of happiness rippled through her. Scarcely, however, had Jeanne been placed in the larger bed than her poor little frame was again seized with violent convulsions. The doctor had removed the shade from the lamp, and a white light was streaming through the room. Then, opening a window, he ordered Rosalie to drag the bed away from the curtains. Helene's heart was again filled with anguish. "Oh, sir, she is dying," she stammered. "Look! look! Ah! I scarcely recognize her."

The doctor did not reply, but watched the paroxysm attentively.

"Step into the alcove," he at last exclaimed. "Hold her hands to prevent her from tearing herself. There now, gently, quietly! Don't make yourself uneasy. The fit must be allowed to run its course."

They both bent over the bed, supporting and holding Jeanne, whose limbs shot out with sudden jerks. The doctor had buttoned up his coat to hide his bare neck, and Helene's shoulders had till now been enveloped in her shawl; but Jeanne in her struggles dragged a corner of the shawl away, and unbuttoned the top of the coat. Still they did not notice it; they never even looked at one another.

At last the convulsion ceased, and the little one then appeared to sink into deep prostration. Doctor Deberle was evidently ill at ease, though he had assured the mother that there was no danger. He kept his gaze fixed on the sufferer, and put some brief questions to Helene as she stood by the bedside.

"How old is the child?"

"Eleven years and six months, sir," was the reply.

Silence again fell between them. He shook his head, and stooped to raise one of Jeanne's lowered eyelids and examine the mucus. Then he resumed his questions, but without raising his eyes to Helene.

"Did she have convulsions when she was a baby?"

"Yes, sir; but they left her after she reached her sixth birthday. Ah! she is very delicate. For some days past she had seemed ill at ease. She was at times taken with cramp, and plunged in a stupor."

"Do you know of any members of your family that have suffered from nervous affections?"

"I don't know. My mother was carried off by consumption."

Here shame made her pause. She could not confess that she had a grandmother who was an inmate of a lunatic asylum. There was something tragic connected with all her ancestry.

"Take care! the convulsions are coming on again!" now hastily exclaimed the doctor.

Jeanne had just opened her eyes, and for a moment she gazed around her with a vacant look, never speaking a word. Her glance then grew fixed, her body was violently thrown backwards, and her limbs became distended and rigid. Her skin, fiery-red, all at once turned livid. Her pallor was the pallor of death; the convulsions began once more.

"Do not lose your hold of her," said the doctor. "Take her other hand."

He ran to the table, where, on entering, he had placed a small med-

icine-case. He came back with a bottle, the contents of which he made
Jeanne inhale; but the effect was like that of a terrible lash; the child
gave such a violent jerk that she slipped from her mother's hands.

"No, no, don't give her ether," exclaimed Helene, warned by the
odor. "It drives her mad."

The two had now scarcely strength enough to keep the child under
control. Her frame was racked and distorted, raised by the heels and
the nape of the neck, as if bent in two. But she fell back again and
began tossing from one side of the bed to the other. Her fists were
clenched, her thumbs bent against the palms of her hands. At times
she would open the latter, and, with fingers wide apart, grasp at phantom bodies in the air, as though to twist them. She touched her mother's
shawl and fiercely clung to it. But Helene's greatest grief was that she
no longer recognized her daughter. The suffering angel, whose face was
usually so sweet, was transformed in every feature, while her eyes swam,
showing balls of a nacreous blue.

"Oh, do something, I implore you," she murmured. "My strength
is exhausted, sir."

She had just remembered how the child of a neighbor at Marseilles
had died of suffocation in a similar fit. Perhaps from feelings of pity the
doctor was deceiving her. Every moment she believed she felt Jeanne's
last breath against her face; for the child's halting respiration seemed
suddenly to cease. Heartbroken and overwhelmed with terror, Helene
then burst into tears, which fell on the body of her child, who had
thrown off the bedclothes.

The doctor meantime was gently kneading the base of the neck
with his long supple fingers. Gradually the fit subsided, and Jeanne,
after a few slight twitches, lay there motionless. She had fallen back in
the middle of the bed, with limbs outstretched, while her head, supported by the pillow, inclined towards her bosom. One might have
thought her an infant Jesus. Helene stooped and pressed a long kiss on
her brow.

"Is it over?" she asked in a whisper. "Do you think she'll have another fit?"

The doctor made an evasive gesture, and then replied:

"In any case the others will be less violent."

He had asked Rosalie for a glass and water-bottle. Half-filling the
glass with water, he took up two fresh medicine phials, and counted

out a number of drops. Helene assisted in raising the child's head, and the doctor succeeded in pouring a spoonful of the liquid between the clenched teeth. The white flame of the lamp was leaping up high and clear, revealing the disorder of the chamber's furnishings. Helene's garments, thrown on the back of an arm-chair before she slipped into bed, had now fallen, and were littering the carpet. The doctor had trodden on her stays, and had picked them up lest he might again find them in his way. An odor of vervain stole through the room. The doctor himself went for the basin, and soaked a linen cloth in it, which he then pressed to Jeanne's temples.

"Oh, madame, you'll take cold," expostulated Rosalie as she stood there shivering. "Perhaps the window might be shut? The air is too raw."

"No, no," cried Helene; "leave the window open. Should it not be so?" she appealed to the doctor.

The wind entered in slight puffs, rustling the curtains to and fro; but she was quite unconscious of it. Yet the shawl had slipped off her shoulders, and her hair had become unwound, some wanton tresses sweeping down to her hips. She had left her arms free and uncovered, that she might be the more ready; she had forgotten all, absorbed entirely in her love for her child. And on his side, the doctor, busy with his work, no longer thought of his unbuttoned coat, or of the shirt-collar that Jeanne's clutch had torn away.

"Raise her up a little," said he to Helene. "No, no, not in that way! Give me your hand."

He took her hand and placed it under the child's head. He wished to give Jeanne another spoonful of the medicine. Then he called Helene close to him, made use of her as his assistant; and she obeyed him reverently on seeing that her daughter was already more calm.

"Now, come," he said. "You must let her head lean against your shoulder, while I listen."

Helene did as he bade her, and he bent over her to place his ear against Jeanne's bosom. He touched her bare shoulder with his cheek, and as the pulsation of the child's heart struck his ear he could also have heard the throbbing of the mother's breast. As he rose up his breath mingled with Helene's.

"There is nothing wrong there," was the quiet remark that filled her with delight. "Lay her down again. We must not worry her more."

However, another, though much less violent, paroxysm followed.

From Jeanne's lips burst some broken words. At short intervals two fresh attacks seemed about to convulse her, and then a great prostration, which again appeared to alarm the doctor, fell on the child. He had placed her so that her head lay high, with the clothes carefully tucked under her chin; and for nearly an hour he remained there watching her, as though awaiting the return of a healthy respiration. On the other side of the bed Helene also waited, never moving a limb.

Little by little a great calm settled on Jeanne's face. The lamp cast a sunny light upon it, and it regained its exquisite though somewhat lengthy oval. Jeanne's fine eyes, now closed, had large, bluish, transparent lids, which veiled—one could divine it—a sombre, flashing glance. A light breathing came from her slender nose, while round her somewhat large mouth played a vague smile. She slept thus, amidst her outspread tresses, which were inky black.

"It has all passed away now," said the doctor in a whisper; and he turned to arrange his medicine bottles prior to leaving.

"Oh, sir," exclaimed Helene, approaching him, "don't leave me yet; wait a few minutes. Another fit might come on, and you, you alone, have saved her!"

He signed to her that there was nothing to fear; yet he tarried, with the idea of tranquillizing her. She had already sent Rosalie to bed; and now the dawn soon broke, still and grey, over the snow which whitened the housetops. The doctor proceeded to close the window, and in the deep quiet the two exchanged a few whispers.

"There is nothing seriously wrong with her, I assure you," said he; "only with one so young great care must be taken. You must see that her days are spent quietly and happily, and without shocks of any kind."

"She is so delicate and nervous," replied Helene after a moment's pause. "I cannot always control her. For the most trifling reasons she is so overcome by joy or sorrow that I grow alarmed. She loves me with a passion, a jealousy, which makes her burst into tears when I caress another child."

"So, so—delicate, nervous, and jealous," repeated the doctor as he shook his head. "Doctor Bodin has attended her, has he not? I'll have a talk with him about her. We shall have to adopt energetic treatment. She has reached an age that is critical in one of her sex."

Recognizing the interest he displayed, Helene gave vent to her gratitude. "How I must thank you, sir, for the great trouble you have taken!"

The loudness of her tones frightened her, however; she might have woke Jeanne, and she bent down over the bed. But no; the child was sound asleep, with rosy cheeks, and a vague smile playing round her lips. The air of the quiet chamber was charged with languor. The whilom drowsiness, as if born again of relief, once more seized upon the curtains, furniture, and littered garments. Everything was steeped restfully in the early morning light as it entered through the two windows.

Helene again stood up close to the bed; on the other side was the doctor, and between them lay Jeanne, lightly sleeping.

"Her father was frequently ill," remarked Helene softly, continuing her answer to his previous question. "I myself enjoy the best of health."

The doctor, who had not yet looked at her, raised his eyes, and could scarcely refrain from smiling, so hale and hearty was she in every way. She greeted his gaze with her own sweet and quiet smile. Her happiness lay in her good health.

However, his looks were still bent on her. Never had he seen such classical beauty. Tall and commanding, she was a nut-brown Juno, of a nut-brown sunny with gleams of gold. When she slowly turned her head, its profile showed the severe purity of a statue. Her grey eyes and pearly teeth lit up her whole face. Her chin, rounded and somewhat pronounced, proved her to be possessed of commonsense and firmness. But what astonished the doctor was the superbness of her whole figure. She stood there, a model of queenliness, chastity, and modesty.

On her side also she scanned him for a moment. Doctor Deberle's years were thirty-five; his face was clean-shaven and a little long; he had keen eyes and thin lips. As she gazed on him she noticed for the first time that his neck was bare. Thus they remained face to face, with Jeanne asleep between them. The distance which but a short time before had appeared immense, now seemed to be dwindling away. Then Helene slowly wrapped the shawl about her shoulders again, while the doctor hastened to button his coat at the neck.

"Mamma! mamma!" Jeanne stammered in her sleep. She was waking, and on opening her eyes she saw the doctor and became uneasy.

"Mamma, who's that?" was her instant question; but her mother kissed her, and replied: "Go to sleep, darling, you haven't been well. It's only a friend."

The child seemed surprised; she did not remember anything.

Drowsiness was coming over her once more, and she fell asleep again, murmuring tenderly: "I'm going to by-by. Good-night, mamma, dear. If he is your friend he will be mine."

The doctor had removed his medicine-case, and, with a silent bow, he left the room. Helene listened for a while to the child's breathing, and then, seated on the edge of the bed, she became oblivious to everything around her; her looks and thoughts wandering far away. The lamp, still burning, was paling in the growing sunlight.

CHAPTER II.

Next day Helene thought it right and proper to pay a visit of thanks to Doctor Deberle. The abrupt fashion in which she had compelled him to follow her, and the remembrance of the whole night which he had spent with Jeanne, made her uneasy, for she realized that he had done more than is usually compassed within a doctor's visit. Still, for two days she hesitated to make her call, feeling a strange repugnance towards such a step. For this she could give herself no reasons. It was the doctor himself who inspired her with this hesitancy; one morning she met him, and shrunk from his notice as though she were a child. At this excess of timidity she was much annoyed. Her quiet, upright nature protested against the uneasiness which was taking possession of her. She decided, therefore, to go and thank the doctor that very day.

Jeanne's attack had taken place during the small hours of Wednesday morning; it was now Saturday, and the child was quite well again. Doctor Bodin, whose fears concerning her had prompted him to make an early call, spoke of Doctor Deberle with the respect that an old doctor with a meagre income pays to another in the same district, who is young, rich, and already possessed of a reputation. He did not forget to add, however, with an artful smile, that the fortune had been bequeathed by the elder Deberle, a man whom all Passy held in veneration. The son had only been put to the trouble of inheriting fifteen hundred thousand francs, together with a splendid practice. "He is, though, a very smart fellow," Doctor Bodin hastened to add, "and I shall be honored by having a consultation with him about the precious health of my little friend Jeanne."

About three o'clock Helene made her way downstairs with her daughter, and had to take but a few steps along the Rue Vineuse before

ringing at the next-door house. Both mother and daughter still wore
deep mourning. A servant, in dress-coat and white tie, opened the door.
Helene easily recognized the large entrance-hall, with its Oriental hangings; on each side of it, however, there were now flower-stands, brilliant
with a profusion of blossoms. The servant having admitted them to a
small drawing-room, the hangings and furniture of which were of a
mignonette hue, stood awaiting their pleasure, and Helene gave her
name—Madame Grandjean.

Thereupon the footman pushed open the door of a drawing-room,
furnished in yellow and black, of dazzling effect, and, moving aside,
announced:

"Madame Grandjean."

Helene, standing on the threshold, started back. She had just noticed at the other end of the room a young woman seated near the fireplace on a narrow couch which was completely covered by her ample
skirts. Facing her sat an elderly person, who had retained her bonnet
and shawl, and was evidently paying a visit.

"I beg pardon," exclaimed Helene. "I wished to see Doctor Deberle."

She had made the child enter the room before her, and now took
her by the hand again. She was both astonished and embarrassed in
meeting this young lady. Why had she not asked for the doctor? She
well knew he was married.

Madame Deberle was just finishing some story, in a quick and rather
shrill voice.

"Oh, it's marvelous, marvelous! She dies with wonderful realism.
She clutches at her bosom like this, throws back her head, and her face
turns green. I declare you ought to see her, Mademoiselle Aurelie!"

Then, rising up, she sailed towards the doorway, rustling her skirts
terribly.

"Be so kind as to walk in, madame," she said with charming gra-
ciousness. "My husband is not at home, but I shall be delighted to receive you, I assure you. This must be the pretty little girl who was so ill
a few nights ago. Sit down for a moment, I beg of you."

Helene was forced to accept the invitation, while Jeanne timidly
perched herself on the edge of another chair. Madame Deberle again
sank down on her little sofa, exclaiming with a pretty laugh,

"Yes, this is my day. I receive every Saturday, you see, and Pierre then announces all comers. A week or two ago he ushered in a colonel suffering from the gout."

"How silly you are, my dear Juliette," expostulated Mademoiselle Aurelie, the elderly lady, an old friend in straitened circumstances, who had seen her come into the world.

There was a short silence, and Helene gazed round at the luxury of the apartment, with its curtains and chairs in black and gold, glittering like constellations. Flowers decorated mantel-shelf, piano, and tables alike, and the clear light streamed through the windows from the garden, in which could be seen the leafless trees and bare soil. The room had almost a hot-house temperature; in the fireplace one large log was glowing with intense heat. After another glance Helene recognized that the gaudy colors had a happy effect. Madame Deberle's hair was inky-black, and her skin of a milky whiteness. She was short, plump, slow in her movements, and withal graceful. Amidst all the golden decorations, her white face assumed a vermeil tint under her heavy, sombre tresses. Helene really admired her.

"Convulsions are so terrible," broke in Madame Deberle. "My Lucien had them when a mere baby. How uneasy you must have been, madame! However, the dear little thing appears to be quite well now."

As she drawled out these words she kept her eyes on Helene, whose superb beauty amazed and delighted her. Never had she seen a woman with so queenly an air in the black garments which draped the widow's commanding figure. Her admiration found vent in an involuntary smile, while she exchanged glances with Mademoiselle Aurelie. Their admiration was so ingenuously and charmingly expressed, that a faint smile also rippled over Helene's face.

Then Madame Deberle stretched herself on the sofa. "You were not at the first night at the Vaudeville yesterday, madame?" she asked, as she played with the fan that hung from her waist.

"I never go to the theatre," was Helene's reply.

"Oh, little Noemi was simply marvelous! Her death scene is so realistic. She clutches her bosom like this, throws back her head, and her face turns green. Oh, the effect is prodigious."

Thereupon she entered into a minute criticism of the actress's playing, which she upheld against the world; and then she passed to the other topics of the day—a fine art exhibition, at which she had seen some most remarkable paintings; a stupid novel about which too much fuss was being made; a society intrigue which she spoke of to Mademoiselle Aurelie in veiled language. And so she went on from one subject to another, without wearying, her tongue ever ready, as though this social atmosphere were peculiarly her own. Helene, a stranger to such society, was content to listen, merely interjecting a remark or brief reply every now and then.

At last the door was again thrown open and the footman announced: "Madame de Chermette! Madame Tissot!"

Two ladies entered, magnificently dressed. Madame Deberle rose eagerly to meet them, and the train of her black silk gown, heavily decked with trimmings, trailed so far behind her that she had to kick it out of her way whenever she happened to turn round. A confused babel of greetings in shrill voices arose.

"Oh, how kind of you. I declare I never see you!"

"You know we come about that lottery."

"Yes: I know, I know."

"Oh, we cannot sit down. We have to call at twenty houses yet."

"Come now, you are not going to run away at once."

And then the visitors finished by sitting down on the edge of a couch; the chatter beginning again, shriller than ever.

"Well, what do you think of yesterday at the Vaudeville?"

"Oh, it was splendid."

"You know she unfastens her dress and lets down her hair. All the effect springs from that."

"People say that she swallows something to make her green."

"No, no, every action is premeditated; but she had to invent and study them all, in the first place."

"It's wonderful."

The two ladies rose and made their exit, and the room regained its tranquil peacefulness. From some hyacinths on the mantel-shelf was wafted an all-pervading perfume. For a time one could hear the noisy twittering of some sparrows quarrelling on the lawn. Before resuming her seat, Madame Deberle proceeded to draw down the embroidered tulle blind of a window facing her, and then returned to her sofa in the mellowed, golden light of the room.

"I beg pardon," she now said. "We have had quite an invasion."

Then, in an affectionate way, she entered into conversation with Helene. She seemed to know some details of her history, doubtless from the gossip of her servants. With a boldness that was yet full of tact, and appeared instinct with much friendliness, she spoke to Helene of her husband, and of his sad death at the Hotel du Var, in the Rue de Richelieu.

"And you had just arrived, hadn't you? You had never been in Paris before. It must be awful to be plunged into mourning, in a strange room, the day after a long journey, and when one doesn't know a single place to go to."

Helene assented with a slow nod. Yes, she had spent some very bitter hours. The disease which carried off her husband had abruptly declared itself on the day after their arrival, just as they were going out together. She knew none of the streets, and was wholly unaware what district she was in. For eight days she had remained at the bedside of the dying man, hearing the rumble of Paris beneath her window, feeling she was alone, deserted, lost, as though plunged in the depths of an abyss. When she stepped out on the pavement for the first time, she was a widow. The mere recalling of that bare room, with its rows of medicine bottles, and with the travelling trunks standing about unpacked, still made her shudder.

"Was your husband, as I've been told, nearly twice your age?" asked Madame Deberle with an appearance of profound interest, while Mademoiselle Aurelie cocked her ears so as not to lose a syllable of the conversation.

"Oh, no," replied Helene. "He was scarcely six years older."

Then she ventured to enter into the story of her marriage, telling in a few brief sentences how her husband had fallen deeply in love with her while she was living with her father, Monsieur Mouret, a hatter in the Rue des Petites-Maries, at Marseilles; how the Grandjean family, who were rich sugar-refiners, were bitterly opposed to the match, on account of her poverty. She spoke, too, of the ill-omened and secret wedding after the usual legal formalities, and of their hand-to-mouth existence, till the day an uncle on dying left them some ten thousand francs a year. It was then that Grandjean, within whom an intense hatred of Marseilles was growing, had decided on coming to Paris, to live there for good.

"And how old were you when you were married?" was Madame Deberle's next question.

"Seventeen."

"You must have been very beautiful."

The conversation suddenly ceased, for Helene had not seemed to hear the remark.

"Madame Manguelin," announced the footman.

A young, retiring woman, evidently ill at ease, was ushered in. Madame Deberle scarcely rose. It was one of her dependents, who had called to thank her for some service performed. The visitor only remained for a few minutes, and left the room with a courtesy.

Madame Deberle then resumed the conversation, and spoke of Abbe Jouve, with whom both were acquainted. The Abbe was a meek officiating priest at Notre-Dame-de-Grace, the parish church of Passy; however, his charity was such that he was more beloved and more respectfully hearkened to than any other priest in the district.

"Oh, he has such pious eloquence," exclaimed Madame Deberle, with a sanctimonious look.

"He has been very kind to us," said Helene. "My husband had formerly known him at Marseilles. The moment he heard of my misfortune he took charge of everything. To him we owe our settling in Passy."

"He has a brother, hasn't he?" questioned Juliette.

"Yes, a step-brother, for his mother married again. Monsieur Rambaud was also acquainted with my husband. He has started a large business in the Rue de Rambuteau, where he sells oils and other Southern produce. I believe he makes a large amount of money by it." And she added, with a laugh: "The Abbe and his brother make up my court."

Jeanne, sitting on the edge of her chair, and wearied to death, now cast an impatient look at her mother. Her long, delicate, lamb-like face wore a pained expression, as if she disliked all this conversation; and she appeared at times to sniff the heavy, oppressive odors floating in the room, while casting suspicious side-glances at the furniture, as though her own exquisite sensibility warned her of some undefined dangers. Finally, however, she turned a look of tyrannical worship on her mother.

Madame Deberle noticed the child's uneasiness.

"Here's a little girl," she said, "who feels tired at being serious, like a grown-up person. There are some picture-books on the table, dear; they will amuse you."

Jeanne took up an album, but her eyes strayed from it to glance imploringly at her mother. Helene, charmed by her hostess's excessive kindness, did not move; there was nothing of the fidget in her, and she would of her own accord remain seated for hours. However, as the servant announced three ladies in succession—Madame Berthier, Madame de Guiraud, and Madame Levasseur—she thought she ought to rise.

"Oh, pray stop," exclaimed Madame Deberle; "I must show you my son."

The semi-circle round the fireplace was increasing in size. The ladies were all gossiping at the same time. One of them declared that she was completely broken down, as for five days she had not gone to bed till four o'clock in the morning. Another indulged in a diatribe against wet nurses; she could no longer find one who was honest. Next the conversation fell on dressmakers. Madame Deberle affirmed no woman tailor could fit you properly; a man was requisite. Two of the ladies, however, were mumbling something under their breath, and, a silence intervening, two or three words became audible. Every one then broke into a laugh, while languidly waving their fans.

"Monsieur Malignon," announced the servant.

A tall young man, dressed in good style, was ushered in. Some exclamations greeted him. Madame Deberle, not taking the trouble to rise, stretched out her hand and inquired: "Well, what of yesterday at the Vaudeville?"

"Vile," was his reply.

"What, vile? She's marvelous when she clutches her bosom and throws back her head—"

"Stop! stop! The whole thing is loathsome in its realism."

And then quite a dispute commenced. It was easy to talk of realism, but the young man would have no realism at all.

"I would not have it in anything, you hear," said he, raising his voice. "No, not in anything, it degrades art."

People would soon be seeing some fine things on the stage, indeed. Why didn't Noemi follow out her actions to their logical conclusion? And he illustrated his remark with a gesture which quite scandalized the ladies. Oh, how horrible! However, when Madame Deberle had declared that the actress produced a great effect, and Madame Levasseur had related how a lady had fainted in the balcony, everybody agreed that the affair was a great success; and with this the discussion stopped short.

The young man sat in an arm-chair, with his legs stretched out

among the ladies' flowing skirts. He seemed to be quite at home in the
doctor's house. He had mechanically plucked a flower from a vase, and
was tearing it to pieces with his teeth. Madame Deberle interrupted
him:

"Have you read that novel which——"

He did not allow her to finish, but replied, with a superior air, that
he only read two novels in the year.

As for the exhibition of paintings at the Art Club, it was not worth
troubling about; and then, every topic being exhausted, he rose and
leaned over Juliette's little sofa, conversing with her in a low voice, while
the other ladies continued chatting together in an animated manner.

At length: "Dear me, he's gone," exclaimed Madame Berthier turning round. "I met him only an hour ago in Madame Robinot's drawing-
room."

"Yes, and he is now going to visit Madame Lecomte," said Madame
Deberle. "He goes about more than any other man in Paris." She turned
to Helene, who had been following the scene, and added: "A very dis-
tinguished young fellow he is, and we like him very much. He has some
interest in a stockbroking business; he's very rich besides, and well
posted in everything."

The other ladies, however, were now going off.

"Good-bye, dear madame. I rely upon you for Wednesday."

"Yes, to be sure; Wednesday."

"Oh, by the way, will you be at that evening party? One doesn't
know whom one may meet. If you go, I'll go."

"Ah, well, I'll go, I promise you. Give my best regards to Monsieur
de Guiraud."

When Madame Deberle returned she found Helene standing in the
middle of the drawing-room. Jeanne had drawn close to her mother,
whose hands she firmly grasped; and thus clinging to her caressingly
and almost convulsively, she was drawing her little by little towards the
doorway.

"Ah, I was forgetting," exclaimed the lady of the house; and ringing the bell for the servant, she said to him: "Pierre, tell Miss Smithson
to bring Lucien here."

During the short interval of waiting that ensued the door was again
opened, but this time in a familiar fashion and without any formal announcement. A good-looking girl of some sixteen years of age entered

in company with an old man, short of stature but with a rubicund, chubby face.

"Good-day, sister," was the girl's greeting, as she kissed Madame Deberle.

"Good-day, Pauline, good-day, father," replied the doctor's wife.

Mademoiselle Aurelie, who had not stirred from her seat beside the fire, rose to exchange greetings with Monsieur Letellier. He owned an extensive silk warehouse on the Boulevard des Capucines. Since his wife's death he had been taking his younger daughter about everywhere, in search of a rich husband for her.

"Were you at the Vaudeville last night?" asked Pauline.

"Oh, it was simply marvelous," repeated Juliette in parrot-fashion, as, standing before a mirror, she rearranged a rebellious curl.

"It is annoying to be so young; one can't go to anything," said Pauline, pouting like a spoiled child. "I went with papa to the theatre-door at midnight, to find out how the piece had taken."

"Yes, and we tumbled upon Malignon," said the father.

"He was extremely pleased with it."

"Really," exclaimed Juliette. "He was here a minute ago, and declared it vile. One never knows how to take him."

"Have you had many visitors to-day?" asked Pauline, rushing off to another subject.

"Oh, several ladies; quite a crowd. The room was never once empty. I'm dead-beat—"

Here she abruptly broke off, remembering she had a formal introduction to make

"My father, my sister—Madame Grandjean."

The conversation was turning on children and the ailments which give mothers so much worry when Miss Smithson, an English governess, appeared with a little boy clinging to her hand. Madame Deberle scolded her in English for having kept them waiting.

"Ah, here's my little Lucien," exclaimed Pauline as she dropped on her knees before the child, with a great rustling of skirts.

"Now, now, leave him alone!" said Juliette. "Come here, Lucien; come and say good-day to this little lady."

The boy came forward very sheepishly. He was no more than seven years old, fat and dumpy, and dressed as coquettishly as a doll. As he saw that they were all looking at him with smiles, he stopped short, and surveyed Jeanne, his blue eyes wide open with astonishment.

"Go on!" urged his mother.

He turned his eyes questioningly on her and advanced a step, evincing all the sullenness peculiar to lads of his age, his head lowered, his thick lips pouting, and his eyebrows bent into a growing frown. Jeanne must have frightened him with the serious look she wore standing there in her black dress. She had not ceased holding her mother's hand, and was nervously pressing her fingers on the bare part of the arm between the sleeve and glove. With head lowered she awaited Lucien's approach uneasily, like a young and timid savage, ready to fly from his caress. But a gentle push from her mother prompted her to step forward.

"Little lady, you will have to kiss him first," Madame Deberle said laughingly. "Ladies always have to begin with him. Oh! the little stupid."

"Kiss him, Jeanne," urged Helene.

The child looked up at her mother; and then, as if conquered by the bashful looks of the little noodle, seized with sudden pity as she gazed on his good-natured face, so dreadfully confused—she smiled divinely. A sudden wave of hidden tenderness rose within her and brightened her features, and she whispered: "Willingly, mamma!"

Then, taking Lucien under the armpits, almost lifting him from the ground, she gave him a hearty kiss on each cheek. He had no further hesitation in embracing her.

"Bravo, capital," exclaimed the onlookers.

With a bow Helene turned to leave, accompanied to the door by Madame Deberle.

"I beg you, madame," said she, "to present my heartiest thanks to the doctor. He relieved me of such dreadful anxiety the other night."

"Is Henri not at home?" broke in Monsieur Letellier.

"No, he will be away some time yet," was Juliette's reply. "But you're not going away; you'll dine with us," she continued, addressing Mademoiselle Aurelie, who had risen as if to leave with Madame Grandjean.

The old maid with each Saturday expected a similar invitation, then decided to relieve herself of shawl and bonnet. The heat in the drawing-room was intense, and Monsieur Letellier hastened to open a window, at which he remained standing, struck by the sight of a lilac bush which was already budding. Pauline, meantime, had begun playfully running after Lucien behind the chairs and couches, left in confusion by the visitors.

On the threshold Madame Deberle held out her hand to Helene with a frank and friendly movement.

"You will allow me," said she. "My husband spoke to me about you, and I felt drawn to you. Your bereavement, your lonely life—in short, I am very glad to have seen you, and you must not be long in coming back."

"I give you my promise, and I am obliged to you," said Helene, moved by these tokens of affection from a woman whom she had imagined rather flighty. They clasped hands, and each looked into the other's face with a happy smile. Juliette's avowal of her sudden friendship was given with a caressing air. "You are too lovely not to be loved!" she said.

Helene broke into a merry laugh, for her beauty never engaged her thoughts, and she called Jeanne, whose eyes were busy watching the pranks of Lucien and Pauline. But Madame Deberle detained the girl for a moment longer.

"You are good friends henceforth," she said; "you must just say *au revoir.*"

Thereupon the two children blew one another a kiss with their finger-tips.

CHAPTER III.

Every Tuesday Helene had Monsieur Rambaud and Abbe Jouve to dine with her. It was they who, during the early days of her bereavement, had broken in on her solitude, and drawn up their chairs to her table with friendly freedom; their object being to extricate her, at least once a week, from the solitude in which she lived. The Tuesday dinners became established institutions, and the partakers in these little feasts appeared punctually at seven o'clock, serenely happy in discharging what they deemed a duty.

That Tuesday Helene was seated at the window, profiting by the last gleams of the twilight to finish some needle work, pending the arrival of her guests. She here spent her days in pleasant peacefulness. The noises of the street died away before reaching such a height. She loved this large, quiet chamber, with its substantial luxury, its rosewood furniture and blue velvet curtains. When her friends had attended to her installation, she not having to trouble about anything, she had at first somewhat suffered from all this sombre luxury, in preparing which Monsieur Rambaud had realized his ideal of comfort, much to the admiration of his brother, who had declined the task. She was not long, however, in feeling happy in a home in which, as in her heart, all was sound and simple. Her only enjoyment during her long hours of work was to gaze before her at the vast horizon, the huge pile of Paris, stretching its roofs, like billows, as far as the eye could reach. Her solitary corner overlooked all that immensity.

"Mamma, I can no longer see," said Jeanne, seated near her on a low chair. And then, dropping her work, the child gazed at Paris, which was darkening over with the shadows of night. She rarely romped about, and her mother even had to exert authority to induce her to go out. In accordance with Doctor Bodin's strict injunction, Helene made her stroll with her two hours each day in the Bois de Boulogne, and this was their only promenade; in eighteen months they had not gone three times into Paris. Nowhere was Jeanne so evidently happy as in their large blue room. Her mother had been obliged to renounce her intention of having her taught music, for the sound of an organ in the silent streets made her tremble and drew tears from her eyes. Her favorite occupation was to assist her mother in sewing linen for the children of the Abbe's poor.

Night had quite fallen when the lamp was brought in by Rosalie, who, fresh from the glare of her range, looked altogether upset. Tuesday's dinner was the one event of the week, which put things topsy-turvy.

"Aren't the gentlemen coming here to-night, madame?" she inquired.

Helene looked at the timepiece: "It's a quarter to seven; they will be here soon," she replied.

Rosalie was a gift from Abbe Jouve, who had met her at the station on the day she arrived from Orleans, so that she did not know a single street in Paris. A village priest, an old schoolmate of Abbe Jouve's, had sent her to him. She was dumpy and plump, with a round face under her narrow cap, thick black hair, a flat nose, and deep red lips; and she was expert in preparing savory dishes, having been brought up at the parsonage by her godmother, servant to the village priest.

"Here is Monsieur Rambaud at last!" she exclaimed, rushing to open the door before there was even a ring.

Full and broad-shouldered, Monsieur Rambaud entered, displaying an expansive countenance like that of a country notary. His forty-five years had already silvered his hair, but his large blue eyes retained a wondering, artless, gentle expression, akin to a child's.

"And here's his reverence; everybody has come now!" resumed Rosalie, as she opened the door once more.

Whilst Monsieur Rambaud pressed Helene's hand and sat down without speaking, smiling like one who felt quite at home, Jeanne threw her arms round the Abbe's neck.

"Good-evening, dear friend," said she. "I've been so ill!"

"So ill, my darling?"

The two men at once showed their anxiety, the Abbe especially. He was a short, spare man, with a large head and awkward manners, and dressed in the most careless way; but his eyes, usually half-closed, now opened to their full extent, all aglow with exquisite tenderness. Jeanne relinquished one of her hands to him, while she gave the other to Monsieur Rambaud. Both held her and gazed at her with troubled looks. Helene was obliged to relate the story of her illness, and the Abbe was on the point of quarrelling with her for not having warned him of it. And then they each questioned her. "The attack was quite over now? She had not had another, had she?" The mother smiled as she listened.

"You are even fonder of her than I am, and I think you'll frighten me in the end," she replied. "No, she hasn't been troubled again, except that she has felt some pains in her limbs and had some headaches. But we shall get rid of these very soon."

The maid then entered to announce that dinner was ready.

The table, sideboard, and eight chairs furnishing the dining-room were of mahogany. The curtains of red reps had been drawn close by Rosalie, and a hanging lamp of white porcelain within a plain brass ring lighted up the tablecloth, the carefully-arranged plates, and the tureen of steaming soup. Each Tuesday's dinner brought round the same remarks, but on this particular day Dr. Deberle served naturally as a subject of conversation. Abbe Jouve lauded him to the skies, though he knew that he was no church-goer. He spoke of him, however, as a man of upright character, charitable to a fault, a good father, and a good husband—in fact, one who gave the best of examples to others. As for Madame Deberle she was most estimable, in spite of her somewhat flighty ways, which were doubtless due to her Parisian education. In a word, he dubbed the couple charming. Helene seemed happy to hear this; it confirmed her own opinions; and the Abbe's remarks determined her to continue the acquaintance, which had at first rather frightened her.

"You shut yourself up too much," declared the priest.

"No doubt," echoed his brother.

Helene beamed on them with her quiet smile, as though to say that they themselves sufficed for all her wants, and that she dreaded new acquaintances. However, ten o'clock struck at last, and the Abbe and his brother took up their hats. Jeanne had just fallen asleep in an easy-chair in the bedroom, and they bent over her, raising their heads with satisfied looks as they observed how tranquilly she slumbered. They stole from the room on tiptoe, and in the lobby whispered their good-byes:

"Till next Tuesday!"

"O, by the way," said the Abbe, returning a step or two, "I was for-getting: Mother Fetu is ill. You should go to see her."

"I will go to-morrow," answered Helene.

The Abbe had a habit of commissioning her to visit his poor. They engaged in all sorts of whispered talk together on this subject, private business which a word or two enabled them to settle together, and which they never referred to in the presence of other persons.

On the morrow Helene went out alone. She decided to leave Jeanne in the house, as the child had been troubled with fits of shivering since paying a visit of charity to an old man who had become paralyzed. Once out of doors, she followed the Rue Vineuse, turned down the Rue Raynouard, and soon found herself in the Passage des Eaux, a strange, steep lane, like a staircase, pent between garden walls, and con-ducting from the heights of Passy to the quay. At the bottom of this de-scent was a dilapidated house, where Mother Fetu lived in an attic lighted by a round window, and furnished with a wretched bed, a rick-ety table, and a seatless chair.

"Oh, my good lady, my good lady," she moaned out, directly she saw Helene enter.

The old woman was in bed. In spite of her wretchedness, her body was plump, swollen out, as it were, while her face was puffy, and her hands seemed numbed as she drew the tattered sheet over her. She had small, keen eyes and a whimpering voice, and displayed a noisy humil-ity in a rush of words.

"Ah, my good lady, how I thank you. Ah, ah, oh, how I suffer! It's just as if dogs were tearing at my side. I'm sure I have a beast inside me—see, just there. The skin isn't broken; the complaint is internal. But, oh, oh, the pain hasn't ceased for two days past. Good Lord, how is it possible to suffer so much? Ah, my good lady, thank you. You don't forget the poor. It will be taken into account up above; yes, yes, it will be taken into account."

Helene had sat down. Noticing on the table a jug of warm *tisane*, she filled a cup which was near at hand, and gave it to the sufferer. Near the jug were placed a packet of sugar, two oranges, and some other comfits.

"Has any one been to see you?" Helene asked.

"Yes, yes,—a little lady. But she doesn't know. That isn't the sort of stuff I need. Oh, if I could get a little meat. My next-door neighbor would cook it for me. Oh, oh, this pain is something dreadful! A dog is tearing at me—oh, if only I had some broth."

In spite of the pains which were racking her limbs, she kept her sharp eyes fixed on Helene, who was now busy fumbling in her pocket, and on seeing her visitor place a ten-franc piece on the table, she whimpered all the more, and tried to rise to a sitting posture. Whilst struggling, she extended her arm, and the money vanished, as she repeated:

"Gracious Heaven, this is another frightful attack. Oh, oh, I cannot stand such agony any longer! God will requite you, my good lady; I will pray to Him to requite you. Bless my soul, how these pains shoot through my whole body! His reverence Abbe Jouve promised me you would come. It's only you who know what I want. I am going to buy some meat. But now the pain's going down into my legs. Help me; I have no strength left—none left at all!"

The old woman wished to turn over, and Helene, drawing off her gloves, gently took hold of her and placed her as she desired. As she was still bending over her the door opened, and a flush of surprise mounted to her cheeks as she saw Dr. Deberle entering. Did he also make visits to which he never referred?

"It's the doctor!" blurted out the old woman. "Oh, Heaven must bless you both for being so good!"

The doctor bowed respectfully to Helene. Mother Fetu had ceased whining on his entrance, but kept up a sibilant wheeze, like that of a child in pain. She had understood at once that the doctor and her benefactress were known to one another; and her eyes never left them, but travelled from one to the other, while her wrinkled face showed that her mind was covertly working. The doctor put some questions to her, and sounded her right side; then, turning to Helene, who had just sat down, he said:

"She is suffering from hepatic colic. She will be on her feet again in a few days."

And, tearing from his memorandum book a leaf on which he had written some lines, he added, addressing Mother Fetu:

"Listen to me. You must send this to the chemist in the Rue de Passy, and every two hours you must drink a spoonful of the draught he will give you."

The old woman burst out anew into blessings. Helene remained seated. The doctor lingered gazing at her; but when their eyes had met, he bowed and discreetly took his leave. He had not gone down a flight ere Mother Fetu's lamentations were renewed.

"Ah, he's such a clever doctor! Ah, if his medicine could do me some good! Dandelions and tallow make a good simple for removing water from the body. Yes, yes, you can say you know a clever doctor. Have you known him long? Gracious goodness, how thirsty I am! I feel burning hot. He has a wife, hasn't he? He deserves to have a good wife and beautiful children. Indeed, it's a pleasure to see kind-hearted people good acquaintances."

Helene had risen to give her a drink.

"I must go now, Mother Fetu," she said. "Good-bye till to-morrow."

"Ah, how good you are. If I only had some linen! Look at my chemise —it's torn in half; and this bed is so dirty. But that doesn't matter. God will requite you, my good lady."

Next day, on Helene's entering Mother Fetu's room, she found Dr. Deberle already there. Seated on the chair, he was writing out a prescription, while the old woman rattled on with whimpering volubility.

"Oh, sir, it now feels like lead in my side—yes, just like lead! It's as heavy as a hundred-pound weight, and prevents me from turning round."

Then, having caught sight of Helene, she went on without a pause: "Ah, here's the good lady! I told the kind doctor you would come. Though the heavens might fall, said I, you would come all the same. You're a very saint, an angel from paradise, and, oh, so beautiful that people might fall on their knees in the streets to gaze on you as you pass! Dear lady, I am no better; just now I have a heavy feeling here. Oh, I have told the doctor what you did for me! The emperor could have done no more. Yes, indeed, it would be a sin not to love you—a great sin."

These broken sentences fell from her lips as, with eyes half closed, she rolled her head on the bolster, the doctor meantime smiling at Helene, who felt very ill at ease.

"Mother Fetu," she said softly, "I have brought you a little linen."

"Oh, thank you, thank you; God will requite you! You're just like this kind, good gentleman, who does more good to poor folks than a host of those who declare it their special work. You don't know what great care he has taken of me for four months past, supplying me with medicine and broth and wine. One rarely finds a rich person so kind to a poor soul. Oh, he's another of God's angels. Dear, dear, I seem to have quite a house in my stomach."

In his turn the doctor now seemed to be embarrassed. He rose and offered his chair to Helene; but although she had come with the intention of remaining a quarter of an hour, she declined to sit down, on the plea that she was in a great hurry.

Meanwhile, Mother Fetu, still rolling her head to and fro, had stretched out her hand, and the parcel of linen had vanished in the bed. Then she resumed:

"Oh, what a couple of good souls you are! I don't wish to offend you; I only say it because it's true. When you have seen one, you have seen the other. Oh, dear Lord! give me a hand and help me to turn round. Kind-hearted people understand one another. Yes, yes, they understand one another."

"Good-bye, Mother Fetu," said Helene, leaving the doctor in sole possession. "I don't think I shall call to-morrow."

The next day, however, found her in the attic again. The old woman was sound asleep, but scarcely had she opened her eyes and recognized Helene in her black dress sitting on the chair than she exclaimed:

"He has been here—oh, I really don't know what he gave me to take, but I am as stiff as a stick. We were talking about you. He asked me all kinds of questions; whether you were generally sad, and whether your look was always the same. Oh, he's such a good man!"

Her words came more slowly, and she seemed to be waiting to see by the expression of Helene's face what effect her remarks might have on her, with that wheedling, anxious air of the poor who are desirous of pleasing people. No doubt she fancied she could detect a flush of displeasure mounting to her benefactress's brow, for her huge, puffed-up face, all eagerness and excitement, suddenly clouded over; and she resumed, in stammering accents:

"I am always asleep. Perhaps I have been poisoned. A woman in the Rue de l'Annonciation was killed by a drug which the chemist gave her in mistake for another."

That day Helene lingered for nearly half an hour in Mother Fetu's room, hearing her talk of Normandy, where she had been born, and where the milk was so good. During a silence she asked the old woman carelessly: "Have you known the doctor a long time?"

Mother Fetu, lying on her back, half-opened her eyes and again closed them.

"Oh, yes!" she answered, almost in a whisper. "For instance, his father attended to me before '48, and he accompanied him then."

"I have been told the father was a very good man."

"Yes, but a little cracked. The son is much his superior. When he touches you you would think his hands were of velvet."

Silence again fell.

"I advise you to do everything he tells you," at last said Helene. "He is very clever; he saved my daughter."

"To be sure!" exclaimed Mother Fetu, again all excitement. "People ought to have confidence in him. Why, he brought a boy to life again when he was going to be buried! Oh, there aren't two persons like him; you won't stop me from saying that! I am very lucky; I fall in with the pick of good-hearted people. I thank the gracious Lord for it every night. I don't forget either of you. You are mingled together in my prayers. May God in His goodness shield you and grant your every wish! May He load you with His gifts! May He keep you a place in Paradise!"

She was now sitting up in bed with hands clasped, seemingly entreating Heaven with devout fervor. Helene allowed her to go on thus for a considerable time, and even smiled. The old woman's chatter, in fact, ended by lulling her into a pleasant drowsiness, and when she went off she promised to give her a bonnet and gown, as soon as she should be able to get about again.

Throughout that week Helene busied herself with Mother Fetu. Her afternoon visit became an item in her daily life. She felt a strange fondness for the Passage des Eaux. She liked that steep lane for its coolness and quietness and its ever-clean pavement, washed on rainy days by the water rushing down from the heights. A strange sensation thrilled her as she stood at the top and looked at the narrow alley with its steep declivity, usually deserted, and only known to the few inhabitants of the neighboring streets. Then she would venture through an archway dividing a house fronting the Rue Raynouard, and trip down the seven flights of broad steps, in which lay the bed of a pebbly stream occupying half of the narrow way. The walls of the gardens on each side bulged out, coated with a grey, leprous growth; umbrageous trees drooped over, foliage rained down, here and there an ivy plant thickly mantled the stonework, and the chequered verdure, which only left glimpses of the blue sky above, made the light very soft and greeny. Halfway down Helene would stop to take breath, gazing at the street-lamp which hung there, and listening to the merry laughter in the gardens, whose doors she had never seen open. At times an old woman panted up with the aid of the black, shiny, iron handrail fixed in the wall to the right; a lady would come, leaning on her parasol as on a walking-stick; or a band of urchins would run down, with a great stamping of feet. But almost always Helene found herself alone, and this steep, secluded, shady descent was to her a veritable delight —like a path in the depths of a forest. At the bottom she would raise her eyes, and the sight of the narrow, precipitous alley she had just descended made her feel somewhat frightened.

She glided into the old woman's room with the quiet and coolness of the Passage des Eaux clinging to her garments. This woefully wretched den no longer affected her painfully. She moved about there as if in her own rooms, opening the round attic window to admit the fresh air, and pushing the table into a corner if it came in her way. The garret's bareness, its whitewashed walls and rickety furniture, realized to her mind an existence whose simplicity she had sometimes dreamt of in her girlhood. But what especially charmed her was the kindly emotion she experienced there. Playing the part of sick nurse, hearing the constant bewailing of the old woman, all she saw and felt within the four walls left her quivering with deep pity. In the end she awaited with evident impatience Doctor Deberle's customary visit. She questioned him as to Mother Fetu's condition; but from this they glided to other subjects, as they stood near each other, face to face. A closer acquaintance was springing up between them, and they were surprised to find they possessed similar tastes. They understood one another without speaking a word, each heart engulfed in the same overflowing charity. Nothing to Helene seemed sweeter than this mutual feeling, which arose in such an unusual way, and to which she yielded without resistance, filled as she was with divine pity. At first she had felt somewhat afraid of the doctor; in her own drawing-room she would have been cold and distrustful, in harmony with her nature. Here, however, in this garret they were far from the world, sharing the one chair, and almost happy in the midst of the wretchedness and poverty which filled their souls with emotion. A week passed, and they knew one another as though they had been intimate for years. Mother Fetu's miserable abode was filled with sunshine, streaming from this fellowship of kindliness.

The old woman grew better very slowly. The doctor was surprised, and charged her with coddling herself when she related that she now felt a dreadful weight in her legs. She always kept up her monotonous moaning, lying on her back and rolling her head to and fro; but she closed her eyes, as though to give her visitors an opportunity for unrestrained talk. One day she was to all appearance sound asleep, but beneath their lids her little black eyes continued watching. At last, however, she had to rise from her bed; and next day Helene presented her with the promised bonnet and gown. When the doctor made his appearance that afternoon the old woman's laggard memory seemed suddenly stirred. "Gracious goodness!" said she, "I've forgotten my neighbor's soup-pot; I promised to attend to it!"

Then she disappeared, closing the door behind her and leaving the couple alone. They did not notice that they were shut in, but continued their conversation. The doctor urged Helene to spend the afternoon occasionally in his garden in the Rue Vineuse.

"My wife," said he, "must return your visit, and she will in person repeat my invitation. It would do your daughter good."

"But I don't refuse," she replied, laughing. "I do not require to be fetched with ceremony. Only—only—I am afraid of being indiscreet. At any rate, we will see."

Their talk continued, but at last the doctor exclaimed in a tone of surprise: "Where on earth can Mother Fetu have gone? It must be a quarter of an hour since she went to see after her neighbor's soup-pot."

Helene then saw that the door was shut, but it did not shock her at the moment. She continued to talk of Madame Deberle, of whom she spoke highly to her husband; but noticing that the doctor constantly glanced towards the door, she at last began to feel uncomfortable.

"It's very strange that she does not come back!" she remarked in her turn.

Their conversation then dropped. Helene, not knowing what to do, opened the window; and when she turned round they avoided looking at one another. The laughter of children came in through the circular window, which, with its bit of blue sky, seemed like a full round moon. They could not have been more alone—concealed from all inquisitive looks, with merely this bit of heaven gazing in on them. The voices of the children died away in the distance; and a quivering silence fell. No one would dream of finding them in that attic, out of the world. Their confusion grew apace, and in the end Helene, displeased with herself, gave the doctor a steady glance.

"I have a great many visits to pay yet," he at once exclaimed. "As she doesn't return, I must leave."

He quitted the room, and Helene then sat down. Immediately afterwards Mother Fetu returned with many protestations:

"Oh! oh! I can scarcely crawl; such a faintness came over me! Has the dear good doctor gone? Well, to be sure, there's not much comfort here! Oh, you are both angels from heaven, coming to spend your time with one so unfortunate as myself! But God in His goodness will requite you. The pain has gone down into my feet to-day, and I had to sit down on a step. Oh, I should like to have some chairs! If I only had an easy-chair! My mattress is so vile too that I am quite ashamed when you come. The whole place is at your disposal, and I would throw myself into the fire if you required it. Yes. Heaven knows it; I always repeat it in my prayers! Oh, kind Lord, grant their utmost desires to these good friends of mine—in the name of the Father, the Son, and the Holy Ghost!"

As Helene listened she experienced a singular feeling of discomfort. Mother Fetu's bloated face filled her with disgust. Never before in this stifling attic had she been affected in a like way; its sordid misery seemed to stare her in the face; the lack of fresh air, the surrounding wretchedness, quite sickened her. So she made all haste to leave, feeling hurt by the blessings which Mother Fetu poured after her.

In the Passage des Eaux an additional sorrow came upon her. Halfway up, on the right-hand side of the path, the wall was hollowed out, and here there was an excavation, some disused well, enclosed by a railing. During the last two days when passing she had heard the wailings of a cat rising from this well, and now, as she slowly climbed the path, these wailings were renewed, but so pitifully that they seemed instinct with the agony of death. The thought that the poor brute, thrown into the disused well, was slowly dying there of hunger, quite rent Helene's heart. She hastened her steps, resolving that she would not venture down this lane again for a long time, lest the cat's death-call should reach her ears.

The day was a Tuesday. In the evening, on the stroke of seven, as

Helene was finishing a tiny bodice, the two wonted rings at the bell were heard, and Rosalie opened the door.

"His reverence is first to-night!" she exclaimed. "Oh, here comes Monsieur Rambaud too!"

They were very merry at dinner. Jeanne was nearly well again now, and the two brothers, who spoiled her, were successful in procuring her permission to eat some salad, of which she was excessively fond, notwithstanding Doctor Bodin's formal prohibition. When she was going to bed, the child in high spirits hung round her mother's neck and pleaded:

"Oh! mamma, darling! let me go with you to-morrow to see the old woman you nurse!"

But the Abbe and Monsieur Rambaud were the first to scold her for thinking of such a thing. They would not hear of her going amongst the poor, as the sight affected her too grievously. The last time she had been on such an expedition she had twice swooned, and for three days her eyes had been swollen with tears, that had flowed even in her sleep.

"Oh! I will be good!" she pleaded. "I won't cry, I promise."

"It is quite useless, my darling," said her mother, caressing her. "The old woman is well now. I shall not go out any more; I'll stay all day with you!"

CHAPTER IV.

During the following week Madame Deberle paid a return visit to Madame Grandjean, and displayed an affability that bordered on affection.

"You know what you promised me," she said, on the threshold, as she was going off. "The first fine day we have, you must come down to the garden, and bring Jeanne with you. It is the doctor's strict injunction."

"Very well," Helene answered, with a smile, "it is understood; we will avail ourselves of your kindness."

Three days later, on a bright February afternoon, she accompanied her daughter down to the garden. The porter opened the door connecting the two houses. At the near end of the garden, in a kind of greenhouse built somewhat in the style of a Japanese pavilion, they found Madame Deberle and her sister Pauline, both idling away their time, for some embroidery, thrown on the little table, lay there neglected.

"Oh, how good of you to come!" cried Juliette. "You must sit down here. Pauline, move that table away! It is still rather cool you know to sit out of doors, but from this pavilion we can keep a watch on the children. Now, little ones, run away and play; but take care not to fall!"

The large door of the pavilion stood open, and on each side were portable mirrors, whose covers had been removed so that they allowed one to view the garden's expanse as from the threshold of a tent. The garden, with a green sward in the center, flanked by beds of flowers, was separated from the Rue Vineuse by a plain iron railing, but against this grew a thick green hedge, which prevented the curious from gazing in. Ivy, clematis, and woodbine clung and wound around the railings, and behind this first curtain of foliage came a second one of lilacs and laburnums. Even in the winter the ivy leaves and the close network of branches sufficed to shut off the view. But the great charm of the garden lay in its having at the far end a few lofty trees, some magnificent elms, which concealed the grimy wall of a five-story house. Amidst all the neighboring houses these trees gave the spot the aspect of a nook in some park, and seemed to increase the dimensions of this little Parisian garden, which was swept like a drawing-room. Between two of the elms hung a swing, the seat of which was green with damp.

Helene leaned forward the better to view the scene.

"Oh, it is a hole!" exclaimed Madame Deberle carelessly. "Still, trees are so rare in Paris that one is happy in having half a dozen of one's own."

"No, no, you have a very pleasant place," murmured Helene.

The sun filled the pale atmosphere that day with a golden dust, its rays streaming slowly through the leafless branches of the trees. These assumed a ruddier tint, and you could see the delicate purple gems softening the cold grey of the bark. On the lawn and along the walks the grass and gravel glittered amidst the haze that seemed to ooze from the ground. No flower was in blossom; only the happy flush which the sunshine cast upon the soil revealed the approach of spring.

"At this time of year it is rather dull," resumed Madame Deberle. "In June it is as cozy as a nest; the trees prevent any one from looking in, and we enjoy perfect privacy." At this point she paused to call: "Lucien, you must come away from that watertap!"

The lad, who was doing the honors of the garden, had led Jeanne towards a tap under the steps. Here he had turned on the water, which he allowed to splash on the tips of his boots. It was a game that he delighted in. Jeanne, with grave face, looked on while he wetted his feet.

"Wait a moment!" said Pauline, rising. "I'll go and stop his nonsense!"

But Juliette held her back.

"You'll do no such thing; you are even more of a madcap than he is. The other day both of you looked as if you had taken a bath. How is it that a big girl like you cannot remain two minutes seated? Lucien!" she continued directing her eyes on her son, "turn off the water at once!"

The child, in his fright, made an effort to obey her. But instead of turning the tap off, he turned it on all the more, and the water gushed forth with a force and a noise that made him lose his head. He recoiled, splashed up to the shoulders.

"Turn off the water at once!" again ordered his mother, whose cheeks were flushing with anger.

Jeanne, hitherto silent, then slowly, and with the greatest caution, ventured near the tap; while Lucien burst into loud sobbing at sight of this cold stream, which terrified him, and which he was powerless to stop. Carefully drawing her skirt between her legs, Jeanne stretched out her bare hands so as not to wet her sleeves, and closed the tap without receiving a sprinkle. The flow instantly ceased. Lucien, astonished and inspired with respect, dried his tears and gazed with swollen eyes at the girl.

"Oh, that child puts me beside myself!" exclaimed Madame Deberle, her complexion regaining its usual pallor, while she stretched herself out, as though wearied to death.

Helene deemed it right to intervene. "Jeanne," she called, "take his hand, and amuse yourselves by walking up and down."

Jeanne took hold of Lucien's hand, and both gravely paced the paths with little steps. She was much taller than her companion, who had to stretch his arm up towards her; but this solemn amusement, which consisted in a ceremonious circuit of the lawn, appeared to absorb them and invest them with a sense of great importance. Jeanne, like a genuine lady, gazed about, preoccupied with her own thoughts; Lucien every now and then would venture a glance at her; but not a word was said by either.

"How droll they are!" said Madame Deberle, smiling, and again at her ease. "I must say that your Jeanne is a dear, good child. She is so obedient, so well behaved—"

"Yes, when she is in the company of others," broke in Helene. "She is a great trouble at times. Still, she loves me, and does her best to be good so as not to vex me."

Then they spoke of children; how girls were more precocious than boys; though it would be wrong to deduce too much from Lucien's unintelligent face. In another year he would doubtless lose all his gawkiness and become quite a gallant. Finally, Madame Deberle resumed her embroidery, making perhaps two stitches in a minute. Helene, who was only happy when busy, begged permission to bring her work the next time she came. She found her companions somewhat dull, and whiled away the time in examining the Japanese pavilion. The walls and ceiling were hidden by tapestry worked in gold, with designs showing bright cranes in full flight, butterflies, and flowers and views in which blue ships were tossing upon yellow rivers. Chairs, and ironwood flower-stands were scattered about; on the floor some fine mats were spread; while the lacquered furnishings were littered with trinkets, small bronzes and vases, and strange toys painted in all the hues of the rainbow. At the far end stood a grotesque idol in Dresden china, with bent legs and bare, protruding stomach, which at the least movement shook its head with a terrible and amusing look.

"Isn't it horribly ugly?" asked Pauline, who had been watching Helene as she glanced round. "I say, sister, you know that all these purchases of yours are so much rubbish! Malignon calls your Japanese museum 'the sixpenny bazaar.' Oh, by the way, talking of him, I met him. He was with a lady, and such a lady—Florence, of the Varietes Theatre."

"Where was it?" asked Juliette immediately. "How I shall tease him!"

"On the boulevards. He's coming here to-day, is he not?"

She was not vouchsafed any reply. The ladies had all at once become uneasy owing to the disappearance of the children, and called to them. However, two shrill voices immediately answered:

"We are here!"

Half hidden by a spindle tree, they were sitting on the grass in the middle of the lawn.

"What are you about?"

"We have put up at an inn," answered Lucien. "We are resting in our room."

Greatly diverted, the women watched them for a time. Jeanne seemed quite contented with the game. She was cutting the grass around her, doubtless with the intention of preparing breakfast. A piece of wood, picked up among the shrubs, represented a trunk. And now they were talking. Jeanne, with great conviction in her tone, was declaring that they were in Switzerland, and that they would set out to see the glaciers, which rather astonished Lucien.

"Ha, here he is!" suddenly exclaimed Pauline.

Madame Deberle turned, and caught sight of Malignon descending the steps. He had scarcely time to make his bow and sit down before she attacked him.

"Oh," she said, "it is nice of you to go about everywhere saying that I have nothing but rubbishy ornaments about me!"

"You mean this little saloon of yours? Oh yes," said he, quite at his ease. "You haven't anything worth looking at here!"

"What! not my china figure?" she asked, quite hurt.

"No, no, everything is quite *bourgeois*. It is necessary for a person to have some taste. You wouldn't allow me to select the things—"

"Your taste, forsooth! just talk about your taste!" she retorted, flushing crimson and feeling quite angry. "You have been seen with a lady—"

"What lady?" he asked, surprised by the violence of the attack.

"A fine choice, indeed! I compliment you on it. A girl whom the whole of Paris knows—"

She suddenly paused, remembering Pauline's presence.

"Pauline," she said, "go into the garden for a minute."

"Oh no," retorted the girl indignantly. "It's so tiresome; I'm always being sent out of the way."

"Go into the garden," repeated Juliette, with increased severity in her tone.

The girl stalked off with a sullen look, but stopped all at once, to exclaim: "Well, then, be quick over your talk!"

As soon as she was gone, Madame Deberle returned to the charge. "How can you, a gentleman, show yourself in public with that actress Florence? She is at least forty. She is ugly enough to frighten one, and all the gentlemen in the stalls thee and thou her on first nights."

"Have you finished?" called out Pauline, who was strolling sulkily under the trees. "I'm not amusing myself here, you know."

Malignon, however, defended himself. He had no knowledge of this girl Florence; he had never in his life spoken a word to her. They had possibly seen him with a lady: he was sometimes in the company of the wife of a friend of his. Besides, who had seen him? He wanted proofs, witnesses.

"Pauline," hastily asked Madame Deberle, raising her voice, "did you not meet him with Florence?"

"Yes, certainly," replied her sister. "I met them on the boulevards opposite Bignon's."

Thereupon, glorying in her victory over Malignon, whose face wore an embarrassed smile, Madame Deberle called out: "You can come back, Pauline; I have finished."

Malignon, who had a box at the Folies-Dramatiques for the following night, now gallantly placed it at Madame Deberle's service, apparently not feeling the slightest ill-will towards her; moreover, they were always quarreling. Pauline wished to know if she might go to see the play that was running, and as Malignon laughed and shook his head, she declared it was very silly; authors ought to write plays fit for girls to see. She was only allowed such entertainments as *La Dame Blanche* and the classic drama could offer.

Meantime, the ladies had ceased watching the children, and all at once Lucien began to raise terrible shrieks.

"What have you done to him, Jeanne?" asked Helene.

"I have done nothing, mamma," answered the little girl. "He has thrown himself on the ground."

The truth was, the children had just set out for the famous glaciers. As Jeanne pretended that they were reaching the mountains, they had lifted their feet very high, as though to step over the rocks. Lucien, however, quite out of breath with his exertions, at last made a false step, and fell sprawling in the middle of an imaginary ice-field. Disgusted, and furious with child-like rage, he no sooner found himself on the ground than he burst into tears.

"Lift him up," called Helene.

"He won't let me, mamma. He is rolling about."

And so saying, Jeanne drew back, as though exasperated and annoyed by such a display of bad breeding. He did not know how to play; he would certainly cover her with dirt. Her mouth curled, as though she were a duchess compromising herself by such companionship. Thereupon Madame Deberle, irritated by Lucien's continued wailing, requested her sister to pick him up and coax him into silence. Nothing loth, Pauline ran, cast herself down beside the child, and for a moment rolled on the ground with him. He struggled with her, unwilling to be lifted, but she at last took him up by the arms, and to appease him, said, "Stop crying, you noisy fellow; we'll have a swing!"

Lucien at once closed his lips, while Jeanne's solemn looks vanished, and a gleam of ardent delight illumined her face. All three ran towards the swing, but it was Pauline who took possession of the seat.

"Push, push!" she urged the children; and they pushed with all the force of their tiny hands; but she was heavy, and they could scarcely stir the swing.

"Push!" she urged again. "Oh, the big sillies, they can't!"

In the pavilion, Madame Deberle had just felt a slight chill. Despite the bright sunshine she thought it rather cold, and she requested Malignon to hand her a white cashmere burnous that was hanging from the handle of a window fastening. Malignon rose to wrap the burnous round her shoulders, and they began chatting familiarly on matters which had little interest for Helene. Feeling fidgety, fearing that Pauline might unwittingly knock the children down, she therefore stepped into the garden, leaving Juliette and the young man to wrangle over some new fashion in bonnets which apparently deeply interested them.

Jeanne no sooner saw her mother than she ran towards her with a wheedling smile, and entreaty in every gesture. "Oh, mamma, mamma!" she implored. "Oh, mamma!"

"No, no, you mustn't!" replied Helene, who understood her meaning very well. "You know you have been forbidden."

Swinging was Jeanne's greatest delight. She would say that she believed herself a bird; the breeze blowing in her face, the lively rush through the air, the continued swaying to and fro in a motion as rythmic as the beating of a bird's wings, thrilled her with an exquisite pleasure; in her ascent towards cloudland she imagined herself on her way to heaven. But it always ended in some mishap. On one occasion she had been found clinging to the ropes of the swing in a swoon, her large eyes wide open, fixed in a vacant stare; at another time she had fallen to the ground, stiff, like a swallow struck by a shot.

"Oh, mamma!" she implored again. "Only a little, a very, very little!"

In the end her mother, in order to win peace, placed her on the seat. The child's face lit up with an angelic smile, and her bare wrists quivered with joyous expectancy. Helene swayed her very gently.

"Higher, mamma, higher!" she murmured.

But Helene paid no heed to her prayer, and retained firm hold of the rope. She herself was glowing all over, her cheeks flushed, and she thrilled with excitement at every push she gave to the swing. Her wonted sedateness vanished as she thus became her daughter's playmate.

"That will do," she declared after a time, taking Jeanne in her arms.

"Oh, mamma, you must swing now!" the child whispered, as she clung to her neck.

She took a keen delight in seeing her mother flying through the air; as she said, her pleasure was still more intense in gazing at her than in having a swing herself. Helene, however, asked her laughingly who would push her; when she went in for swinging, it was a serious matter; why, she went higher than the treetops! While she was speaking it happened that Monsieur Rambaud made his appearance under the guidance of the doorkeeper. He had met Madame Deberle in Helene's rooms, and thought he would not be deemed presuming in presenting himself here when unable to find her. Madame Deberle proved very gracious, pleased as she was with the good-natured air of the worthy man; however, she soon returned to a lively discussion with Malignon.

"*Bon ami* will push you, mamma! *Bon ami* will push you!" Jeanne called out, as she danced round her mother.

"Be quiet! We are not at home!" said her mother with mock gravity.

"Bless me! if it will please you, I am at your disposal," exclaimed Monsieur Rambaud. "When people are in the country—"

Helene let herself be persuaded. When a girl she had been accustomed to swing for hours, and the memory of those vanished pleasures created a secret craving to taste them once more. Moreover, Pauline, who had sat down with Lucien at the edge of the lawn, intervened with the boldness of a girl freed from the trammels of childhood.

"Of course he will push you, and he will swing me after you. Won't you, sir?"

This determined Helene. The youth which dwelt within her, in spite of the cold demureness of her great beauty, displayed itself in a charming, ingenuous fashion. She became a thorough school-girl, unaffected and gay. There was no prudishness about her. She laughingly declared that she must not expose her legs, and asked for some cord to tie her skirts securely round her ankles. That done, she stood upright on the swing, her arms extended and clinging to the ropes.

"Now, push, Monsieur Rambaud," she exclaimed delightedly. "But gently at first!"

Monsieur Rambaud had hung his hat on the branch of a tree. His broad, kindly face beamed with a fatherly smile. First he tested the strength of the ropes, and, giving a look at the trees, determined to give a slight push. That day Helene had for the first time abandoned her widow's weeds; she was wearing a grey dress set off with mauve bows. Standing upright, she began to swing, almost touching the ground, and as if rocking herself to sleep.

"Quicker! quicker!" she exclaimed.

Monsieur Rambaud, with his hands ready, caught the seat as it came back to him, and gave it a more vigorous push. Helene went higher, each ascent taking her farther. However, despite the motion, she did not lose her sedateness; she retained almost an austre demeanor; her eyes shone very brightly in her beautiful, impassive face; her nostrils only were inflated, as though to drink in the air.

Not a fold of her skirts was out of place, but a plait of her hair slipped down.

"Quicker! quicker!" she called.

An energetic push gave her increased impetus. Up in the sunshine she flew, even higher and higher. A breeze sprung up with her motion, and blew through the garden; her flight was so swift that they could scarcely distinguish her figure aright. Her face was now all smiles, and flushed with a rosy red, while her eyes sparkled here, then there, like shooting stars. The loosened plait of hair rustled against her neck. Despite the cords which bound them, her skirts now waved about, and you could divine that she was at her ease, her bosom heaving in its free enjoyment as though the air were indeed her natural place.

"Quicker! quicker!"

Monsieur Rambaud, his face red and bedewed with perspiration, exerted all his strength. A cry rang out. Helene went still higher.

"Oh, mamma! Oh, mamma!" repeated Jeanne in her ecstasy.

She was sitting on the lawn gazing at her mother, her little hands clasped on her bosom, looking as though she herself had drunk in all the air that was stirring. Her breath failed her; with a rythmical movement of the shoulders she kept time with the long strokes of the swing. And she cried, "Quicker! quicker!" while her mother still went higher, her feet grazing the lofty branches of the trees.

"Higher, mamma! oh, higher, mamma!"

But Helene was already in the very heavens. The trees bent and cracked as beneath a gale. Her skirts, which were all they could see, flapped with a tempestuous sound. When she came back with arms stretched out and bosom distended she lowered her head slightly and for a moment hovered; but then she rose again and sank backwards, her head tilted, her eyes closed, as though she had swooned. These ascensions and descents which made her giddy were delightful. In her flight she entered into the sunshine—the pale yellow February sunshine that rained down like golden dust. Her chestnut hair gleamed with amber tints; and a flame seemed to have leaped up around her, as the mauve bows on her whitening dress flashed like burning flowers. Around her the springtide was maturing into birth, and the purple-tinted gems of the trees showed like delicate lacquer against the blue sky.

Jeanne clasped her hands. Her mother seemed to her a saint with a golden glory round her head, winging her way to paradise, and she again stammered: "Oh, mamma! oh! mamma!"

Madame Deberle and Malignon had now grown interested, and had stepped under the trees. Malignon declared the lady to be very bold.

"I should faint, I'm sure," said Madame Deberle, with a frightened air.

Helene heard them, for she dropped these words from among the branches: "Oh, my heart is all right! Give a stronger push, Monsieur Rambaud!"

And indeed her voice betrayed no emotion. She seemed to take no heed of the two men who were onlookers. They were doubtless nothing to her. Her tress of hair had become entangled, and the cord that confined her skirts must have given way, for the drapery flapped in the wind like a flag. She was going still higher.

All at once, however, the exclamation rang out:

"Enough, Monsieur Rambaud, enough!"

Doctor Deberle had just appeared on the house steps. He came forward, embraced his wife tenderly, took up Lucien and kissed his brow. Then he gazed at Helene with a smile.

"Enough, enough!" she still continued exclaiming.

"Why?" asked he. "Do I disturb you?"

She made no answer; a look of gravity had suddenly come over her face. The swing, still continuing its rapid flights, owing to the impetus given to it, would not stop, but swayed to and fro with a regular motion which still bore Helene to a great height. The doctor, surprised and charmed, beheld her with admiration; she looked so superb, so tall and strong, with the pure figure of an antique statue whilst swinging thus gently amid the spring sunshine. But she seemed annoyed, and all at once leaped down.

"Stop! stop!" they all cried out.

From Helene's lips came a dull moan; she had fallen upon the gravel of a pathway, and her efforts to rise were fruitless.

"Good heavens!" exclaimed the doctor, his face turning very pale. "How imprudent!"

They all crowded round her. Jeanne began weeping so bitterly that Monsieur Rambaud, with his heart in his mouth, was compelled to take her in his arms. The doctor, meanwhile, eagerly questioned Helene.

"Is it the right leg you fell on? Cannot you stand upright?" And as she remained dazed, without answering, he asked: "Do you suffer?"

"Yes, here at the knee; a dull pain," she answered, with difficulty.

He at once sent his wife for his medicine case and some bandages, and repeated:

"I must see, I must see. No doubt it is a mere nothing."

He knelt down on the gravel and Helene let him do so; but all at once she struggled to her feet and said: "No, no!"

"But I must examine the place," he said.

A slight quiver stole over her, and she answered in a yet lower tone: "It is not necessary. It is nothing at all."

He looked at her, at first astounded. Her neck was flushing red; for a moment their eyes met, and seemed to read each other's soul; he was disconcerted, and slowly rose, remaining near her, but without pressing her further.

Helene had signed to Monsieur Rambaud. "Fetch Doctor Bodin," she whispered in his ear, "and tell him what has happened to me."

Ten minutes later, when Doctor Bodin made his appearance, she, with superhuman courage, regained her feet, and leaning on him and Monsieur Rambaud, contrived to return home. Jeanne followed, quivering with sobs.

"I shall wait," said Doctor Deberle to his brother physician. "Come down and remove our fears."

In the garden a lively colloquy ensued. Malignon was of opinion that women had queer ideas. Why on earth had that lady been so foolish as to jump down? Pauline, excessively provoked at this accident, which deprived her of a pleasure, declared it was silly to swing so high. On his side Doctor Deberle did not say a word, but seemed anxious.

"It is nothing serious," said Doctor Bodin, as he came down again —"only a sprain. Still, she will have to keep to an easy-chair for at least a fortnight."

Thereupon Monsieur Deberle gave a friendly slap on Malignon's shoulder. He wished his wife to go in, as it was really becoming too cold. For his own part, taking Lucien in his arms, he carried him into the house, covering him with kisses the while.

CHAPTER V.

Both windows of the bedroom were wide open, and in the depths below the house, which was perched on the very summit of the hill, lay Paris, rolling away in a mighty flat expanse. Ten o'clock struck; the lovely February morning had all the sweetness and perfume of spring.

Helene reclined in an invalid chair, reading in front of one of the windows, her knee still in bandages. She suffered no pain; but she had been confined to her room for a week past, unable even to take up her customary needlework. Not knowing what to do, she had opened a book which she had found on the table—she, who indulged in little or no reading at any time. This book was the one she used every night as a shade for the night-lamp, the only volume which she had taken within eighteen months from the small but irreproachable library selected by Monsieur Rambaud. Novels usually seemed to her false to life and puerile; and this one, Sir Walter Scott's "Ivanhoe," had at first wearied her to death. However, a strange curiosity had grown upon her, and she was finishing it, at times affected to tears, and at times rather bored, when she would let it slip from her hand for long minutes and gaze fixedly at the far-stretching horizon.

That morning Paris awoke from sleep with a smiling indolence. A mass of vapor, following the valley of the Seine, shrouded the two banks from view. This mist was light and milky, and the sun, gathering strength, was slowly tinging it with radiance. Nothing of the city was distinguishable through this floating muslin. In the hollows the haze thickened and assumed a bluish tint; while over certain broad expanses delicate transparencies appeared, a golden dust, beneath which you could divine the depths of the streets; and up above domes and steeples rent the mist, rearing grey outlines to which clung shreds of the haze which they had pierced. At times cloudlets of yellow smoke would, like giant birds, heavy of wing, slowly soar on high, and then mingle with the atmosphere which seemed to absorb them. And above all this immensity, this mass of cloud, hanging in slumber over Paris, a sky of extreme purity, of a faint and whitening blue, spread out its mighty vault. The sun was climbing the heavens, scattering a spray of soft rays; a pale golden light, akin in hue to the flaxen tresses of a child, was streaming down like rain, filling the atmosphere with the warm quiver of its sparkle. It was like a festival of the infinite, instinct with sovereign peacefulness and gentle gaiety, whilst the city, chequered with golden beams, still remained lazy and sleepy, unwilling to reveal itself by casting off its coverlet of lace.

For eight days it had been Helene's diversion to gaze on that mighty expanse of Paris, and she never wearied of doing so. It was as unfathomable and varying as the ocean—fair in the morning, ruddy with fire at night, borrowing all the joys and sorrows of the heavens reflected in its depths. A flash of sunshine came, and it would roll in waves of gold; a cloud would darken it and raise a tempest. Its aspect was ever changing. A complete calm would fall, and all would assume an orange hue; gusts of wind would sweep by from time to time, and turn everything livid; in keen, bright weather there would be a shimmer of light on every housetop; whilst when showers fell, blurring both heaven and earth, all would be plunged in chaotic confusion. At her window Helene experienced all the hopes and sorrows that pertain to the open sea. As the keen wind blew in her face she imagined it wafted a saline fragrance; even the ceaseless noise of the city seemed to her like that of a surging tide beating against a rocky cliff.

The book fell from her hands. She was dreaming, with a far-away look in her eyes. When she stopped reading thus it was from a desire to linger and understand what she had already perused. She took a delight in denying her curiosity immediate satisfaction. The tale filled her soul with a tempest of emotion. Paris that morning was displaying the same vague joy and sorrow as that which disturbed her heart. In this lay a great charm—to be ignorant, to guess things dimly, to yield to slow initiation, with the vague thought that her youth was beginning again.

How full of lies were novels! She was assuredly right in not reading them. They were mere fables, good for empty heads with no proper conception of life. Yet she remained entranced, dreaming unceasingly of the knight Ivanhoe, loved so passionately by two women—Rebecca, the beautiful Jewess, and the noble Lady Rowena. She herself thought she could have loved with the intensity and patient serenity of the latter maiden. To love! to love! She did not utter the words, but they thrilled her through and through in the very thought, astonishing her, and irradiating her face with a smile. In the distance some fleecy cloudlets, driven by the breeze, now floated over Paris like a flock of swans. Huge gaps were being cleft in the fog; a momentary glimpse was given of the left bank, indistinct and clouded, like a city of fairydom seen in a dream; but suddenly a thick curtain of mist swept down, and the fairy city was engulfed, as though by an inundation. And then the vapors, spreading equally over every district, formed, as it were, a beautiful lake, with milky, placid waters. There was but one denser streak, indicating the grey, curved course of the Seine. And slowly over those milky, placid waters shadows passed, like vessels with pink sails, which the young woman followed with a dreamy gaze. To love! to love! She smiled as her dream sailed on.

However, she again took up her book. She had reached the chapter describing the attack on the castle, wherein Rebecca nurses the wounded Ivanhoe, and recounts to him the incidents of the fight, which she gazes at from a window. Helene felt that she was in the midst of a beautiful falsehood, but roamed through it as through some mythical garden, whose trees are laden with golden fruit, and where she imbibed all sorts of fancies. Then, at the conclusion of the scene, when Rebecca, wrapped in her veil, exhales her love beside the sleeping knight, Helene again allowed the book to slip from her hand; her heart was so brimful of emotion that she could read no further.

Heavens! could all those things be true? she asked, as she lay back in her easy-chair, numbed by her enforced quiescence, and gazing on Paris, shrouded and mysterious, beneath the golden sun. The events of her life now arose before her, conjured up by the perusal of the novel. She saw herself a young girl in the house of her father, Mouret, a hatter at Marseilles. The Rue des Petites-Maries was black and dismal, and the house, with its vat of steaming water ready to the hand of the hatter, exhaled a rank odor of dampness, even in fine weather. She also saw her mother, who was ever an invalid, and who kissed her with pale lips, without speaking. No gleam of the sun penetrated into her little room. Hard work went on around her; only by dint of toil did her father gain a workingman's competency. That summed up her early life, and till her marriage nothing intervened to break the monotony of days ever the same. One morning, returning from market with her mother, a basketful of vegetables on her arm, she jostled against young Grandjean. Charles turned round and followed them. The love-romance of her life was in this incident. For three months she was always meeting him, while he, bashful and awkward, could not pluck up courage to speak to her. She was sixteen years of age, and a little proud of her lover, who, she knew, belonged to a wealthy family. But she deemed him bad-looking, and often laughed at him, and no thought of him disturbed her sleep in the large, gloomy, damp house. In the end they were married, and this marriage yet filled her with surprise. Charles worshipped her, and would fling himself on the floor to kiss her bare feet. She beamed on him, her smile full of kindness, as she rebuked him for such childishness. Then another dull life began. During twelve years no event of sufficient interest had occurred for her to bear in mind. She was very quiet and very happy, tormented by no fever either of body or heart; her whole attention being given to the daily cares of a poor household. Charles was still wont to kiss her fair white feet, while she showed herself indulgent and motherly towards him. But other feeling she had none. Then there abruptly came before her the room in the Hotel du Var, her husband in his coffin, and her widow's robe hanging over a chair. She had wept that day as on the winter's night when her mother died. Then once more the days glided on; for two months with her daughter she had again enjoyed peace and happiness. Heaven! did that sum up everything? What, then, did that book mean when it spoke of transcendent loves which illumine one's existence?

While she thus reflected prolonged quivers were darting over the sleeping lake of mist on the horizon. Suddenly it seemed to burst, gaps appeared, a rending sped from end to end, betokening a complete break-up. The sun, ascending higher and higher, scattering its rays in glorious triumph, was victoriously attacking the mist. Little by little the great lake seemed to dry up, as though some invisible sluice were draining the plain. The fog, so dense but a moment before, was losing its consistency and becoming transparent, showing all the bright hues of the rainbow. On the left bank of the Seine all was of a heavenly blue, deepening into violet over towards the Jardin des Plantes. Upon the right bank a pale pink, flesh-like tint suffused the Tuileries district; while away towards Montmartre there was a fiery glow, carmine flaming amid gold. Then, farther off, the working-men's quarters deepened to a dusty brick-color, changing more and more till all became a slatey, bluish grey. The eye could not yet distinguish the city, which quivered and receded like those subaqueous depths divined through the crystalline waves, depths with awful forests of huge plants, swarming with horrible things and monsters faintly espied. However, the watery mist was quickly falling. It became at last no more than a fine muslin drapery; and bit by bit this muslin vanished, and Paris took shape and emerged from dreamland.

To love! to love! Why did these words ring in Helene's ears with such sweetness as the darkness of the fog gave way to light? Had she not loved her husband, whom she had tended like a child? But a bitter memory stirred within her—the memory of her dead father, who had hung himself three weeks after his wife's decease in a closet where her gowns still dangled from their hooks. There he had gasped out his last agony, his body rigid, and his face buried in a skirt, wrapped round by the clothes which breathed of her whom he had ever worshipped. Then Helene's reverie took a sudden leap. She began thinking of her own home-life, of the month's bills which she had checked with Rosalie that very morning; and she felt proud of the orderly way in which she regulated her household. During more than thirty years she had lived with self-respect and strength of mind. Uprightness alone impassioned her. When she questioned her past, not one hour revealed a sin; in her mind's eye she saw herself ever treading a straight and level path. Truly, the days might slip by; she would walk on peacefully as before, with no impediment in her way. The very thought of this made her stern, and her spirit rose in angry contempt against those lying lives whose apparent heroism disturbs the heart. The only true life was her own, following its course amidst such peacefulness. But over Paris there now only hung a thin smoke, a fine, quivering gauze, on the point of floating away; and emotion suddenly took possession of her. To love! to love! everything brought her back to that caressing phrase —even the pride born of her virtue. Her dreaming became so light, she no longer thought, but lay there, steeped in springtide, with moist eyes.

At last, as she was about to resume her reading, Paris slowly came into view. Not a breath of wind had stirred; it was as if a magician had waved his wand. The last gauzy film detached itself, soared and vanished in the air; and the city spread out without a shadow, under the conquering sun. Helene, with her chin resting on her hand, gazed on this mighty awakening.

A far-stretching valley appeared, with a myriad of buildings huddled together. Over the distant range of hills were scattered close-set roofs, and you could divine that the sea of houses rolled afar off behind the undulating ground, into the fields hidden from sight. It was as the ocean, with all the infinity and mystery of its waves. Paris spread out as vast as the heavens on high. Burnished with the sunshine that lovely morning, the city looked like a field of yellow corn; and the huge picture was all simplicity, compounded of two colors only, the pale blue of the sky, and the golden reflections of the housetops. The stream of light from the spring sun invested everything with the beauty of a new birth. So pure was the light that the minutest objects became visible. Paris, with its chaotic maze of stonework, shone as though under glass. From time to time, however, a breath of wind passed athwart this bright, quiescent serenity; and then the outlines of some districts grew faint, and quivered as if they were being viewed through an invisible flame.

Helene took interest at first in gazing on the large expanse spread under her windows, the slope of the Trocadero, and the far-stretching quays. She had to lean out to distinguish the deserted square of the Champ-de-Mars, barred at the farther end by the sombre Military School. Down below, on thoroughfare and pavement on each side of the Seine, she could see the passers-by—a busy cluster of black dots, moving like a swarm of ants. A yellow omnibus shone out like a spark of fire; drays and cabs crossed the bridge, mere child's toys in the distance, with miniature horses like pieces of mechanism; and amongst others traversing the grassy slopes was a servant girl, with a white apron which set a bright spot in all the greenery. Then Helene raised her eyes; but the crowd scattered and passed out of sight, and even the vehicles looked like mere grains of sand; there remained naught but the gigantic carcass of the city, seemingly untenanted and abandoned, its life limited to the dull trepidation by which it was agitated. There, in the foreground to the left, some red roofs were shining, and the tall chimneys of the Army Bakehouse slowly poured out their smoke; while, on the other side of the river, between the Esplanade and the Champ-de-Mars, a grove of lofty elms clustered, like some patch of a park, with bare branches, rounded tops, and young buds already bursting forth, quite clear to the eye. In the center of the picture, the Seine spread out and reigned between its grey banks, to which rows of casks, steam cranes, and carts drawn up in line, gave a seaport kind of aspect. Helene's eyes were always turning towards this shining river, on which boats passed to and fro like birds with inky plumage. Her looks involuntarily followed the water's stately course, which, like a silver band, cut Paris atwain. That morning the stream rolled liquid sunlight; no greater resplendency could be seen on the horizon. And the young woman's glance encountered first the Pont des Invalides, next the Pont de la Concorde, and then the Pont Royal. Bridge followed bridge, they appeared to get closer, to rise one above the other like viaducts forming a flight of steps, and pierced with all kinds of arches; while the river, wending its way beneath these airy structures, showed here and there small patches of its blue robe, patches which became narrower and narrower, more and more indistinct. And again did Helene raise her eyes, and over yonder the stream forked amidst a jumble of houses; the bridges on either side of the island of La Cite were like mere films stretching from one bank to the other; while the golden towers of Notre-Dame sprang up like boundary-marks of the horizon, beyond which river, buildings, and clumps of trees became naught but sparkling sunshine. Then Helene, dazzled, withdrew her gaze from this the triumphant heart of Paris, where the whole glory of the city appeared to blaze.

On the right bank, amongst the clustering trees of the Champs-Elysees she saw the crystal buildings of the Palace of Industry glittering with a snowy sheen; farther away, behind the roof of the Madeleine, which looked like a tombstone, towered the vast mass of the Opera House; then there were other edifices, cupolas and towers, the Vendome Column, the church of Saint-Vincent de Paul, the tower of Saint-Jacques; and nearer in, the massive cube-like pavilions of the new Louvre and the Tuileries, half-hidden by a wood of chestnut trees. On the left bank the dome of the Invalides shone with gilding; beyond it the two irregular towers of Saint-Sulpice paled in the bright light; and yet farther in the rear, to the right of the new spires of Sainte-Clotilde, the bluish Pantheon, erect on a height, its fine colonnade showing against the sky, overlooked the city, poised in the air, as it were, motionless, with the silken hues of a captive balloon.

Helene's gaze wandered all over Paris. There were hollows, as could be divined by the lines of roofs; the Butte des Moulins surged upward, with waves of old slates, while the line of the principal boulevards dipped downward like a gutter, ending in a jumble of houses whose tiles even could no longer be seen. At this early hour the oblique sun did not light up the house-fronts looking towards the Trocadero; not a window-pane of these threw back its rays. The skylights on some roofs alone sparkled with the glittering reflex of mica amidst the red of the adjacent chimney-pots. The houses were mostly of a sombre grey, warmed by reflected beams; still rays of light were transpiercing certain districts, and long streets, stretching in front of Helene, set streaks of sunshine amidst the shade. It was only on the left that the far-spreading horizon, almost perfect in its circular sweep, was broken by the heights of Montmartre and Pere-Lachaise. The details so clearly defined in the foreground, the innumerable denticles of the chimneys, the little black specks of the thousands of windows, grew less and less distinct as you gazed farther and farther away, till everything became mingled in confusion—the pell-mell of an endless city, whose faubourgs, afar off, looked like shingly beaches, steeped in a violet haze under the bright, streaming, vibrating light that fell from the heavens.

Helene was watching the scene with grave interest when Jeanne burst gleefully into the room.

"Oh, mamma! look here!"

The child had a big bunch of wall-flowers in her hand. She told, with some laughter, how she had waylaid Rosalie on her return from market to peep into her basket of provisions. To rummage in this basket was a great delight to her.

"Look at it, mamma! It lay at the very bottom. Just smell it; what a lovely perfume!"

From the tawny flowers, speckled with purple, there came a penetrating odor which scented the whole room. Then Helene, with a passionate movement, drew Jeanne to her breast, while the nosegay fell on her lap. To love! to love! Truly, she loved her child. Was not that intense love which had pervaded her life till now sufficient for her wants? It ought to satisfy her; it was so gentle, so tranquil; no lassitude could put an end to its continuance. Again she pressed her daughter to her, as though to conjure away thoughts which threatened to separate them. In the meantime Jeanne surrendered herself to the shower of kisses. Her

eyes moist with tears, she turned her delicate neck upwards with a coaxing gesture, and pressed her face against her mother's shoulder. Then
she slipped an arm round her waist and thus remained, very demure, her
cheek resting on Helene's bosom. The perfume of the wall-flowers ascended between them.

For a long time they did not speak; but at length, without moving,
Jeanne asked in a whisper:

"Mamma, you see that rosy-colored dome down there, close to the
river; what is it?"

It was the dome of the Institute, and Helene looked towards it for
a moment as though trying to recall the name.

"I don't know, my love," she answered gently.

The child appeared content with this reply, and silence again fell.
But soon she asked a second question.

"And there, quite near, what beautiful trees are those?" she said,
pointing with her finger towards a corner of the Tuileries garden.

"Those beautiful trees!" said her mother. "On the left, do you
mean? I don't know, my love."

"Ah!" exclaimed Jeanne; and after musing for a little while she added
with a pout: "We know nothing!"

Indeed they knew nothing of Paris. During eighteen months it had
lain beneath their gaze every hour of the day, yet they knew not a stone
of it. Three times only had they gone down into the city; but on returning home, suffering from terrible headaches born of all the agitation they had witnessed, they could find in their minds no distinct
memory of anything in all that huge maze of streets.

However, Jeanne at times proved obstinate. "Ah! you can tell me
this!" said she: "What is that glass building which glitters there? It is so
big you must know it."

She was referring to the Palais de l'Industrie. Helene, however, hesitated.

"It's a railway station," said she. "No, I'm wrong, I think it is a theatre."

Then she smiled and kissed Jeanne's hair, at last confessing as before: "I do not know what it is, my love."

So they continued to gaze on Paris, troubling no further to identify
any part of it. It was very delightful to have it there before them, and
yet to know nothing of it; it remained the vast and the unknown. It was

as though they had halted on the threshold of a world which ever unrolled its panorama before them, but into which they were unwilling to descend. Paris often made them anxious when it wafted them a hot, disturbing atmosphere; but that morning it seemed gay and innocent, like a child, and from its mysterious depths only a breath of tenderness rose gently to their faces.

Helene took up her book again while Jeanne, clinging to her, still gazed upon the scene. In the dazzling, tranquil sky no breeze was stirring. The smoke from the Army Bakehouse ascended perpendicularly in light cloudlets which vanished far aloft. On a level with the houses passed vibrating waves of life, waves of all the life pent up there. The loud voices of the streets softened amidst the sunshine into a languid murmur. But all at once a flutter attracted Jeanne's notice. A flock of white pigeons, freed from some adjacent dovecot, sped through the air in front of the window; with spreading wings like falling snow, the birds barred the line of view, hiding the immensity of Paris.

With eyes again dreamily gazing upward, Helene remained plunged in reverie. She was the Lady Rowena; she loved with the serenity and intensity of a noble mind. That spring morning, that great, gentle city, those early wall-flowers shedding their perfume on her lap, had little by little filled her heart with tenderness.

CHAPTER VI.

One morning Helene was arranging her little library, the various books of which had got out of order during the past few days, when Jeanne skipped into the room, clapping her hands.

"A soldier, mamma! a soldier!" she cried.

"What? a soldier?" exclaimed her mother. "What do you want, you and your soldier?"

But the child was in one of her paroxysms of extravagant delight; she only jumped about the more, repeating: "A soldier! a soldier!" without deigning to give any further explanation. She had left the door wide open behind her, and so, as Helene rose, she was astonished to see a soldier—a very little soldier too—in the ante-room. Rosalie had gone out, and Jeanne must have been playing on the landing, though strictly forbidden to do so by her mother.

"What do you want, my lad?" asked Helene.

The little soldier was very much confused on seeing this lady, so lovely and fair, in her dressing-gown trimmed with lace; he shuffled one foot to and fro over the floor, bowed, and at last precipitately stammered: "I beg pardon—excuse—"

But he could get no further, and retreated to the wall, still shuffling his feet. His retreat was thus cut off, and seeing the lady awaited his reply with an involuntary smile, he dived into his right-hand pocket, from which he dragged a blue handkerchief, a knife, and a hunk of bread. He gazed on each in turn, and thrust them all back again. Then he turned his attention to the left-hand pocket, from which were produced a twist of cord, two rusty nails, and some pictures wrapped in part of a newspaper. All these he pushed back to their resting-place, and began tapping his thighs with an anxious air. And again he stammered in bewilderment:

"I beg pardon—excuse—"

But all at once he raised his finger to his nose, and exclaimed with a loud laugh: "What a fool I am! I remember now!"

He then undid two buttons of his greatcoat, and rummaged in his breast, into which he plunged his arm up to the elbow. After a time he drew forth a letter, which he rustled violently before handing to Helene, as though to shake some dust from it.

"A letter for me! Are you sure?" said she.

On the envelope were certainly inscribed her name and address in a heavy rustic scrawl, with pothooks and hangers tumbling over one another. When at last she made it all out, after being repeatedly baffled by the extraordinary style and spelling, she could not but smile again. It was a letter from Rosalie's aunt, introducing Zephyrin Lacour, who had fallen a victim to the conscription, "in spite of two masses having been said by his reverence." However, as Zephyrin was Rosalie's "intended" the aunt begged that madame would be so good as to allow the young folks to see each other on Sundays. In the three pages which the letter comprised this question was continually cropping up in the same words, the confusion of the epistle increasing through the writer's vain efforts to say something she had not said before. Just above the signature, however, she seemed to have hit the nail on the head, for she had written: "His reverence gives his permission"; and had then broken her pen in the paper, making a shower of blots.

Helene slowly folded the letter. Two or three times, while deciphering its contents, she had raised her head to glance at the soldier. He still remained close to the wall, and his lips stirred, as though to emphasize each sentence in the letter by a slight movement of the chin. No doubt he knew its contents by heart.

"Then you are Zephyrin Lacour, are you not?" asked Helene.

He began to laugh and wagged his head.

"Come in, my lad; don't stay out there."

He made up his mind to follow her, but he continued standing close to the door, while Helene sat down. She had scarcely seen him in the darkness of the ante-room. He must have been just as tall as Rosalie; a third of an inch less, and he would have been exempted from service. With red hair, cut very short, he had a round, freckled, beardless face, with two little eyes like gimlet holes. His new greatcoat, much too large for him, made him appear still more dumpy, and with his red-trousered legs wide apart, and his large peaked cap swinging before him, he presented both a comical and pathetic sight—his plump, stupid little person plainly betraying the rustic, although he wore a uniform.

Helene desired to obtain some information from him.

"You left Beauce a week ago?" she asked.

"Yes, madame!"

"And here you are in Paris. I suppose you are not sorry?"

"No, madame."

He was losing his bashfulness, and now gazed all over the room, evidently much impressed by its blue velvet hangings.

"Rosalie is out," Helene began again, "but she will be here very soon. Her aunt tells me you are her sweetheart."

To this the little soldier vouchsafed no reply, but hung his head, laughing awkwardly, and scraping the carpet with the tip of his boot.

"Then you will have to marry her when you leave the army?" Helene continued questioning.

"Yes, to be sure!" exclaimed he, his face turning very red. "Yes, of course; we are engaged!" And, won over by the kindly manners of the lady, he made up his mind to speak out, his fingers still playing with his cap. "You know it's an old story. When we were quite children, we used to go thieving together. We used to get switched; oh yes, that's true! I must tell you that the Lacours and the Pichons lived in the same lane, and were next-door neighbors. And so Rosalie and myself were almost brought up together. Then her people died, and her aunt Marguerite took her in. But she, the minx, was already as strong as a demon."

He paused, realizing that he was warming up, and asked hesitatingly:

"But perhaps she has told you all this?"

"Yes, yes; but go on all the same," said Helene, who was greatly amused.

"In short," continued he, "she was awfully strong, though she was no bigger than a tomtit. It was a treat to see her at her work! How she did get through it! One day she gave a slap to a friend of mine—by God! such a slap! I had the mark of it on my arm for a week! Yes, that was the way it all came about. All the gossips declared we must marry one another. Besides, we weren't ten years old before we had agreed on that! And, we have stuck to it, madame, we have stuck to it!"

He placed one hand upon his heart, with fingers wide apart. Helene, however, had now become very grave. The idea of allowing a soldier in her kitchen somewhat worried her. His reverence, no doubt, had given his sanction, but she thought it rather venturesome. There is too much license in the country, where lovers indulge in all sorts of pleasantries. So she gave expression to her apprehensions. When Zephyrin at last gathered her meaning, his first inclination was to laugh, but his awe for Helene restrained him.

"Oh, madame, madame!" said he, "you don't know her, I can see! I have received slaps enough from her! Of course young men like to laugh! isn't that so? Sometimes I pinched her, and she would turn round and hit me right on the nose. Her aunt's advice always was, 'Look here, my girl, don't put up with any nonsense!' His reverence, too, interfered in it, and maybe that had a lot to do with our keeping up sweethearting. We were to have been married after I had drawn for a soldier. But it was all my eye! Things turned out badly. Rosalie declared she would go to service in Paris, to earn a dowry while she was waiting for me. And so, and so—"

He swung himself about, dangling his cap, now from one hand now from the other. But still Helene never said a word, and he at last fancied that she distrusted him. This pained him dreadfully.

"You think, perhaps, that I shall deceive her?" he burst out angrily. "Even, too, when I tell you we are betrothed? I shall marry her, as surely as the heaven shines on us. I'm quite ready to pledge my word in writing. Yes, if you like, I'll write it down for you."

Deep emotion was stirring him. He walked about the room gazing around in the hope of finding pen and ink. Helene quickly tried to appease him, but he still went on:

"I would rather sign a paper for you. What harm would it do you? Your mind would be all the easier with it."

However, just at that moment Jeanne, who had again run away, returned, jumping and clapping her hands.

"Rosalie! Rosalie! Rosalie!" she chanted in a dancing tune of her own composition.

Through the open doorway one could hear the panting of the maid as she climbed up the stairs laden with her basket. Zephyrin started back into a corner of the room, his mouth wide agape from ear to ear in silent laughter, and the gimlet holes of his eyes gleaming with rustic roguery. Rosalie came straight into the room, as was her usual practice, to show her mistress her morning's purchase of provisions.

"Madame," said she, "I've brought some cauliflowers. Look at them! Only eighteen sous for two; it isn't dear, is it?"

She held out the basket half open, but on lifting her head noticed Zephyrin's grinning face. Surprise nailed her to the carpet. Two or three seconds slipped away; she had doubtless at first failed to recognize him in his uniform. But then her round eyes dilated, her fat little face blanched, and her coarse black hair waved in agitation.

"Oh!" she simply said.

But her astonishment was such that she dropped her basket. The provisions, cauliflowers, onions, apples, rolled on to the carpet. Jeanne gave a cry of delight, and falling on her knees, began hunting for the apples, even under the chairs and the wardrobe. Meanwhile Rosalie, as though paralyzed, never moved, though she repeated:

"What! it's you! What are you doing here? what are you doing here? Say!"

Then she turned to Helene with the question: "Was it you who let him come in?"

Zephyrin never uttered a word, but contented himself with winking slily. Then Rosalie gave vent to her emotion in tears; and, to show her delight at seeing him again, could hit on nothing better than to quiz him.

"Oh! go away!" she began, marching up to him. "You look neat and pretty I must say in that guise of yours! I might have passed you in the street, and not even have said: 'God bless you.' Oh! you've got a nice rig-out. You just look as if you had your sentry-box on your back; and they've cut your hair so short that folks might take you for the sexton's poodle. Good heavens! what a fright you are; what a fright!"

Zephyrin, very indignant, now made up his mind to speak. "It's not my fault, that's sure! Oh! if you joined a regiment we should see a few things."

They had quite forgotten where they were; everything had vanished—the room, Helene and Jeanne, who was still gathering the apples together. With hands folded over her apron, the maid stood upright in front of the little soldier.

"Is everything all right down there?" she asked.

"Oh, yes, excepting Guignard's cow is ill. The veterinary surgeon came and said she'd got the dropsy."

"If she's got the dropsy, she's done for. Excepting that, is everything all right?"

"Yes, yes! The village constable has broken his arm. Old Canivet's dead. And, by the way, his reverence lost his purse with thirty sous in it as he was a-coming back from Grandval. But otherwise, things are all right."

Then silence fell on them, and they looked at one another with sparkling eyes, their compressed lips slowly making an amorous grimace. This, indeed, must have been the manner in which they expressed their love, for they had not even stretched out their hands in greeting. Rosalie, however, all at once ceased her contemplation, and began to lament at sight of the vegetables on the floor. Such a nice mess! and it was he who had caused it all! Madame ought to have made him wait on the stairs! Scolding away as fast as she could, she dropped on her knees and began putting the apples, onions, and cauliflowers into the basket again, much to the disgust of Jeanne, who would fain have done it all herself. And as she turned, with the object of betaking herself into her kitchen, never deigning another look in Zephyrin's direction, Helene, conciliated by the healthy tranquility of the lovers, stopped her to say:

"Listen a moment, my girl. Your aunt has asked me to allow this young man to come and see you on Sundays. He will come in the afternoon, and you will try not to let your work fall behind too much."

Rosalie paused, merely turning her head. Though she was well pleased, she preserved her doleful air.

"Oh, madame, he will be such a bother," she declared. But at the same time she glanced over her shoulder at Zephyrin, and again made an affectionate grimace at him. The little soldier remained for a minute stock-still, his mouth agape from ear to ear with its silent laugh. Then he retired backwards, with his cap against his heart as he thanked Helene profusely. The door had been shut upon him, when on the landing he still continued bowing.

"Is that Rosalie's brother, mamma?" asked Jeanne.

Helene was quite embarrassed by the question. She regretted the permission which she had just given in a sudden impulse of kindliness which now surprised her. She remained thinking for some seconds, and then replied, "No, he is her cousin."

"Ah!" said the child gravely.

Rosalie's kitchen looked out on the sunny expanse of Doctor Deberle's garden. In the summer the branches of the elms swayed in
through the broad window. It was the cheeriest room of the suite, always flooded with light, which was sometimes so blinding that Rosalie
had put up a curtain of blue cotton stuff, which she drew of an afternoon. The only complaint she made about the kitchen was its smallness;
and indeed it was a narrow strip of a place, with a cooking-range on the
right-hand side, while on the left were the table and dresser. The various utensils and furnishings, however, had all been so well arranged
that she had contrived to keep a clear corner beside the window, where
she worked in the evening. She took a pride in keeping everything,
stewpans, kettles, and dishes, wonderfully clean; and so, when the sun
veered round to the window, the walls became resplendent, the copper
vessels sparkled like gold, the tin pots showed bright discs like silver
moons, while the white-and-blue tiles above the stove gleamed pale in
the fiery glow.

On the evening of the ensuing Saturday Helene heard so great a
commotion in the kitchen that she determined to go and see what was
the matter.

"What is it?" asked she: "are you fighting with the furniture?"

"I am scouring, madame," replied Rosalie, who, sweating and dishevelled, was squatting on the tiled floor and scrubbing it with all the
strength of her arms.

This over, she sponged it with clear water. Never had the kitchen
displayed such perfection of cleanliness. A bride might have slept in it;
all was white as for a wedding. So energetically had she exerted her
hands that it seemed as if table and dresser had been freshly planed.
And the good order of everything was a sight to see; stewpans and pots
taking rank by their size, each on its own hook, even the frying-pan and
gridiron shining brightly without one grimy stain. Helene looked on for
a moment in silence, and then with a smile disappeared.

Every Saturday afterwards there was a similar furbishing, a tornado
of dust and water lasting for four hours. It was Rosalie's wish to display
her neatness to Zephyrin on the Sunday. That was her reception day. A
single cobweb would have filled her with shame; but when everything
shone resplendent around her she became amiable, and burst into song.
At three o'clock she would again wash her hands and don a cap gay
with ribbons. Then the curtain being drawn halfway, so that only the

subdued light of a boudoir came in, she awaited Zephyrin's arrival amidst all this primness, through which a pleasant scent of thyme and laurel was borne.

At half-past three exactly Zephyrin made his appearance; he would walk about the street until the clocks of the neighborhood had struck the half-hour. Rosalie listened to the beat of his heavy shoes on the stairs, and opened the door the moment he halted on the landing. She had forbidden him to ring the bell. At each visit the same greeting passed between them.

"Is it you?"

"Yes, it's me!"

And they stood face to face, their eyes sparkling and their lips compressed. Then Zephyrin followed Rosalie; but there was no admission vouchsafed to him till she had relieved him of shako and sabre. She would have none of these in her kitchen; and so the sabre and shako were hidden away in a cupboard. Next she would make him sit down in the corner she had contrived near the window, and thenceforth he was not allowed to budge.

"Sit still there! You can look on, if you like, while I get madame's dinner ready."

But he rarely appeared with empty hands. He would usually spend the morning in strolling with some comrades through the woods of Meudon, lounging lazily about, inhaling the fresh air, which inspired him with regretful memories of his country home. To give his fingers something to do he would cut switches, which he tapered and notched with marvelous figurings, and his steps gradually slackening he would come to a stop beside some ditch, his shako on the back of his head, while his eyes remained fixed on the knife with which he was carving the stick. Then, as he could never make up his mind to discard his switches, he carried them in the afternoon to Rosalie, who would throw up her hands, and exclaim that they would litter her kitchen. But the truth was, she carefully preserved them; and under her bed was gathered a bundle of these switches, of all sorts and sizes.

One day he made his appearance with a nest full of eggs, which he had secreted in his shako under the folds of a handkerchief. Omelets made from the eggs of wild birds, so he declared, were very nice—a statement which Rosalie received with horror; the nest, however, was preserved and laid away in company with the switches. But Zephyrin's pockets were always full to overflowing. He would pull curiosities from them, transparent pebbles found on the banks of the Seine, pieces of old iron, dried berries, and all sorts of strange rubbish, which not even a rag-picker would have cared for. His chief love, however, was for pictures; as he sauntered along he would seize on all the stray papers that had served as wrappers for chocolate or cakes of soap, and on which were black men, palm-trees, dancing-girls, or clusters of roses. The tops of old broken boxes, decorated with figures of languid, blonde ladies, the glazed prints and silver paper which had once contained sugar-sticks and had been thrown away at the neighboring fairs, were great windfalls that filled his bosom with pride. All such booty was speedily transferred to his pockets, the choicer articles being enveloped in a fragment of an old newspaper. And on Sunday, if Rosalie had a moment's leisure between the preparation of a sauce and the tending of the joint, he would exhibit his pictures to her. They were hers if she cared for them; only as the paper around them was not always clean he would cut them out, a pastime which greatly amused him. Rosalie got angry, as the shreds of paper blew about even into her plates; and it was a sight to see with what rustic cunning he would at last gain possession of her scissors. At times, however, in order to get rid of him, she would give them up without any asking.

Meanwhile some brown sauce would be simmering on the fire. Rosalie watched it, wooden spoon in hand; while Zephyrin, his head bent and his breadth of shoulder increased by his epaulets, continued cutting out the pictures. His head was so closely shaven that the skin of his skull could be seen; and the yellow collar of his tunic yawned widely behind, displaying his sunburnt neck. For a quarter of an hour at a time neither would utter a syllable. When Zephyrin raised his head, he watched Rosalie while she took some flour, minced some parsley, or salted and peppered some dish, his eyes betraying the while intense interest. Then, at long intervals, a few words would escape him:

"By God! that does smell nice!"

The cook, busily engaged, would not vouchsafe an immediate reply; but after a lengthy silence she perhaps exclaimed: "You see, it must simmer properly."

Their talk never went beyond that. They no longer spoke of their native place even. When a reminiscence came to them a word sufficed, and they chuckled inwardly the whole afternoon. This was pleasure enough, and by the time Rosalie turned Zephyrin out of doors both of them had enjoyed ample amusement.

"Come, you will have to go! I must wait on madame," said she; and restoring him his shako and sabre, she drove him out before her, afterwards waiting on madame with cheeks flushed with happiness; while he walked back to barracks, dangling his arms, and almost intoxicated by the goodly odors of thyme and laurel which still clung to him.

During his earlier visits Helene judged it right to look after them. She popped in sometimes quite suddenly to give an order, and there was Zephyrin always in his corner, between the table and the window, close to the stone filter, which forced him to draw in his legs. The moment madame made her appearance he rose and stood upright, as though shouldering arms, and if she spoke to him his reply never went beyond a salute and a respectful grunt. Little by little Helene grew somewhat easier; she saw that her entrance did not disturb them, and that their faces only expressed the quiet content of patient lovers.

At this time, too, Rosalie seemed even more wide awake than Zephyrin. She had already been some months in Paris, and under its influence was fast losing her country rust, though as yet she only knew three streets—the Rue de Passy, the Rue Franklin, and the Rue Vineuse. Zephyrin, soldier though he was, remained quite a lubber. As Rosalie confided to her mistress, he became more of a blockhead every day. In the country he had been much sharper. But, added she, it was the uniform's fault; all the lads who donned the uniform became sad dolts. The fact is, his change of life had quite muddled Zephyrin, who, with his staring round eyes and solemn swagger, looked like a goose. Despite his epaulets he retained his rustic awkwardness and heaviness; the barracks had taught him nothing as yet of the fine words and victorious attitudes of the ideal Parisian fire-eater. "Yes, madame," Rosalie would wind up by saying, "you don't need to disturb yourself; it is not in him to play any tricks!"

Thus the girl began to treat him in quite a motherly way. While dressing her meat on the spit she would preach him a sermon, full of good counsel as to the pitfalls he should shun; and he in all obedience vigorously nodded approval of each injunction. Every Sunday he had to swear to her that he had attended mass, and that he had solemnly repeated his prayers morning and evening. She strongly inculcated the necessity of tidiness, gave him a brush down whenever he left her, stitched on a loose button of his tunic, and surveyed him from head to foot to see if aught were amiss in his appearance. She also worried herself about his health, and gave him cures for all sorts of ailments. In return for her kindly care Zephyrin professed himself anxious to fill her filter for her; but this proposal was long-rejected, through the fear that he might spill the water. One day, however, he brought up two buckets without letting a drop of their contents fall on the stairs, and from that time he replenished the filter every Sunday. He would also make himself useful in other ways, doing all the heavy work and was extremely handy in running to the greengrocer's for butter, had she forgotten to purchase any. At last, even, he began to share in the duties of kitchen-maid. First he was permitted to peel the vegetables; later on the mincing was assigned to him. At the end of six weeks, though still forbidden to touch the sauces, he watched over them with wooden spoon in hand. Rosalie had fairly made him her helpmate, and would sometimes burst out laughing as she saw him, with his red trousers and yellow collar, working busily before the fire with a dishcloth over his arm, like some scullery-servant.

One Sunday Helene betook herself to the kitchen. Her slippers deadened the sound of her footsteps, and she reached the threshold unheard by either maid or soldier. Zephyrin was seated in his corner over a basin of steaming broth. Rosalie, with her back turned to the door, was occupied in cutting some long sippets of bread for him.

"There, eat away, my dear!" she said. "You walk too much; it is that which makes you feel so empty! There! have you enough? Do you want any more?"

Thus speaking, she watched him with a tender and anxious look. He, with his round, dumpy figure, leaned over the basin, devouring a sippet with each mouthful of broth. His face, usually yellow with freckles, was becoming quite red with the warmth of the steam which circled round him.

"Heavens!" he muttered, "what grand juice! What do you put in it?"

"Wait a minute," she said; "if you like leeks—"

However, as she turned round she suddenly caught sight of her mistress. She raised an exclamation, and then, like Zephyrin, seemed turned to stone. But a moment afterwards she poured forth a torrent of excuses.

"It's my share, madame—oh, it's my share! I would not have taken any more soup, I swear it! I told him, 'If you would like to have my bowl of soup, you can have it.' Come, speak up, Zephyrin; you know that was how it came about!"

The mistress remained silent, and the servant grew uneasy, thinking she was annoyed. Then in quavering tones she continued:

"Oh, he was dying of hunger, madame; he stole a raw carrot for me! They feed him so badly! And then, you know, he had walked goodness knows where all along the river-side. I'm sure, madame, you would have told me yourself to give him some broth!"

Gazing at the little soldier, who sat with his mouth full, not daring to swallow, Helene felt she could no longer remain stern. So she quietly said:

"Well, well, my girl, whenever the lad is hungry you must keep him to dinner—that's all. I give you permission"

Face to face with them, she had again felt within her that tender feeling which once already had banished all thoughts of rigor from her mind. They were so happy in that kitchen! The cotton curtain, drawn half-way, gave free entry to the sunset beams. The burnished copper pans set the end wall all aglow, lending a rosy tint to the twilight lingering in the room. And there, in the golden shade, the lovers' little round faces shone out, peaceful and radiant, like moons. Their love was instinct with such calm certainty that no neglect was even shown in keeping the kitchen utensils in their wonted good order. It blossomed amidst the savory odors of the cooking-stove, which heightened their appetites and nourished their hearts.

"Mamma," asked Jeanne, one evening after considerable meditation, "why is it Rosalie's cousin never kisses her?"

"And why should they kiss one another?" asked Helene in her turn. "They will kiss on their birthdays."

CHAPTER VII.

The soup had just been served on the following Tuesday evening, when Helene, after listening attentively, exclaimed:

"What a downpour! Don't you hear? My poor friends, you will get drenched to-night!"

"Oh, it's only a few drops," said the Abbe quietly, though his old cassock was already wet about the shoulders.

"I've got a good distance to go," said Monsieur Rambaud. "But I shall return home on foot all the same; I like it. Besides, I have my umbrella."

Jeanne was reflecting as she gazed gravely on her last spoonful of vermicelli; and at last her thoughts took shape in words: "Rosalie said you wouldn't come because of the wretched weather; but mamma said you would come. You are very kind; you always come."

A smile lit up all their faces. Helene addressed a nod of affectionate approval to the two brothers. Out of doors the rain was falling with a dull roar, and violent gusts of wind beat angrily against the window-shutters. Winter seemed to have returned. Rosalie had carefully drawn the red repp curtains; and the small, cosy dining-room, illumined by the steady light of the white hanging-lamp, looked, amidst the buffeting of the storm, a picture of pleasant, affectionate intimacy. On the mahogany sideboard some china reflected the quiet light; and amidst all this indoor peacefulness the four diners leisurely conversed, awaiting the good pleasure of the servant-maid, as they sat round the table, where all, if simple, was exquisitely clean.

"Oh! you are waiting; so much the worse!" said Rosalie familiarly, as she entered with a dish. "These are fillets of sole *au gratin* for Monsieur Rambaud; they require to be lifted just at the last moment."

Monsieur Rambaud pretended to be a gourmand, in order to amuse Jeanne, and give pleasure to Rosalie, who was very proud of her accomplishments as a cook. He turned towards her with the question: "By the way, what have you got for us to-day? You are always bringing in some surprise or other when I am no longer hungry."

"Oh," said she in reply, "there are three dishes as usual, and no more. After the sole you will have a leg of mutton and then some Brussels sprouts. Yes, that's the truth; there will be nothing else."

From the corner of his eye Monsieur Rambaud glanced towards Jeanne. The child was boiling over with glee, her hands over her mouth to restrain her laughter, while she shook her head, as though to insinuate that the maid was deceiving them. Monsieur Rambaud thereupon clacked his tongue as though in doubt, and Rosalie pretended great indignation.

"You don't believe me because Mademoiselle Jeanne laughs so," said she. "Ah, very well! believe what you like. Stint yourself, and see if you won't have a craving for food when you get home."

When the maid had left the room, Jeanne, laughing yet more loudly, was seized with a longing to speak out.

"You are really too greedy!" she began. "I myself went into the kitchen—" However, she left her sentence unfinished: "No, no, I won't tell; it isn't right, is it, mamma? There's nothing more—nothing at all! I only laughed to cheat you."

This interlude was re-enacted every Tuesday with the same unvarying success. Helene was touched by the kindliness with which Monsieur Rambaud lent himself to the fun; she was well aware that, with Provencal frugality, he had long limited his daily fare to an anchovy and half-a-dozen olives. As for Abbe Jouve, he never knew what he was eating, and his blunders and forgetfulness supplied an inexhaustible fund of amusement. Jeanne, meditating some prank in this respect, was even now stealthily watching him with her glittering eyes.

"How nice this whiting is!" she said to him, after they had all been served.

"Very nice, my dear," he answered. "Bless me, you are right—it is whiting; I thought it was turbot."

And then, as every one laughed, he guilelessly asked why. Rosalie, who had just come into the room again, seemed very much hurt, and burst out:

"A fine thing indeed! The priest in my native place knew much better what he was eating. He could tell the age of the fowl he was carving to a week or so, and didn't require to go into the kitchen to find out what there was for dinner. No, the smell was quite sufficient. Goodness gracious! had I been in the service of a priest like your reverence, I should not know yet even how to turn an omelet."

The Abbe hastened to excuse himself with an embarrassed air, as though his inability to appreciate the delights of the table was a failing he despaired of curing. But, as he said, he had too many other things to think about.

"There! that is a leg of mutton!" exclaimed Rosalie, as she placed on the table the joint referred to.

Everybody once more indulged in a peal of laughter, the Abbe Jouve being the first to do so. He bent forward to look, his little eyes twinkling with glee.

"Yes, certainly," said he; "it is a leg of mutton. I think I should have known it."

Despite this remark, there was something about the Abbe that day which betokened unusual absent-mindedness. He ate quickly, with the haste of a man who is bored by a long stay at table, and lunches standing when at home. And, having finished, himself, he would wait the convenience of the others, plunged in deep thought, and simply smiling in reply to the questions put to him. At every moment he cast on his brother a look in which encouragement and uneasiness were mingled. Nor did Monsieur Rambaud seen possessed of his wonted tranquility that evening; but his agitation manifested itself in a craving to talk and fidget on his chair, which seemed rather inconsistent with his quiet disposition. When the Brussels sprouts had disappeared, there was a delay in the appearance of the dessert, and a spell of silence ensued. Out of doors the rain was beating down with still greater force, rattling noisily against the house. The dining-room was rather close, and it suddenly dawned on Helene that there was something strange in the air—that the two brothers had some worry of which they did not care to speak. She looked at them anxiously, and at last spoke:

"Dear, dear! What dreadful rain! isn't it? It seems to be influencing both of you, for you look out of sorts."

They protested, however, that such was not the case, doing their utmost to clear her mind of the notion. And as Rosalie now made her appearance with an immense dish, Monsieur Rambaud exclaimed, as though to veil his emotion: "What did I say! Still another surprise!"

The surprise of the day was some vanilla cream, one of the cook's triumphs. And thus it was a sight to see her broad, silent grin, as she deposited her burden on the table. Jeanne shouted and clapped her hands.

"I knew it, I knew it! I saw the eggs in the kitchen!"

"But I have no more appetite," declared Monsieur Rambaud, with a look of despair. "I could not eat any of it!"

Thereupon Rosalie became grave, full of suppressed wrath. With a dignified air, she remarked: "Oh, indeed! A cream which I made specially for you! Well, well! just try not to eat any of it—yes, try!"

He had to give in and accept a large helping of the cream. Meanwhile the Abbe remained thoughtful. He rolled up his napkin and rose before the dessert had come to an end, as was frequently his custom. For a little while he walked about, with his head hanging down; and when Helene in her turn quitted the table, he cast at Monsieur Rambaud a look of intelligence, and led the young woman into the bedroom. The door being left open behind them, they could almost immediately afterwards be heard conversing together, though the words which they slowly exchanged were indistinguishable.

"Oh, do make haste!" said Jeanne to Monsieur Rambaud, who seemed incapable of finishing a biscuit. "I want to show you my work."

However, he evinced no haste, though when Rosalie began to clear the table it became necessary for him to leave his chair.

"Wait a little! wait a little!" he murmured, as the child strove to drag him towards the bedroom, And, overcome with embarrassment and timidity, he retreated from the doorway. Then, as the Abbe raised his voice, such sudden weakness came over him that he had to sit down again at the table. From his pocket he drew a newspaper.

"Now," said he, "I'm going to make you a little coach."

Jeanne at once abandoned her intention of entering the adjoining room. Monsieur Rambaud always amazed her by his skill in turning a sheet of paper into all sorts of playthings. Chickens, boats, bishops' mitres, carts, and cages, were all evolved under his fingers. That day, however, so tremulous were his hands that he was unable to perfect anything. He lowered his head whenever the faintest sound came from the adjacent room. Nevertheless, Jeanne took interest in watching him, and leaned on the table at his side.

"Now," said she, "you must make a chicken to harness to the carriage."

Meantime, within the bedroom, Abbe Jouve remained standing in the shadow thrown by the lamp-shade upon the floor. Helene had sat down in her usual place in front of the round table; and, as on Tuesdays she refrained from ceremony with her friends, she had taken up her needlework, and, in the circular glare of light, only her white hands could be seen sewing a child's cap.

"Jeanne gives you no further worry, does she?" asked the Abbe.

Helene shook her head before making a reply.

"Doctor Deberle seems quite satisfied," said she. "But the poor darling is still very nervous. Yesterday I found her in her chair in a fainting fit."

"She needs exercise," resumed the priest. "You stay indoors far too much; you should follow the example of other folks and go about more than you do."

He ceased speaking, and silence followed. He now, without doubt, had what he had been seeking,—a suitable inlet for his discourse; but the moment for speaking came, and he was still communing with himself. Taking a chair, he sat down at Helene's side.

"Hearken to me, my dear child," he began. "For some time past I have wished to talk with you seriously. The life you are leading here can entail no good results. A convent existence such as yours is not consistent with your years; and this abandonment of worldly pleasures is as injurious to your child as it is to yourself. You are risking many dangers—dangers to health, ay, and other dangers, too."

Helene raised her head with an expression of astonishment. "What do you mean, my friend?" she asked.

"Dear me! I know the world but little," continued the priest, with some slight embarrassment, "yet I know very well that a woman incurs great risk when she remains without a protecting arm. To speak frankly, you keep to your own company too much, and this seclusion in which you hide yourself is not healthful, believe me. A day must come when you will suffer from it."

"But I make no complaint; I am very happy as I am," she exclaimed with spirit.

The old priest gently shook his large head.

"Yes, yes, that is all very well. You feel completely happy. I know all that. Only, on the downhill path of a lonely, dreamy life, you never know where you are going. Oh! I understand you perfectly; you are incapable of doing any wrong. But sooner or later you might lose your peace of mind. Some morning, when it is too late, you will find that blank which you now leave in your life filled by some painful feeling not to be confessed."

As she sat there in the shadow, a blush crimsoned Helene's face. Had the Abbe, then, read her heart? Was he aware of this restlessness which was fast possessing her—this heart-trouble which thrilled her every-day life, and the existence of which she had till now been unwilling to admit? Her needlework fell on her lap. A sensation of weakness pervaded her, and she awaited from the priest something like a pious complicity which would allow her to confess and particularize the vague feelings which she buried in her innermost being. As all was known to him, it was for him to question her, and she would strive to answer.

"I leave myself in your hands, my friend," she murmured. "You are well aware that I have always listened to you."

The priest remained for a moment silent, and then slowly and solemnly said:

"My child, you must marry again."

She remained speechless, with arms dangling, in a stupor this counsel brought upon her. She awaited other words, failing, as it were, to understand him. And the Abbe continued putting before her the arguments which should incline her towards marriage.

"Remember, you are still young. You must not remain longer in this out-of-the-way corner of Paris, scarcely daring to go out, and wholly ignorant of the world. You must return to the every-day life of humanity, lest in the future you should bitterly regret your loneliness. You yourself have no idea how the effects of your isolation are beginning to tell on you, but your friends remark your pallor, and feel uneasy."

With each sentence he paused, in the hope that she might break in and discuss his proposition. But no; she sat there as if lifeless, seemingly benumbed with astonishment.

"No doubt you have a child," he resumed. "That is always a delicate matter to surmount. Still, you must admit that even in Jeanne's interest a husband's arm would be of great advantage. Of course, we must find someone good and honorable, who would be a true father—"

However, she did not let him finish. With violent revolt and repulsion she suddenly spoke out: "No, no; I will not! Oh, my friend, how can you advise me thus? Never, do you hear, never!"

Her whole heart was rising; she herself was frightened by the violence of her refusal. The priest's proposal had stirred up that dim nook in her being whose secret she avoided reading, and, by the pain she experienced, she at last understood all the gravity of her ailment. With the open, smiling glance of the priest still bent on her, she plunged into contention.

"No, no; I do not wish it! I love nobody!"

And, as he still gazed at her, she imagined he could read her lie on her face. She blushed and stammered:

"Remember, too, I only left off my mourning a fortnight ago. No, it could not be!"

"My child!" quietly said the priest, "I thought over this a great deal before speaking. I am sure your happiness is wrapped up in it. Calm yourself; you need never act against your own wishes."

The conversation came to a sudden stop. Helene strove to keep pent within her bosom the angry protests that were rushing to her lips. She resumed her work, and, with head lowered, contrived to put in a few stitches. And amid the silence, Jeanne's shrill voice could be heard in the dining-room.

"People don't put a chicken to a carriage; it ought to be a horse! You don't know how to make a horse, do you?"

"No, my dear; horses are too difficult," said Monsieur Rambaud. "But if you like I'll show you how to make carriages."

This was always the fashion in which their game came to an end. Jeanne, all ears and eyes, watched her kindly playfellow folding the paper into a multitude of little squares, and afterwards she followed his example; but she would make mistakes and then stamp her feet in vexation. However, she already knew how to manufacture boats and bishops' mitres.

"You see," resumed Monsieur Rambaud patiently, "you make four corners like that; then you turn them back—"

With his ears on the alert, he must during the last moment have heard some of the words spoken in the next room; for his poor hands were now trembling more and more, while his tongue faltered, so that he could only half articulate his sentences.

Helene, who was unable to quiet herself, now began the conversation anew. "Marry again! And whom, pray?" she suddenly asked the priest, as she laid her work down on the table. "You have someone in view, have you not?"

Abbe Jouve rose from his chair and stalked slowly up and down. Without halting, he nodded assent.

"Well! tell me who he is," she said.

For a moment he lingered before her erect, then, shrugging his shoulders, said: "What's the good, since you decline?"

"No matter, I want to know," she replied. "How can I make up my mind when I don't know?"

He did not answer her immediately, but remained standing there, gazing into her face. A somewhat sad smile wreathed his lips. At last he exclaimed, almost in a whisper: "What! have you not guessed?"

No, she could not guess. She tried to do so, with increasing wonder, whereupon he made a simple sign—nodding his head in the direction of the dining-room.

"He!" she exclaimed, in a muffled tone, and a great seriousness fell upon her. She no longer indulged in violent protestations; only sorrow and surprise remained visible on her face. She sat for a long time plunged in thought, her gaze turned to the floor. Truly, she had never dreamed of such a thing; and yet, she found nothing in it to object to. Monsieur Rambaud was the only man in whose hand she could put her own honestly and without fear. She knew his innate goodness; she did not smile at his *bourgeois* heaviness. But despite all her regard for him, the idea that he loved her chilled her to the soul.

Meanwhile the Abbe had again begun walking from one to the other end of the room, and on passing the dining-room door he gently called Helene. "Come here and look!"

She rose and did as he wished.

Monsieur Rambaud had ended by seating Jeanne in his own chair; and he, who had at first been leaning against the table, had now slipped down at the child's feet. He was on his knees before her, encircling her with one of his arms. On the table was the carriage drawn by the chicken, with some boats, boxes, and bishops' mitres.

"Now, do you love me well?" he asked her. "Tell me that you love me well!"

"Of course, I love you well; you know it."

He stammered and trembled, as though he were making some declaration of love.

"And what would you say if I asked you to let me stay here with you always?"

"Oh, I should be quite pleased. We would play together, wouldn't we? That would be good fun."

"Ah, but you know I should always be here."

Jeanne had taken up a boat which she was twisting into a gendarme's hat. "You would need to get mamma's leave," she murmured.

By this reply all his fears were again stirred into life. His fate was being decided.

"Of course," said he. "But if mamma gave me leave, would you say yes, too?"

Jeanne, busy finishing her gendarme's hat, sang out in a rapturous strain: "I would say yes! yes! yes! I would say yes! yes! yes! Come, look how pretty my hat is!"

Monsieur Rambaud, with tears in his eyes, rose to his knees and kissed her, while she threw her arms round his neck. He had entrusted the asking of Helene's consent to his brother, whilst he himself sought to secure that of Jeanne.

"You see," said the priest, with a smile, "the child is quite content."

Helene still retained her grave air, and made no further inquiry. The Abbe, however, again eloquently took up his plea, and emphasized his brother's good qualities. Was he not a treasure-trove of a father for Jeanne? She was well acquainted with him; in trusting him she gave no hostages to fortune. Then, as she still remained silent, the Abbe with great feeling and dignity declared that in the step he had taken he had not thought of his brother, but of her and her happiness.

"I believe you; I know how you love me," Helene promptly answered. "Wait; I want to give your brother his answer in your presence."

The clock struck ten. Monsieur Rambaud made his entry into the bedroom. With outstretched hands she went to meet him.

"I thank you for your proposal, my friend," said she. "I am very grateful; and you have done well in speaking—"

She was gazing calmly into his face, holding his big hand in her grasp. Trembling all over, he dared not lift his eyes.

"Yet I must have time to consider," she resumed. "You will perhaps have to give me a long time."

"Oh! as long as you like—six months, a year, longer if you please," exclaimed he with a light heart, well pleased that she had not forthwith sent him about his business.

His excitement brought a faint smile to her face. "But I intend that we shall still continue friends," said she. "You will come here as usual, and simply give me your promise to remain content till I speak to you about the matter. Is that understood?"

He had withdrawn his hand, and was now feverishly hunting for his hat, signifying his acquiescence by a continuous bobbing of the head. Then, at the moment of leaving, he found his voice once more.

"Listen to me," said he. "You now know that I am there—don't you? Well, whatever happens I shall always be there. That's all the Abbe should have told you. In ten years, if you like; you will only have to make a sign. I shall obey you!"

And it was he who a last time took Helene's hand and gripped it as though he would crush it. On the stairs the two brothers turned round with the usual good-bye:

"Till next Tuesday!"

"Yes, Tuesday," answered Helene.

On returning to her room a fresh downfall of rain beating against the shutters filled her with grave concern. Good heavens! what an obstinate downpour, and how wet her poor friends would get! She opened the window and looked down into the street. Sudden gusts of wind were making the gaslights flicker, and amid the shiny puddles and shimmering rain she could see the round figure of Monsieur Rambaud, as he went off with dancing gait, exultant in the darkness, seemingly caring nothing for the drenching torrent.

Jeanne, however, was very grave, for she had overheard some of her playfellow's last words. She had just taken off her little boots, and was sitting on the edge of the bed in her nightgown, in deep cogitation. On entering the room to kiss her, her mother discovered her thus.

"Good-night, Jeanne; kiss me."

Then, as the child did not seem to hear her, Helene sank down in front of her, and clasped her round the waist, asking her in a whisper: "So you would be glad if he came to live with us?"

The question seemed to bring no surprise to Jeanne. She was doubtless pondering over this very matter. She slowly nodded her head.

"But you know," said her mother, "he would be always beside us—

night and day, at table—everywhere!"

A great trouble dawned in the clear depths of the child's eyes. She nestled her cheek against her mother's shoulder, kissed her neck, and finally, with a quiver, whispered in her ear: "Mamma, would he kiss you?"

A crimson flush rose to Helene's brow. In her first surprise she was at a loss to answer, but at last she murmured: "He would be the same as your father, my darling!"

Then Jeanne's little arms tightened their hold, and she burst into loud and grievous sobbing. "Oh! no, no!" she cried chokingly. "I don't want it then! Oh! mamma, do please tell him I don't. Go and tell him I won't have it!"

She gasped, and threw herself on her mother's bosom, covering her with tears and kisses. Helene did her utmost to appease her, assuring her she would make it all right; but Jeanne was bent on having a definite answer at once.

"Oh! say no! say no, darling mother! You know it would kill me. Never! Oh, never! Eh?"

"Well, I'll promise it will never be. Now, be good and lie down."

For some minutes longer the child, speechless with emotion, clasped her mother in her arms, as though powerless to tear herself away, and intent on guarding her against all who might seek to take her from her. After some time Helene was able to put her to bed; but for a part of the night she had to watch beside her. Jeanne would start violently in her sleep, and every half-hour her eyes would open to make sure of her mother's presence, and then she would doze off again, with her lips pressed to Helene's hand.

CHAPTER VIII.

It was a month of exquisite mildness. The April sun had draped the garden in tender green, light and delicate as lace. Twining around the railing were the slender shoots of the lush clematis, while the budding honeysuckle filled the air with its sweet, almost sugary perfume. On both sides of the trim and close-shaven lawn red geraniums and white stocks gave the flower beds a glow of color; and at the end of the garden the clustering elms, hiding the adjacent houses, reared the green drapery of their branches, whose little leaves trembled with the least breath of air.

For more than three weeks the sky had remained blue and cloudless. It was like a miraculous spring celebrating the new youth and blossoming that had burst into life in Helene's heart. Every afternoon she went down into the garden with Jeanne. A place was assigned her against the first elm on the right. A chair was ready for her; and on the morrow she would still find on the gravel walk the scattered clippings of thread that had fallen from her work on the previous afternoon.

"You are quite at home," Madame Deberle repeated every evening, displaying for Helene one of those affections of hers, which usually lasted some six months. "You will come to-morrow, of course; and try to come earlier, won't you?"

Helene, in truth, felt thoroughly at her ease there. By degrees she became accustomed to this nook of greenery, and looked forward to her afternoon visit with the longing of a child. What charmed her most in this garden was the exquisite trimness of the lawn and flower beds. Not a single weed interfered with the symmetry of the plants. Helene spent her time there, calmly and restfully. The neatly laid out flower beds, and the network of ivy, the withered leaves of which were carefully removed by the gardener, could exercise no disturbing influence on her spirit. Seated beneath the deep shadow of the elm-trees, in this quiet spot which Madame Deberle's presence perfumed with a faint odor of musk, she could have imagined herself in a drawing-room; and only the sight of the blue sky, when she raised her head, reminded her that she was out-of-doors, and prompted her to breathe freely.

Often, without seeing a soul, the two women would thus pass the afternoon. Jeanne and Lucien played at their feet. There would be long intervals of silence, and then Madame Deberle, who disliked reverie, would chatter for hours, quite satisfied with the silent acquiescence of Helene, and rattling off again if the other even so much as nodded. She would tell endless stories concerning the ladies of her acquaintance, get up schemes for parties during the coming winter, vent magpie opinions on the day's news and the society trifling which filled her narrow brain, the whole intermingled with affectionate outbursts over the children, and sentimental remarks on the delights of friendship. Helene allowed her to squeeze her hands. She did not always lend an attentive ear; but, in this atmosphere of unceasing tenderness, she showed herself greatly touched by Juliette's caresses, and pronounced her to be a perfect angel of kindness.

Sometimes, to Madame Deberle's intense delight, a visitor would drop in. Since Easter she had ceased receiving on Saturdays, as was usual at this time of the year. But she dreaded solitude, and a casual unceremonious visit paid her in her garden gave her the greatest pleasure. She was now busily engaged in settling on the watering-place where she would spend her holiday in August. To every visitor she retailed the same talk; discoursed on the fact that her husband would not accompany her to the seaside; and then poured forth a flood of questions, as she could not make up her mind where to go. She did not ask for herself, however; no, it was all on Lucien's account. When the foppish youth Malignon came he seated himself astride a rustic chair. He, indeed, loathed the country; one must be mad, he would declare, to exile oneself from Paris with the idea of catching influenza beside the sea. However, he took part in the discussions on the merits of the various watering-places, all of which were horrid, said he; apart from Trouville there was not a place worthy of any consideration whatever. Day after day Helene listened to the same talk, yet without feeling wearied; indeed, she even derived pleasure from this monotony, which lulled her into dreaming of one thing only. The last day of the month came, and still Madame Deberle had not decided where to go.

As Helene was leaving one evening, her friend said to her: "I must go out to-morrow; but that needn't prevent you from coming down here. Wait for me; I shan't be back late."

Helene consented; and, alone in the garden, there spent a delicious afternoon. Nothing stirred, save the sparrows fluttering in the trees overhead. This little sunny nook entranced her, and, from that day, her happiest afternoons were those on which her friend left her alone.

A closer intimacy was springing up between the Deberles and herself. She dined with them like a friend who is pressed to stay when the family sits down to table; when she lingered under the elm-trees and Pierre came down to announce dinner, Juliette would implore her to remain, and she sometimes yielded. They were family dinners, enlivened by the noisy pranks of the children. Doctor Deberle and Helene seemed good friends, whose sensible and somewhat reserved natures sympathized well. Thus it was that Juliette frequently declared: "Oh, you two would get on capitally! Your composure exasperates me!"

The doctor returned from his round of visits at about six o'clock every evening. He found the ladies in the garden, and sat down beside them. On the earlier occasions, Helene started up with the idea of leaving her friends to themselves, but her sudden departure displeased Juliette greatly, and she now perforce had to remain. She became almost a member of this family, which appeared to be so closely united. On the doctor's arrival his wife held up her cheek to him, always with the same loving gesture, and he kissed her; then, as Lucien began clambering up his legs, he kept him on his knees while chatting away. The child would clap his tiny hands on his father's mouth, pull his hair, and play so many pranks that in the upshot he had to be put down, and told to go and play with Jeanne. The fun would bring a smile to Helene's face, and she neglected her work for the moment, to gaze at father, mother, and child. The kiss of the husband and wife gave her no pain, and Lucien's tricks filled her with soft emotion. It might have been said that she had found a haven of refuge amidst this family's quiet content.

Meanwhile the sun would sink into the west, gilding the tree tops with its rays. Serene peacefulness fell from the grey heavens. Juliette, whose curiosity was insatiable, even in company with strangers, plagued her husband with ceaseless questions, and often lacked the patience to wait his replies. "Where have you been? What have you been about?"

Thereupon he would describe his round of visits to them, repeat any news of what was going on, or speak of some cloth or piece of furniture he had caught a glimpse of in a shop window. While he was speaking, his eyes often met those of Helene, but neither turned away the head. They gazed into each other's face for a moment with grave looks, as though heart were being revealed to heart; but after a little they smiled and their eyes dropped. Juliette, fidgety and sprightly, though she would often assume a studied languor, allowed them no opportunity for lengthy conversation, but burst with her interruptions into any talk whatever. Still they exchanged a few words, quite commonplace, slowly articulated sentences which seemed to assume a deep meaning, and to linger in the air after having been spoken. They approvingly punctuated each word the other uttered, as though they had thoughts in common. It was an intimate sympathy that was growing up between them, springing from the depths of their beings, and becoming closer even when they were silent. Sometimes Juliette, rather ashamed of monopolizing all the talk, would cease her magpie chatter.

"Dear me!" she would exclaim, "you are getting bored, aren't you? We are talking of matters which can have no possible interest for you."

"Oh, never mind me," Helene answered blithely. "I never tire. It is a pleasure to me to listen and say nothing."

She was uttering no untruth. It was during the lengthy periods of silence that she experienced most delight in being there. With her head bent over her work, only lifting her eyes at long intervals to exchange with the doctor those interminable looks that riveted their hearts the closer, she willingly surrendered herself to the egotism of her emotion. Between herself and him, she now confessed it, there existed a secret sentiment, a something very sweet—all the sweeter because no one in the world shared it with them. But she kept her secret with a tranquil mind, her sense of honor quite unruffled, for no thought of evil ever disturbed her. How good he was to his wife and child! She loved him the more when he made Lucien jump or kissed Juliette on the cheek. Since she had seen him in his own home their friendship had greatly increased. She was now as one of the family; she never dreamt that the intimacy could be broken. And within her own breast she called him Henri—naturally, too, from hearing Juliette address him so. When her lips said "Sir," through all her being "Henri" was re-echoed.

One day the doctor found Helene alone under the elms. Juliette now went out nearly every afternoon.

"Hello! is my wife not with you?" he exclaimed.

"No, she has left me to myself," she answered laughingly. "It is true you have come home earlier than usual."

The children were playing at the other end of the garden. He sat down beside her. Their *tete-a-tete* produced no agitation in either of them. For nearly an hour they spoke of all sorts of matters, without for a moment feeling any desire to allude to the tenderness which filled their hearts. What was the good of referring to that? Did they not well know what might have been said? They had no confession to make. Theirs was the joy of being together, of talking of many things, of surrendering themselves to the pleasure of their isolation without a shadow of regret, in the very spot where every evening he embraced his wife in her presence.

That day he indulged in some jokes respecting her devotion to work. "Do you know," said he, "I do not even know the color of your eyes? They are always bent on your needle."

She raised her head and looked straight into his face, as was her custom. "Do you wish to tease me?" she asked gently.

But he went on. "Ah! they are grey—grey, tinged with blue, are they not?"

This was the utmost limit to which they dared go; but these words, the first that had sprung to his lips, were fraught with infinite tenderness. From that day onwards he frequently found her alone in the twilight. Despite themselves, and without their having any knowledge of it, their intimacy grew apace. They spoke in an altered voice, with caressing inflections, which were not apparent when others were present. And yet, when Juliette came in, full of gossip about her day in town, they could keep up the talk they had already begun without even troubling themselves to draw their chairs apart. It seemed as though this lovely springtide and this garden, with its blossoming lilac, were prolonging within their hearts the first rapture of love.

Towards the end of the month, Madame Deberle grew excited over a grand idea. The thought of giving a children's ball had suddenly struck her. The season was already far advanced, but the scheme took such hold on her foolish brain that she hurried on the preparations with reckless haste. She desired that the affair should be quite perfect; it was

to be a fancy-dress ball. And, in her own home, and in other people's
houses, everywhere, in short, she now spoke of nothing but her ball.
The conversations on the subject which took place in the garden were
endless. The foppish Malignon thought the project rather stupid, still he
condescended to take some interest in it, and promised to bring a comic
singer with whom he was acquainted.

One afternoon, while they were all sitting under the trees, Juliette
introduced the grave question of the costumes which Lucien and
Jeanne should wear.

"It is so difficult to make up one's mind," said she. "I have been
thinking of a clown's dress in white satin."

"Oh, that's too common!" declared Malignon. "There will be a
round dozen of clowns at your ball. Wait, you must have something
novel." Thereupon he began gravely pondering, sucking the head of
his cane all the while.

Pauline came up at the moment, and proclaimed her desire to appear as a soubrette.

"You!" screamed Madame Deberle, in astonishment. "You won't
appear in costume at all! Do you think yourself a child, you great stupid? You will oblige me by coming in a white dress."

"Oh, but it would have pleased me so!" exclaimed Pauline, who,
despite her eighteen years and plump girlish figure, liked nothing better than to romp with a band of little ones.

Meanwhile Helene sat at the foot of her tree working away, and
raising her head at times to smile at the doctor and Monsieur Rambaud,
who stood in front of her conversing. Monsieur Rambaud had now become quite intimate with the Deberle family.

"Well," said the doctor, "and how are you going to dress, Jeanne?"

He got no further, for Malignon burst out: "I've got it! I've got it!
Lucien must be a marquis of the time of Louis XV."

He waved his cane with a triumphant air; but, as no one of the
company hailed his idea with enthusiasm, he appeared astonished.
"What, don't you see it? Won't it be for Lucien to receive his little
guests? So you place him, dressed as a marquis, at the drawing-room
door, with a large bouquet of roses on his coat, and he bows to the
ladies."

"But there will be dozens of marquises at the ball!" objected Juliette.

"What does that matter?" replied Malignon coolly. "The more marquises the greater the fun. I tell you it is the best thing you can hit upon. The master of the house must be dressed as a marquis, or the ball will be a complete failure."

Such was his conviction of his scheme's success that at last it was adopted by Juliette with enthusiasm. As a matter of fact, a dress in the Pompadour style, white satin embroidered with posies, would be altogether charming.

"And what about Jeanne?" again asked the doctor.

The little girl had just buried her head against her mother's shoulder in the caressing manner so characteristic of her; and as an answer was about to cross Helene's lips, she murmured:

"Oh! mamma, you know what you promised me, don't you?"

"What was it?" asked those around her.

Then, as her daughter gave her an imploring look, Helene laughingly replied: "Jeanne does not wish her dress to be known."

"Yes, that's so," said the child; "you don't create any effect when you tell your dress beforehand."

Every one was tickled with this display of coquetry, and Monsieur Rambaud thought he might tease the child about it. For some time past Jeanne had been ill-tempered with him, and the poor man, at his wits' end to hit upon a mode of again gaining her favor, thought teasing her the best method of conciliation. Keeping his eyes on her face, he several times repeated: "I know; I shall tell, I shall tell!"

Jeanne, however, became quite livid. Her gentle, sickly face assumed an expression of ferocious anger; her brow was furrowed by two deep wrinkles, and her chin drooped with nervous agitation.

"You!" she screamed excitedly; "you will say nothing!" And, as he still feigned a resolve to speak, she rushed at him madly, and shouted out: "Hold your tongue! I will have you hold your tongue! I will! I will!"

Helene had been unable to prevent this fit of blind anger, such as sometimes took possession of the child, and with some harshness exclaimed: "Jeanne, take care; I shall whip you!"

But Jeanne paid no heed, never once heard her. Trembling from head to foot, stamping on the ground, and choking with rage, she again and again repeated, "I will! I will!" in a voice that grew more and more hoarse and broken; and her hands convulsively gripped hold of Monsieur Rambaud's arm, which she twisted with extraordinary strength. In vain did Helene threaten her. At last, perceiving her inability to quell

her by severity, and grieved to the heart by such a display before so
many people, she contented herself by saying gently: "Jeanne, you are
grieving me very much."

The child immediately quitted her hold and turned her head. And
when she caught sight of her mother, with disconsolate face and eyes
swimming with repressed tears, she on her side burst into loud sobs,
and threw herself on Helene's neck, exclaiming in her grief: "No,
mamma! no, mamma!"

She passed her hands over her mother's face, as though to prevent
her weeping. Helene, however, slowly put her from her, and then the little one, broken-hearted and distracted, threw herself on a seat a short
distance off, where her sobs broke out louder than ever. Lucien, to
whom she was always held up as an example to follow, gazed at her surprised and somewhat pleased. And then, as Helene folded up her work,
apologizing for so regrettable an incident, Juliette remarked to her:

"Dear me! we have to pardon children everything. Besides, the little one has the best of hearts, and is grieved so much, poor darling,
that she has been already punished too severely."

So saying she called Jeanne to come and kiss her; but the child remained on her seat, rejecting the offer of forgiveness, and still choking
with tears.

Monsieur Rambaud and the doctor, however, walked to her side,
and the former, bending over her, asked, in tones husky with emotion:
"Tell me, my pet, what has vexed you? What have I done to you?"

"Oh!" she replied, drawing away her hands and displaying a face
full of anguish, "you wanted to take my mamma from me!"

The doctor, who was listening, burst into laughter. Monsieur Rambaud at first failed to grasp her meaning.

"What is this you're talking of?"

"Yes, indeed, the other Tuesday! Oh! you know very well; you were
on your knees, and asked me what I should say if you were to stay
with us!"

The smile vanished from the doctor's face; his lips became ashy
pale, and quivered. A flush, on the other hand, mounted to Monsieur
Rambaud's cheek, and he whispered to Jeanne: "But you said yourself
that we should always play together?"

"No, no; I did not know at the time," the child resumed excitedly.
"I tell you I don't want it. Don't ever speak to me of it again, and then

we shall be friends."

Helene was on her feet now, with her needlework in its basket, and the last words fell on her ear. "Come, let us go up, Jeanne," she said; "your tears are not pleasant company."

She bowed, and pushed the child before her. The doctor, with livid face, gazed at her fixedly. Monsieur Rambaud was in dismay. As for Madame Deberle and Pauline, they had taken hold of Lucien, and were making him turn between them, while excitedly discussing the question of his Pompadour dress.

On the morrow Helene was left alone under the elms. Madame Deberle was running about in the interests of her ball, and had taken Lucien and Jeanne with her. On the doctor's return home, at an earlier hour than usual, he hurried down the garden steps. However, he did not seat himself, but wandered aimlessly round the young woman, at times tearing strips of bark from the trees with his finger-nails. She lifted her eyes for a moment, feeling anxious at sight of his agitation; and then again began plying her needle with a somewhat trembling hand.

"The weather is going to break up," said she, feeling uncomfortable as the silence continued. "The afternoon seems quite cold."

"We are only in April, remember," he replied, with a brave effort to control his voice.

Then he appeared to be on the point of leaving her, but turned round, and suddenly asked: "So you are going to get married?"

This abrupt question took her wholly by surprise, and her work fell from her hands. Her face blanched, but by a supreme effort of will remained unimpassioned, as though she were a marble statue, fixing dilated eyes upon him. She made no reply, and he continued in imploring tones:

"Oh! I pray you, answer me. One word, one only. Are you going to get married?"

"Yes, perhaps. What concern is it of yours?" she retorted, in a tone of icy indifference.

He made a passionate gesture, and exclaimed:

"It is impossible!"

"Why should it be?" she asked, still keeping her eyes fixed on his face.

Her glance stayed the words upon his lips, and he was forced to silence. For a moment longer he remained near her, pressing his hands to his brow, and then fled away, with a feeling of suffocation in his throat, dreading lest he might give expression to his despair; while she, with assumed tranquility, once more turned to her work.

But the spell of those delicious afternoons was gone. Next day shone fair and sunny, and Helene seemed ill at ease from the moment she found herself alone with him. The pleasant intimacy, the happy trustfulness, which sanctioned their sitting side by side in blissful security, and revelling in the unalloyed joy of being together, no longer existed. Despite his intense carefulness to give her no cause for alarm, he would sometimes gaze at her and tremble with sudden excitement, while his face crimsoned with a rush of blood. From her own heart had fled its wonted happy calm; quivers ran through her frame; she felt languid; her hands grew weary, and forsook their work.

She now no longer allowed Jeanne to wander from her side. Between himself and her the doctor found this constant onlooker, watching him with large, clear eyes. But what pained Helene most was that she now felt ill at ease in Madame Deberle's company. When the latter returned of an afternoon, with her hair swept about by the wind, and called her "my dear" while relating the incidents of some shopping expedition, she no longer listened with her former quiet smile. A storm arose from the depths of her soul, stirring up feelings to which she dared not give a name. Shame and spite seemed mingled in them. However, her honorable nature gained the mastery, and she gave her hand to Juliette, but without being able to repress the shudder which ran through her as she pressed her friend's warm fingers.

The weather had now broken up. Frequent rain forced the ladies to take refuge in the Japanese pavilion. The garden, with its whilom exquisite order, became transformed into a lake, and no one dared venture on the walks, on account of the mud. However, whenever the sun peeped out from behind the clouds, the dripping greenery soon dried; pearls hung from each little blossom of the lilac trees; and under the elms big drops fell splashing on the ground.

"At last I've arranged it; it will be on Saturday," said Madame Deberle one day. "My dear, I'm quite tired out with the whole affair. Now, you'll be here at two o'clock, won't you? Jeanne will open the ball with Lucien."

And thereupon, surrendering to a flow of tenderness, in ecstasy over the preparations for her ball, she embraced both children, and, laughingly catching hold of Helene, pressed two resounding kisses on her cheeks.

"That's my reward!" she exclaimed merrily. "You know I deserve it; I have run about enough. You'll see what a success it will be!"

But Helene remained chilled to the heart, while the doctor, with Lucien clinging to his neck, gazed at them over the child's fair head.

CHAPTER IX.

In the hall of the doctor's house stood Pierre, in dress coat and white cravat, throwing open the door as each carriage rolled up. Puffs of dank air rushed in; the afternoon was rainy, and a yellow light illumined the narrow hall, with its curtained doorways and array of green plants. It was only two o'clock, but the evening seemed as near at hand as on a dismal winter's day.

However, as soon as the servant opened the door of the first drawing-room, a stream of light dazzled the guests. The shutters had been closed, and the curtains carefully drawn, and no gleam from the dull sky could gain admittance. The lamps standing here and there on the furniture, and the lighted candles of the chandelier and the crystal wall-brackets, gave the apartment somewhat the appearance of a brilliantly illuminated chapel. Beyond the smaller drawing-room, whose green hangings rather softened the glare of the light, was the large black-and-gold one, decorated as magnificently as for the ball which Madame Deberle gave every year in the month of January.

The children were beginning to arrive, while Pauline gave her attention to the ranging of a number of chairs in front of the dining-room doorway, where the door had been removed from its hinges and replaced by a red curtain.

"Papa," she cried, "just lend me a hand! We shall never be ready."

Monsieur Letellier, who, with his arms behind his back, was gazing at the chandelier, hastened to give the required assistance. Pauline carried the chairs about herself. She had paid due deference to her sister's request, and was robed in white; only her dress opened squarely at the neck and displayed her bosom.

"At last we are ready," she exclaimed: "they can come when they like. But what is Juliette dreaming about? She has been ever so long dressing Lucien!"

Just at that moment Madame Deberle entered, leading the little marquis, and everybody present began raising admiring remarks. "Oh! what a love! What a darling he is!" His coat was of white satin embroidered with flowers, his long waistcoat was embroidered with gold, and his knee-breeches were of cherry-colored silk. Lace clustered round his chin, and delicate wrists. A sword, a mere toy with a great rose-red knot, rattled against his hip.

"Now you must do the honors," his mother said to him, as she led him into the outer room.

For eight days past he had been repeating his lesson, and struck a cavalier attitude with his little legs, his powdered head thrown slightly back, and his cocked hat tucked under his left arm. As each of his lady-guests was ushered into the room, he bowed low, offered his arm, exchanged courteous greetings, and returned to the threshold. Those near him laughed over his intense seriousness in which there was a dash of effrontery. This was the style in which he received Marguerite Tissot, a little lady five years old, dressed in a charming milkmaid costume, with a milk-can hanging at her side; so too did he greet the Berthier children, Blanche and Sophie, the one masquerading as Folly, the other dressed in soubrette style; and he had even the hardihood to tackle Valentine de Chermette, a tall young lady of some fourteen years, whom her mother always dressed in Spanish costume, and at her side his figure appeared so slight that she seemed to be carrying him along. However, he was profoundly embarrassed in the presence of the Levasseur family, which numbered five girls, who made their appearance in a row of increasing height, the youngest being scarcely two years old, while the eldest was ten. All five were arrayed in Red Riding-Hood costumes, their head-dresses and gowns being in poppy-colored satin with black velvet bands, with which their lace aprons strikingly contrasted. At last Lucien, making up his mind, bravely flung away his three-cornered hat, and led the two elder girls, one hanging on each arm, into the drawing-room, closely followed by the three others. There was a good deal of laughter at it, but the little man never lost his self-possession for a moment.

In the meantime Madame Deberle was taking her sister to task in a corner.

"Good gracious! is it possible! what a fearfully low-necked dress you are wearing!"

"Dear, dear! what have I done now? Papa hasn't said a word," answered Pauline coolly. "If you're anxious, I'll put some flowers at my breast."

She plucked a handful of blossoms from a flower-stand where they were growing and allowed them to nestle in her bosom; while Madame Deberle was surrounded by several mammas in stylish visiting-dresses, who were already profuse in their compliments about her ball. As Lucien was passing them, his mother arranged a loose curl of his powdered hair, while he stood on tip-toe to whisper in her ear:

"Where's Jeanne?"

"She will be here immediately, my darling. Take good care not to fall. Run away, there comes little Mademoiselle Guiraud. Ah! she is wearing an Alsatian costume."

The drawing-room was now filling rapidly; the rows of chairs fronting the red curtain were almost all occupied, and a hubbub of children's voices was rising. The boys were flocking into the room in groups. There were already three Harlequins, four Punches, a Figaro, some Tyrolese peasants, and a few Highlanders. Young Master Berthier was dressed as a page. Little Guiraud, a mere bantling of two-and-a-half summers, wore his clown's costume in so comical a style that every one as he passed lifted him up and kissed him.

"Here comes Jeanne," exclaimed Madame Deberle, all at once. "Oh, she is lovely!"

A murmur ran round the room; heads were bent forward, and every one gave vent to exclamations of admiration. Jeanne was standing on the threshold of the outer room, awaiting her mother, who was taking off her cloak in the hall. The child was robed in a Japanese dress of unusual splendor. The gown, embroidered with flowers and strange-looking birds, swept to her feet, which were hidden from view; while beneath her broad waist-ribbon the flaps, drawn aside, gave a glimpse of a green petticoat, watered with yellow. Nothing could be more strangely bewitching than her delicate features seen under the shadow of her hair, coiled above her head with long pins thrust through it, while her chin and oblique eyes, small and sparkling, pictured to the life a young lady of Yeddo, strolling amidst the perfume of tea and benzoin. And she lingered there hesitatingly, with all the sickly languor of a tropical flower pining for the land of its birth.

Behind her, however, appeared Helene. Both, in thus suddenly passing from the dull daylight of the street into the brilliant glare of the
wax candles, blinked their eyes as though blinded, while their faces were
irradiated with smiles. The rush of warm air and the perfumes, the scent
of violets rising above all else, almost stifled them, and brought a flush
of red to their cheeks. Each guest, on passing the doorway, wore a similar air of surprise and hesitancy.

"Why, Lucien! where are you?" exclaimed Madame Deberle.

The boy had not caught sight of Jeanne. But now he rushed forward and seized her arm, forgetting to make his bow. And they were so
dainty, so loving, the little marquis in his flowered coat, and the Japanese maiden in her purple embroidered gown, that they might have been
taken for two statuettes of Dresden china, daintily gilded and painted,
into which life had been suddenly infused.

"You know, I was waiting for you," whispered Lucien. "Oh, it is so
nasty to give everybody my arm! Of course, we'll keep beside each
other, eh?"

And he sat himself down with her in the first row of chairs, wholly
oblivious of his duties as host.

"Oh, I was so uneasy!" purred Juliette into Helene's ear. "I was beginning to fear that Jeanne had been taken ill."

Helene proffered apology; dressing children, said she, meant endless labor. She was still standing in a corner of the drawing-room, one
of a cluster of ladies, when her heart told her that the doctor was approaching behind her. He was making his way from behind the red curtain, beneath which he had dived to give some final instructions. But
suddenly he came to a standstill. He, too, had divined her presence,
though she had not yet turned her head. Attired in a dress of black
grenadine, she had never appeared more queenly in her beauty; and a
thrill passed through him as he breathed the cool air which she had
brought with her from outside, and wafted from her shoulders and
arms, gleaming white under their transparent covering.

"Henri has no eyes for anybody," exclaimed Pauline, with a laugh.
"Ah, good-day, Henri!"

Thereupon he advanced towards the group of ladies, with a courteous greeting. Mademoiselle Aurelie, who was amongst them, engaged
his attention for the moment to point out to him a nephew whom she

had brought with her. He was all complaisance. Helene, without speaking, gave him her hand, encased in its black glove, but he dared not clasp it with marked force.

"Oh! here you are!" said Madame Deberle, as she appeared beside them. "I have been looking for you everywhere. It is nearly three o'clock; they had better begin."

"Certainly; at once," was his reply.

The drawing-room was now crowded. All round it, in the brilliant glare thrown from the chandelier, sat the fathers and mothers, their walking costumes serving to fringe the circle with less vivid colors. Some ladies, drawing their chairs together, formed groups; men standing motionless along the walls filled up the gaps; while in the doorway leading to the next room a cluster of frock-coated guests could be seen crowding together and peering over each other's shoulders. The light fell wholly on the little folks, noisy in their glee, as they rustled about in their seats in the center of the large room. There were almost a hundred children packed together; in an endless variety of gay costumes, bright with blue and red. It was like a sea of fair heads, varying from pale yellow to ruddy gold, with here and there bows and flowers gleaming vividly—or like a field of ripe grain, spangled with poppies and cornflowers, and waving to and fro as though stirred by a breeze. At times, amidst this confusion of ribbons and lace, of silk and velvet, a face was turned round—a pink nose, a pair of blue eyes, a smiling or pouting little mouth. There were some, no higher than one's boots, who were buried out of sight between big lads of ten years of age, and whom their mothers sought from a distance, but in vain. A few of the boys looked bored and foolish by the side of girls who were busy spreading out their skirts. Some, however, were already very venturesome, jogging the elbows of their fair neighbors with whom they were unacquainted, and laughing in their faces. But the royalty of the gathering remained with the girls, some of whom, clustering in groups, stirred about in such a way as to threaten destruction to their chairs, and chattered so loudly that the grown-up folks could no longer hear one another speaking. And all eyes were intently gazing at the red curtain.

Slowly was it drawn aside, and in the recess of the doorway appeared a puppet-show. There was a hushed silence. Then all at once Punch sprang in, with so ferocious a yell that baby Guiraud could not

restrain a responsive cry of terror and delight. It was one of those
bloodthirsty dramas in which Punch, having administered a sound beating to the magistrate, murders the policeman, and tramples with ferocious glee on every law, human and divine. At every cudgelling
bestowed on the wooden heads the pitiless audience went into shrieks
of laughter; and the sharp thrusts delivered by the puppets at each
other's breasts, the duels in which they beat a tattoo on one another's
skulls as though they were empty pumpkins, the awful havoc of legs and
arms, reducing the characters to a jelly, served to increase the roars of
laughter which rang out from all sides. But the climax of enjoyment
was reached when Punch sawed off the policeman's head on the edge
of the stage; an operation provocative of such hysterical mirth that the
rows of juveniles were plunged into confusion, swaying to and fro with
glee till they all but fell on one another. One tiny girl, but four years
old, all pink and white, considered the spectacle so entrancing that she
pressed her little hands devoutly to her heart. Others burst into applause, while the boys laughed, with mouths agape, their deeper voices
mingling with the shrill peals from the girls.

"How amused they are!" whispered the doctor. He had returned to
his place near Helene. She was in high spirits like the children. Behind
her, he sat inhaling the intoxicating perfume which came from her hair.
And as one puppet on the stage dealt another an exceptionally hard
knock she turned to him and exclaimed: "Do you know, it is awfully
funny!"

The youngsters, crazy with excitement, were now interfering with
the action of the drama. They were giving answers to the various characters. One young lady, who must have been well up in the plot, was
busy explaining what would next happen.

"He'll beat his wife to death in a minute! Now they are going to
hang him!"

The youngest of the Levasseur girls, who was two years old,
shrieked out all at once:

"Mamma, mamma, will they put him on bread and water?"

All sorts of exclamations and reflections followed. Meanwhile Helene, gazing into the crowd of children, remarked: "I cannot see Jeanne.
Is she enjoying herself?"

Then the doctor bent forward, with head perilously near her own,
and whispered: "There she is, between that harlequin and the Norman

peasant maiden! You can see the pins gleaming in her hair. She is laughing very heartily."

He still leaned towards her, her cool breath playing on his cheek. Till
now no confession had escaped them; preserving silence, their intimacy
had only been marred for a few days past by a vague sensation of discomfort. But amidst these bursts of happy laughter, gazing upon the little folks before her, Helene became once more, in sooth, a very child,
surrendering herself to her feelings, while Henri's breath beat warm
upon her neck. The whacks from the cudgel, now louder than ever,
filled her with a quiver which inflated her bosom, and she turned towards him with sparkling eyes.

"Good heavens! what nonsense it all is!" she said each time. "See
how they hit one another!"

"Oh! their heads are hard enough!" he replied, trembling.

This was all his heart could find to say. Their minds were fast lapsing into childhood once more. Punch's unedifying life was fostering
languor within their breasts. When the drama drew to its close with the
appearance of the devil, and the final fight and general massacre ensued, Helene in leaning back pressed against Henri's hand, which was
resting on the back of her arm-chair; while the juvenile audience, shouting and clapping their hands, made the very chairs creak with their enthusiasm.

The red curtain dropped again, and the uproar was at its height
when Malignon's presence was announced by Pauline, in her customary style: "Ah! here's the handsome Malignon!"

He made his way into the room, shoving the chairs aside, quite out
of breath.

"Dear me! what a funny idea to close the shutters!" he exclaimed,
surprised and hesitating. "People might imagine that somebody in the
house was dead." Then, turning towards Madame Deberle, who was
approaching him, he continued: "Well, you can boast of having made
me run about! Ever since the morning I have been hunting for
Perdiguet; you know whom I mean, my singer fellow. But I haven't been
able to lay my hands on him, and I have brought you the great Morizot
instead."

The great Morizot was an amateur who entertained drawing-rooms
by conjuring with juggler-balls. A gipsy table was assigned to him, and
on this he accomplished his most wonderful tricks; but it all passed off

without the spectators evincing the slightest interest. The poor little darlings were pulling serious faces; some of the tinier mites fell fast asleep, sucking their thumbs. The older children turned their heads and smiled towards their parents, who were themselves yawning behind their hands. There was thus a general feeling of relief when the great Morizot decided to take his table away.

"Oh! he's awfully clever," whispered Malignon into Madame Deberle's neck.

But the red curtain was drawn aside once again, and an entrancing spectacle brought all the little folks to their feet.

Along the whole extent of the dining-room stretched the table, laid and bedecked as for a grand dinner, and illumined by the bright radiance of the central lamp and a pair of large candelabra. There were fifty covers laid; in the middle and at either end were shallow baskets, full of flowers; between these towered tall *epergnes*, filled to overflowing with crackers in gilded and colored paper. Then there were mountains of decorated cakes, pyramids of iced fruits, piles of sandwiches, and, less prominent, a whole host of symmetrically disposed plates, bearing sweetmeats and pastry: buns, cream puffs, and *brioches* alternating with dry biscuits, cracknals, and fancy almond cakes. Jellies were quivering in their glass dishes. Whipped creams waited in porcelain bowls. And round the table sparkled the silver helmets of champagne bottles, no higher than one's hand, made specially to suit the little guests. It all looked like one of those gigantic feasts which children conjure up in dreamland—a feast served with the solemnity that attends a repast of grown-up folks—a fairy transformation of the table to which their own parents sat down, and on which the horns of plenty of innumerable pastry-cooks and toy dealers had been emptied.

"Come, come, give the ladies your arms!" said Madame Deberle, her face covered with smiles as she watched the delight of the children.

But the filing off in couples proved a lure. Lucien, who had triumphantly taken Jeanne's arm, went first. But the others following behind fell somewhat into confusion, and the mothers were forced to come and assign them places, remaining close at hand, especially behind the babies, whom they watched lest any mischance should befall them. Truth to tell, the guests at first seemed rather uncomfortable; they looked at one another, felt afraid to lay hands on the good things, and were vaguely disquieted by this new social organization in which everything appeared to be topsy-turvy, the children seated at table while their parents remained standing. At length the older ones gained confidence and commenced the attack. And when the mothers entered into the fray, and cut up the large cakes, helping those in their vicinity, the feast speedily became very animated and noisy. The exquisite symmetry of the table was destroyed as though by a tempest. The two Berthier girls, Blanche and Sophie, laughed at the sight of their plates, which had been filled with something of everything—jam, custard, cake, and fruit. The five young ladies of the Levasseur family took sole possession of a corner laden with dainties, while Valentine, proud of her fourteen years, acted the lady's part, and looked after the comfort of her little neighbors. Lucien, however, impatient to display his politeness, uncorked a bottle of champagne, but in so clumsy a way that the whole contents spurted over his cherry silk breeches. There was quite a to-do about it.

"Kindly leave the bottles alone! I am to uncork the champagne," shouted Pauline.

She bustled about in an extraordinary fashion, purely for her own amusement. On the entry of a servant with the chocolate pot, she seized it and filled the cups with the greatest glee, as active in the performance as any restaurant waiter. Next she took round some ices and glasses of syrup and water, set them down for a moment to stuff a little baby-girl who had been overlooked, and then went off again, asking everyone questions.

"What is it you wish, my pet? Eh? A cake? Yes, my darling, wait a moment; I am going to pass you the oranges. Now eat away, you little stupids, you shall play afterwards."

Madame Deberle, calm and dignified, declared that they ought to be left alone, and would acquit themselves very well.

At one end of the room sat Helene and some other ladies laughing at the scene which the table presented; all the rosy mouths were eating with the full strength of their beautiful white teeth. And nothing could eclipse in drollery the occasional lapses from the polished behavior of well-bred children to the outrageous freaks of young savages. With both hands gripping their glasses, they drank to the very dregs, smeared their faces, and stained their dresses. The clamor grew worse. The last of the dishes were plundered. Jeanne herself began dancing on her chair as she heard the strains of a quadrille coming from the drawing-room; and on her mother approaching to upbraid her with having eaten too much, she replied: "Oh! mamma, I feel so happy to-day!"

But now the other children were rising as they heard the music. Slowly the table thinned, until there only remained a fat, chubby infant right in the middle. He seemingly cared little for the attractions of the piano; with a napkin round his neck, and his chin resting on the table-cloth—for he was a mere chit—he opened his big eyes, and protruded his lips each time that his mamma offered him a spoonful of chocolate. The contents of the cup vanished, and he licked his lips as the last mouthful went down his throat, with eyes more agape than ever.

"By God! my lad, you eat heartily!" exclaimed Malignon, who was watching him with a thoughtful air.

Now came the division of the "surprise" packets. Each child, on leaving the table, bore away one of the large gilt paper twists, the coverings of which were hastily torn off and from them poured forth a host of toys, grotesque hats made of tissue paper, birds and butterflies. But the joy of joys was the possession of a cracker. Every "surprise" packet had its cracker; and these the lads pulled at gallantly, delighted with the noise, while the girls shut their eyes, making many tries before the explosion took place. For a time the sharp crackling of all this musketry alone could be heard; and the uproar was still lasting when the children returned to the drawing-room, where lively quadrille music resounded from the piano.

"I could enjoy a cake," murmured Mademoiselle Aurelie, as she sat down.

At the table, which was now deserted, but covered with all the litter of the huge feast, a few ladies—some dozen or so, who had preferred to wait till the children had retired—now sat down. As no servant could be found, Malignon bustled hither and thither in attendance. He poured out all that remained in the chocolate pot, shook up the dregs of the bottles, and was even successful in discovering some ices. But amidst all these gallant doings of his, he could not quit one idea, and that was—why had they decided on closing the shutters?

"You know," he asserted, "the place looks like a cellar."

Helene had remained standing, engaged in conversation with Madame Deberle. As the latter directed her steps towards the drawing-room, her companion prepared to follow, when she felt a gentle touch. Behind her was the doctor, smiling; he was ever near her.

"Are you not going to take anything?" he asked. And the trivial question cloaked so earnest an entreaty that her heart was filled with profound emotion. She knew well enough that each of his words was eloquent of another thing. The excitement springing from the gaiety which pulsed around her was slowly gaining on her. Some of the fever of all these little folks, now dancing and shouting, coursed in her own veins. With flushed cheeks and sparkling eyes, she at first declined.

"No, thank you, nothing at all."

But he pressed her, and in the end, ill at ease and anxious to get rid of him, she yielded. "Well, then, a cup of tea."

He hurried off and returned with the cup, his hands trembling as he handed it to her. While she was sipping the tea he drew nearer to her, his lips quivering nervously with the confession springing from his heart. She in her turn drew back from him, and, returning him the empty cup, made her escape while he was placing it on a sideboard, thus leaving him alone in the dining-room with Mademoiselle Aurelie, who was slowly masticating, and subjecting each dish in succession to a close scrutiny.

Within the drawing-room the piano was sending forth its loudest strains, and from end to end of the floor swept the ball with its charming drolleries. A circle of onlookers had gathered round the quadrille party with which Lucien and Jeanne were dancing. The little marquis became rather mixed over the figures; he only got on well when he had occasion to take hold of Jeanne; and then he gripped her by the waist and whirled around. Jeanne preserved her equilibrium, somewhat vexed by his rumpling her dress; but the delights of the dance taking full possession of her, she caught hold of him in her turn and lifted him off his feet. The white satin coat embroidered with nosegays mingled with the folds of the gown woven with flowers and strange birds, and the two little figures of old Dresden ware assumed all the grace and novelty of some whatnot ornaments. The quadrille over, Helene summoned Jeanne to her side, in order to rearrange her dress.

"It is his fault, mamma," was the little one's excuse. "He rubs against me—he's a dreadful nuisance."

Around the drawing-room the faces of the parents were wreathed with smiles. As soon as the music began again all the little ones were once more in motion. Seeing, however, that they were observed they felt distrustful, remained grave, and checked their leaps in order to keep up appearances. Some of them knew how to dance; but the majority were

ignorant of the steps, and their limbs were evidently a source of embarrassment to them. But Pauline interposed: "I must see to them! Oh,
you little sillies!"

She threw herself into the midst of the quadrille, caught hold of
two of them, one grasping her right hand the other her left, and managed to infuse such life into the dance that the wooden flooring creaked
beneath them. The only sounds now audible rose from the hurrying
hither and thither of tiny feet beating wholly out of time, the piano
alone keeping to the dance measure. Some more of the older people
joined in the fun. Helene and Madame Deberle, noticing some little
maids who were too bashful to venture forth, dragged them into the
thickest of the throng. It was they who led the figures, pushed the lads
forward, and arranged the dancing in rings; and the mothers passed
them the youngest of the babies, so that they might make them skip
about for a moment, holding them the while by both hands. The ball
was now at its height. The dancers enjoyed themselves to their hearts'
content, laughing and pushing each other about like some boarding
school mad with glee over the absence of the teacher. Nothing, truly,
could surpass in unalloyed gaiety this carnival of youngsters, this assemblage of miniature men and women—akin to a veritable micro-
cosm, wherein the fashions of every people mingled with the fantastic
creations of romance and drama. The ruddy lips and blue eyes, the
faces breathing love, invested the dresses with the fresh purity of childhood. The scene realized to the mind the merrymaking of a fairy-tale
to which trooped Cupids in disguise to honor the betrothal of some
Prince Charming.

"I'm stifling!" exclaimed Malignon. "I'm off to inhale some fresh
air."

As he left the drawing-room he threw the door wide open. The
daylight from the street then entered in a lurid stream, bedimming the
glare of lamps and candles. In this fashion every quarter of an hour
Malignon opened the door to let in some fresh air.

Still there was no cessation of the piano-playing. Little Guiraud, in
her Alsatian costume, with a butterfly of black ribbon in her golden
hair, swung round in the dance with a harlequin twice her height. A
Highlander whirled Marguerite Tissot round so madly that she lost her
milk-pail. The two Berthier girls, Blanche and Sophie, who were insep-
arables, were dancing together; the soubrette in the arms of Folly,

whose bells were jingling merrily. A glance could not be thrown over the assemblage without one of the Levasseur girls coming into view; the Red Riding-Hoods seemed to increase in number; caps and gowns of gleaming red satin slashed with black velvet everywhere leaped into sight. Meanwhile some of the older boys and girls had found refuge in the adjacent saloon, where they could dance more at their ease. Valentine de Chermette, cloaked in the mantilla of a Spanish senorita, was executing some marvelous steps in front of a young gentleman who had donned evening dress. Suddenly there was a burst of laughter which drew every one to the sight; behind a door in a corner, baby Guiraud, the two-year-old clown, and a mite of a girl of his own age, in peasant costume, were holding one another in a tight embrace for fear of tumbling, and gyrating round and round like a pair of slyboots, with cheek pressed to cheek.

"I'm quite done up," remarked Helene, as she leaned against the dining-room door.

She fanned her face, flushed with her exertions in the dance. Her bosom rose and fell beneath the transparent grenadine of her bodice. And she was still conscious of Henri's breath beating on her shoulders; he was still close to her—ever behind her. Now it flashed on her that he would speak, yet she had no strength to flee from his avowal. He came nearer and whispered, breathing on her hair: "I love you! oh, how I love you!"

She tingled from head to foot, as though a gust of flame had beaten on her. O God! he had spoken; she could no longer feign the pleasurable quietude of ignorance. She hid behind her fan, her face purple with blushes. The children, whirling madly in the last of the quadrilles, were making the floor ring with the beating of their feet. There were silvery peals of laughter, and bird-like voices gave vent to exclamations of pleasure. A freshness arose from all that band of innocents galloping round and round like little demons.

"I love you! oh, how I love you!"

She shuddered again; she would listen no further. With dizzy brain she fled into the dining-room, but it was deserted, save that Monsieur Letellier sat on a chair, peacefully sleeping. Henri had followed her, and had the hardihood to seize her wrists even at the risk of a scandal, his face convulsed with such passion that she trembled before him. And he still repeated the words:

"I love you! I love you!"

"Leave me," she murmured faintly. "You are mad—"

And, close by, the dancing still went on, with the trampling of tiny feet. Blanche Berthier's bells could be heard ringing in unison with the softer notes of the piano; Madame Deberle and Pauline were clapping their hands, by way of beating time. It was a polka, and Helene caught a glimpse of Jeanne and Lucien, as they passed by smiling, with arms clasped round each other.

But with a sudden jerk she freed herself and fled to an adjacent room —a pantry into which streamed the daylight. That sudden brightness blinded her. She was terror-stricken—she dared not return to the drawing-room with the tale of passion written so legibly on her face. So, hastily crossing the garden, she climbed to her own home, the noises of the ball-room still ringing in her ears.

CHAPTER X.

Upstairs, in her own room, in the peaceful, convent-like atmosphere she found there, Helene experienced a feeling of suffocation. Her room astonished her, so calm, so secluded, so drowsy did it seem with its blue velvet hangings, while she came to it hotly panting with the emotion which thrilled her. Was this indeed her room, this dreary, lifeless nook, devoid of air? Hastily she threw open a window, and leaned out to gaze on Paris.

The rain had ceased, and the clouds were trooping off like some herd of monsters hurrying in disorderly array into the gloom of the horizon. A blue gap, that grew larger by degrees, had opened up above the city. But Helene, her elbows trembling on the window-rail, still breathless from her hasty ascent, saw nothing, and merely heard her heart beating against her swelling breast. She drew a long breath, but it seemed to her that the spreading valley with its river, its two millions of people, its immense city, its distant hills, could not hold air enough to enable her to breathe peacefully and regularly again.

For some minutes she remained there distracted by the fever of passion which possessed her. It seemed as though a torrent of sensations and confused ideas were pouring down on her, their roar preventing her from hearing her own voice or understanding aught. There was a buzzing in her ears, and large spots of light swam slowly before her eyes. Then she suddenly found herself examining her gloved hands, and remembering that she had omitted to sew on a button that had come off the left-hand glove. And afterwards she spoke aloud, repeating several times, in tones that grew fainter and fainter: "I love you! I love you! oh, how I love you!"

Instinctively she buried her face in her hands, and pressed her fingers to her eyelids as though to intensify the darkness in which she sought to plunge. It was a wish to annihilate herself, to see no more, to be utterly alone, girt in by the gloom of night. Her breathing grew calmer. Paris blew its mighty breath upon her face; she knew it lay before her, and though she had no wish to look on it, she felt full of terror at the thought of leaving the window, and of no longer having beneath her that city whose vastness lulled her to rest.

Ere long she grew unmindful of all around her. The love-scene and confession, despite her efforts, again woke to life in her mind. In the inky darkness Henri appeared to her, every feature so distinct and vivid that she could perceive the nervous twitching of his lips. He came nearer and hung over her. And then she wildly darted back. But, nevertheless, she felt a burning breath on her shoulders and a voice exclaimed: "I love you! I love you!" With a mighty effort she put the phantom to flight, but it again took shape in the distance, and slowly swelled to its whilom proportions; it was Henri once more following her into the dining-room, and still murmuring: "I love you! I love you!" These words rang within her breast with the sonorous clang of a bell; she no longer heard anything but them, pealing their loudest throughout her frame. Nevertheless, she desired to reflect, and again strove to escape from the apparition. He had spoken; never would she dare to look on his face again. The brutal passion of the man had tainted the tenderness of their love. She conjured up past hours, in which he had loved her without being so cruel as to say it; hours spent in the garden amidst the tranquility of the budding springtime God! he had spoken— the thought clung to her so stubbornly, lowered on her in such immensity and with such weight, that the instant destruction of Paris by a thunderbolt before her eyes would have seemed a trivial matter. Her heart was rent by feelings of indignant protest and haughty anger, commingling with a secret and unconquerable pleasure, which ascended from her inner being and bereft her of her senses. He had spoken, and was speaking still, he sprang up unceasingly before her, uttering those passionate words: "I love you! I love you!"—words that swept into oblivion all her past life as wife and mother.

In spite of her brooding over this vision, she retained some consciousness of the vast expanse which stretched beneath her, beyond the darkness that curtained her sight. A loud rumbling arose, and waves of life seemed to surge up and circle around her. Echoes, odors, and

even light streamed against her face, though her hands were still nervously pressed to it. At times sudden gleams appeared to pierce her
closed eyelids, and amidst the radiance she imagined she saw monuments, steeples, and domes standing out in the diffuse light of dreamland. Then she lowered her hands and, opening her eyes, was dazzled.
The vault of heaven expanded before her, and Henri had vanished.

A line of clouds, a seeming mass of crumbling chalk-hills, now
barred the horizon far away. Across the pure, deep blue heavens overhead, merely a few light, fleecy cloudlets were slowly drifting, like a
flotilla of vessels with full-blown sails. On the north, above Montmartre, hung a network of extreme delicacy, fashioned as it were of
pale-hued silk, and spread over a patch of sky as though for fishing in
those tranquil waters. Westward, however, in the direction of the slopes
of Meudon, which Helene could not see, the last drops of the downpour must still have been obscuring the sun, for, though the sky above
was clear, Paris remained gloomy, dismal beneath the vapor of the dry-
ing house-roofs. It was a city of uniform hue—the bluey-grey of slate,
studded with black patches of trees—but withal very distinct, with the
sharp outlines and innumerable windows of its houses. The Seine
gleamed with the subdued brightness of old silver. The edifices on either bank looked as though they had been smeared with soot. The
Tower of St. Jacques rose up like some rust-eaten museum curio,
whilst the Pantheon assumed the aspect of a gigantic catafalque above
the darkened district which it overlooked. Gleams of light peeped
only from the gilding of the dome of the Invalides, like lamps burning in the daytime, sad and vague amidst the crepuscular veil of
mourning in which the city was draped. All the usual effects of distance had vanished; Paris resembled a huge yet minutely executed
charcoal drawing, showing very vigorously through its cloudy veil,
under the limpid heavens.

Gazing upon this dismal city, Helene reflected that she really knew
nothing of Henri. She felt strong and brave now that his image no
longer pursued her. A rebellious impulse stirred her soul to reject the
mastery which this man had gained over her within a few weeks. No,
she did not know him. She knew nothing of him, of his actions or his
thoughts; she could not even have determined whether he possessed
talent. Perhaps he was even more lacking in qualities of the heart than
of the mind. And thus she gave way to every imagining, her heart full

of bitterness, ever finding herself confronted by her ignorance, that barrier which separated her from Henri, and checked her in her efforts to know him. She knew nothing, she would never know anything. She pictured him, hissing out those burning words, and creating within her the one trouble which had, till now, broken in on the quiet happiness of her life. Whence had he sprung to lay her life desolate in this fashion? She suddenly thought that but six weeks before she had had no existence for him, and this thought was insufferable. Angels in heaven! to live no more for one another, to pass each other without recognition, perhaps never to meet again! In her despair she clasped her hands, and her eyes filled with tears.

Then Helene gazed fixedly on the towers of Notre-Dame in the far distance. A ray of light from between two clouds tinged them with gold. Her brain was heavy, as though surcharged with all the tumultuous thoughts hurtling within it. It made her suffer; she would fain have concerned herself with the sight of Paris, and have sought to regain her life-peace by turning on that sea of roofs the tranquil glances of past days. To think that at other times, at the same hour, the infinitude of the city—in the stillness of a lovely twilight—had lulled her into tender musing!

At present Paris was brightening in the sunshine. After the first ray had fallen on Notre-Dame, others had followed, streaming across the city. The luminary, dipping in the west, rent the clouds asunder, and the various districts spread out, motly with ever-changing lights and shadows. For a time the whole of the left bank was of a leaden hue, while the right was speckled with spots of light which made the verge of the river resemble the skin of some huge beast of prey. Then these resemblances varied and vanished at the mercy of the wind, which drove the clouds before it. Above the burnished gold of the housetops dark patches floated, all in the same direction and with the same gentle and silent motion. Some of them were very large, sailing along with all the majestic grace of an admiral's ship, and surrounded by smaller ones, preserving the regular order of a squadron in line of battle. Then one vast shadow, with a gap yawning like a serpent's mouth, trailed along, and for a while hid Paris, which it seemed ready to devour. And when it had reached the far-off horizon, looking no larger than a worm, a gush of light streamed from a rift in a cloud, and fell into the void which it had left. The golden cascade could be seen descending first like a

thread of fine sand, then swelling into a huge cone, and raining in a
continuous shower on the Champs-Elysees district, which it inundated
with a splashing, dancing radiance. For a long time did this shower of
sparks descend, spraying continuously like fireworks.

Ah, well! this love was her fate, and Helene ceased to resist. She
could battle no longer against her feelings. And in ceasing to struggle
she tasted immeasurable delight. Why should she grudge herself happiness any longer? The memory of her past life inspired her with disgust and aversion. How had she been able to drag on that cold, dreary
existence, of which she was formerly so proud? A vision rose before
her of herself as a young girl living in the Rue des Petites-Maries, at
Marseilles, where she had ever shivered; she saw herself a wife, her
heart's blood frozen in the companionship of a big child of a husband,
with little to take any interest in, apart from the cares of her household; she saw herself through every hour of her life following the same
path with the same even tread, without a trouble to mar her peace; and
now this monotony in which she had lived, her heart fast asleep, enraged her beyond expression. To think that she had fancied herself
happy in thus following her path for thirty years, her passions silent,
with naught but the pride of virtue to fill the blank in her existence.
How she had cheated herself with her integrity and nice honor, which
had girt her round with the empty joys of piety! No, no; she had had
enough of it; she wished to live! And an awful spirit of ridicule woke
within her as she thought of the behests of reason. Her reason, forsooth! she felt a contemptuous pity for it; during all the years she had
lived it had brought her no joy to be compared with that she had tasted
during the past hour. She had denied the possibility of stumbling, she
had been vain and idiotic enough to think that she would go on to the
end without her foot once tripping against a stone. Ah, well! to-day she
almost longed to fall. Oh that she might disappear, after tasting for one
moment the happiness which she had never enjoyed!

Within her soul, however, a great sorrow lingered, a heart-burning
and a consciousness of a gloomy blank. Then argument rose to her
lips. Was she not free? In her love for Henri she deceived nobody; she
could deal as she pleased with her love. Then, did not everything ex-
culpate her? What had been her life for nearly two years? Her widow-
hood, her unrestricted liberty, her loneliness—everything, she realized,
had softened and prepared her for love. Love must have been smol-

dering within her during the long evenings spent between her two old friends, the Abbe and his brother, those simple hearts whose serenity had lulled it to rest; it had been growing whilst she remained shut up within those narrow walls, far away from the world, and gazed on Paris rumbling noisily on the horizon; it had been growing even when she leaned from that window in the dreamy mood which she had scarce been conscious of, but which little by little had rendered her so weak. And a recollection came to her of that radiant spring morning when Paris had shone out fair and clear, as though in a glass mirror, when it had worn the pure, sunny hue of childhood, as she lazily surveyed it, stretched in her easy-chair with a book upon her knees. That morning love had first awoke—a scarcely perceptible feeling that she had been unable to define, and against which she had believed herself strongly armed. To-day she was in the same place, but devoured by overpowering passion, while before her eyes the dying sun illumined the city with flame. It seemed to her that one day had sufficed for all, that this was the ruddy evening following upon that limpid morning; and she imagined she could feel those fiery beams scorching her heart.

But a change had come over the sky. The sun, in its descent towards the slopes of Meudon, had just burst through the last clouds in all its splendor. The azure vault was illuminated with glory; deep on the horizon the crumbling ridge of chalk clouds, blotting out the distant suburbs of Charenton and Choisy-le-Roi, now reared rocks of a tender pink, outlined with brilliant crimson; the flotilla of cloudlets drifting slowly through the blue above Paris, was decked with purple sails; while the delicate network, seemingly fashioned of white silk thread, above Montmartre, was suddenly transformed into golden cord, whose meshes would snare the stars as soon as they should rise.

Beneath the flaming vault of heaven lay Paris, a mass of yellow, striped with huge shadows. On the vast square below Helene, in an orange-tinted haze, cabs and omnibuses crossed in all directions, amidst a crowd of pedestrians, whose swarming blackness was softened and irradiated by splashes of light. The students of a seminary were hurrying in serried ranks along the Quai de Billy, and the trail of cassocks acquired an ochraceous hue in the diffuse light. Farther away, vehicles and foot-passengers faded from view; it was only by their gleaming lamps that you were made aware of the vehicles which, one behind the other, were crossing some distant bridge. On the left the straight, lofty,

pink chimneys of the Army Bakehouse were belching forth whirling
clouds of flesh-tinted smoke; whilst, across the river, the beautiful elms
of the Quai d'Orsay rose up in a dark mass transpierced by shafts of
light.

The Seine, whose banks the oblique rays were enfilading, was rolling
dancing wavelets, streaked with scattered splashes of blue, green, and
yellow; but farther up the river, in lieu of this blotchy coloring, suggestive of an Eastern sea, the waters assumed a uniform golden hue,
which became more and more dazzling. You might have thought that
some ingot were pouring forth from an invisible crucible on the horizon, broadening out with a coruscation of bright colors as it gradually
grew colder. And at intervals over this brilliant stream, the bridges, with
curves growing ever more slender and delicate, threw, as it were, grey
bars, till there came at last a fiery jumble of houses, above which rose
the towers of Notre-Dame, flaring red like torches. Right and left alike
the edifices were all aflame. The glass roof of the Palais de l'Industrie
appeared like a bed of glowing embers amidst the Champs-Elysees
groves. Farther on, behind the roof of the Madeline, the huge pile of
the Opera House shone out like a mass of burnished copper; and the
summits of other buildings, cupolas, and towers, the Vendome column,
the church of Saint-Vincent de Paul, the tower of Saint-Jacques, and,
nearer in, the pavilions of the new Louvre and the Tuileries, were
crowned by a blaze, which lent them the aspect of sacrificial pyres. The
dome of the Invalides was flaring with such brilliancy that you instinctively feared lest it should suddenly topple down and scatter burning
flakes over the neighborhood. Beyond the irregular towers of Saint-
Sulpice, the Pantheon stood out against the sky in dull splendor, like
some royal palace of conflagration reduced to embers. Then, as the
sun declined, the pyre-like edifices gradually set the whole of Paris on
fire. Flashes sped over the housetops, while black smoke lingered in the
valleys. Every frontage turned towards the Trocadero seemed to be red-
hot, the glass of the windows glittering and emitting a shower of sparks,
which darted upwards as though some invisible bellows were ever urg-
ing the huge conflagration into greater activity. Sheaves of flame were
also ever rising afresh from the adjacent districts, where the streets
opened, now dark and now all ablaze. Even far over the plain, from a
ruddy ember-like glow suffusing the destroyed faubourgs, occasional
flashes of flame shot up as from some fire struggling again into life. Ere

long a furnace seemed raging, all Paris burned, the heavens became yet more empurpled, and the clouds hung like so much blood over the vast city, colored red and gold.

With the ruddy tints falling upon her, yielding to the passion which was devouring her, Helene was still gazing upon Paris all ablaze, when a little hand was placed on her shoulder, and she gave a start. It was Jeanne, calling her. "Mamma! mamma!"

She turned her head, and the child went on: "At last! Didn't you hear me before? I have called you at least a dozen times."

The little girl, still in her Japanese costume, had sparkling eyes, and cheeks flushed with pleasure. She gave her mother no time for answer.

"You ran away from me nicely! Do you know, they were hunting for you everywhere? Had it not been for Pauline, who came with me to the bottom of the staircase, I shouldn't have dared to cross the road."

With a pretty gesture, she brought her face close to her mother's lips, and, without pausing, whispered the question: "Do you love me?"

Helene kissed her somewhat absently. She was amazed and impatient at her early return. Had an hour really gone by since she had fled from the ball-room? However, to satisfy the child, who seemed uneasy, she told her that she had felt rather unwell. The fresh air was doing her good; she only needed a little quietness.

"Oh! don't fear; I'm too tired," murmured Jeanne. "I am going to stop here, and be very, very good. But, mamma dear, I may talk, right?"

She nestled close to Helene, full of joy at the prospect of not being undressed at once. She was in ecstasies over her embroidered purple gown and green silk petticoat; and she shook her head to rattle the pendants hanging from the long pins thrust through her hair. At last there burst from her lips a rush of hasty words. Despite her seeming demureness, she had seen everything, heard everything, and remembered everything; and she now made ample amends for her former assumed dignity, silence, and indifference.

"Do you know, mamma, it was an old fellow with a grey beard who made Punch move his arms and legs? I saw him well enough when the curtain was drawn aside. Yes, and the little boy Guiraud began to cry. How stupid of him, wasn't it? They told him the policeman would come and put some water in his soup; and at last they had to carry him off, for he wouldn't stop crying. And at lunch, too, Marguerite stained her milkmaid's dress all over with jam. Her mamma wiped it off and said to her: 'Oh, you dirty girl!' She even had a lot of it in her hair. I never opened my mouth, but it did amuse me to see them all rush at the cakes! Were they not bad-mannered, mamma dear?"

She paused for a few seconds, absorbed in some reminiscence, and then asked, with a thoughtful air: "I say, mamma, did you eat any of those yellow cakes with white cream inside? Oh! they were nice! they were nice! I kept the dish beside me the whole time."

Helene was not listening to this childish chatter. But Jeanne talked to relieve her excited brain. She launched out again, giving the minutest details about the ball, and investing each little incident with the greatest importance.

"You did not see that my waistband came undone just as we began dancing. A lady, whose name I don't know, pinned it up for me. So I said to her: 'Madame, I thank you very much.' But while I was dancing with Lucien the pin ran into him, and he asked me: 'What have you got in front of you that pricks me so?' Of course I knew nothing about it, and told him I had nothing there to prick him. However, Pauline came and put the pin in its proper place. Ah! but you've no idea how they pushed each other about; and one great stupid of a boy gave Sophie a blow on the back which made her fall. The Levasseur girls jumped about with their feet close together. I am pretty certain that isn't the way to dance. But the best of it all came at the end. You weren't there; so you can't know. We all took one another by the arms, and then whirled round; it was comical enough to make one die laughing. Besides, some of the big gentlemen were whirling around as well. It's true; I am not telling fibs. Why, don't you believe me, mamma dear?"

Helene's continued silence was beginning to vex Jeanne. She nestled closer, and gave her mother's hand a shake. But, perceiving that she drew only a few words from her, she herself, by degrees, lapsed into silence, into thought of the incidents of that ball of which her heart was full. Both mother and daughter now sat mutely gazing on Paris all aflame. It seemed to them yet more mysterious than ever, as it lay there illumined by blood-red clouds, like some city of an old-world tale expiating its lusts under a rain of fire.

"Did you have any round dances?" all at once asked Helene, as if wakening with a start.

"Yes, yes!" murmured Jeanne, engrossed in her turn.

"And the doctor—did he dance!"

"I should think so; he had a turn with me. He lift me up and asked me: 'Where is your mamma? where is your mamma?' and then he kissed me."

Helene unconsciously smiled. What need had she of knowing Henri well? It appeared sweeter to her not to know him—ay, never to know him well —and to greet him simply as the one whose coming she had awaited so long. Why should she feel astonished or disquieted? At the fated hour he had met her on her life-journey. Her frank nature accepted whatever might be in store; and quietude, born of the knowledge that she loved and was beloved, fell on her mind. She told her heart that she would prove strong enough to prevent her happiness from being marred.

But night was coming on and a chilly breeze arose. Jeanne, still plunged in reverie, began to shiver. She reclined her head on her mother's bosom, and, as though the question were inseparably connected with her deep meditation, she murmured a second time: "Do you love me?"

Then Helene, her face still glad with smiles, took her head within her hands and for a moment examined her face closely. Next she pressed a long kiss near her mouth, over a ruddy spot on her skin. It was there, she could divine it, that Henri had kissed the child!

The gloomy ridge of the Meudon hills was already partially concealing the disc of the sun. Over Paris the slanting beams of light had yet lengthened. The shadow cast by the dome of the Invalides—increased to stupendous proportions—covered the whole of the Saint-Germain district; while the Opera-House, the Saint-Jacques tower, the columns and the steeples, threw streaks of darkness over the right bank dwellings. The lines of house-fronts, the yawning streets, the islands of roofs, were burning with a more sullen glow. The flashes of fire died away in the darkening windows, as though the houses were reduced to embers. Distant bells rang out; a rumbling noise fell on the ears, and then subsided. With the approach of night the expanse of sky grew more vast, spreading a vault of violet, streaked with gold and purple, above the ruddy city. But all at once the conflagration flared afresh with formidable intensity, a last great flame shot up from Paris, illumining its entire expanse, and even its hitherto hidden suburbs. Then it seemed as if a grey, ashy dust were falling; and though the clustering districts remained erect, they wore the gloomy, unsubstantial aspect of coals which had ceased to burn.

CHAPTER XI.

One morning in May, Rosalie ran in from the kitchen, dish-cloth in hand, screaming out in the familiar fashion of a favorite servant: "Oh, madame, come quick! His reverence the Abbe is digging the ground down in the doctor's garden."

Helene made no responsive movement, but Jeanne had already rushed to have a look. On her return, she exclaimed:

"How stupid Rosalie is! he is not digging at all. He is with the gardener, who is putting some plants into a barrow. Madame Deberle is plucking all her roses."

"They must be for the church," quietly said Helene, who was busy with some tapestry-work.

A few minutes later the bell rang, and Abbe Jouve made his appearance. He came to say that his presence must not be expected on the following Tuesday. His evenings would be wholly taken up with the ceremonies incident to the month of Mary. The parish priest had assigned him the task of decorating the church. It would be a great success. All the ladies were giving him flowers. He was expecting two palm-trees about fourteen feet high, and meant to place them to the right and left of the altar.

"Oh! mamma, mamma!" murmured Jeanne, listening, wonderstruck.

"Well," said Helene, with a smile, "since you cannot come to us, my old friend, we will go to see you. Why, you've quite turned Jeanne's head with your talk about flowers."

She had few religious tendencies; she never even went to mass, on the plea that her daughter's health suffered from the shivering fits which seized her when she came out of a church. In her presence the old priest avoided all reference to religion. It was his wont to say, with good-natured indulgence, that good hearts carve out their own salvation by deeds of loving kindness and charity. God would know when and how to touch her.

Till the evening of the following day Jeanne thought of nothing but the month of Mary. She plagued her mother with questions; she dreamt of the church adorned with a profusion of white roses, filled with thousands of wax tapers, with the sound of angels' voices, and sweet perfumes. And she was very anxious to go near the altar, that she might have a good look at the Blessed Virgin's lace gown, a gown worth a fortune, according to the Abbe. But Helene bridled her excitement with a threat not to take her should she make herself ill beforehand.

However, the evening came at last, and they set out. The nights were still cold, and when they reached the Rue de l'Annonciation, where the church of Notre-Dame-de-Grace stands, the child was shivering all over.

"The church is heated," said her mother. "We must secure a place near a hot-air pipe."

She pushed open the padded door, and as it gently swung back to its place they found themselves in a warm atmosphere, with brilliant lights streaming on them, and chanting resounding in their ears. The ceremony had commenced, and Helene, perceiving that the nave was crowded, signified her intention of going down one of the aisles. But there seemed insuperable obstacles in her way; she could not get near the altar. Holding Jeanne by the hand, she for a time patiently pressed forward, but at last, despairing of advancing any farther, took the first unoccupied chairs she could find. A pillar hid half of the choir from view.

"I can see nothing," said the child, grievously discontented. "This is a very nasty place."

However, Helene signed to her to keep silent, and she lapsed into a fit of sulks. In front of her she could only perceive the broad back of a fat old lady. When her mother next turned towards her she was standing upright on her chair.

"Will you come down!" said Helene in a low voice. "You are a nuisance."

But Jeanne was stubborn.

"Hist! mamma," she said, "there's Madame Deberle. Look! she is down there in the center, beckoning to us."

The young woman's annoyance on hearing this made her very im-patient, and she shook her daughter, who still refused to sit down. Dur-ing the three days that had intervened since the ball, Helene had avoided any visit to the doctor's house on the plea of having a great deal to do.

"Mamma," resumed Jeanne with a child's wonted stubbornness, "she is looking at you; she is nodding good-day to you."

At this intimation Helene was forced to turn round and exchange greetings; each bowed to the other. Madame Deberle, in a striped silk gown trimmed with white lace, sat in the center of the nave but a short distance from the choir, looking very fresh and conspicuous. She had brought her sister Pauline, who was now busy waving her hand. The chanting still continued, the elder members of the congregation pour-ing forth a volume of sound of falling scale, while now and then the shrill voice of the children punctuated the slow, monotonous rhythm of the canticle.

"They want us to go over to them, you see," exclaimed Jeanne, with some triumph in her remark.

"It is useless; we shall be all right here."

"Oh, mamma, do let us go over to them! There are two chairs empty."

"No, no; come and sit down."

However, the ladies smilingly persisted in making signs, heedless to the last degree of the slight scandal they were causing; nay, delighted at being the observed of all observers. Helene thus had to yield. She pushed the gratified Jeanne before her, and strove to make her way through the congregation, her hands all the while trembling with re-pressed anger. It was no easy business. Devout female worshippers, un-willing to disturb themselves, glared at her with furious looks, whilst all agape they kept on singing. She pressed on in this style for five long minutes, the tempest of voices ringing around her with ever-increasing violence. Whenever she came to a standstill, Jeanne, squeezing close beside her, gazed at those cavernous, gaping mouths. However, at last they reached the vacant space in front of the choir, and then had but a few steps to make.

"Come, be quick," whispered Madame Deberle. "The Abbe told me you would be coming, and I kept two chairs for you."

Helene thanked her, and, to cut the conversation short, at once began turning over the leaves of her missal. But Juliette was as worldly here as elsewhere; as much at her ease, as agreeable and talkative, as in her drawing-room. She bent her head towards Helene and resumed:

"You have become quite invisible. I intended to pay you a visit to-morrow. Surely you haven't been ill, have you?"

"No, thank you. I've been very busy."

"Well, listen to me. You must come and dine with us to-morrow. Quite a family dinner, you know."

"You are very kind. We will see."

She seemed to retire within herself, intent on following the service, and on saying nothing more. Pauline had taken Jeanne beside her that she might be nearer the hot-air flue over which she toasted herself lux-uriously, as happy as any chilly mortal could be. Steeped in the warm air, the two girls raised themselves inquisitively and gazed around on every-thing, the low ceiling with its woodwork panels, the squat pillars, con-nected by arches from which hung chandeliers, and the pulpit of carved oak; and over the ocean of heads which waved with the rise and fall of the canticle, their eyes wandered towards the dark corners of the aisles, towards the chapels whose gilding faintly gleamed, and the baptistery enclosed by a railing near the chief entrance. However, their gaze always returned to the resplendent choir, decorated with brilliant colors and dazzling gilding. A crystal chandelier, flaming with light, hung from the vaulted ceiling; immense candelabra, filled with rows of wax tapers, that glittered amidst the gloom of the church like a profusion of stars in orderly array, brought out prominently the high altar, which seemed one huge bouquet of foliage and flowers. Over all, standing amidst a profusion of roses, a Virgin, dressed in satin and lace, and crowned with pearls, was holding a Jesus in long clothes on her arm.

"I say, are you warm?" asked Pauline. "It's nice, eh?"

But Jeanne, in ecstasy, was gazing on the Virgin amongst the flow-ers. The scene thrilled her. A fear crept over her that she might do something wrong, and she lowered her eyes in the endeavor to restrain her tears by fixing her attention on the black-and-white pavement. The vibrations of the choir-boys' shrill voices seemed to stir her tresses like puffs of air.

Meanwhile Helene, with face bent over her prayer-book, drew her-self away whenever Juliette's lace rustled against her. She was in no wise prepared for this meeting. Despite the vow she had sworn within herself, to be ever pure in her love for Henri, and never yield to him, she felt great discomfort at the thought that she was a traitoress to the confiding, happy woman who sat by her side. She was possessed by one idea—she would not go to that dinner. She sought for reasons which would enable her to break off these relations so hateful to her honor. But the swelling voices of the choristers, so near to her, drove all reflection from her mind; she could decide on no precise course, and surrendered herself to the soothing influences of the chant, tasting a pious joy such as she had never before found inside a church.

"Have you been told about Madame de Chermette?" asked Juliette, unable any longer to restrain her craving for a gossip.

"No, I know nothing."

"Well, well; just imagine. You have seen her daughter, so womanish and tall, though she is only fifteen, haven't you? There is some talk about her getting married next year to that dark young fellow who is always hanging to her mother's skirts. People are talking about it with a vengeance."

"Ah!" muttered Helene, who was not paying the least attention.

Madame Deberle went into particulars, but of a sudden the chant ceased, and the organ-music died away in a moan. Astounded at the loudness of her own voice breaking upon the stillness which ensued, she lapsed into silence. A priest made his appearance at this moment in the pulpit. There was a rustling, and then he spoke. No, certainly not; Helene would not join that dinner-party. With her eyes fixed on the priest she pictured to herself the next meeting with Henri, that meeting which for three days she had contemplated with terror; she saw him white with anger, reproaching her for hiding herself, and she dreaded lest she might not display sufficient indifference. Amidst her dream the priest had disappeared, his thrilling tones merely reaching her in casual sentences: "No hour could be more ineffable than that when the Virgin, with bent head, answered: 'I am the handmaiden of the Lord!'"

Yes, she would be brave; all her reason had returned to her. She would taste the joy of being loved, but would never avow her love, for her heart told her that such an avowal would cost her peace. And how intensely would she love, without confessing it, gratified by a word, a look from Henri, exchanged at lengthy intervals on the occasion of a chance meeting! It was a dream that brought her some sense of the infinite. The church around her became a friend and comforter. The priest was now exclaiming:

"The angel vanished and Mary plunged into contemplation of the divine mystery working within her, her heart bathed in sunshine and love."

"He speaks very well," whispered Madame Deberle, leaning towards her. "And he's quite young, too, scarcely thirty, don't you think?"

Madame Deberle was affected. Religion pleased her because the emotions it prompted were in good taste. To present flowers for the decoration of churches, to have petty dealings with the priests, who were so polite and discreet, to come to church attired in her best and assume an air of worldly patronage towards the God of the poor—all this had for her special delights; the more so as her husband did not interest himself in religion, and her devotions thus had all the sweetness of forbidden fruit. Helene looked at her and answered with a nod; her face was ashy white with faintness, while the other's was lit up by smiles. There was a stirring of chairs and a rustling of handkerchiefs, as the priest quitted the pulpit with the final adjuration

"Oh! give wings unto your love, souls imbued with Christian piety. God has made a sacrifice of Himself for your sakes, your hearts are full of His presence, your souls overflow with His grace!"

Of a sudden the organ sounded again, and the litanies of the Virgin began with their appeals of passionate tenderness. Faint and distant the chanting rolled forth from the side-aisles and the dark recesses of the chapels, as though the earth were giving answer to the angel voices of the chorister-boys. A rush of air swept over the throng, making the flames of the tapers leap, while amongst the flowers, fading as they exhaled their last perfume, the Divine Mother seemed to incline her head to smile on her infant Jesus.

All at once, seized with an instinctive dread, Helene turned. "You're not ill, Jeanne, are you?" she asked.

The child, with face ashy white and eyes glistening, her spirit borne aloft by the fervent strains of the litanies, was gazing at the altar, where in imagination she could see the roses multiplying and falling in cascades.

"No, no, mamma," she whispered; "I am pleased, I am very well pleased." And then she asked: "But where is our dear old friend?"

She spoke of the Abbe. Pauline caught sight of him; he was seated in the choir, but Jeanne had to be lifted up in order that she might perceive him.

"Oh! He is looking at us," said she; "he is blinking." According to Jeanne, the Abbe blinked when he laughed inwardly. Helene hastened to exchange a friendly nod with him. And then the tranquility within her seemed to increase, her future serenity appeared to be assured, thus endearing the church to her and lulling her into a blissful condition of patient endurance. Censers swung before the altar and threads of smoke ascended; the benediction followed, and the holy monstrance was slowly raised and waved above the heads lowered to the earth. Helene was still on her knees in happy meditation when she heard Madame Deberle exclaiming: "It's over now; let us go."

There ensued a clatter of chairs and a stamping of feet which reverberated along the arched aisles. Pauline had taken Jeanne's hand, and, walking away in front with the child, began to question her:

"Have you ever been to the theatre?"

"No. Is it finer than this?"

As she spoke, the little one, giving vent to great gasps of wonder, tossed her head as though ready to express the belief that nothing could be finer. To her question, however, Pauline deigned no reply, for she had just come to a standstill in front of a priest who was passing in his surplice. And when he was a few steps away she exclaimed aloud, with such conviction in her tones that two devout ladies of the congregation turned around:

"Oh! what a fine head!"

Helene, meanwhile, had risen from her knees. She stepped along by the side of Juliette among the crowd which was making its way out with difficulty. Her heart was full of tenderness, she felt languid and enervated, and her soul no longer rebelled at the other being so near. At one moment their bare hands came in contact and they smiled. They were almost stifling in the throng, and Helene would fain have had Juliette go first. All their old friendship seemed to blossom forth once more.

"Is it understood that we can rely on you for to-morrow evening?" asked Madame Deberle.

Helene no longer had the will to decline. She would see whether it were possible when she reached the street. It finished by their being the last to leave. Pauline and Jeanne already stood on the opposite pavement awaiting them. But a tearful voice brought them to a halt.

"Ah, my good lady, what a time it is since I had the happiness of seeing you!"

It was Mother Fetu, who was soliciting alms at the church door. Barring Helene's way, as though she had lain in wait for her, she went on:

"Oh, I have been so very ill always here, in the stomach, you know. Just now I feel as if a hammer were pounding away inside me; and I have nothing at all, my good lady. I didn't dare to send you word about it—May the gracious God repay you!"

Helene had slipped a piece of money into her hand, and promised to think about her.

"Hello!" exclaimed Madame Deberle, who had remained standing within the porch, "there's someone talking with Pauline and Jeanne. Why, it is Henri."

"Yes, yes" Mother Fetu hastened to add as she turned her ferret-like eyes on the ladies, "it is the good doctor. I have seen him there all through the service; he has never budged from the pavement; he has been waiting for you, no doubt. Ah! he's a saint of a man! I swear that to be the truth in the face of God who hears us. Yes, I know you, madame; he is a husband who deserves to be happy. May Heaven hearken to your prayers, may every blessing fall on you! In the name of the Father, the Son, and the Holy Ghost!"

Amidst the myriad furrows of her face, which was wrinkled like a withered apple, her little eyes kept gleaming in malicious unrest, darting a glance now on Juliette, now on Helene, so that it was impossible to say with any certainty whom she was addressing while speaking of "the good doctor." She followed them, muttering on without a stop, mingling whimpering entreaty with devout outbursts.

Henri's reserve alike astonished and moved Helene. He scarcely had the courage to raise his eyes towards her. On his wife quizzing him about the opinions which restrained him from entering a church, he merely explained that to smoke a cigar was his object in coming to meet them; but Helene understood that he had wished to see her again, to prove to her how wrong she was in fearing some fresh outrage. Doubtless, like herself, he had sworn to keep within the limits of reason. She never questioned whether his sincerity could be real. She simply experienced a feeling of unhappiness at seeing him unhappy. Thus it came about, that on leaving them it the Rue Vineuse, she said cheerfully:

"Well, it is settled then; to-morrow at seven."

In this way the old friendship grew closer than ever, and a charming life began afresh. To Helene it seemed as if Henri had never yielded to that moment of folly; it was but a dream of hers; each loved the other, but they would never breathe a word of their love, they were content with knowing its existence. They spent delicious hours, in which, without their tongues giving evidence of their passion, they displayed it constantly; a gesture, an inflexion of the voice sufficed, ay, even a silence. Everything insensibly tended towards their love, plunged them more and more deeply into a passion which they bore away with them whenever they parted, which was ever with them, which formed, as it were, the only atmosphere they could breathe. And their excuse was their honesty; with eyes wide open they played this comedy of affection; not even a hand-clasp did they allow each other and their restraint infused unalloyed delight into the simple greetings with which they met.

Every evening the ladies went to church. Madame Deberle was enchanted with the novel pleasure she was enjoying. It was so different from evening dances, concerts, and first nights; she adored fresh sensations, and nuns and priests were now constantly in her company. The store of religion which she had acquired in her school-days now found new life in her giddy brain, taking shape in all sorts of trivial observances, as though she were reviving the games of her childhood. Helene, who on her side had grown up without any religious training, surrendered herself to the bliss of these services of the month of Mary, happy also in the delight with which they appeared to inspire Jeanne. They now dined earlier; they gave Rosalie no peace lest she should cause them to be late, and prevent their securing good seats. Then they called for Juliette on the way. One day Lucien was taken, but he behaved so badly that he was afterward left at home. On entering the warm church, with its glare of wax candles, a feeling of tenderness and calm, which by degrees grew necessary to Helene, came over her. When doubts sprang up within her during the day, and the thought of Henri filled her with indefinable anxiety, with the evening the church once more brought her peace. The chants arose overflowing with divine passion; the flowers, newly culled, made the close atmosphere of the building still heavier. It was here that she breathed all the first rapture of springtide, amidst that adoration of woman raised to the status of a cult; and her senses swam as she contemplated the mystery of love and purity—Mary, virgin and mother, beaming beneath her wreath of white roses. Each day she remained longer on her knees. She found herself at times with hands joined in entreaty. When the ceremony came to an end, there followed the happiness of the return home. Henri awaited their appearance at the door; the evenings grew warmer, and they wended their way through the dark, still streets of Passy, while scarce a word passed between them.

"How devout you are getting, my dear!" said Madame Deberle one night, with a laugh.

Yes, it was true; Helene was widely opening the portals of her heart to pious thoughts. Never could she have fancied that such happiness would attend her love. She returned to the church as to a spot where her heart would melt, for under its roof she could give free vent to her tears, remain thoughtless, plunged in speechless worship. For an hour each evening she put no restraint on herself. The bursting love within her, prisoned throughout the day, at length escaped from her bosom on the wings of prayer, amidst the pious quiver of the throng. The muttered supplications, the bendings of the knee, the reverences —words and gestures seemingly interminable—all lulled her to rest; to her they ever expressed the same thing; it was always the same passion speaking in the same phrase, or the same gesture. She felt a need of faith, and basked enraptured by the Divine goodness.

Helene was not the only person whom Juliette twitted; she feigned a belief that Henri himself was becoming religious. What, had he not now entered the church to wait for them?—he, atheist and scoffer, who had been wont to assert that he had sought for the soul with his scalpel, and had not yet discovered its existence! As soon as she perceived him standing behind a pillar in the shadow of the pulpit, she would instantly jog Helene's arm.

"Look, look, he is there already! Do you know, he wouldn't confess when we got married! See how funny he looks; he gazes at us with so comical an expression; quick, look!"

Helene did not at the moment raise her head. The service was coming to an end, clouds of incense were rising, and the organ-music pealed forth joyfully. But her neighbor was not a woman to leave her alone, and she was forced to speak in answer.

"Yes, yes, I see him," she whispered, albeit she never turned her eyes.

She had on her own side divined his presence amidst the song of praise that mounted from the worshipping throng. It seemed to her that Henri's breath was wafted on the wings of the music and beat against her neck, and she imagined she could see behind her his glances shedding their light along the nave and haloing her, as she knelt, with a golden glory. And then she felt impelled to pray with such fervor that words failed her. The expression on his face was sober, as unruffled as any husband might wear when looking for ladies in a church, the same, indeed, as if he had been waiting for them in the lobby of a theatre. But when they came together, in the midst of the slowly-moving crowd of worshippers, they felt that the bonds of their love had been drawn closer by the flowers and the chanting; and they shunned all conversation, for their hearts were on their lips.

A fortnight slipped away, and Madame Deberle grew wearied. She ever jumped from one thing to the other, consumed with the thirst of doing what every one else was doing. For the moment charity bazaars had become her craze; she would toil up sixty flights of stairs of an afternoon to beg paintings of well-known artists, while her evenings were spent in presiding over meetings of lady patronesses, with a bell handy to call noisy members to order. Thus it happened that one Thursday evening Helene and her daughter went to church without their companions. On the conclusion of the sermon, while the choristers were commencing the *Magnificat*, the young woman, forewarned by some impulse of her heart, turned her head. Henri was there, in his usual place. Thereupon she remained with looks riveted to the ground till the service came to an end, waiting the while for the return home.

"Oh, how kind of you to come!" said Jeanne, with all a child's frankness, as they left the church. "I should have been afraid to go alone through these dark streets."

Henri, however, feigned astonishment, asserting that he had expected to meet his wife. Helene allowed the child to answer him, and followed them without uttering a word. As the trio passed under the porch a pitiful voice sang out: "Charity, charity! May God repay you!"

Every night Jeanne dropped a ten-sou piece into Mother Fetu's hand. When the latter saw the doctor alone with Helene, she nodded her head knowingly, instead of breaking out into a storm of thanks, as was her custom. The church was now empty, and she began to follow them, mumbling inaudible sentences. Sometimes, instead of returning by the Rue de Passy, the ladies, when the night was fine, went homewards by the Rue Raynouard, the way being thus lengthened by five or six minutes' walk. That night also Helene turned into the Rue Raynouard, craving for gloom and stillness, and entranced by the loneliness of the long thoroughfare, which was lighted by only a few gas-lamps, without the shadow of a single passer-by falling across its pavement.

At this hour Passy seemed out of the world; sleep had already fallen over it; it had all the quietude of a provincial town. On each side of the street loomed mansions, girls' schools, black and silent, and dining places, from the kitchens of which lights still streamed. There was not, however, a single shop to throw the glare of its frontage across the dimness. To Henri and Helene the loneliness was pregnant with intense charm. He had not ventured to offer her his arm. Jeanne walked between them in the middle of the road, which was gravelled like a walk in some park. At last the houses came to an end, and then on each side were walls, over which spread mantling clematis and clusters of lilac blossoms. Immense gardens parted the mansions, and here and there through the railings of an iron gate they could catch glimpses of a gloomy background of verdure, against which the tree-dotted turf assumed a more delicate hue. The air was filled with the perfume of irises growing in vases which they could scarce distinguish. All three paced on slowly through the warm spring night, which was steeping them in its odors, and Jeanne, with childish artlessness, raised her face to the heavens, and exclaimed:

"Oh, mamma, see what a number of stars!"

But behind them, like an echo of their own, came the footfall of Mother Fetu. Nearer and nearer she approached, till they could hear her muttering the opening words of the Angelic Salutation "*Ave Marie, gratia plena*," repeating them over and over again with the same confused persistency. She was telling her beads on her homeward way.

"I have still something left—may I give it to her?" Jeanne asked her mother.

And thereupon, without waiting for a reply, she left them, running towards the old woman, who was on the point of entering the Passage des Eaux. Mother Fetu clutched at the coin, calling upon all the angels of Heaven to bless her. As she spoke, however, she grasped the child's hand and detained her by her side, then asking in changed tones:

"The other lady is ill, is she not?"

"No," answered Jeanne, surprised.

"May Heaven shield her! May it shower its favors on her and her husband! Don't run away yet, my dear little lady. Let me say an *Ave Maria* for your mother's sake, and you will join in the 'Amen' with me. Oh! your mother will allow you; you can catch her up."

Meanwhile Henri and Helene trembled as they found themselves suddenly left alone in the shadow cast by a line of huge chestnut trees that bordered the road. They quietly took a few steps. The chestnut trees had strewn the ground with their bloom, and they were walking upon this rosy-tinted carpet. On a sudden, however, they came to a stop, their hearts filled with such emotion that they could go no farther.

"Forgive me," said Henri simply.

"Yes, yes," ejaculated Helene. "But oh! be silent, I pray you."

She had felt his hand touch her own, and had started back. Fortunately Jeanne ran towards them at the moment.

"Mamma, mamma!" she cried; "she made me say an *Ave*; she says it will bring you good luck."

The three then turned into the Rue Vineuse, while Mother Fetu crept down the steps of the Passage des Eaux, busy completing her rosary.

The month slipped away. Two or three more services were attended by Madame Deberle. One Sunday, the last one, Henri once more ventured to wait for Helene and Jeanne. The walk home thrilled them with joy. The month had been one long spell of wondrous bliss. The little church seemed to have entered into their lives to soothe their love and render its way pleasant. At first a great peace had settled on Helene's soul; she had found happiness in this sanctuary where she imagined she could without shame dwell on her love; however, the undermining had continued, and when her holy rapture passed away she was again in the grip of her passion, held by bonds that would have plucked at her heart-strings had she sought to break them asunder. Henri still preserved his respectful demeanor, but she could not do otherwise than see the passion burning in his face. She dreaded some outburst, and even grew afraid of herself.

One afternoon, going homewards after a walk with Jeanne, she passed along the Rue de l'Annonciation and entered the church. The child was complaining of feeling very tired. Until the last day she had been unwilling to admit that the evening services exhausted her, so intense was the pleasure she derived from them; but her cheeks had grown waxy-pale, and the doctor advised that she should take long walks.

"Sit down here," said her mother. "It will rest you; we'll only stay ten minutes."

She herself walked towards some chairs a short way off, and knelt down. She had placed Jeanne close to a pillar. Workmen were busy at the other end of the nave, taking down the hangings and removing the flowers, the ceremonials attending the month of Mary having come to an end the evening before. With her face buried in her hands Helene saw nothing and heard nothing; she was eagerly catechising her heart, asking whether she ought not to confess to Abbe Jouve what an awful life had come upon her. He would advise her, perhaps restore her lost peace. Still, within her there arose, out of her very anguish, a fierce flood of joy. She hugged her sorrow, dreading lest the priest might succeed in finding a cure for it. Ten minutes slipped away, then an hour. She was overwhelmed by the strife raging within her heart.

At last she raised her head, her eyes glistening with tears, and saw Abbe Jouve gazing at her sorrowfully. It was he who was directing the workmen. Having recognized Jeanne, he had just come forward.

"Why, what is the matter, my child?" he asked of Helene, who hastened to rise to her feet and wipe away her tears.

She was at a loss what answer to give; she was afraid lest she should once more fall on her knees and burst into sobs. He approached still nearer, and gently resumed:

"I do not wish to cross-question you, but why do you not confide in me? Confide in the priest and forget the friend."

"Some other day," she said brokenly, "some other day, I promise you."

Jeanne meantime had at first been very good and patient, finding amusement in looking at the stained-glass windows, the statues over the great doorway, and the scenes of the journey to the Cross depicted in miniature bas-reliefs along the aisles. By degrees, however, the cold air of the church had enveloped her as with a shroud; and she remained plunged in a weariness that even banished thought, a feeling of discomfort waking within her with the holy quiet and far-reaching echoes, which the least sound stirred in this sanctuary where she imagined she was going to die. But a grievous sorrow rankled in her heart—the flowers were being borne away. The great clusters of roses were vanishing, and the altar seemed to become more and more bare and chill. The marble looked icy-cold now that no wax-candle shone on it and there was no smoking incense. The lace-robed Virgin moreover was being moved, and after suddenly tottering fell backward into the arms of two workmen. At the sight Jeanne uttered a faint cry, stretched out her arms, and fell back rigid; the illness that had been threatening her for some days had at last fallen upon her.

And when Helene, in distraction, carried her child, with the assistance of the sorrowing Abbe, into a cab, she turned towards the porch with outstretched, trembling hands.

"It's all this church! it's all this church!" she exclaimed, with a vehemence instinct with regret and self-reproach as she thought of the month of devout delight which she herself had tasted there.

CHAPTER XII.

When evening came Jeanne was somewhat better. She was able to get up, and, in order to remove her mother's fears, persisted in dragging herself into the dining-room, where she took her seat before her empty plate.

"I shall be all right," she said, trying to smile. "You know very well that the least thing upsets me. Get on with your dinner, mamma; I want you to eat."

And in the end she pretended an appetite she did not feel, for she observed that her mother sat watching her paling and trembling, without being able to swallow a morsel. She promised to take some jam, and Helene then hurried through her dinner, while the child, with a never-fading smile and her head nodding tremblingly, watched her with worshipping looks. On the appearance of the dessert she made an effort to carry out her promise, but tears welled into her eyes.

"You see I can't get it down my throat," she murmured. "You mustn't be angry with me."

The weariness that overwhelmed her was terrible. Her legs seemed lifeless, her shoulders pained her as though gripped by a hand of iron. But she was very brave through it all, and choked at their source the moans which the shooting pains in her neck awakened. At one moment, however, she forgot herself, her head felt too heavy, and she was bent double by pain. Her mother, as she gazed on her, so faint and feeble, was wholly unable to finish the pear which she was trying to force down her throat. Her sobs choked her, and throwing down her napkin, she clasped Jeanne in her arms.

"My child! my child!" she wailed, her heart bursting with sorrow, as her eyes ranged round the dining-room where her darling, when in good health, had so often enlivened her by her fondness for tid-bits.

At last Jeanne woke to life again, and strove to smile as of old.

"Don't worry, mamma," said she; "I shall be all right soon. Now that you have done you must put me to bed. I only wanted to see you have your dinner. Oh! I know you; you wouldn't have eaten as much as a morsel of bread."

Helene bore her away in her arms. She had brought the little crib close to her own bed in the blue room. When Jeanne had stretched out her limbs, and the bedclothes were tucked up under her chin, she declared she felt much better. There were no more complaints about dull pains at the back of her head; but she melted into tenderness, and her passionate love seemed to grow more pronounced. Helene was forced to caress her, to avow intense affection for her, and to promise that she would again kiss her when she came to bed.

"Never mind if I'm sleeping," said Jeanne. "I shall know you're there all the same."

She closed her eyes and fell into a doze. Helene remained near her, watching over her slumber. When Rosalie entered on tip-toe to ask permission to go to bed, she answered "Yes" with a nod. At last eleven o'clock struck, and Helene was still watching there, when she imagined she heard a gentle tapping at the outer door. Bewildered with astonishment, she took up the lamp and left the room to make sure.

"Who is there?"

"'Tis I; open the door," replied a voice in stifled tones.

It was Henri's voice. She quickly opened the door, thinking his coming only natural. No doubt he had but now been informed of Jeanne's illness, and had hastened to her, although she had not summoned him to her assistance, feeling a certain shame at the thought of allowing him to share in attending on her daughter.

However, he gave her no opportunity to speak. He followed her into the dining-room, trembling, with inflamed visage.

"I beseech you, pardon me," he faltered, as he caught hold of her hand. "I haven't seen you for three days past, and I cannot resist the craving to see you."

Helene withdrew her hand. He stepped back, but, with his gaze still fixed on her, continued: "Don't be afraid; I love you. I would have waited at the door had you not opened it. Oh! I know very well it is simple madness, but I love you, I love you all the same!"

Her face was grave as she listened, eloquent with a dumb reproach which tortured him, and impelled him to pour forth his passionate love.

But Helene still remained standing, wholly unmoved. At last she spoke. "You know nothing, then?" asked she.

He had taken her hand, and was raising it to his lips, when she started back with a gesture of impatience.

"Oh! leave me!" she exclaimed. "You see that I am not even listening to you. I have something far different to think about!"

Then becoming more composed, she put her question to him a second time. "You know nothing? Well, my daughter is ill. I am pleased to see you; you will dispel my fears."

She took up the lamp and walked on before him, but as they were passing through the doorway, she turned, and looking at him, said firmly:

"I forbid you beginning again here. Oh! you must not!"

He entered behind her, scarcely understanding what had been enjoined on him. His temples throbbed convulsively, as he leaned over the child's little crib.

"She is asleep; look at her," said Helene in a whisper.

He did not hear her; his passion would not be silenced. She was hanging over the bed in front of him, and he could see her rosy neck, with its wavy hair. He shut his eyes that he might escape the temptation of kissing her, as she said to him:

"Doctor, look at her, she is so feverish. Oh, tell me whether it is serious!"

Then, yielding to professional habit, despite the tempest raging in his brain, he mechanically felt Jeanne's pulse. Nevertheless, so fierce was the struggle that he remained for a time motionless, seemingly unaware that he held this wasted little hand in his own.

"Is it a violent fever?" asked Helene.

"A violent fever! Do you think so?" he repeated.

The little hand was scorching his own. There came another silence; the physician was awakening within him, and passion was dying from his eyes. His face slowly grew paler; he bent down uneasily, and examined Jeanne.

"You are right; this is a very severe attack," he exclaimed. "My God! the poor child!"

His passion was now dead; he was solely consumed by a desire to be of service to her. His coolness at once returned; he sat down, and was questioning the mother respecting the child's condition previous to this attack of illness, when Jeanne awoke, moaning loudly. She again complained of a terrible pain in the head. The pangs which were darting through her neck and shoulders had attained such intensity that her every movement wrung a sob from her. Helene knelt on the other side of the bed, encouraging her, and smiling on her, though her heart almost broke at the sight of such agony.

"There's someone there, isn't there, mamma?" Jeanne asked, as she turned round and caught sight of the doctor.

"It is a friend, whom you know."

The child looked at him for a time with thoughtful eyes, as if in doubt; but soon a wave of affection passed over her face. "Yes, yes, I know him; I love him very much." And with her coaxing air she added: "You will have to cure me, won't you, sir, to make mamma happy? Oh, I'll be good; I'll drink everything you give me."

The doctor again felt her pulse, while Helene grasped her other hand; and, as she lay there between them, her eyes travelled attentively from one to the other, as though no such advantageous opportunity of seeing and comparing them had ever occurred before. Then her head shook with a nervous trembling; she grew agitated; and her tiny hands caught hold of her mother and the doctor with a convulsive grip.

"Do not go away; I'm so afraid. Take care of me; don't let all the others come near me. I only want you, only you two, near me. Come closer up to me, together!" she stammered.

Drawing them nearer, with a violent effort she brought them close to her, still uttering the same entreaty: "Come close, together, together!"

Several times did she behave in the same delirious fashion. Then came intervals of quiet, when a heavy sleep fell on her, but it left her breathless and almost dead. When she started out of these short dozes she heard nothing, saw nothing—a white vapor shrouded her eyes. The doctor remained watching over her for a part of the night, which proved a very bad one. He only absented himself for a moment to procure some medicine. Towards morning, when he was about to leave, Helene, with terrible anxiety in her face accompanied him into the ante-room.

"Well?" asked she.

"Her condition is very serious," he answered; "but you must not fear; rely on me; I will give you every assistance. I shall come back at ten o'clock."

When Helene returned to the bedroom she found Jeanne sitting up in bed, gazing round her with bewildered looks.

"You left me! you left me!" she wailed. "Oh! I'm afraid; I don't want to be left all alone."

To console her, her mother kissed her, but she still gazed round the room:

"Where is he?" she faltered. "Oh! tell him not to go away; I want him to be here, I want him—"

"He will come back, my darling!" interrupted Helene, whose tears were mingling with Jeanne's own. "He will not leave us, I promise you. He loves us too well. Now, be good and lie down. I'll stay here till he comes back."

"Really? really?" murmured the child, as she slowly fell back into deep slumber.

Terrible days now began, three weeks full of awful agony. The fever did not quit its victim for an hour. Jeanne only seemed tranquil when the doctor was present; she put one of her little hands in his, while her mother held the other. She seemed to find safety in their presence; she gave each of them an equal share of her tyrannical worship, as though she well knew beneath what passionate kindness she was sheltering herself. Her nervous temperament, so exquisite in its sensibility, the keener since her illness, inspired her, no doubt, with the thought that only a miraculous effort of their love could save her. As the hours slipped away she would gaze on them with grave and searching looks as they sat on each side of her crib. Her glances remained instinct with human passion, and though she spoke not she told them all she desired by the warm pressure of her hands, with which she besought them not to leave her, giving them to understand what peace was hers when they were present. Whenever the doctor entered after having been away her joy became supreme, and her eyes, which never quitted the door, flashed with light; and then she would fall quietly asleep, all her fears fleeing as she heard her mother and him moving around her and speaking in whispers.

On the day after the attack Doctor Bodin called. But Jeanne suddenly turned away her head and refused to allow him to examine her.

"I don't want him, mamma," she murmured, "I don't want him! I beg of you."

As he made his appearance on the following day, Helene was forced to inform him of the child's dislike, and thus it came about that the venerable doctor made no further effort to enter the sick-room. Still, he climbed the stairs every other day to inquire how Jeanne was getting on, and sometimes chatted with his brother professional, Doctor Deberle, who paid him all the deference due to an elder.

Moreover, it was useless to try to deceive Jeanne. Her senses had become wondrously acute. The Abbe and Monsieur Rambaud paid a visit every night; they sat down and spent an hour in sad silence. One evening, as the doctor was going away, Helene signed to Monsieur Rambaud to take his place and clasp the little one's hand, so that she might not notice the departure of her beloved friend. But two or three minutes had scarcely passed ere Jeanne opened her eyes and quickly drew her hand away. With tears flowing she declared that they were behaving ill to her.

"Don't you love me any longer? won't you have me beside you?" asked poor Monsieur Rambaud, with tears in his eyes.

She looked at him, deigning no reply; it seemed as if her heart was set on knowing him no more. The worthy man, grievously pained, returned to his corner. He always ended by thus gliding into a window-recess, where, half hidden behind a curtain, he would remain during the evening, in a stupor of grief, his eyes the while never quitting the sufferer. The Abbe was there as well, with his large head and pallid face showing above his scraggy shoulders. He concealed his tears by blowing his nose loudly from time to time. The danger in which he saw his little friend lying wrought such havoc within him that his poor were for the time wholly forgotten.

But it was useless for the two brothers to retire to the other end of the room; Jeanne was still conscious of their presence. They were a source of vexation to her, and she would turn round with a harassed look, even though drowsy with fever. Her mother bent over her to catch the words trembling on her lips.

"Oh! mamma, I feel so ill. All this is choking me; send everybody away —quick, quick!"

Helene with the utmost gentleness then explained to the two brothers the child's wish to fall asleep; they understood her meaning, and quitted the room with drooping heads. And no sooner had they gone than Jeanne breathed with greater freedom, cast a glance round the chamber, and once more fixed a look of infinite tenderness on her mother and the doctor.

"Good-night," she whispered; "I feel well again; stay beside me."

For three weeks she thus kept them by her side. Henri had at first paid two visits each day, but soon he spent the whole night with them, giving every hour he could spare to the child. At the outset he had feared it was a case of typhoid fever; but so contradictory were the symptoms that he soon felt himself involved in perplexity. There was no doubt he was confronted by a disease of the chlorosis type, presenting the greatest difficulty in treatment, with the possibility of very dangerous complications, as the child was almost on the threshold of womanhood. He dreaded first a lesion of the heart and then the setting in of consumption. Jeanne's nervous excitement, wholly beyond his control, was a special source of uneasiness; to such heights of delirium did the fever rise, that the strongest medicines were of no avail. He brought all his fortitude and knowledge to bear on the case, inspired with the one thought that his own happiness and life were at stake. On his mind there had now fallen a great stillness; not once during those three anxious weeks did his passion break its bonds. Helene's breath no longer woke tremors within him, and when their eyes met they were only eloquent of the sympathetic sadness of two souls threatened by a common misfortune.

Nevertheless every moment brought their hearts nearer. They now lived only with the one idea. No sooner had he entered the bed-chamber than by a glance he gathered how Jeanne had spent the night; and there was no need for him to speak for Helene to learn what he thought of the child's condition. Besides, with all the innate bravery of a mother, she had forced from him a declaration that he would not deceive her, but allow her to know his fears. Always on her feet, not having had three hours' uninterrupted sleep for three weeks past, she displayed superhuman endurance and composure, and quelled her despair without a tear in order that she might concentrate her whole soul upon the struggle with the dread enemy. Within and without her heart there was nothing but emptiness; the world around her, the usual thoughts of each hour, the consciousness of life itself, had all faded into darkness. Existence held nothing for her. Nothing now bound her to life but her suffering darling and this man who promised her a miracle. It was he, and he only, to whom she looked, to whom she listened, whose most trivial words were to her of the first importance, and into whose breast she would fain have transfused her own soul in order to increase his energy. Insensibly, and without break, this idea wrought out its own accomplishment. Almost every evening, when the fever was raging at its worst and Jeanne lay in imminent peril, they were there beside her in silence; and as though eager to remind themselves that they stood shoulder to shoulder struggling against death, their hands met on the edge of the bed in a caressing clasp, while they trembled with solicitude and pity till a faint smile breaking over the child's face, and the sound of quiet and regular breathing, told them that the danger was past. Then each encouraged the other by an inclination of the head. Once again had their love triumphed; and every time the mute caress grew more demonstrative their hearts drew closer together.

One night Helene divined that Henri was concealing something from her. For ten minutes, without a word crossing his lips, he had been examining Jeanne. The little one complained of intolerable thirst; she seemed choking, and there was an incessant wheezing in her parched throat. Then a purple flush came over her face, and she lapsed into a stupor which prevented her even from raising her eyelids. She lay motionless; it might have been imagined she was dead but for the sound coming from her throat.

"You consider her very ill, do you not?" gasped Helene.

He answered in the negative; there was no change. But his face was ashy-white, and he remained seated, overwhelmed by his powerlessness. Thereupon she also, despite the tension of her whole being, sank upon a chair on the other side of the bed.

"Tell me everything. You promised to tell me all. Is she beyond hope?"

He still sat silent, and she spoke again more vehemently:

"You know how brave I am. Have I wept? have I despaired? Speak: I want to know the truth."

Henri fixed his eyes on her. The words came slowly from his lips. "Well," said he, "if in an hour hence she hasn't awakened from this stupor, it will be all over."

Not a sob broke from Helene; but icy horror possessed her and raised her hair on end. Her eyes turned on Jeanne; she fell on her knees and clasped her in her arms with a superb gesture eloquent of ownership, as though she could preserve her from ill, nestling thus against her shoulder. For more than a minute she kept her face close to the child's, gazing at her intently, eager to give her breath from her own nostrils, ay, and her very life too. The labored breathing of the little sufferer grew shorter and shorter.

"Can nothing be done?" she exclaimed, as she lifted her head. "Why do you remain there? Do something!" But he made a disheartened gesture. "Do something!" she repeated. "There must be something to be done. You are not going to let her die oh, surely not!"

"I will do everything possible," the doctor simply said.

He rose up, and then a supreme struggle began. All the coolness and nerve of the practitioner had returned to him. Till now he had not ventured to try any violent remedies, for he dreaded to enfeeble the little frame already almost destitute of life. But he no longer remained undecided, and straightway dispatched Rosalie for a dozen leeches. And he did not attempt to conceal from the mother that this was a desperate remedy which might save or kill her child. When the leeches were brought in, her heart failed her for a moment.

"Gracious God! gracious God!" she murmured. "Oh, if you should kill her!"

He was forced to wring consent from her.

"Well, put them on," said she; "but may Heaven guide your hand!"

She had not ceased holding Jeanne, and refused to alter her position, as she still desired to keep the child's little head nestling against her shoulder. With calm features he meantime busied himself with the last resource, not allowing a word to fall from his lips. The first application of the leeches proved unsuccessful. The minutes slipped away. The only sound breaking the stillness of the shadowy chamber was the merciless, incessant tick-tack of the timepiece. Hope departed with every second. In the bright disc of light cast by the lamp, Jeanne lay stretched among the disordered bedclothes, with limbs of waxen pallor. Helene, with tearless eyes, but choking with emotion, gazed on the little body already in the clutches of death, and to see a drop of her daughter's blood appear, would willingly have yielded up all her own. And at last a ruddy drop trickled down—the leeches had made fast their hold; one by one they commenced sucking. The child's life was in the balance. These were terrible moments, pregnant with anguish. Was that sigh the exhalation of Jeanne's last breath, or did it mark her return to life? For a time Helene's heart was frozen within her; she believed that the little one was dead; and there came to her a violent impulse to pluck away the creatures which were sucking so greedily; but some supernatural power restrained her, and she remained there with open mouth and her blood chilled within her. The pendulum still swung to and fro; the room itself seemed to wait the issue in anxious expectation.

At last the child stirred. Her heavy eyelids rose, but dropped again, as though wonder and weariness had overcome her. A slight quiver passed over her face; it seemed as if she were breathing. Finally there was a trembling of the lips; and Helene, in an agony of suspense, bent over her, fiercely awaiting the result.

"Mamma! mamma!" murmured Jeanne.

Henri heard, and walking to the head of the bed, whispered in the mother's ear: "She is saved."

"She is saved! she is saved!" echoed Helene in stammering tones, her bosom filled with such joy that she fell on the floor close to the bed, gazing now at her daughter and now at the doctor with distracted looks. But she rose and giving way to a mighty impulse, threw herself on Henri's neck.

"I love you!" she exclaimed.

This was her avowal—the avowal imprisoned so long, but at last poured forth in the crisis of emotion which had come upon her. Mother and lover were merged in one; she proffered him her love in a fiery rush of gratitude.

Through her sobs she spoke to him in endearing words. Her tears, dried at their source for three weeks, were now rolling down her cheeks. But at last she fell upon her knees, and took Jeanne in her arms to lull her to deeper slumber against her shoulder; and at intervals whilst her child thus rested she raised to Henri's eyes glistening with passionate tears.

Stretched in her cot, the bedclothes tucked under her chin, and her head, with its dark brown tresses, resting in the center of the pillow, Jeanne lay, relieved, but prostrate. Her eyelids were closed, but she did not sleep. The lamp, placed on the table, which had been rolled close to the fireplace, lit but one end of the room, and the shade encompassed Helene and Henri, seated in their customary places on each side of the bed. But the child did not part them; on the contrary, she served as a closer bond between them, and her innocence was intermingled with their love on this first night of its avowal. At times Helene rose on tiptoe to fetch the medicine, to turn up the lamp, or give some order to Rosalie; while the doctor, whose eyes never quitted her, would sign to her to walk gently. And when she had sat down again they smiled at one another. Not a word was spoken; all their interest was concentrated on Jeanne, who was to them as their love itself. Sometimes when the coverlet was being pulled up, or the child's head was being raised, their hands met and rested together in sweet forgetfulness. This undesigned, stealthy caress was the only one in which they indulged.

"I am not sleeping," murmured Jeanne. "I know very well you are there."

On hearing her speak they were overjoyed. Their hands parted; beyond this they had no desires. The improvement in the child's condition was to them satisfaction and peace.

"Are you feeling better, my darling?" asked Helene, when she saw her stirring.

Jeanne made no immediate reply, and when she spoke it was dreamingly.

"Oh, yes! I don't feel anything now. But I can hear you, and that pleases me."

After the lapse of a moment, she opened her eyes with an effort and looked at them. Then an angelic smile crossed her face, and her eyelids dropped once more.

On the morrow, when the Abbe and Monsieur Rambaud made their appearance, Helene gave way to a shrug of impatience. They were now a disturbing element in her happy nest. As they went on questioning her, shaking with fear lest they might receive bad tidings, she had the cruelty to reply that Jeanne was no better. She spoke without consideration, driven to this strait by the selfish desire of treasuring for herself and Henri the bliss of having rescued Jeanne from death, and of alone knowing this to be so. What was their reason for seeking a share in her happiness? It belonged to Henri and herself, and had it been known to another would have seemed to her impaired in value. To her imagination it would have been as though a stranger were participating in her love.

The priest, however, approached the bed.

"Jeanne, 'tis we, your old friends. Don't you know us?"

She nodded gravely to them in recognition, but she was unwilling to speak to them; she was in a thoughtful mood, and she cast a look full of meaning on her mother. The two poor men went away more heartbroken than on any previous evening.

Three days later Henri allowed his patient her first boiled egg. It was a matter of the highest importance. Jeanne's mind was made up to eat it with none present but her mother and the doctor, and the door must be closed. As it happened, Monsieur Rambaud was present at the moment; and when Helene began to spread a napkin, by way of table-cloth, on the bed, the child whispered in her ear: "Wait a moment—when he has gone."

And as soon as he had left them she burst out: "Now, quick! quick! It's far nicer when there's nobody but ourselves."

Helene lifted her to a sitting posture, while Henri placed two pillows behind her to prop her up; and then, with the napkin spread before her and a plate on her knees, Jeanne waited, smiling.

"Shall I break the shell for you?" asked her mother.

"Yes, do, mamma."

"And I will cut you three little bits of bread," added the doctor.

"Oh! four; you'll see if I don't eat four."

It was now the doctor's turn to be addressed endearingly. When he gave her the first slice, she gripped his hand, and as she still clasped her mother's, she rained kisses on both with the same passionate tenderness.

"Come, come; you will have to be good," entreated Helene, who observed that she was ready to burst into tears; "you must please us by eating your egg."

At this Jeanne ventured to begin; but her frame was so enfeebled that with the second sippet of bread she declared herself wearied. As she swallowed each mouthful, she would say, with a smile, that her teeth were tender. Henri encouraged her, while Helene's eyes were brimful of tears. Heaven! she saw her child eating! She watched the bread disappear, and the gradual consumption of this first egg thrilled her to the heart. To picture Jeanne stretched dead beneath the sheets was a vision of mortal terror; but now she was eating, and eating so prettily, with all an invalid's characteristic dawdling and hesitancy!

"You won't be angry, mamma? I'm doing my best. Why, I'm at my third bit of bread! Are you pleased?"

"Yes, my darling, quite pleased. Oh! you don't know all the joy the sight gives me!"

And then, in the happiness with which she overflowed, Helene forgetfully leaned against Henri's shoulder. Both laughed gleefully at the child, but over her face there suddenly crept a sullen flush; she gazed at them stealthily, and drooped her head, and refused to eat any more, her features glooming the while with distrust and anger. At last they had to lay her back in bed again.

CHAPTER XIII.

Months slipped away, and Jeanne was still convalescent. August came, and she had not quitted her bed. When evening fell she would rise for an hour or two; but even the crossing of the room to the window—where she reclined on an invalid-chair and gazed out on Paris, flaming with the ruddy light of the dying sun—seemed too great a strain for her wearied frame. Her attenuated limbs could scarce bear their burden, and she would declare with a wan smile that the blood in her veins would not suffice for a little bird, and that she must have plenty of soup. Morsels of raw meat were dipped in her broth. She had grown to like this mixture, as she longed to be able to go down to play in the garden.

The weeks and the months which slipped by were ever instinct with the same delightful monotony, and Helene forgot to count the days. She never left the house; at Jeanne's side she forgot the whole world. No news from without reached her ears. Her retreat, though it looked down on Paris, which with its smoke and noise stretched across the horizon, was as secret and secluded as any cave of holy hermit amongst the hills. Her child was saved, and the knowledge of it satisfied all her desires. She spent her days in watching over her return to health, rejoicing in a shade of bright color returning to her cheeks, in a lively look, or in a gesture of gladness. Every hour made her daughter more like what she had been of old, with lovely eyes and wavy hair. The slower Jeanne's recovery, the greater joy was yielded to Helene, who recalled the olden days when she had suckled her, and, as she gazed on her gathering strength, felt even a keener emotion than when in the past she had measured her two little feet in her hand to see if she would soon be able to walk.

At the same time some anxiety remained to Helene. On several occasions she had seen a shadow come over Jeanne's face—a shadow of sudden distrust and sourness. Why was her laughter thus abruptly turned to sulkiness? Was she suffering? was she hiding some quickening of the old pain?

"Tell me, darling, what is the matter? You were laughing just a moment ago, and now you are nearly crying! Speak to me: do you feel a pain anywhere?"

But Jeanne abruptly turned away her head and buried her face in the pillow.

"There's nothing wrong with me," she answered curtly. "I want to be left alone."

And she would lie brooding the whole afternoon, with her eyes fixed on the wall, showing no sign of affectionate repentance, but plunged in a sadness which baffled her forlorn mother. The doctor knew not what to say; these fits of gloom would always break out when he was there, and he attributed them to the sufferer's nervousness. He impressed on Helene the necessity of crossing her in nothing.

One afternoon Jeanne had fallen asleep. Henri, who was pleased with her progress, had lingered in the room, and was carrying on a whispered conversation with Helene, who was once more busy with her everlasting needlework at her seat beside the window. Since the terrible night when she had confessed she loved him both had lived on peacefully in the consciousness of their mutual passions, careless of the morrow, and without a thought of the world. Around Jeanne's bed, in this room that still reverberated with her agony, there was an atmosphere of purity which shielded them from any outburst. The child's innocent breath fell on them with a quieting influence. But as the little invalid slowly grew well again, their love in very sympathy took new strength, and they would sit side by side with beating hearts, speaking little, and then only in whispers, lest the little one might be awakened. Their words were without significance, but struck re-echoing chords within the breast of each. That afternoon their love revealed itself in a thousand ways.

"I assure you she is much better," said the doctor. "In a fortnight she will be able to go down to the garden."

Helene went on stitching quickly.

"Yesterday she was again very sad," she murmured, "but this morning she was laughing and happy. She has given me her promise to be good."

A long silence followed. The child was still plunged in sleep, and their souls were enveloped in a profound peace. When she slumbered thus, their relief was intense; they seemed to share each other's hearts the more.

"Have you not seen the garden yet?" asked Henri. "Just now it's full of flowers."

"The asters are out, aren't they?" she questioned.

"Yes; the flower-bed looks magnificent. The clematises have wound their way up into the elms. It is quite a nest of foliage."

There was another silence. Helene ceased sewing, and gave him a smile. To their fancy it seemed as though they were strolling together along high-banked paths, dim with shadows, amidst which fell a shower of roses. As he hung over her he drank in the faint perfume of vervain that arose from her dressing-gown. However, all at once a rustling of the sheets disturbed them.

"She is wakening!" exclaimed Helene, as she started up.

Henri drew himself away, and simultaneously threw a glance towards the bed. Jeanne had but a moment before gripped the pillow with her arms, and, with her chin buried in it, had turned her face towards them. But her eyelids were still shut, and judging by her slow and regular breathing, she had again fallen asleep.

"Are you always sewing like this?" asked Henri, as he came nearer to Helene.

"I cannot remain with idle hands," she answered. "It is mechanical enough, but it regulates my thoughts. For hours I can think of the same thing without wearying."

He said no more, but his eye dwelt on the needle as the stitching went on almost in a melodious cadence; and it seemed to him as if the thread were carrying off and binding something of their lives together. For hours she could have sewn on, and for hours he could have sat there, listening to the music of the needle, in which, like a lulling refrain, re-echoed one word that never wearied them. It was their wish to live their days like this in that quiet nook, to sit side by side while the child was asleep, never stirring from their places lest they might awaken her. How sweet was that quiescent silence, in which they could listen to the pulsing of hearts, and bask in the delight of a dream of everlasting love!

"How good you are!" were the words which came several times from his lips, the joy her presence gave him only finding expression in that one phrase.

Again she raised her head, never for a moment deeming it strange that she should be so passionately worshipped. Henri's face was near her own, and for a second they gazed at one another.

"Let me get on with my work," she said in a whisper. "I shall never have it finished."

But just then an instinctive dread prompted her to turn round, and indeed there lay Jeanne, lowering upon them with deadly pale face and great inky-black eyes. The child had not made the least movement; her chin was still buried in the downy pillow, which she clasped with her little arms. She had only opened her eyes a moment before and was contemplating them.

"Jeanne, what's the matter?" asked Helene. "Are you ill? do you want anything?"

The little one made no reply, never stirred, did not even lower the lids of her great flashing eyes. A sullen gloom was on her brow, and in her pallid cheeks were deep hollows. She seemed about to throw back her hands as though a convulsion was imminent. Helene started up, begging her to speak; but she remained obstinately stiff, darting such black looks on her mother that the latter's face became purple with blushes, and she murmured:

"Doctor, see; what is the matter with her?"

Henri had drawn his chair away from Helene's. He ventured near the bed, and was desirous of taking hold of one of the little hands which so fiercely gripped the pillow. But as he touched Jeanne she trembled in every limb, turned with a start towards the wall, and exclaimed:

"Leave me alone; you, I mean! You are hurting me!"

She pulled the coverlet over her face, and for a quarter of an hour they attempted, without success, to soothe her with gentle words. At last, as they still persevered, she sat up with her hands clasped in supplication: "Oh, please leave me alone; you are tormenting me! Leave me alone!"

Helene, in her bewilderment, once more sat down at the window, but Henri did not resume his place beside her. They now understood: Jeanne was devoured by jealousy. They were unable to speak another word. For a minute or two the doctor paced up and down in silence, and then slowly quitted the room, well understanding the meaning of the anxious glances which the mother was darting towards the bed. As soon as he had gone, she ran to her daughter's side and pressed her passionately to her breast, with a wild outburst of words.

"Hear me, my pet, I am alone now; look at me, speak to me. Are you in pain? Have I vexed you then? Tell me everything! Is it I whom you are angry with? What are you troubled about?"

But it was useless to pray for an answer, useless to plead with all sorts of questions; Jeanne declared that she was quite well. Then she started up with a frenzied cry: "You don't love me any more, mamma! you don't love me any more!"

She burst into grievous sobbing, and wound her arms convulsively round her mother's neck, raining greedy kisses on her face. Helene's heart was rent within her, she felt overwhelmed with unspeakable sadness, and strained her child to her bosom, mingling her tears with her own, and vowing to her that she would never love anybody save herself.

From that day onward a mere word or glance would suffice to awaken Jeanne's jealousy. While she was in the perilous grip of death some instinct had led her to put her trust in the loving tenderness with which they had shielded and saved her. But now strength was returning to her, and she would allow none to participate in her mother's love. She conceived a kind of spite against the doctor, a spite which stealthily grew into hate as her health improved. It was hidden deep within her self-willed brain, in the innermost recesses of her suspicious and silent nature. She would never consent to explain things; she herself knew not what was the matter with her; but she felt ill whenever the doctor drew too near to her mother; and would press her hands violently to her bosom. Her torment seemed to sear her very heart, and furious passion choked her and made her cheeks turn pale. Nor could she place any restraint on herself; she imagined every one unjust, grew stiff and haughty, and deigned no reply when she was charged with being very ill-tempered. Helene, trembling with dismay, dared not press her to explain the source of her trouble; indeed, her eyes turned away whenever this eleven-year-old child darted at her a glance in which was concentrated the premature passion of a woman.

"Oh, Jeanne, you are making me very wretched!" she would sometimes say to her, the tears standing in her eyes as she observed her stifling in her efforts to restrain a sudden bubbling up of mad anger.

But these words, once so potent for good, which had so often drawn the child weeping to Helene's arms, were now wholly without influence. There was a change taking place in her character. Her humors varied ten times a day. Generally she spoke abruptly and imperiously, addressing her mother as though she were Rosalie, and constantly plaguing her with the pettiest demands, ever impatient and loud in complaint.

"Give me a drink. What a time you take! I am left here dying of thirst!" And when Helene handed the glass to her she would exclaim: "There's no sugar in it; I won't have it!"

Then she would throw herself back on her pillow, and a second time push away the glass, with the complaint that the drink was too sweet. They no longer cared to attend to her, she would say; they were doing it purposely. Helene, dreading lest she might infuriate her to a yet greater extent, made no reply, but gazed on her with tears trembling on her cheeks.

However, Jeanne's anger was particularly visible when the doctor made his appearance. The moment he entered the sick-room she would lay herself flat in bed, or sullenly hang her head in the manner of savage brutes who will not suffer a stranger to come near. Sometimes she refused to say a word, allowing him to feel her pulse or examine her while she remained motionless with her eyes fixed on the ceiling. On other days she would not even look at him, but clasp her hands over her eyes with such a gust of passion that to remove them would have necessitated the violent twisting of her arms. One night, as her mother was about to give her a spoonful of medicine, she burst out with the cruel remark: "I won't have it; it will poison me."

Helene's heart, pierced to the quick, sank within her, and she dreaded to elicit what the remark might mean.

"What are you saying, my child?" she asked. "Do you understand what you are talking about? Medicine is never nice to take. You must drink this."

But Jeanne lay there in obstinate silence, and averted her head in order to get rid of the draught. From that day onward she was full of caprices, swallowing or rejecting her medicines according to the humor of the moment. She would sniff at the phials and examine them suspiciously as they stood on the night-table. Should she have refused to drink the contents of one of them she never forgot its identity, and would have died rather than allow a drop from it to pass her lips. Honest Monsieur Rambaud alone could persuade her at times. It was he whom she now overwhelmed with the most lavish caresses, especially if the doctor were looking on; and her gleaming eyes were turned towards her mother to note if she were vexed by this display of affection towards another.

"Oh, it's you, old friend!" she exclaimed the moment he entered. "Come and sit down near me. Have you brought me any oranges?"

She sat up and laughingly fumbled in his pockets, where goodies were always secreted. Then she embraced him, playing quite a love comedy, while her revenge found satisfaction in the anguish which she imagined she could read on her mother's pallid face. Monsieur Rambaud beamed with joy over his restoration to his little sweetheart's good graces. But Helene, on meeting him in the ante-room, was usually able to acquaint him with the state of affairs, and all at once he would look at the draught standing on the table and exclaim: "What! are you having syrup?"

Jeanne's face clouded over, and, in a low voice, she replied: "No, no, it's nasty, it's nauseous; I can't take it."

"What! you can't drink this?" questioned Monsieur Rambaud gaily. "I can wager it's very good. May I take a little of it?"

Then without awaiting her permission he poured out a large spoonful, and swallowed it with a grimace that seemed to betoken immeasurable satisfaction.

"How delicious!" he murmured. "You are quite wrong; see, just take a little to try."

Jeanne, amused, then made no further resistance. She would drink whatever Monsieur Rambaud happened to taste. She watched his every motion greedily, and appeared to study his features with a view to observing the effects of the medicine. The good man for a month gorged himself in this way with drugs, and, on Helene gratefully thanking him, merely shrugged his shoulders.

"Oh! it's very good stuff!" he declared, with perfect conviction, making it his pleasure to share the little one's medicines.

He passed his evenings at her bedside. The Abbe, on the other hand, came regularly every second day. Jeanne retained them with her as long as possible, and displayed vexation when she saw them take up their hats. Her immediate dread lay in being left alone with her mother

and the doctor, and she would fain have always had company in the
room to keep these two apart. Frequently, without reason, she called
Rosalie to her. When they were alone with her, her eyes never quitted
them, but pursued them into every corner of the bedroom. Whenever
their hands came together, her face grew ashy white. If a whispered
word was exchanged between them, she started up in anger, demand-
ing to know what had been said. It was a grievance to her that her
mother's gown should sweep against the doctor's foot. They could not
approach or look at one another without the child falling immediately
into violent trembling. The extreme sensitiveness of her innocent little
being induced in her an exasperation which would suddenly prompt
her to turn round, should she guess that they were smiling at one another behind her. She could divine the times when their love was at its
height by the atmosphere wafted around her. It was then that her gloom
became deeper, and her agonies were those of nervous women at the
approach of a terrible storm.

Every one about Helene now looked on Jeanne as saved, and she
herself had slowly come to recognize this as a certainty. Thus it happened that Jeanne's fits were at last regarded by her as the bad humors
of a spoilt child, and as of little or no consequence. A craving to live
sprang up within her after the six weeks of anguish which she had just
spent. Her daughter was now well able to dispense with her care for
hours; and for her, who had so long become unconscious of life, these
hours opened up a vista of delight, of peace, and pleasure. She rummaged in her drawers, and made joyous discoveries of forgotten things;
she plunged into all sorts of petty tasks, in the endeavor to resume the
happy course of her daily existence. And in this upwelling of life her
love expanded, and the society of Henri was the reward she allowed
herself for the intensity of her past sufferings. In the shelter of that
room they deemed themselves beyond the world's ken, and every hin-
drance in their path was forgotten. The child, to whom their love had
proved a terror, alone remained a bar between them.

Jeanne became, indeed, a veritable scourge to their affections. An
ever-present barrier, with her eyes constantly upon them, she compelled
them to maintain a continued restraint, an affectation of indifference,
with the result that their hearts were stirred with even greater motion
than before. For days they could not exchange a word; they knew intu-
itively that she was listening even when she was seemingly wrapped in

slumber. One evening, when Helene had quitted the room with Henri, to escort him to the front door, Jeanne burst out with the cry, "Mamma! mamma!" in a voice shrill with rage. Helene was forced to return, for she heard the child leap from her bed; and she met her running towards her, shivering with cold and passion. Jeanne would no longer let her remain away from her. From that day forward they could merely exchange a clasp of the hand on meeting and parting. Madame Deberle was now spending a month at the seaside, and the doctor, though he had all his time at his own command, dared not pass more than ten minutes in Helene's company. Their long chats at the window had come to an end.

What particularly tortured their hearts was the fickleness of Jeanne's humor. One night, as the doctor hung over her, she gave way to tears. For a whole day her hate changed to feverish tenderness, and Helene felt happy once more; but on the morrow, when the doctor entered the room, the child received him with such a display of sourness that the mother besought him with a look to leave them. Jeanne had fretted the whole night in angry regret over her own good-humor. Not a day passed but what a like scene was enacted. And after the blissful hours the child brought them in her moods of impassioned tenderness these hours of misery fell on them with the torture of the lash.

A feeling of revulsion at last awoke within Helene. To all seeming her daughter would be her death. Why, when her illness had been put to flight, did the ill-natured child work her utmost to torment her? If one of those intoxicating dreams took possession of her imagination— a mystic dream in which she found herself traversing a country alike unknown and entrancing with Henri by her side Jeanne's face, harsh and sullen, would suddenly start up before her and thus her heart was ever being rent in twain. The struggle between her maternal affection and her passion became fraught with the greatest suffering.

One evening, despite Helene's formal edict of banishment, the doctor called. For eight days they had been unable to exchange a word together. She would fain that he had not entered; but he did so on learning that Jeanne was in a deep sleep. They sat down as of old, near the window, far from the glare of the lamp, with the peaceful shadows around them. For two hours their conversation went on in such low whispers that scarcely a sound disturbed the silence of the large room. At times they turned their heads and glanced at the delicate profile of Jeanne, whose little hands, clasped together, were reposing on the coverlet. But in the end they grew forgetful of their surroundings, and their talk incautiously became louder. Then, all at once, Jeanne's voice rang out.

"Mamma! mamma!" she cried, seized with sudden agitation, as though suffering from nightmare.

She writhed about in her bed, her eyelids still heavy with sleep, and then struggled to reach a sitting posture.

"Hide, I beseech you!" whispered Helene to the doctor in a tone of anguish. "You will be her death if you stay here."

In an instant Henri vanished into the window-recess, concealed by the blue velvet curtain; but it was in vain, the child still kept up her pitiful cry: "Oh, mamma! mamma! I suffer so much."

"I am here beside you, my darling; where do you feel the pain?"

"I don't know. Oh, see, it is here! Oh, it is scorching me!" With eyes wide open and features distorted, she pressed her little hands to her bosom. "It came on me in a moment. I was asleep, wasn't I? But I felt something like a burning coal."

"But it's all gone now. You're not pained any longer, are you?"

"Yes, yes, I feel it still."

She glanced uneasily round the room. She was now wholly awake; the sullen gloom crept over her face once more, and her cheeks became livid.

"Are you by yourself, mamma?" she asked.

"Of course I am, my darling!"

Nevertheless Jeanne shook her head and gazed about, sniffing the air, while her agitation visibly increased. "No, you're not; I know you're not. There's someone—Oh, mamma! I'm afraid, I'm afraid! You are telling me a story; you are not by yourself."

She fell back in bed in an hysterical fit, sobbing loudly and huddling herself beneath the coverlet, as though to ward off some danger. Helene, crazy with alarm, dismissed Henri without delay, despite his wish to remain and look after the child. But she drove him out forcibly, and on her return clasped Jeanne in her arms, while the little one gave vent to the one pitiful cry, with every utterance of which her sobbing was renewed louder than ever: "You don't love me any more! You don't love me any more!"

"Hush, hush, my angel! don't say that," exclaimed the mother in agony. "You are all the world to me. You'll see yet whether I love you or not."

She nursed her until the morning broke, intent on yielding up to her all her heart's affections, though she was appalled at realizing how completely the love of herself possessed this darling child. Next day she deemed a consultation necessary. Doctor Bodin, dropping in as though by chance, subjected the patient with many jokes to a careful examination; and a lengthy discussion ensued between him and Doctor Deberle, who had remained in the adjacent room. Both readily agreed that there were no serious symptoms apparent at the moment, but they were afraid of complex developments, and cross-questioned Helene for some time. They realized that they were dealing with one of those nervous affections which have a family history, and set medical skill at defiance. She told them, what they already partly knew, that her grandmother was confined in the lunatic asylum of Les Tulettes at a short distance from Plassans, and that her mother had died from galloping consumption, after many years of brain affection and hysterical fits. She herself took more after her father; she had his features and the same gravity of temperament. Jeanne, on the other hand, was the facsimile of her grandmother; but she never would have her strength, commanding figure, or sturdy, bony frame. The two doctors enjoined on her once more that the greatest care was requisite. Too many precautions could not be taken in dealing with chloro-anaemical affections, which tend to develop a multitude of dangerous diseases.

Henri had listened to old Doctor Bodin with a deference which he had never before displayed for a colleague. He besought his advice on Jeanne's case with the air of a pupil who is full of doubt. Truth to tell, this child inspired him with dread; he felt that her case was beyond his science, and he feared lest she might die under his hands and her mother be lost to him for ever. A week passed away. He was no longer admitted by Helene into the little one's presence; and in the end, sad and sick at heart, he broke off his visits of his own accord.

As the month of August verged on its close, Jeanne recovered sufficient strength to rise and walk across the room. The lightness of her heart spoke in her laughter. A fortnight had elapsed since the recurrence of any nervous attack. The thought that her mother was again all her own and would ever cling to her had proved remedy enough. At first distrust had rankled in her mind; while letting Helene kiss her she had remained uneasy at her least movement, and had imperiously besought her hand before she fell asleep, anxious to retain it in her own during her slumber. But at last, with the knowledge that nobody came near, she had regained confidence, enraptured by the prospect of a re-opening of the old happy life when they had sat side by side, working at the window. Every day brought new roses to her cheeks; and Rosalie declared that she was blossoming brighter and brighter every hour.

There were times, however, as night fell, when Helene broke down. Since her daughter's illness her face had remained grave and somewhat pale, and a deep wrinkle, never before visible, furrowed her brow. When Jeanne caught sight of her in these hours of weariness, despair, and voidness, she herself would feel very wretched, her heart heavy with vague remorse. Gently and silently she would then twine her arms around her neck.

"Are you happy, mother darling?" came the whisper.

A thrill ran through Helene's frame, and she hastened to answer: "Yes, of course, my pet."

Still the child pressed her question:

"Are you, oh! are you happy? Quite sure?"

"Quite sure. Why should I feel unhappy?"

With this Jeanne would clasp her closer in her little arms, as though to requite her. She would love her so well, she would say—so well, in-deed, that nowhere in all Paris could a happier mother be found.

CHAPTER XIV.

During August Doctor Deberle's garden was like a well of foliage. The railings were hidden both by the twining branches of the lilac and laburnum trees and by the climbing plants, ivy, honeysuckle, and clematis, which sprouted everywhere in luxuriance, and glided and intermingled in inextricable confusion, drooping down in leafy canopies, and running along the walls till they reached the elms at the far end, where the verdure was so profuse that you might have thought a tent were stretched between the trees, the elms serving as its giant props. The garden was so small that the least shadow seemed to cover it. At noon the sun threw a disc of yellow light on the center, illumining the lawn and its two flower-beds. Against the garden steps was a huge rose-bush, laden with hundreds of large tea-roses. In the evening when the heat subsided their perfume became more penetrating, and the air under the elms grew heavy with their warm breath. Nothing could exceed the charm of this hidden, balmy nook, into which no neighborly inquisition could peep, and which brought one a dream of the forest primeval, albeit barrel-organs were playing polkas in the Rue Vineuse, near by.

"Why, madame, doesn't mademoiselle go down to the garden?" Rosalie daily asked. "I'm sure it would do her good to romp about under the trees."

One of the elms had invaded Rosalie's kitchen with its branches. She would pull some of the leaves off as she gazed with delight on the clustering foliage, through which she could see nothing.

"She isn't strong enough yet," was Helene's reply. "The cold, shady garden might be harmful to her."

Rosalie was in no wise convinced. A happy thought with her was not easily abandoned. Madame must surely be mistaken in imagining that it would be cold or harmful. Perhaps madame's objection sprang rather from the fear that she would be in somebody's way; but that was nonsense. Mademoiselle would of a truth be in nobody's way; not a living soul made any appearance there. The doctor shunned the spot, and as for madame, his wife, she would remain at the seaside till the middle of September. This was so certain that the doorkeeper had asked Zephyrin to give the garden a rake over, and Zephyrin and she herself had spent two Sunday afternoons there already. Oh! it was lovely, lovelier than one could imagine.

Helene, however, still declined to act on the suggestion. Jeanne seemed to have a great longing to enjoy a walk in the garden, which had been the ceaseless topic of her discourse during her illness; but a vague feeling of embarrassment made her eyes droop and closed her mouth on the subject in her mother's presence. At last when Sunday came round again the maid hurried into the room exclaiming breathlessly:

"Oh! madame, there's nobody there, I give you my word! Only myself and Zephyrin, who is raking! Do let her come. You can't imagine how fine it is outside. Come for a little, only a little while, just to see!"

Her conviction was such that Helene gave way. She cloaked Jeanne in a shawl, and told Rosalie to take a heavy wrap with her. The child was in an ecstasy, which spoke silently from the depths of her large sparkling eyes; she even wished to descend the staircase without help in order that her strength might be made plain. However, her mother's arms were stretched out behind her, ready to lend support. When they had reached the foot of the stairs and entered the garden, they both gave vent to an exclamation. So little did this umbrageous, thicket-girt spot resemble the trim nook they had seen in the springtime that they failed to recognize it.

"Ah! you wouldn't believe me!" declared Rosalie, in triumphant tones.

The clumps of shrubbery had grown to great proportions, making the paths much narrower, and, in walking, their skirts caught in some of the interwoven branches. To the fancy it seemed some far-away recess in a wood, arched over with foliage, from which fell a greeny light of delightful charm and mystery. Helene directed her steps towards the elm beneath which she had sat in April.

"But I don't wish her to stay here," said she. "It is shady and coldish."

"Well, well, you will see in a minute," answered the maid.

Three steps farther on they emerged from the seeming forest, and, in the midst of the leafy profusion they found the sun's golden rays streaming on the lawn, warm and still as in a woodland clearing. As they looked up they saw the branches standing out against the blue of the sky with the delicacy of guipure. The tea-roses on the huge bush, faint in the heat, dropped slumberously from their stems. The flower-beds were full of red and white asters, looking with their old-world air like blossoms woven in some ancient tapestry.

"Now you'll see," said Rosalie. "I'm going to put her all right myself."

She had folded and placed the wrap on the edge of a walk, where the shadow came to an end. Here she made Jeanne sit down, covering her shoulders with a shawl, and bidding her stretch out her little legs. In this fashion the shade fell on the child's head, while her feet lay in the sunshine.

"Are you all right, my darling?" Helene asked.

"Oh, yes," was her answer. "I don't feel cold a bit, you know. I almost think I am sweltering before a big fire. Ah! how well one can breathe! How pleasant it is!"

Thereupon Helene, whose eyes had turned uneasily towards the closed window-shutters of the house, expressed her intention of returning upstairs for a little while, and loaded Rosalie with a variety of injunctions. She would have to watch the sun; she was not to leave Jeanne there for more than half an hour; and she must not lose sight of her for a moment.

"Don't be alarmed, mamma," exclaimed the child, with a laugh. "There are no carriages to pass along here."

Left to amuse herself, she gathered a handful of gravel from the path at her side, and took pleasure in letting it fall from her clasped hands like a shower of rain. Zephyrin meantime was raking. On catching sight of madame and her daughter he had slipped on his great-coat, which he had previously hung from the branch of a tree; and in token of respect had stood stock-still, with his rake idle in his hand. Throughout Jeanne's illness he had come every Sunday as usual; but so great had been the caution with which he had slipped into the kitchen, that Helene would scarcely have dreamt of his presence had not Rosalie on each occasion been deputed as his messenger to inquire about the invalid's progress, and convey his condolences. Yes, so ran her comments, he was now laying claim to good manners; Paris was giving him some polish! And at present here he was, leaning on his rake, and mutely addressing Jeanne with a sympathetic nod. As soon as she saw him, her face broke into smiles.

"I have been very ill," she said.

"Yes, I know, mademoiselle," he replied as he placed his hand on his heart. And inspired with the wish to say something pretty or comical, which might serve to enliven the meeting, he added: "You see, your health has been taking a rest. Now it will indulge in a snore."

Jeanne had again gathered up a handful of gravel, while he, perfectly satisfied, and opening his mouth wide from ear to ear in a burst of silent laughter, renewed his raking with all the strength of his arms. As the rake travelled over the gravel a regular, strident sound arose. When a few minutes had elapsed Rosalie, seeing her little charge absorbed in her amusement, seemingly happy and at ease, drew gradually farther away from her, as though lured by the grating of this rake. Zephyrin was now working away in the full glare of the sun, on the other side of the lawn.

"You are sweating like an ox," she whispered to him. "Take off your great-coat. Be quick; mademoiselle won't be offended."

He relieved himself of the garment, and once more suspended it from a branch. His red trousers, supported by a belt round the waist, reached almost to his chest, while his shirt of stout, unbleached linen, held at the neck by a narrow horsehair band, was so stiff that it stuck out and made him look even rounder than he was. He tucked up his sleeves with a certain amount of affectation, as though to show Rosalie a couple of flaming hearts, which, with the inscription "For Ever," had been tattooed on them at the barracks.

"Did you go to mass this morning?" asked Rosalie, who usually tackled him with this question every Sunday.

"To mass! to mass!" he repeated, with a chuckle.

His red ears seemed to stand out from his head, shorn to the very skin, and the whole of his diminutive barrel-like body expressed a spirit of banter.

At last the confession came. "Of course I went to mass."

"You are lying," Rosalie burst out violently. "I know you are lying; your nose is twitching. Oh, Zephyrin, you are going to the dogs—you have left off going to church! Beware!"

His answer, lover-like, was an attempt to put his arm round her waist, but to all appearance she was shocked, for she exclaimed:

"I'll make you put on your coat again if you don't behave yourself. Aren't you ashamed? Why, there's mademoiselle looking at you!"

Thereupon Zephyrin turned to his raking once more. In truth, Jeanne had raised her eyes towards them. Her amusement was palling on her somewhat; the gravel thrown aside, she had been gathering leaves and plucking grass; but a feeling of indolence crept over her, and now she preferred to do nothing but gaze at the sunshine as it fell on her more and more. A few moments previously only her legs, as far as the knees, had been bathed in this warm cascade of sunshine, but now it reached her waist, the heat increasing like an entrancing caress. What particularly amused her were the round patches of light, of a beautiful golden yellow, which danced over her shawl, for all the world like living creatures. She tossed back her head to see if they were perchance creeping towards her face, and meanwhile clasped her little hands together in the glare of the sunshine. How thin and transparent her hands seemed! The sun's rays passed through them, but all the same they appeared to her very pretty, pinky like shells, delicate and attenuated like the tiny hands of an infant Christ. Then too the fresh air, the gigantic trees around her, and the warmth, had lulled her somewhat into a trance. Sleep, she imagined, had come upon her, and yet she could still see and hear. It all seemed to her very nice and pleasant.

"Mademoiselle, please draw back a bit," said Rosalie, who had approached her. "The sun's heat is too warm for you."

But with a wave of her hand Jeanne declined to stir. For the time her attention was riveted on the maid and the little soldier. She pretended to direct her glances towards the ground, with the intention of making them believe that she did not see them; but in reality, despite her apparent drowsiness, she kept watching them from beneath her long eyelashes.

Rosalie stood near her for a minute or two longer, but was powerless against the charms of the grating rake. Once more she slowly dragged herself towards Zephyrin, as if in spite of her will. She resented the change in manner which he was now displaying, and yet her heart was bursting with mute admiration. The little soldier had used to good purpose his long strolls with his comrades in the Jardin des Plantes and round the Place du Chateau-d'Eau, where his barracks stood, and the result was the acquisition of the swaying, expansive graces of the Parisian fire-eater. He had learnt the flowery talk, gallant readiness, and involved style of language so dear to the hearts of the ladies. At times she was thrilled with intense pleasure as she listened to the phrases which he repeated to her with a swagger of the shoulders, phrases full of incomprehensible words that inflamed her cheeks with a flush of pride. His uniform no longer sat awkwardly on him; he swung his arms to and fro with a knowing air, and had an especially noticeable style of wearing his shako on the back of his head, with the result that his round face with its tip of a nose became extremely prominent, while his headgear swayed gently with the rolling of his body. Besides, he was growing quite free and easy, quaffed his dram, and ogled the fair sex. With his sneering ways and affectation of reticence, he now doubtless knew a great deal more than she did. Paris was fast taking all the remaining rust off him; and Rosalie stood before him, delighted yet angry, undecided whether to scratch his face or let him give utterance to foolish prattle.

Zephyrin, meanwhile, raking away, had turned the corner of the path. He was now hidden by a big spindle-tree, and was darting side-glances at Rosalie, luring her on against her will with the strokes of his rake. When she had got near him, he pinched her roughly.

"Don't cry out; that's only to show you how I love you!" he said in a husky whisper. "And take that over and above."

So saying he kissed her where he could, his lips lighting somewhere on her ear. Then, as Rosalie gave him a fierce nip in reply, he retaliated by another kiss, this time on her nose. Though she was well pleased, her face turned fiery-red; she was furious that Jeanne's presence should prevent her from giving him a box on the ear.

"I have pricked my finger," she declared to Jeanne as she returned to her, by way of explaining the exclamation that escaped her lips.

However, betwixt the spare branches of the spindle-tree the child had seen the incident. Amid the surrounding greenery the soldier's red trousers and greyish shirt were clearly discernible. She slowly raised her eyes to Rosalie, and looked at her for a moment, while the maid blushed the more. Then Jeanne's gaze fell to the ground again, and she gathered another handful of pebbles, but lacked the will or strength to play with them, and remained in a dreamy state, with her hands resting on the warm ground, amidst the vibrations of the sunrays. Within her a wave of health was swelling and stifling her. The trees seemed to take Titanic shape, and the air was redolent of the perfume of roses. In wonder and delight, she dreamt of all sorts of vague things.

"What are you thinking of, mademoiselle?" asked Rosalie uneasily.

"I don't know—of nothing," was Jeanne's reply. "Yes, I do know. You see, I should like to live to be very old."

However, she could not explain these words. It was an idea, she said, that had come into her head. But in the evening, after dinner, as her dreamy fit fell on her again, and her mother inquired the cause, she suddenly put the question:

"Mamma, do cousins ever marry?"

"Yes, of course," said Helene. "Why do you ask me that?"

"Oh, nothing; only I wanted to know."

Helene had become accustomed to these extraordinary questions. The hour spent in the garden had so beneficial an effect on the child that every sunny day found her there. Helene's reluctance was gradually dispelled; the house was still shut up. Henri never ventured to show himself, and ere long she sat down on the edge of the rug beside Jeanne. However, on the following Sunday morning she found the windows thrown open, and felt troubled at heart.

"Oh! but of course the rooms must be aired," exclaimed Rosalie, as an inducement for them to go down. "I declare to you nobody's there!"

That day the weather was still warmer. Through the leafy screen the sun's rays darted like golden arrows. Jeanne, who was growing strong, strolled about for ten minutes, leaning on her mother's arm. Then, somewhat tired, she turned towards her rug, a corner of which she assigned to Helene. They smiled at one another, amused at thus finding themselves side by side on the ground. Zephyrin had given up his raking, and was helping Rosalie to gather some parsley, clumps of which were growing along the end wall.

All at once there was an uproar in the house, and Helene was thinking of flight, when Madame Deberle made her appearance on the garden-steps. She had just arrived, and was still in her travelling dress, speaking very loudly, and seemingly very busy. But immediately she caught sight of Madame Grandjean and her daughter, sitting on the ground in the front of the lawn, she ran down, overwhelmed them with embraces, and poured a deafening flood of words into their ears.

"What, is it you? How glad I am to see you! Kiss me, my little

Jeanne! Poor puss, you've been very ill, have you not? But you're getting better; the roses are coming back to your cheeks! And you, my dear, how often I've thought of you! I wrote to you: did my letters reach you? You must have spent a terrible time: but it's all over now! Will you let me kiss you?"

Helene was now on her feet, and was forced to submit to a kiss on each cheek and return them. This display of affection, however, chilled her to the heart.

"You'll excuse us for having invaded your garden," she said.

"You're joking," retorted Juliette impetuously. "Are you not at home here?"

But she ran off for a moment, hastened up the stairs, and called across the open rooms: "Pierre, don't forget anything; there are seventeen packages!"

Then, at once coming back, she commenced chattering about her holiday adventures. "Oh! such a splendid season! We went to Trouville, you know. The beach was always thronged with people. It was quite a crush. and people of the highest spheres, you know. I had visitors too. Papa came for a fortnight with Pauline. All the same, I'm glad to get home again. But I haven't given you all my news. Oh! I'll tell you later on!"

She stooped down and kissed Jeanne again; then suddenly becoming serious, she asked:

"Am I browned by the sun?"

"No; I don't see any signs of it," replied Helene as she gazed at her.

Juliette's eyes were clear and expressionless, her hands were plump, her pretty face was full of amiability; age did not tell on her; the sea air itself was powerless to affect her expression of serene indifference. So far as appearances went, she might have just returned from a shopping expedition in Paris. However, she was bubbling over with affection, and the more loving her outbursts, the more weary, constrained, and ill became Helene. Jeanne meantime never stirred from the rug, but merely raised her delicate, sickly face, while clasping her hands with a chilly air in the sunshine.

"Wait, you haven't seen Lucien yet," exclaimed Juliette. "You must see him; he has got so fat."

When the lad was brought on the scene, after the dust of the journey had been washed from his face by a servant girl, she pushed and

turned him about to exhibit him. Fat and chubby-cheeked, his skin
tanned by playing on the beach in the salt breeze, Lucien displayed ex-
uberant health, but he had a somewhat sulky look because he had just
been washed. He had not been properly dried, and one check was still
wet and fiery-red with the rubbing of the towel. When he caught sight
of Jeanne he stood stock-still with astonishment. She looked at him
out of her poor, sickly face, as colorless as linen against the background
of her streaming black hair, whose tresses fell in clusters to her shoulders. Her beautiful, sad, dilated eyes seemed to fill up her whole countenance; and, despite the excessive heat, she shivered somewhat, and
stretched out her hands as though chilled and seeking warmth from a
blazing fire.

"Well! aren't you going to kiss her?" asked Juliette.

But Lucien looked rather afraid. At length he made up his mind,
and very cautiously protruded his lips so that he might not come too
near the invalid. This done, he started back expeditiously. Helene's eyes
were brimming over with tears. What health that child enjoyed! whereas
her Jeanne was breathless after a walk round the lawn! Some mothers
were very fortunate! Juliette all at once understood how cruel Lucien's
conduct was, and she rated him soundly.

"Good gracious! what a fool you are! Is that the way to kiss young
ladies? You've no idea, my dear, what a nuisance he was at Trouville."

She was getting somewhat mixed. But fortunately for her the doctor now made his appearance, and she extricated herself from her difficulty by exclaiming: "Oh, here's Henri."

He had not been expecting their return until the evening, but she
had travelled by an earlier train. She plunged into a discursive explanation, without in the least making her reasons clear. The doctor listened
with a smiling face. "At all events, here you are," he said. "That's all
that's necessary."

A minute previously he had bowed to Helene without speaking. His
glance for a moment fell on Jeanne, but feeling embarrassed he turned
away his head. Jeanne bore his look with a serious face, and unclasping
her hands instinctively grasped her mother's gown and drew closer to
her side.

"Ah! the rascal," said the doctor, as he raised Lucien and kissed him
on each cheek. "Why, he's growing like magic."

"Yes; and am I to be forgotten?" asked Juliette, as she held up her head. Then, without putting Lucien down, holding him, indeed, on one arm, the doctor leaned over to kiss his wife. Their three faces were lit up with smiles.

Helene grew pale, and declared she must now go up. Jeanne, however, was unwilling; she wished to see what might happen, and her glances lingered for a while on the Deberles and then travelled back to her mother. When Juliette had bent her face upwards to receive her husband's kiss, a bright gleam had come into the child's eyes.

"He's too heavy," resumed the doctor as he set Lucien down again. "Well, was the season a good one? I saw Malignon yesterday, and he was telling me about his stay there. So you let him leave before you, eh?"

"Oh! he's quite a nuisance!" exclaimed Juliette, over whose face a serious, embarrassed expression had now crept. "He tormented us to death the whole time."

"Your father was hoping for Pauline's sake—He hasn't declared his intentions then?"

"What! Malignon!" said she, as though astonished and offended. And then with a gesture of annoyance she added, "Oh! leave him alone; he's cracked! How happy I am to be home again!"

Without any apparent transition, she thereupon broke into an amazing outburst of tenderness, characteristic of her bird-like nature. She threw herself on her husband's breast and raised her face towards him. To all seeming they had forgotten that they were not alone.

Jeanne's eyes, however, never quitted them. Her lips were livid and trembled with anger; her face was that of a jealous and revengeful woman. The pain she suffered was so great that she was forced to turn away her head, and in doing so she caught sight of Rosalie and Zephyrin at the bottom of the garden, still gathering parsley. Doubtless with the intent of being in no one's way, they had crept in among the thickest of the bushes, where both were squatting on the ground. Zephyrin, with a sly movement, had caught hold of one of Rosalie's feet, while she, without uttering a syllable, was heartily slapping him. Between two branches Jeanne could see the little soldier's face, chubby and round as a moon and deeply flushed, while his mouth gaped with an amorous grin. Meantime the sun's rays were beating down vertically, and the trees were peacefully sleeping, not a leaf stirring among them all. From beneath the elms came the heavy odor of soil untouched by the spade.

And elsewhere floated the perfume of the last tea-roses, which were casting their petals one by one on the garden steps. Then Jeanne, with swelling heart, turned her gaze on her mother, and seeing her motionless and dumb in presence of the Deberles, gave her a look of intense anguish—a child's look of infinite meaning, such as you dare not question.

But Madame Deberle stepped closer to them, and said: "I hope we shall see each other frequently now. As Jeanne is feeling better, she must come down every afternoon."

Helene was already casting about for an excuse, pleading that she did not wish to weary her too much. But Jeanne abruptly broke in: "No, no; the sun does me a great deal of good. We will come down, madame. You will keep my place for me, won't you?"

And as the doctor still remained in the background, she smiled towards him.

"Doctor, please tell mamma that the fresh air won't do me any harm."

He came forward, and this man, inured to human suffering, felt on his cheeks a slight flush at being thus gently addressed by the child.

"Certainly not," he exclaimed; "the fresh air will only bring you nearer to good health."

"So you see, mother darling, we must come down," said Jeanne, with a look of ineffable tenderness, whilst a sob died away in her throat.

But Pierre had reappeared on the steps and announced the safe arrival of madame's seventeen packages. Then, followed by her husband and Lucien, Juliette retired, declaring that she was frightfully dirty, and intended to take a bath. When they were alone, Helene knelt down on the rug, as though about to tie the shawl round Jeanne's neck, and whispered in the child's ear:

"You're not angry any longer with the doctor, then?"

With a prolonged shake of the head the child replied "No, mamma."

There was a silence. Helene's hands were seized with an awkward trembling, and she was seemingly unable to tie the shawl. Then Jeanne murmured: "But why does he love other people so? I won't have him love them like that."

And as she spoke, her black eyes became harsh and gloomy, while her little hands fondled her mother's shoulders. Helene would have replied, but the words springing to her lips frightened her. The sun was now low, and mother and daughter took their departure. Zephyrin meanwhile had reappeared to view, with a bunch of parsley in his hand, the stalks of which he continued pulling off while darting murderous glances at Rosalie. The maid followed at some distance, inspired with distrust now that there was no one present. Just as she stooped to roll up the rug he tried to pinch her, but she retaliated with a blow from her fist which made his back re-echo like an empty cask. Still it seemed to delight him, and he was yet laughing silently when he re-entered the kitchen busily arranging his parsley.

Thenceforth Jeanne was stubbornly bent on going down to the garden as soon as ever she heard Madame Deberle's voice there. All Rosalie's tittle-tattle regarding the next-door house she drank in greedily, ever restless and inquisitive concerning its inmates and their doings; and she would even slip out of the bedroom to keep watch from the kitchen window. In the garden, ensconced in a small arm-chair which was brought for her use from the drawing-room by Juliette's direction, her eyes never quitted the family. Lucien she now treated with great reserve, annoyed it seemed by his questions and antics, especially when the doctor was present. On those occasions she would stretch herself out as if wearied, gazing before her with her eyes wide open. For Helene the afternoons were pregnant with anguish. She always returned, however, returned in spite of the feeling of revolt which wrung her whole being. Every day when, on his arrival home, Henri printed a kiss on Juliette's hair, her heart leaped in its agony. And at those moments, if to hide the agitation of her face she pretended to busy herself with Jeanne, she would notice that the child was even paler than herself, with her black eyes glaring and her chin twitching with repressed fury. Jeanne shared in her suffering. When the mother turned away her head, heartbroken, the child became so sad and so exhausted that she had to be carried upstairs and put to bed. She could no longer see the doctor approach his wife without changing countenance; she would tremble, and turn on him a glance full of all the jealous fire of a deserted mistress.

"I cough in the morning," she said to him one day. "You must come and see for yourself."

Rainy weather ensued, and Jeanne became quite anxious that the doctor should commence his visits once more. Yet her health had much improved. To humor her, Helene had been constrained to accept two or three invitations to dine with the Deberles.

At last the child's heart, so long torn by hidden sorrow, seemingly regained quietude with the complete re-establishment of her health. She would again ask Helene the old question—"Are you happy, mother darling?"

"Yes, very happy, my pet," was the reply.

And this made her radiant. She must be pardoned her bad temper in the past, she said. She referred to it as a fit which no effort of her own will could prevent, the result of a headache that came on her suddenly. Something would spring up within her—she wholly failed to understand what it was. She was tempest-tossed by a multitude of vague imaginings—nightmares that she could not even have recalled to memory. However, it was past now; she was well again, and those worries would nevermore return.

CHAPTER XV.

The night was falling. From the grey heaven, where the first of the stars were gleaming, a fine ashy dust seemed to be raining down on the great city, raining down without cessation and slowly burying it. The hollows were already hidden deep in gloom, and a line of cloud, like a stream of ink, rose upon the horizon, engulfing the last streaks of daylight, the wavering gleams which were retreating towards the west. Below Passy but a few stretches of roofs remained visible; and as the wave rolled on, darkness soon covered all.

"What a warm evening!" ejaculated Helene, as she sat at the window, overcome by the heated breeze which was wafted upwards from Paris.

"A grateful night for the poor," exclaimed the Abbe, who stood behind her. "The autumn will be mild."

That Tuesday Jeanne had fallen into a doze at dessert, and her mother, perceiving that she was rather tired, had put her to bed. She was already fast asleep in her cot, while Monsieur Rambaud sat at the table gravely mending a toy—a mechanical doll, a present from himself, which both spoke and walked, and which Jeanne had broken. He excelled in such work as this. Helene on her side feeling the want of fresh air—for the lingering heats of September were oppressive—had thrown the window wide open, and gazed with relief on the vast gloomy ocean of darkness that rolled before her. She had pushed an easy-chair to the window in order to be alone, but was suddenly surprised to hear the Abbe speaking to her. "Is the little one warmly covered?" he gently asked. "On these heights the air is always keen."

She made no reply, however; her heart was craving for silence. She was tasting the delights of the twilight hour, the vanishing of all surrounding objects, the hushing of every sound. Gleams, like those of

night-lights, tipped the steeples and towers; that on Saint-Augustin died
out first, the Pantheon for a moment retained a bluish light, and then
the glittering dome of the Invalides faded away, similar to a moon setting in a rising sea of clouds. The night was like the ocean, its extent
seemingly increased by the gloom, a dark abyss wherein you divined
that a world lay hid. From the unseen city blew a mighty yet gentle wind.
There was still a hum; sounds ascended faint yet clear to Helene's ears—
the sharp rattle of an omnibus rolling along the quay, the whistle of a
train crossing the bridge of the Point-du-Jour; and the Seine, swollen
by the recent storms, and pulsing with the life of a breathing soul,
wound with increased breadth through the shadows far below. A warm
odor steamed upwards from the scorched roofs, while the river, amidst
this exhalation of the daytime heat, seemed to give forth a cooling
breeze. Paris had vanished, sunk in the dreamy repose of a colossus
whose limbs the night has enveloped, and who lies motionless for a
time, but with eyes wide open.

Nothing affected Helene more than this momentary pause in the
great city's life. For the three months during which she had been a close
prisoner, riveted to Jeanne's bedside, she had had no other companion
in her vigil than the huge mass of Paris spreading out towards the horizon. During the summer heats of July and August the windows had almost always been left open; she could not cross the room, could not stir
or turn her head, without catching a glimpse of the ever-present
panorama. It was there, whatever the weather, always sharing in her
griefs and hopes, like some friend who would never leave her side. She
was still quite ignorant respecting it; never had it seemed farther away,
never had she given less thought to its streets and its citizens, and yet
it peopled her solitude. The sick-room, whose door was kept shut to the
outside world, looked out through its two windows upon this city.
Often, with her eyes fixed on its expanse, Helene had wept, leaning on
the window-rail in order to hide her tears from her ailing child. One
day, too—the very day when she had imagined her daughter to be at the
point of death—she had remained for a long time, overcome and
choked with grief, watching the smoke which curled up from the Army
Bakehouse. Frequently, moreover, in hours of hopefulness she had here
confided the gladsome feelings of her heart to the dim and distant suburbs. There was not a single monument which did not recall to her
some sensation of joy or sorrow. Paris shared in her own existence; and

never did she love it better than when the twilight came, and its day's work over, it surrendered itself to an hour's quietude, forgetfulness, and reverie, whilst waiting for the lighting of its gas.

"What a multitude of stars!" murmured Abbe Jouve. "There are thousands of them gleaming."

He had just taken a chair and sat down at her side. On hearing him, she gazed upwards into the summer night. The heaven was studded with golden lights. On the very verge of the horizon a constellation was sparkling like a carbuncle, while a dust of almost invisible stars sprinkled the vault above as though with glittering sand. Charles's-Wain was slowly turning its shaft in the night.

"Look!" said Helene in her turn, "look at that tiny bluish star! See —far away up there. I recognize it night after night. But it dies and fades as the night rolls on."

The Abbe's presence no longer annoyed her. With him by her side, she imagined the quiet was deepening around. A few words passed between them after long intervals of silence. Twice she questioned him on the names of the stars—the sight of the heavens had always interested her —but he was doubtful and pleaded ignorance.

"Do you see," she asked, "that lovely star yonder whose lustre is so exquisitely clear?"

"On the left, eh?" he replied, "near another smaller, greenish one? Ah! there are so many of them that my memory fails me."

They again lapsed into silence, their eyes still turned upwards, dazzled, quivering slightly at the sight of that stupendous swarming of luminaries. In the vast depths of the heavens, behind thousands of stars, thousands of others twinkled in ever-increasing multitudes, with the clear brilliancy of gems. The Milky Way was already whitening, displaying its solar specks, so innumerable and so distant that in the vault of the firmament they form but a trailing scarf of light.

"It fills me with fear," said Helene in a whisper; and that she might see it all no more she bent her head and glanced down on the gaping abyss in which Paris seemed to be engulfed. In its depths not a light could yet be seen; night had rolled over it and plunged it into impenetrable darkness. Its mighty, continuous rumble seemed to have sunk into a softer key.

"Are you weeping?" asked the Abbe, who had heard a sound of sobbing.

"Yes," simply answered Helene.

They could not see each other. For a long time she continued weeping, her whole being exhaling a plaintive murmur. Behind them, meantime, Jeanne lay at rest in innocent sleep, and Monsieur Rambaud, his whole attention engrossed, bent his grizzled head over the doll which he had dismembered. At times he could not prevent the loosened springs from giving out a creaking noise, a childlike squeaking which his big fingers, though plied with the utmost gentleness, drew from the disordered mechanism. If the doll vented too loud a sound, however, he at once stopped working, distressed and vexed with himself, and turning towards Jeanne to see if he had roused her. Then once more he would resume his repairing, with great precautions, his only tools being a pair of scissors and a bodkin.

"Why do you weep, my daughter?" again asked the Abbe. "Can I not afford you some relief?"

"Ah! let me be," said Helene; "these tears do me good. By-and-by, by-and-by—"

A stifling sensation checked any further words. Once before, in this very place, she had been convulsed by a storm of tears; but then she had been alone, free to sob in the darkness till the emotion that wrung her was dried up at its source. However, she knew of no cause of sorrow; her daughter was well once more, and she had resumed the old monotonous delightful life. But it was as though a keen sense of awful grief had abruptly come upon her; it seemed as if she were rolling into a bottomless abyss which she could not fathom, sinking with all who were dear to her in a limitless sea of despair. She knew not what misfortune hung over her head; but she was without hope, and could only weep.

Similar waves of feeling had swept over her during the month of the Virgin in the church laden with the perfume of flowers. And, as twilight fell, the vastness of Paris filled her with a deep religious impression. The stretch of plain seemed to expand, and a sadness rose up from the two millions of living beings who were being engulfed in darkness. And when it was night, and the city with its subdued rumbling had vanished from view, her oppressed heart poured forth its sorrow, and her tears overflowed, in presence of that sovereign peace. She could have clasped her hands and prayed. She was filled with an intense craving for faith, love, and a lapse into heavenly forgetfulness; and the first glinting of the stars overwhelmed her with sacred terror and enjoyment.

A lengthy interval of silence ensued, and then the Abbe spoke once more, this time more pressingly.

"My daughter, you must confide in me. Why do you hesitate?"

She was still weeping, but more gently, like a wearied and powerless child.

"The Church frightens you," he continued. "For a time I thought you had yielded your heart to God. But it has been willed otherwise. Heaven has its own purposes. Well, since you mistrust the priest, why should you refuse to confide in the friend?"

"You are right," she faltered. "Yes, I am sad at heart, and need your consolation. I must tell you of it all. When I was a child I seldom, if ever, entered a church; now I cannot be present at a service without feeling touched to the very depths of my being. Yes; and what drew tears from me just now was that voice of Paris, sounding like a mighty organ, that immeasurable night, and those beauteous heavens. Oh! I would fain believe. Help me; teach me."

Abbe Jouve calmed her somewhat by lightly placing his hand on her own.

"Tell me everything," he merely said.

She struggled for a time, her heart wrung with anguish.

"There's nothing to tell, I assure you. I'm hiding nothing from you. I weep without cause, because I feel stifled, because my tears gush out of their own accord. You know what my life has been. No sorrow, no sin, no remorse could I find in it to this hour. I do not know—I do not know—"

Her voice died away, and from the priest's lips slowly came the words, "You love, my daughter!"

She started; she dared not protest. Silence fell on them once more. In the sea of shadows that slumbered before them a light had glimmered forth. It seemed at their feet, somewhere in the abyss, but at what precise spot they would have been unable to specify. And then, one by one, other lights broke through the darkness, shooting into instant life, and remaining stationary, scintillating like stars. It seemed as though thousands of fresh planets were rising on the surface of a gloomy lake. Soon they stretched out in double file, starting from the Trocadero, and nimbly leaping towards Paris. Then these files were intersected by others, curves were described, and a huge, strange, mag-

nificent constellation spread out. Helene never breathed a word, but
gazed on these gleams of light, which made the heavens seemingly descend below the line of the horizon, as though indeed the earth had
vanished and the vault of heaven were on every side. And Helene's
heart was again flooded with emotion, as a few minutes before when
Charles's-Wain had slowly begun to revolve round the Polar axis, its
shaft in the air. Paris, studded with lights, stretched out, deep and sad,
prompting fearful thoughts of a firmament swarming with unknown
worlds.

Meanwhile the priest, in the monotonous, gentle voice which he
had acquired by years of duty in the confessional, continued whispering in her ear. One evening in the past he had warned her; solitude, he
had said, would be harmful to her welfare. No one could with impunity
live outside the pale of life. She had imprisoned herself too closely, and
the door had opened to perilous thoughts.

"I am very old now, my daughter," he murmured, "and I have frequently seen women come to us weeping and praying, with a craving to
find faith and religion. Thus it is that I cannot be deceiving myself to-
day. These women, who seem to seek God in so zealous a manner, are
but souls rendered miserable by passion. It is a man whom they worship in our churches."

She was not listening; a strife was raging in her bosom, amidst her
efforts to read her innermost thoughts aright. And at last confession
came from her in a broken whisper:

"Oh! yes, I love, and that is all! Beyond that I know nothing —
nothing!"

He now forbore to interrupt her; she spoke in short feverish sentences, taking a mournful pleasure in thus confessing her love, in
sharing with that venerable priest the secret which had so long burdened her.

"I swear I cannot read my thoughts. This has come to me without
my knowing its presence. Perhaps it came in a moment. Only in time
did I realize its sweetness. Besides, why should I deem myself stronger
than I am? I have made no effort to flee from it; I was only too happy,
and to-day I have yet less power of resistance. My daughter was ill; I almost lost her. Well! my love has been as intense as my sorrow; it came
back with sovereign power after those days of terror—and it possesses
me, I feel transported—"

She shivered and drew a breath.

"In short, my strength fails me. You were right, my friend, in thinking it would be a relief to confide in you. But, I beseech you, tell me what is happening in the depths of my heart. My life was once so peaceful; I was so happy. A thunderbolt has fallen on me. Why on me? Why not on another? I had done nothing to bring it on; I imagined myself well protected. Ah, if you only knew—I know myself no longer! Help me, save me!"

Then as she became silent, the priest, with the wonted freedom of the confessor, mechanically asked the question:

"The name? tell me his name?"

She was hesitating, when a peculiar noise prompted her to turn her head. It came from the doll which, in Monsieur Rambaud's hands, was by degrees renewing its mechanical life, and had just taken three steps on the table, with a creaking of wheels and springs which showed that there was still something faulty in its works. Then it had fallen on its back, and but for the worthy man would have rebounded onto the ground. He followed all its movements with outstretched hands, ready to support it, and full of paternal anxiety. The moment he perceived Helene turn, he smiled confidently towards her, as if to give her an assurance that the doll would recover its walking powers. And then he once more dived with scissors and bodkin into the toy. Jeanne still slept on.

Thereupon Helene, her nerves relaxing under the influence of the universal quiet, whispered a name in the priest's ear. He never stirred; in the darkness his face could not be seen. A silence ensued, and he responded:

"I knew it, but I wanted to hear it from your own lips. My daughter, yours must be terrible suffering."

He gave utterance to no truisms on the subject of duty. Helene, overcome, saddened to the heart by this unemotional pity, gazed once more on the lights which spangled the gloomy veil enshrouding Paris. They were flashing everywhere in myriads, like the sparks that dart over the blackened refuse of burnt paper. At first these twinkling dots had started from the Trocadero towards the heart of the city. Soon another coruscation had appeared on the left in the direction of Montmartre; then another had burst into view on the right behind the Invalides, and still another, more distant near the Pantheon. From all these centers flights of flames were simultaneously descending.

"You remember our conversation," slowly resumed the Abbe. "My opinion has not changed. My daughter, you must marry."

"I!" she exclaimed, overwhelmed with amazement. "But I have just confessed to you—Oh, you know well I cannot—"

"You must marry," he repeated with greater decision. "You will wed an honest man."

Within the folds of his old cassock he seemed to have grown more commanding. His large comical-looking head, which, with eyes half-closed, was usually inclined towards one shoulder, was now raised erect, and his eyes beamed with such intensity that she saw them sparkling in the darkness.

"You will marry an honest man, who will be a father to Jeanne, and will lead you back to the path of goodness."

"But I do not love him. Gracious Heaven! I do not love him!"

"You will love him, my daughter. He loves you, and he is good in heart."

Helene struggled, and her voice sank to a whisper as she heard the slight noise that Monsieur Rambaud made behind them. He was so patient and so strong in his hope, that for six months he had not once intruded his love on her. Disposed by nature to the most heroic self-sacrifice, he waited in serene confidence. The Abbe stirred, as though about to turn round.

"Would you like me to tell him everything? He would stretch out his hand and save you. And you would fill him with joy beyond compare."

She checked him, utterly distracted. Her heart revolted. Both of these peaceful, affectionate men, whose judgment retained perfect equilibrium in presence of her feverish passion, were sources of terror to her. What world could they abide in to be able to set at naught that which caused her so much agony? The priest, however, waved his hand with an all-comprehensive gesture.

"My daughter," said he, "look on this lovely night, so supremely still in presence of your troubled spirit. Why do you refuse happiness?"

All Paris was now illumined. The tiny dancing flames had speckled the sea of shadows from one end of the horizon to the other, and now, as in a summer night, millions of fixed stars seemed to be serenely gleaming there. Not a puff of air, not a quiver of the atmosphere stirred these lights, to all appearance suspended in space. Paris, now invisible, had fallen into the depths of an abyss as vast as a firmament. At times, at the base of the Trocadero, a light—the lamp of a passing cab or omnibus—would dart across the gloom, sparkling like a shooting star; and here amidst the radiance of the gas-jets, from which streamed a yellow haze, a confused jumble of house-fronts and clustering trees—green like the trees in stage scenery—could be vaguely discerned. To and fro, across the Pont des Invalides, gleaming lights flashed without ceasing; far below, across a band of denser gloom, appeared a marvelous train of comet-like coruscations, from whose lustrous tails fell a rain of gold. These were the reflections in the Seine's black waters of the lamps on the bridge. From this point, however, the unknown began. The long curve of the river was merely described by a double line of lights, which ever and anon were coupled to other transverse lines, so that the whole looked like some glittering ladder, thrown across Paris, with its ends on the verge of the heavens among the stars.

To the left there was another trench excavated athwart the gloom; an unbroken chain of stars shone forth down the Champs-Elysees from the Arc-de-Triomphe to the Place de la Concorde, where a new cluster of Pleiades was flashing; next came the gloomy stretches of the Tuileries and the Louvre, the blocks of houses on the brink of the water, and the Hotel-de-Ville away at the extreme end—all these masses of darkness being parted here and there by bursts of light from some large square or other; and farther and farther away, amidst the endless confusion of roofs, appeared scattered gleams, affording faint glimpses of the hollow of a street below, the corner of some boulevard, or the brilliantly illuminated meeting-place of several thoroughfares. On the opposite bank, on the right, the Esplanade alone could be discerned with any distinctness, its rectangle marked out in flame, like an Orion of a winter's night bereft of his baldrick. The long streets of the Saint-Germain district seemed gloomy with their fringe of infrequent lamps; but the thickly populated quarters beyond were speckled with a multitude of tiny flames, clustering like nebulae. Away towards the outskirts, girdling the whole of the horizon, swarmed street-lamps and lighted windows, filling these distant parts with a dust, as it were, of those myriads of suns, those planetary atoms which the naked eye cannot discover. The public edifices had vanished into the depths of the darkness; not a lamp marked out their spires and towers. At times you might have imagined you were gazing on some gigantic festival, some illuminated cyclopean monument, with staircases, balusters, windows, pediments, and terraces —a veritable cosmos of stone, whose wondrous architecture was outlined by the gleaming lights of a myriad lamps. But there was always a speedy return of the feeling that new constellations were springing into being, and that the heavens were spreading both above and below.

Helene, in compliance with the all-embracing sweep of the priest's hand, cast a lingering look over illumined Paris. Here too she knew not the names of those seeming stars. She would have liked to ask what the blaze far below on the left betokened, for she saw it night after night. There were others also which roused her curiosity, and some of them she loved, whilst some inspired her with uneasiness or vexation.

"Father," said she, for the first time employing that appellation of affection and respect, "let me live as I am. The loveliness of the night has agitated me. You are wrong; you would not know how to console me, for you cannot understand my feelings."

The priest stretched out his arms, then slowly dropped them to his side resignedly. And after a pause he said in a whisper:

"Doubtless that was bound to be the case. You call for succor and reject salvation. How many despairing confessions I have received! What tears I have been unable to prevent! Listen, my daughter, promise me one thing only; if ever life should become too heavy a burden for you, think that one honest man loves you and is waiting for you. To regain content you will only have to place your hand in his."

"I promise you," answered Helene gravely.

As she made the avowal a ripple of laughter burst through the room. Jeanne had just awoke, and her eyes were riveted on her doll pacing up and down the table. Monsieur Rambaud, enthusiastic over the success of his tinkering, still kept his hands stretched out for fear lest any accident should happen. But the doll retained its stability, strutted about on its tiny feet, and turned its head, whilst at every step repeating the same words after the fashion of a parrot.

"Oh! it's some trick or other!" murmured Jeanne, who was still half asleep. "What have you done to it—tell me? It was all smashed, and now it's walking. Give it me a moment; let me see. Oh, you *are* a darling!"

Meanwhile over the gleaming expanse of Paris a rosy cloud was ascending higher and higher. It might have been thought the fiery breath of a furnace. At first it was shadowy-pale in the darkness—a reflected glow scarcely seen. Then slowly, as the evening progressed, it assumed a ruddier hue; and, hanging in the air, motionless above the city, deriving its being from all the lights and noisy life which breathed from below, it seemed like one of those clouds, charged with flame and lightning, which crown the craters of volcanoes.

CHAPTER XVI.

The finger-glasses had been handed round the table, and the ladies were daintily wiping their hands. A momentary silence reigned, while Madame Deberle gazed on either side to see if every one had finished; then, without speaking, she rose, and amidst a noisy pushing back of chairs, her guests followed her example. An old gentleman who had been seated at her right hand hastened to offer her his arm.

"No, no," she murmured, as she led him towards a doorway. "We will now have coffee in the little drawing-room."

The guests, in couples, followed her. Two ladies and two gentlemen, however, lagged behind the others, continuing their conversation, without thought of joining the procession. The drawing-room reached, all constraint vanished, and the joviality which had marked the dessert made its reappearance. The coffee was already served on a large lacquer tray on a table. Madame Deberle walked round like a hostess who is anxious to satisfy the various tastes of her guests. But it was Pauline who ran about the most, and more particularly waited on the gentlemen. There were a dozen persons present, about the regulation number of people invited to the house every Wednesday, from December onwards. Later in the evening, at ten o'clock, a great many others would make their appearance.

"Monsieur de Guiraud, a cup of coffee," exclaimed Pauline, as she halted in front of a diminutive, bald-headed man. "Ah! no, I remember, you don't take any. Well, then, a glass of Chartreuse?"

But she became confused in discharging her duties, and brought him a glass of cognac. Beaming with smiles, she made the round of the guests, perfectly self-possessed, and looking people straight in the face, while her long train dragged with easy grace behind her. She wore a magnificent gown of white Indian cashmere trimmed with swan's-down, and cut square at the bosom. When the gentlemen were all standing up, sipping their coffee, each with cup in hand and chin high in the air, she began to tackle a tall young fellow named Tissot, whom she considered rather handsome.

Helene had not taken any coffee. She had seated herself apart, with a somewhat wearied expression on her face. Her black velvet gown, unrelieved by any trimming, gave her an air of austerity. In this small drawing-room smoking was allowed, and several boxes of cigars were placed beside her on the pier-table. The doctor drew near; as he selected a cigar he asked her: "Is Jeanne well?"

"Yes, indeed," she replied. "We walked to the Bois to-day, and she romped like a madcap. Oh, she must be sound asleep by now."

They were both chatting in friendly tones, with the smiling intimacy of people who see each other day after day, when Madame Deberle's voice rose high and shrill:

"Stop! stop! Madame Grandjean can tell you all about it. Didn't I come back from Trouville on the 10th of September? It was raining, and the beach had become quite unbearable!"

Three or four of the ladies were gathered round her while she rattled on about her holliday at the seaside. Helene found it necessary to rise and join the group.

"We spent a month at Dinard," said Madame de Chermette. "Such a delightful place, and such charming society!"

"Behind our chalet was a garden, and we had a terrace overlooking the sea," went on Madame Deberle. "As you know, I decided on taking my landau and coachman with me. It was very much handier when I wanted a drive. Then Madame Levasseur came to see us—"

"Yes, one Sunday," interrupted that lady. "We were at Cabourg. Your establishment was perfect, but a little too dear, I think."

"By the way," broke in Madame Berthier, addressing Juliette, "didn't Monsieur Malignon give you lessons in swimming?"

Helene noticed a shadow of vexation, of sudden annoyance, pass over Madame Deberle's face. Several times already she had fancied that, on Malignon's name being brought unexpectedly into the conversation, Madame Deberle suddenly seemed perturbed. However, the young woman immediately regained her equanimity.

"A fine swimmer, indeed!" she exclaimed. "The idea of him ever giving lessons to any one! For my part, I have a mortal fear of cold water —the very sight of people bathing curdles my blood."

She gave an eloquent shiver, with a shrug of her plump shoulders, as though she were a duck shaking water from her back.

"Then it's a fable?" questioned Madame de Guiraud.

"Of course; and one, I presume, of his own invention. He detests me since he spent a month with us down there."

People were now beginning to pour in. The ladies, with clusters of flowers in their hair, and round, plump arms, entered smiling and nodding; while the men, each in evening dress and hat in hand, bowed and ventured on some commonplace remark. Madame Deberle, never ceasing her chatter for a moment, extended the tips of her fingers to the friends of the house, many of whom said nothing, but passed on with a bow. However, Mademoiselle Aurelie had just appeared on the scene, and at once went into raptures over Juliette's dress, which was of dark-blue velvet, trimmed with faille silk. At this all the ladies standing round seemed to catch their first glimpse of the dress, and declared it was exquisite, truly exquisite. It came, they learned, from Worth's, and they discussed it for five minutes. The guests who had drunk their coffee had placed their empty cups here and there on the tray and on the pier-tables; only one old gentleman had not yet finished, as between every mouthful he paused to converse with a lady. A warm perfume, the aroma of the coffee and the ladies' dresses intermingled, permeated the apartment.

"You know I have had nothing," remonstrated young Monsieur Tissot with Pauline, who had been chatting with him about an artist to whose studio her father had escorted her with a view to examining the pictures.

"What! have you had nothing? Surely I brought you a cup of coffee?"

"No, mademoiselle, I assure you."

"But I insist on your having something. See, here is some Chartreuse."

Madame Deberle had just directed a meaning nod towards her husband. The doctor, understanding her, thereupon opened the door of a large drawing-room, into which they all filed, while a servant removed the coffee-tray. There was almost a chill atmosphere in this spacious apartment, through which streamed the white light of six lamps and a chandelier with ten wax candles. There were already some ladies there, sitting in a semi-circle round the fireplace, but only two or three men were present, standing amidst the sea of outspread skirts. And through the open doorway of the smaller drawing-room rang the shrill voice of Pauline, who had lingered behind in company with young Tissot.

"Now that I have poured it out, I'm determined you shall drink it. What would you have me do with it? Pierre has carried off the tray."

Then she entered the larger room, a vision in white, with her dress trimmed with swan's-down. Her ruddy lips parted, displaying her teeth, as she smilingly announced: "Here comes Malignon, the exquisite!"

Hand-shaking and bowing were now the order of the day. Monsieur Deberle had placed himself near the door. His wife, seated with some other ladies on an extremely low couch, rose every other second. When Malignon made his appearance, she affected to turn away her head. He was dressed to perfection; his hair had been curled, and was parted behind, down to his very neck. On the threshold he had stuck an eye-glass in his right eye with a slight grimace, which, according to Pauline, was just the thing; and now he cast a glance around the room. Having nonchalantly and silently shaken hands with the doctor, he made his way towards Madame Deberle, in front of whom he respectfully bent his tall figure.

"Oh, it's you!" she exclaimed, in a voice loud enough to be heard by everybody. "It seems you go in for swimming now."

He did not guess her meaning, but nevertheless replied, by way of a joke:

"Certainly; I once saved a Newfoundland dog from drowning."

The ladies thought this extremely funny, and even Madame Deberle seemed disarmed.

"Well, I'll allow you to save Newfoundlands," she answered, "but you know very well I did not bathe once at Trouville."

"Oh! you're speaking of the lesson I gave you!" he exclaimed. "Didn't I tell you one night in your dining-room how to move your feet and hands about?"

All the ladies were convulsed with mirth—he was delightful! Juliette shrugged her shoulders; it was impossible to engage him in a serious talk. Then she rose to meet a lady whose first visit this was to her house, and who was a superb pianist. Helene, seated near the fire, her lovely face unruffled by any emotion, looked on and listened. Malignon, es-

pecially, seemed to interest her. She saw him execute a strategical movement which brought him to Madame Deberle's side, and she could hear
the conversation that ensued behind her chair. Of a sudden there was
a change in the tones, and she leaned back to gather the drift of what
was being said.

"Why didn't you come yesterday?" asked Malignon. "I waited for
you till six o'clock."

"Nonsense; you are mad," murmured Juliette.

Thereupon Malignon loudly lisped: "Oh! you don't believe the story
about my Newfoundland! Yet I received a medal for it, and I'll show it
to you."

Then he added, in a whisper: "You gave me your promise—remember."

A family group now entered the drawing-room, and Juliette broke
into complimentary greetings, while Malignon reappeared amongst the
ladies, glass in eye. Helene had become quite pale since overhearing
those hastily spoken words. It was as though a thunderbolt, or something equally unforeseen and horrible, had fallen on her. How could
thoughts of treachery enter into the mind of that woman whose life
was so happy, whose face betrayed no signs of sorrow, whose cheeks
had the freshness of the rose? She had always known her to be devoid
of brains, displaying an amiable egotism which seemed a guarantee that
she would never commit a foolish action. And over such a fellow as
Malignon, too! The scenes in the garden of an afternoon flashed back
on her memory—she recalled Juliette smiling lovingly as the doctor
kissed her hair. Their love for one another had seemed real enough. An
inexplicable feeling of indignation with Juliette now pervaded Helene,
as though some wrong had been done herself. She felt humiliated for
Henri's sake; she was consumed with jealous rage; and her perturbed
feelings were so plainly mirrored in her face that Mademoiselle Aurelie
asked her: "What is the matter with you? Do you feel ill?"

The old lady had sunk into a seat beside her immediately she had
observed her to be alone. She had conceived a lively friendship for Helene, and was charmed with the kindly manner in which so sedate and
lovely a woman would listen for hours to her tittle-tattle.

But Helene made no reply. A wild desire sprang up within her to
gaze on Henri, to know what he was doing, and what was the expression of his face. She sat up, and glancing round the drawing-room, at

last perceived him. He stood talking with a stout, pale man, and looked completely at his ease, his face wearing its customary refined smile. She scanned him for a moment, full of a pity which belittled him somewhat, though all the while she loved him the more with an affection into which entered some vague idea of watching over him. Her feelings, still in a whirl of confusion, inspired her with the thought that she ought to bring him back the happiness he had lost.

"Well, well!" muttered Mademoiselle Aurelie; "it will be pleasant if Madame de Guiraud's sister favors us with a song. It will be the tenth time I have heard her sing the 'Turtle-Doves.' That is her stock song this winter. You know that she is separated from her husband. Do you see that dark gentleman down there, near the door? They are most intimate together, I believe. Juliette is compelled to have him here, for otherwise she wouldn't come!"

"Indeed!" exclaimed Helene.

Madame Deberle was bustling about from one group to another, requesting silence for a song from Madame de Guiraud's sister. The drawing-room was now crowded, some thirty ladies being seated in the center whispering and laughing together; two, however, had remained standing, and were talking loudly and shrugging their shoulders in a pretty way, while five or six men sat quite at home amongst the fair ones, almost buried beneath the folds of their skirts and trains. A low "Hush!" ran round the room, the voices died away, and a stolid look of annoyance crept into every face. Only the fans could be heard rustling through the heated atmosphere.

Madame de Guiraud's sister sang, but Helene never listened. Her eyes were now riveted on Malignon, who feigned an intense love of music, and appeared to be enraptured with the "Turtle Doves." Was it possible? Could Juliette have turned a willing ear to the amorous chatter of the young fop? It was at Trouville, no doubt, that some dangerous game had been played. Malignon now sat in front of Juliette, marking the time of the music by swaying to and fro with the air of one who is enraptured. Madame Deberle's face beamed in admiring complacency, while the doctor, good-natured and patient, silently awaited the last notes of the song in order to renew his talk with the stout, pale man.

There was a murmur of applause as the singer's voice died away, and two or three exclaimed in tones of transport: "Delightful! magnificent!"

Malignon, however, stretching his arms over the ladies'
3 head-dresses, noiselessly clapped his gloved hands, and repeated
"Brava! brava!" in a voice that rose high above the others.

The enthusiasm promptly came to an end, every face relaxed and
smiled, and a few of the ladies rose, while, with the feeling of general
relief, the buzz of conversation began again. The atmosphere was
growing much warmer, and the waving fans wafted an odor of musk
from the ladies' dresses. At times, amidst the universal chatter, a peal of
pearly laughter would ring out, or some word spoken in a loud tone
would cause many to turn round. Thrice already had Juliette swept into
the smaller drawing-room to request some gentleman who had escaped
thither not to desert the ladies in so rude a fashion. They returned at her
request, but ten minutes afterwards had again vanished.

"It's intolerable," she muttered, with an air of vexation; "not one of
them will stay here."

In the meantime Mademoiselle Aurelie was running over the ladies'
names for Helene's benefit, as this was only the latter's second evening
visit to the doctor's house. The most substantial people of Passy, some
of them rolling in riches, were present. And the old maid leaned towards Helene and whispered in her ear: "Yes, it seems it's all arranged.
Madame de Chermette is going to marry her daughter to that tall fair
fellow with whom she has flirted for the last eighteen months. Well,
never mind, that will be one mother-in-law who'll be fond of her son-
in-law."

She stopped short, and then burst out in a tone of intense surprise:
"Good gracious! there's Madame Levasseur's husband speaking to that
man. I thought Juliette had sworn never to have them here together."

Helene's glances slowly travelled round the room. Even amongst
such seemingly estimable and honest people as these could there be
women of irregular conduct? With her provincial austerity she was astounded at the manner in which wrongdoing was winked at in Paris.
She railed at herself for her own painful repugnance when Juliette had
shaken hands with her. Madame Deberle had now seemingly become
reconciled with Malignon; she had curled up her little plump figure in
an easy-chair, where she sat listening gleefully to his jests. Monsieur Deberle happened to pass them.

"You're surely not quarrelling to-night?" asked he.

"No," replied Juliette, with a burst of merriment. "He's talking too much silly nonsense. If you had heard all the nonsense he's been saying!"

There now came some more singing, but silence was obtained with greater difficulty. The aria selected was a duet from *La Favorita*, sung by young Monsieur Tissot and a lady of ripened charms, whose hair was dressed in childish style. Pauline, standing at one of the doors, amidst a crowd of black coats, gazed at the male singer with a look of undisguised admiration, as though she were examining a work of art.

"What a handsome fellow!" escaped from her lips, just as the accompaniment subsided into a softer key, and so loud was her voice that the whole drawing-room heard the remark.

As the evening progressed the guests' faces began to show signs of weariness. Ladies who had occupied the same seat for hours looked bored, though they knew it not,—they were even delighted at being able to get bored here. In the intervals between the songs, which were only half listened to, the murmur of conversation again resounded, and it seemed as though the deep notes of the piano were still echoing. Monsieur Letellier related how he had gone to Lyons for the purpose of inspecting some silk he had ordered, and how he had been greatly impressed by the fact that the Saone did not mingle its waters with those of the Rhone. Monsieur de Guiraud, who was a magistrate, gave vent to some sententious observations on the need of stemming the vice of Paris. There was a circle round a gentleman who was acquainted with a Chinaman, and was giving some particulars of his friend. In a corner two ladies were exchanging confidences about the failings of their servants; whilst literature was being discussed by those among whom Malignon sat enthroned. Madame Tissot declared Balzac to be unreadable, and Malignon did not deny it, but remarked that here and there, at intervals far and few, some very fine passages occurred in Balzac.

"A little silence, please!" all at once exclaimed Pauline; "she's just going to play."

The lady whose talent as a musician had been so much spoken of had just sat down to the piano. In accordance with the rules of politeness, every head was turned towards her. But in the general stillness which ensued the deep voices of the men conversing in the small drawing-room could be heard. Madame Deberle was in despair.

"They are a nuisance!" she muttered. "Let them stay there, if they don't want to come in; but at least they ought to hold their tongues!"

She gave the requisite orders to Pauline, who, intensely delighted, ran into the adjacent apartment to carry out her instructions.

"You must know, gentlemen, that a lady is going to play," she said, with the quiet boldness of a maiden in queenly garb. "You are requested to keep silence."

She spoke in a very loud key, her voice being naturally shrill. And, as she lingered with the men, laughing and quizzing, the noise grew more pronounced than ever. There was a discussion going on among these males, and she supplied additional matter for argument. In the larger drawing-room Madame Deberle was in agony. The guests, moreover, had been sated with music, and no enthusiasm was displayed; so the pianist resumed her seat, biting her lips, notwithstanding the laudatory compliments which the lady of the house deemed it her duty to lavish on her.

Helene was pained. Henri scarcely seemed to see her; he had made no attempt to approach her, and only at intervals smiled to her from afar. At the earlier part of the evening she had felt relieved by his prudent reserve; but since she had learnt the secret of the two others she wished for something—she knew not what—some display of affection, or at least interest, on his part. Her breast was stirred with confused yearnings, and every imaginable evil thought. Did he no longer care for her, that he remained so indifferent to her presence? Oh! if she could have told him everything! If she could apprise him of the unworthiness of the woman who bore his name! Then, while some short, merry catches resounded from the piano, she sank into a dreamy state. She imagined that Henri had driven Juliette from his home, and she was living with him as his wife in some far-away foreign land, the language of which they knew not.

All at once a voice startled her.

"Won't you take anything?" asked Pauline.

The drawing-room had emptied, and the guests were passing into the dining-room to drink some tea. Helene rose with difficulty. She was dazed; she thought she had dreamt it all—the words she had heard, Juliette's secret intrigue, and its consequences. If it had all been true, Henri would surely have been at her side and ere this both would have quitted the house.

"Will you take a cup of tea?"

She smiled and thanked Madame Deberle, who had kept a place

for her at the table. Plates loaded with pastry and sweetmeats covered the cloth, while on glass stands arose two lofty cakes, flanking a large *brioche*. The space was limited, and the cups of tea were crowded together, narrow grey napkins with long fringes lying between each two. The ladies only were seated. They held biscuits and preserved fruits with the tips of their ungloved fingers, and passed each other the cream-jugs and poured out the cream with dainty gestures. Three or four, however, had sacrificed themselves to attend on the men, who were standing against the walls, and, while drinking, taking all conceivable precautions to ward off any push which might be unwittingly dealt them. A few others lingered in the two drawing-rooms, waiting for the cakes to come to them. This was the hour of Pauline's supreme delight. There was a shrill clamor of noisy tongues, peals of laughter mingled with the ringing clatter of silver plate, and the perfume of musk grew more powerful as it blended with the all-pervading fragrance of the tea.

"Kindly pass me some cake," said Mademoiselle Aurelie to Helene, close to whom she happened to find herself. "These sweetmeats are frauds!"

She had, however, already emptied two plates of them. And she continued, with her mouth full:

"Oh! some of the people are beginning to go now. We shall be a little more comfortable."

In truth, several ladies were now leaving, after shaking hands with Madame Deberle. Many of the gentlemen had already wisely vanished, and the room was becoming less crowded. Now came the opportunity for the remaining gentlemen to sit down at table in their turn. Mademoiselle Aurelie, however, did not quit her place, though she would much have liked to secure a glass of punch.

"I will get you one," said Helene, starting to her feet.

"No, no, thank you. You must not inconvenience yourself so much."

For a short time Helene had been watching Malignon. He had just shaken hands with the doctor, and was now bidding farewell to Juliette at the doorway. She had a lustrous face and sparkling eyes, and by her complacent smile it might have been imagined that she was receiving some commonplace compliments on the evening's success. While Pierre was pouring out the punch at a sideboard near the door, Helene stepped forward in such wise as to be hidden from view by the curtain, which had been drawn back. She listened.

"I beseech you," Malignon was saying, "come the day after to-morrow. I shall wait for you till three o'clock."

"Why cannot you talk seriously," replied Madame Deberle, with a laugh. "What foolish things you say!"

But with greater determination he repeated: "I shall wait for you—the day after to-morrow."

Then she hurriedly gave a whispered reply:

"Very well—the day after to-morrow."

Malignon bowed and made his exit. Madame de Chermette followed in company with Madame Tissot. Juliette, in the best of spirits, walked with them into the hall, and said to the former of these ladies with her most amiable look:

"I shall call on you the day after to-morrow. I have a lot of calls to make that day."

Helene stood riveted to the floor, her face quite white. Pierre, in the meanwhile, had poured out the punch, and now handed the glass to her. She grasped it mechanically and carried it to Mademoiselle Aurelie, who was making an inroad on the preserved fruits.

"Oh, you are far too kind!" exclaimed the old maid. "I should have made a sign to Pierre. I'm sure it's a shame not offering the punch to ladies. Why, when people are my age—"

She got no further, however, for she observed the ghastliness of Helene's face. "You surely are in pain! You must take a drop of punch!"

"Thank you, it's nothing. The heat is so oppressive—"

She staggered, and turned aside into the deserted drawing-room, where she dropped into an easy-chair. The lamps were shedding a reddish glare; and the wax candles in the chandelier, burnt to their sockets, threatened imminent destruction to the crystal sconces. From the dining-room were wafted the farewells of the departing guests. Helene herself had lost all thoughts of going; she longed to linger where she was, plunged in thought. So it was no dream after all; Juliette would visit that man the day after to-morrow—she knew the day. Then the thought struck her that she ought to speak to Juliette and warn her against sin. But this kindly thought chilled her to the heart, and she drove it from her mind as though it were out of place, and deep in meditation gazed at the grate, where a smouldering log was crackling. The air was still heavy and oppressive with the perfumes from the ladies' hair.

"What! you are here!" exclaimed Juliette as she entered. "Well, you are kind not to run away all at once. At last we can breathe!"

Helene was surprised, and made a movement as though about to rise; but Juliette went on: "Wait, wait, you are in no hurry. Henri, get me my smelling-salts."

Three or four persons, intimate friends, had lingered behind the others. They sat before the dying fire and chatted with delightful freedom, while the vast room wearily sank into a doze. The doors were open, and they saw the smaller drawing-room empty, the dining-room deserted, the whole suite of rooms still lit up and plunged in unbroken silence. Henri displayed a tender gallantry towards his wife; he had run up to their bedroom for her smelling-salts, which she inhaled with closed eyes, whilst he asked her if she had not fatigued herself too much. Yes, she felt somewhat tired; but she was delighted —everything had gone off so well. Next she told them that on her reception nights she could not sleep, but tossed about till six o'clock in the morning. Henri's face broke into a smile, and some quizzing followed. Helene looked at them, and quivered amidst the benumbing drowsiness which little by little seemed to fall upon the whole house.

However, only two guests now remained. Pierre had gone in search of a cab. Helene remained the last. One o'clock struck. Henri, no longer standing on ceremony, rose on tiptoe and blew out two candles in the chandelier which were dangerously heating their crystal sconces. As the lights died out one by one, it seemed like a bedroom scene, the gloom of an alcove spreading over all.

"I am keeping you up!" exclaimed Helene, as she suddenly rose to her feet. "You must turn me out."

A flush of red dyed her face; her blood, racing through her veins, seemed to stifle her. They walked with her into the hall, but the air there was chilly, and the doctor was somewhat alarmed for his wife in her low dress.

"Go back; you will do yourself harm. You are too warm."

"Very well; good-bye," said Juliette, embracing Helene, as was her wont in her most endearing moments. "Come and see me oftener."

Henri had taken Helene's fur coat in his hand, and held it outstretched to assist her in putting it on. When she had slipped her arms into the sleeves, he turned up the collar with a smile, while they stood in front of an immense mirror which covered one side of the hall. They were alone, and saw one another in the mirror's depths. For three months, on meeting and parting they had simply shaken hands in friendly greeting; they would fain that their love had died. But now Helene was overcome, and sank back into his arms. The smile vanished from his face, which became impassioned, and, still clasping her, he kissed her on the neck. And she, raising her head, returned his kiss.

CHAPTER XVII.

That night Helene was unable to sleep. She turned from side to side in feverish unrest, and whenever a drowsy stupor fell on her senses, the old sorrows would start into new life within her breast. As she dozed and the nightmare increased, one fixed thought tortured her—she was eager to know where Juliette and Malignon would meet. This knowledge, she imagined, would be a source of relief to her. Where, where could it be? Despite herself, her brain throbbed with the thought, and she forgot everything save her craving to unravel this mystery, which thrilled her with secret longings.

When day dawned and she began to dress, she caught herself saying loudly: "It will be to-morrow!"

With one stocking on, and hands falling helpless to her side, she lapsed for a while into a fresh dreamy fit. "Where, where was it that they had agreed to meet?"

"Good-day, mother, darling!" just then exclaimed Jeanne who had awakened in her turn.

As her strength was now returning to her, she had gone back to sleep in her cot in the closet. With bare feet and in her nightdress she came to throw herself on Helene's neck, as was her every-day custom; then back again she rushed, to curl herself up in her warm bed for a little while longer. This jumping in and out amused her, and a ripple of laughter stole from under the clothes. Once more she bounded into the bedroom, saying: "Good-morning, mammy dear!"

And again she ran off, screaming with laughter. Then she threw the sheet over her head, and her cry came, hoarse and muffled, from beneath it: "I'm not there! I'm not there!"

But Helene was in no mood for play, as on other mornings; and

Jeanne, dispirited, fell asleep again. The day was still young. About eight
o'clock Rosalie made her appearance to recount the morning's chapter
of accidents. Oh! the streets were awful outside; in going for the milk
her shoes had almost come off in the muddy slush. All the ice was
thawing; and it was quite mild too, almost oppressive. Oh! by the way,
she had almost forgotten! an old woman had come to see madame the
night before.

"Why!" she said, as there came a pull at the bell, "I expect that's
she!"

It was Mother Fetu, but Mother Fetu transformed, magnificent in
a clean white cap, a new gown, and tartan shawl wrapped round her
shoulders. Her voice, however, still retained its plaintive tone of entreaty.

"Dear lady, it's only I, who have taken the liberty of calling to ask
you about something!"

Helene gazed at her, somewhat surprised by her display of finery.

"Are you better, Mother Fetu?"

"Oh yes, yes; I feel better, if I may venture to say so. You see I always have something queer in my inside; it knocks me about dreadfully,
but still I'm better. Another thing, too; I've had a stroke of luck; it was
a surprise, you see, because luck hasn't often come in my way. But a
gentleman has made me his housekeeper—and oh! it's such a story!"

Her words came slowly, and her small keen eyes glittered in her
face, furrowed by a thousand wrinkles. She seemed to be waiting for
Helene to question her; but the young woman sat close to the fire which
Rosalie had just lit, and paid scant attention to her, engrossed as she
was in her own thoughts, with a look of pain on her features.

"What do you want to ask me?" she at last said to Mother Fetu.

The old lady made no immediate reply. She was scrutinizing the
room, with its rosewood furniture and blue velvet hangings. Then, with
the humble and fawning air of a pauper, she muttered: "Pardon me,
madame, but everything is so beautiful here. My gentleman has a room
like this, but it's all in pink. Oh! it's such a story! Just picture to yourself
a young man of good position who has taken rooms in our house. Of
course, it isn't much of a place, but still our first and second floors are
very nice. Then, it's so quiet, too! There's no traffic; you could imagine
yourself in the country. The workmen have been in the house for a
whole fortnight; they have made such a jewel of his room!"

She here paused, observing that Helene's attention was being aroused.

"It's for his work," she continued in a drawling voice; "he says it's for his work. We have no doorkeeper, you know, and that pleases him. Oh! my gentleman doesn't like doorkeepers, and he is quite right, too!"

Once more she came to a halt, as though an idea had suddenly occurred to her.

"Why, wait a minute; you must know him—of course you must. He visits one of your lady friends!"

"Ah!" exclaimed Helene, with colorless face.

"Yes, to be sure; the lady who lives close by—the one who used to go with you to church. She came the other day."

Mother Fetu's eyes contracted, and from under the lids she took note of her benefactress's emotion. But Helene strove to question her in a tone that would not betray her agitation.

"Did she go up?"

"No, she altered her mind; perhaps she had forgotten something. But I was at the door. She asked for Monsieur Vincent, and then got back into her cab again, calling to the driver to return home, as it was too late. Oh! she's such a nice, lively, and respectable lady. The gracious God doesn't send many such into the world. Why, with the exception of yourself, she's the best—well, well, may Heaven bless you all!"

In this way Mother Fetu rambled on with the pious glibness of a devotee who is perpetually telling her beads. But the twitching of the myriad wrinkles of her face showed that her mind was still working, and soon she beamed with intense satisfaction.

"Ah!" she all at once resumed in inconsequent fashion, "how I should like to have a pair of good shoes! My gentleman has been so very kind, I can't ask him for anything more. You see I'm dressed; still I must get a pair of good shoes. Look at those I have; they are all holes; and when the weather's muddy, as it is to-day, one's apt to get very ill. Yes, I was down with colic yesterday; I was writhing all the afternoon, but if I had a pair of good shoes—"

"I'll bring you a pair, Mother Fetu," said Helene, waving her towards the door.

Then, as the old woman retired backwards, with profuse curtseying and thanks, she asked her: "At what hour are you alone?"

"My gentleman is never there after six o'clock," she answered. "But don't give yourself the trouble; I'll come myself, and get them from your doorkeeper. But you can do as you please. You are an angel from heaven. God on high will requite you for all your kindness!"

When she had reached the landing she could still be heard giving vent to her feelings. Helene sat a long time plunged in the stupor which the information, supplied by this woman with such fortuitous season-ableness, had brought upon her. She now knew the place of assignation. It was a room, with pink decorations, in that old tumbledown house! She once more pictured to herself the staircase oozing with damp, the yellow doors on each landing, grimy with the touch of greasy hands, and all the wretchedness which had stirred her heart to pity when she had gone during the previous winter to visit Mother Fetu; and she also strove to conjure up a vision of that pink chamber in the midst of such repulsive, poverty-stricken surroundings. However, whilst she was still absorbed in her reverie, two tiny warm hands were placed over her eyes, which lack of sleep had reddened, and a laughing voice inquired: "Who is it? who is it?"

It was Jeanne, who had slipped into her clothes without assistance. Mother Fetu's voice had awakened her; and perceiving that the closet door had been shut, she had made her toilet with the utmost speed in order to give her mother a surprise.

"Who is it? who is it?" she again inquired, convulsed more and more with laughter.

She turned to Rosalie, who entered at the moment with the break-fast.

"You know; don't you speak. Nobody is asking you any question."

"Be quiet, you little madcap!" exclaimed Helene. "I suppose it's you!"

The child slipped on to her mother's lap, and there, leaning back and swinging to and fro, delighted with the amusement she had de-vised, she resumed:

"Well, it might have been another little girl! Eh? Perhaps some lit-tle girl who had brought you a letter of invitation to dine with her mamma. And she might have covered your eyes, too!"

"Don't be silly," exclaimed Helene, as she set her on the floor. "What are you talking about? Rosalie, let us have breakfast."

The maid's eyes, however, were riveted on the child, and she com-mented upon her little mistress being so oddly dressed. To tell the truth, so great had been Jeanne's haste that she had not put on her shoes. She had drawn on a short flannel petticoat which allowed a glimpse of her chemise, and had left her morning jacket open, so that you could see her delicate, undeveloped bosom. With her hair streaming behind her, stamping about in her stockings, which were all awry, she looked charming, all in white like some child of fairyland.

She cast down her eyes to see herself, and immediately burst into laughter.

"Look, mamma, I look nice, don't I? Won't you let me be as I am? It is nice!"

Repressing a gesture of impatience, Helene, as was her wont every morning, inquired: "Are you washed?"

"Oh, mamma!" pleaded the child, her joy suddenly dashed. "Oh, mamma! it's raining; it's too nasty!"

"Then, you'll have no breakfast. Wash her, Rosalie."

She usually took this office upon herself, but that morning she felt altogether out of sorts, and drew nearer to the fire, shivering, although the weather was so balmy. Having spread a napkin and placed two white china bowls on a small round table, Rosalie had brought the latter close to the fireplace. The coffee and milk steamed before the fire in a silver pot, which had been a present from Monsieur Rambaud. At this early hour the disorderly, drowsy room seemed delightfully homelike.

"Mamma, mamma!" screamed Jeanne from the depths of the closet, "she's rubbing me too hard. It's taking my skin off. Oh dear! how awfully cold!"

Helene, with eyes fixed on the coffee-pot, remained engrossed in thought. She desired to know everything, so she would go. The thought of that mysterious place of assignation in so squalid a nook of Paris was an ever-present pain and vexation. She judged such taste hateful, but in it she identified Malignon's leaning towards romance.

"Mademoiselle," declared Rosalie, "if you don't let me finish with you, I shall call madame."

"Stop, stop: you are poking the soap into my eyes," answered Jeanne, whose voice was hoarse with sobs. "Leave me alone; I've had enough of it. The ears can wait till to-morrow."

But the splashing of water went on, and the squeezing of the sponge into the basin could be heard. There was a clamor and a struggle, the child was sobbing; but almost immediately afterward she made her appearance, shouting gaily: "It's over now; it's over now!"

Her hair was still glistening with wet, and she shook herself, her face glowing with the rubbing it had received and exhaling a fresh and pleasant odor. In her struggle to get free her jacket had slipped from her shoulders, her petticoat had become loosened, and her stockings had tumbled down, displaying her bare legs. According to Rosalie, she looked like an infant Jesus. Jeanne, however, felt very proud that she was clean; she had no wish to be dressed again.

"Look at me, mamma; look at my hands, and my neck, and my ears. Oh! you must let me warm myself; I am so comfortable. You don't say anything; surely I've deserved my breakfast to-day."

She had curled herself up before the fire in her own little easy-chair. Then Rosalie poured out the coffee and milk. Jeanne took her bowl on her lap, and gravely soaked her toast in its contents with all the airs of a grown-up person. Helene had always forbidden her to eat in this way, but that morning she remained plunged in thought. She did not touch her own bread, and was satisfied with drinking her coffee. Then Jeanne, after swallowing her last morsel, was stung with remorse. Her heart filled, she put aside her bowl, and gazing on her mother's pale face, threw herself on her neck: "Mamma, are you ill now? I haven't vexed you, have I?—say."

"No, no, my darling, quite the contrary; you're very good," murmured Helene as she embraced her. "I'm only a little wearied; I haven't slept well. Go on playing: don't be uneasy."

The thought occurred to her that the day would prove a terribly long one. What could she do whilst waiting for the night? For some time past she had abandoned her needlework; sewing had become a terrible weariness. For hours she lingered in her seat with idle hands, almost suffocating in her room, and craving to go out into the open air for breath, yet never stirring. It was this room which made her ill; she hated it, in angry exasperation over the two years which she had spent within its walls; its blue velvet and the vast panorama of the mighty city disgusted her, and her thoughts dwelt on a lodging in some busy street, the uproar of which would have deafened her. Good heavens! how long were the hours! She took up a book, but the fixed idea that engrossed her mind continually conjured up the same visions between her eyes and the page of print.

In the meantime Rosalie had been busy setting the room in order;

Jeanne's hair also had been brushed, and she was dressed. While her mother sat at the window, striving to read, the child, who was in one of her moods of obstreperous gaiety, began playing a grand game. She was all alone; but this gave her no discomfort; she herself represented three or four persons in turn with comical earnestness and gravity. At first she played the lady going on a visit. She vanished into the dining-room, and returned bowing and smiling, her head nodding this way and that in the most coquettish style.

"Good-day, madame! How are you, madame? How long it is since I've seen you! A marvelously long time, to be sure! Dear me, I've been so ill, madame! Yes; I've had the cholera; it's very disagreeable. Oh! it doesn't show; no, no, it makes you look younger, on my word of honor. And your children, madame? Oh! I've had three since last summer!"

So she rattled on, never ceasing her curtseying to the round table, which doubtless represented the lady she was visiting. Next she ventured to bring the chairs closer together, and for an hour carried on a general conversation, her talk abounding in extraordinary phrases.

"Don't be silly," said her mother at intervals, when the chatter put her out of patience.

"But, mamma, I'm paying my friend a visit. She's speaking to me, and I must answer her. At tea nobody ought to put the cakes in their pockets, ought they?"

Then she turned and began again:

"Good-bye, madame; your tea was delicious. Remember me most kindly to your husband."

The next moment came something else. She was going out shopping in her carriage, and got astride of a chair like a boy.

"Jean, not so quick; I'm afraid. Stop! stop! here is the milliner's! Mademoiselle, how much is this bonnet? Three hundred francs; that isn't dear. But it isn't pretty. I should like it with a bird on it—a bird big like that! Come, Jean, drive me to the grocer's. Have you some honey? Yes, madame, here is some. Oh, how nice it is! But I don't want any of it; give me two sous' worth of sugar. Oh! Jean, look, take care! There! we have had a spill! Mr. Policeman, it was the cart which drove against us. You're not hurt, madame, are you? No, sir, not in the least. Jean, Jean! home now. Gee-up! gee-up. Wait a minute; I must order some chemises. Three dozen chemises for madame. I want some boots too and some stays. Gee-up! gee-up! Good gracious, we shall never get back again."

Then she fanned herself, enacting the part of the lady who has returned home and is finding fault with her servants. She never remained quiet for a moment; she was in a feverish ecstasy, full of all sorts of whimsical ideas; all the life she knew surged up in her little brain and escaped from it in fragments. Morning and afternoon she thus moved about, dancing and chattering; and when she grew tired, a footstool or parasol discovered in a corner, or some shred of stuff lying on the floor, would suffice to launch her into a new game in which her effervescing imagination found fresh outlet. Persons, places, and incidents were all of her own creation, and she amused herself as much as though twelve children of her own age had been beside her.

But evening came at last. Six o'clock was about to strike. And Helene, rousing herself from the troubled stupor in which she had spent the afternoon, hurriedly threw a shawl over her shoulders.

"Are you going out, mamma?" asked Jeanne in her surprise.

"Yes, my darling, just for a walk close by. I won't be long; be good."

Outside it was still thawing. The footways were covered with mud. In the Rue de Passy, Helene entered a boot shop, to which she had taken Mother Fetu on a previous occasion. Then she returned along the Rue Raynouard. The sky was grey, and from the pavement a mist was rising. The street stretched dimly before her, deserted and fear-inspiring, though the hour was yet early. In the damp haze the infrequent gas-lamps glimmered like yellow spots. She quickened her steps, keeping close to the houses, and shrinking from sight as though she were on the way to some assignation. However, as she hastily turned into the Passage des Eaux, she halted beneath the archway, her heart giving way to genuine terror. The passage opened beneath her like some black gulf. The bottom of it was invisible; the only thing she could see in this black tunnel was the quivering gleam of the one lamp which lighted it. Eventually she made up her mind, and grasped the iron railing to prevent herself from slipping. Feeling her way with the tip of her boots she landed successively on the broad steps. The walls, right and left, grew closer, seemingly prolonged by the darkness, while the bare branches of the trees above cast vague shadows, like those of gigantic arms with closed or outstretched hands. She trembled as she thought that one of the garden doors might open and a man spring out upon her. There were no passers-by, however, and she stepped down as quickly as possible. Suddenly from out of the darkness loomed a shadow which coughed, and she was frozen with fear; but it was only an old woman creeping with difficulty up the path. Then she felt less uneasy, and carefully raised her dress, which had been trailing in the mud. So thick was the latter that her boots were constantly sticking to the steps. At the bottom she turned aside instinctively. From the branches the raindrops dripped fast into the passage, and the lamp glimmered like that of some miner, hanging to the side of a pit which infiltrations have rendered dangerous.

Helene climbed straight to the attic she had so often visited at the top of the large house abutting on the Passage. But nothing stirred, although she rapped loudly. In considerable perplexity she descended the stairs again. Mother Fetu was doubtless in the rooms on the first floor, where, however, Helene dared not show herself. She remained five minutes in the entry, which was lighted by a petroleum lamp. Then again she ascended the stairs hesitatingly, gazing at each door, and was on the point of going away, when the old woman leaned over the balusters.

"What! it's you on the stairs, my good lady!" she exclaimed. "Come in, and don't catch cold out there. Oh! it is a vile place—enough to kill one."

"No, thank you," said Helene; "I've brought you your pair of shoes, Mother Fetu."

She looked at the door which Mother Fetu had left open behind her, and caught a glimpse of a stove within.

"I'm all alone, I assure you," declared the old woman. "Come in. This is the kitchen here. Oh! you're not proud with us poor folks; we can talk to you!"

Despite the repugnance which shame at the purpose of her coming created within her, Helene followed her.

"God in Heaven! how can I thank you! Oh, what lovely shoes! Wait, and I'll put them on. There's my whole foot in; it fits me like a glove. Bless the day! I can walk with these without being afraid of the rain. Oh! my good lady, you are my preserver; you've given me ten more years of life. No, no, it's no flattery; it's what I think, as true as there's a lamp shining on us. No, no, I don't flatter!"

She melted into tears as she spoke, and grasping Helene's hands kissed them. In a stewpan on the stove some wine was being heated, and on the table, near the lamp, stood a half-empty bottle of Bordeaux with its tapering neck. The only other things placed there were four dishes, a glass, two saucepans, and an earthenware pot. It could be seen that Mother Fetu camped in this bachelor's kitchen, and that the fires were lit for herself only. Seeing Helene's glance turn towards the stewpan, she coughed, and once more put on her dolorous expression.

"It's gripping me again," she groaned. "Oh! it's useless for the doctor to talk; I must have some creature in my inside. And then, a drop of wine relieves me so. I'm greatly afflicted, my good lady. I wouldn't have a soul suffer from my trouble; it's too dreadful. Well, I'm nursing myself a bit now; and when a person has passed through so much, isn't it fair she should do so? I have been so lucky in falling in with a nice gentleman. May Heaven bless him!"

With this outburst she dropped two large lumps of sugar into her wine. She was now getting more corpulent than ever, and her little eyes had almost vanished from her fat face. She moved slowly with a beatifical expression of felicity. Her life's ambition was now evidently satisfied. For this she had been born. When she put her sugar away again Helene caught a glimpse of some tid-bits secreted at the bottom of a cupboard—a jar of preserves, a bag of biscuits, and even some cigars, all doubtless pilfered from the gentleman lodger.

"Well, good-bye, Mother Fetu, I'm going away," she exclaimed.

The old lady, however, pushed the saucepan to one side of the stove and murmured: "Wait a minute; this is far too hot, I'll drink it by-and-by. No, no; don't go out that way. I must beg pardon for having received you in the kitchen. Let us go round the rooms."

She caught up the lamp, and turned into a narrow passage. Helene, with beating heart, followed close behind. The passage, dilapidated and smoky, was reeking with damp. Then a door was thrown open, and she found herself treading a thick carpet. Mother Fetu had already advanced into a room which was plunged in darkness and silence.

"Well?" she asked, as she lifted up the lamp; "it's very nice, isn't it?"

There were two rooms, each of them square, communicating with one another by folding-doors, which had been removed, and replaced by curtains. Both were hung with pink cretonne of a Louis Quinze pattern, picturing chubby-checked cupids disporting themselves amongst garlands of flowers. In the first apartment there was a round table, two lounges, and some easy-chairs; and in the second, which was somewhat smaller, most of the space was occupied by the bed. Mother Fetu drew attention to a crystal lamp with gilt chains, which hung from the ceiling. To her this lamp was the veritable acme of luxury.

Then she began explaining things: "You can't imagine what a funny fellow he is! He lights it up in mid-day, and stays here, smoking a cigar and gazing into vacancy. But it amuses him, it seems. Well, it doesn't matter; I've an idea he must have spent a lot of money in his time."

Helene went through the rooms in silence. They seemed to her in bad taste. There was too much pink everywhere; the furniture also looked far too new.

"He calls himself Monsieur Vincent," continued the old woman, rambling on. "Of course, it's all the same to me. As long as he pays, my gentleman—"

"Well, good-bye, Mother Fetu," said Helene, in whose throat a feeling of suffocation was gathering.

She was burning to get away, but on opening a door she found herself threading three small rooms, the bareness and dirt of which were repulsive. The paper hung in tatters from the walls, the ceilings were grimy, and old plaster littered the broken floors. The whole place was pervaded by a smell of long prevalent squalor.

"Not that way! not that way!" screamed Mother Fetu. "That door is generally shut. These are the other rooms which they haven't attempted to clean. My word! it's cost him quite enough already! Yes, indeed, these aren't nearly so nice! Come this way, my good lady—come this way!"

On Helene's return to the pink boudoir, she stopped to kiss her hand once more.

"You see, I'm not ungrateful! I shall never forget the shoes. How well they fit me! and how warm they are! Why, I could walk half-a-dozen miles with them. What can I beg Heaven to grant you? O Lord, hearken to me, and grant that she may be the happiest of women—in the name of the Father, the Son, and the Holy Ghost!" A devout enthusiasm had suddenly come upon Mother Fetu; she repeated the sign of the cross again and again, and bowed the knee in the direction of the crystal lamp. This done, she opened the door conducting to the landing, and whispered in a changed voice into Helene's ear:

"Whenever you like to call, just knock at the kitchen door; I'm always there!"

Dazed, and glancing behind her as though she were leaving a place of dubious repute, Helene hurried down the staircase, reascended the Passage des Eaux, and regained the Rue Vineuse, without consciousness

of the ground she was covering. The old woman's last words still rang
in her ears. In truth, no; never again would she set foot in that house,
never again would she bear her charity thither. Why should she ever
rap at the kitchen door again? At present she was satisfied; she had seen
what was to be seen. And she was full of scorn for herself —for everybody. How disgraceful to have gone there! The recollection of the place
with its tawdry finery and squalid surroundings filled her with mingled
anger and disgust.

"Well, madame," exclaimed Rosalie, who was awaiting her return
on the staircase, "the dinner will be nice. Dear, oh dear! it's been burning for half an hour!"

At table Jeanne plagued her mother with questions. Where had she
been? what had she been about? However, as the answers she received
proved somewhat curt, she began to amuse herself by giving a little
dinner. Her doll was perched near her on a chair, and in a sisterly fashion she placed half of her dessert before it.

"Now, mademoiselle, you must eat like a lady. See, wipe your mouth.
Oh, the dirty little thing! She doesn't even know how to wear her napkin! There, you're nice now. See, here is a biscuit. What do you say? You
want some preserve on it. Well, I should think it better as it is! Let me
pare you a quarter of this apple!"

She placed the doll's share on the chair. But when she had emptied
her own plate she took the dainties back again one after the other and
devoured them, speaking all the time as though she were the doll.

"Oh! it's delicious! I've never eaten such nice jam! Where did you
get this jam, madame? I shall tell my husband to buy a pot of it. Do
those beautiful apples come from your garden, madame?"

She fell asleep while thus playing, and stumbled into the bedroom
with the doll in her arms. She had given herself no rest since morning.
Her little legs could no longer sustain her—she was helpless and wearied to death. However, a ripple of laughter passed over her face even
in sleep; in her dreams she must have been still continuing her play.

At last Helene was alone in her room. With closed doors she spent
a miserable evening beside the dead fire. Her will was failing her;
thoughts that found no utterance were stirring within the innermost
recesses of her heart. At midnight she wearily sought her bed, but there
her torture passed endurance. She dozed, she tossed from side to side
as though a fire were beneath her. She was haunted by visions which

sleeplessness enlarged to a gigantic size. Then an idea took root in her brain. In vain did she strive to banish it; it clung to her, surged and clutched her at the throat till it entirely swayed her. About two o'clock she rose, rigid, pallid, and resolute as a somnambulist, and having again lighted the lamp she wrote a letter in a disguised hand; it was a vague denunciation, a note of three lines, requesting Doctor Deberle to repair that day to such a place at such an hour; there was no explanation, no signature. She sealed the envelope and dropped the letter into the pocket of her dress which was hanging over an arm-chair. Then returning to bed, she immediately closed her eyes, and in a few minutes was lying there breathless, overpowered by leaden slumber.

CHAPTER XVIII.

It was nearly nine o'clock the next morning before Rosalie was able to serve the coffee. Helene had risen late. She was weary and pale with the nightmare that had broken her rest. She rummaged in the pocket of her dress, felt the letter there, pressed it to the very bottom, and sat down at the table without opening her lips. Jeanne too was suffering from headache, and had a pale, troubled face. She quitted her bed regretfully that morning, without any heart to indulge in play. There was a sooty color in the sky, and a dim light saddened the room, while from time to time sudden downpours of rain beat against the windows.

"Mademoiselle is in the blues," said Rosalie, who monopolized all the talk. "She can't keep cheerful for two days running. That's what comes of dancing about too much yesterday."

"Do you feel ill, Jeanne?" asked Helene.

"No, mamma," answered the child. "It's only the nasty weather."

Helene lapsed once more into silence. She finished her coffee, and sat in her chair, plunged in thought, with her eyes riveted on the flames. While rising she had reflected that it was her duty to speak to Juliette and bid her renounce the afternoon assignation. But how? She could not say. Still, the necessity of the step was impressed on her, and now her one urgent, all-absorbing thought was to attempt it. Ten o'clock struck, and she began to dress. Jeanne gazed at her, and, on seeing her take up her bonnet, clasped her little hands as though stricken with cold, while over her face crept a pained look. It was her wont to take umbrage whenever her mother went out; she was unwilling to quit her side, and craved to go with her everywhere.

"Rosalie," said Helene, "make haste and finish the room. Don't go out. I'll be back in a moment."

She stooped and gave Jeanne a hasty kiss, not noticing her vexation. But the moment she had gone a sob broke from the child, who had hitherto summoned all her dignity to her aid to restrain her emotion.

"Oh, mademoiselle, how naughty!" exclaimed the maid by way of consolation. "Gracious powers! no one will rob you of your mamma. You must allow her to see after her affairs. You can't always be hanging to her skirts!"

Meanwhile Helene had turned the corner of the Rue Vineuse, keeping close to the wall for protection against the rain. It was Pierre who opened the door; but at sight of her he seemed somewhat embarrassed.

"Is Madame Deberle at home?"

"Yes, madame; but I don't know whether—"

Helene, in the character of a family friend, was pushing past him towards the drawing-room; but he took the liberty of stopping her.

"Wait, madame; I'll go and see."

He slipped into the room, opening the door as little as he could; and immediately afterwards Juliette could be heard speaking in a tone of irritation. "What! you've allowed someone to come in? Why, I forbade it peremptorily. It's incredible!! I can't be left quiet for an instant!"

Helene, however, pushed open the door, strong in her resolve to do that which she imagined to be her duty.

"Oh, it's you!" said Juliette, as she perceived her. "I didn't catch who it was!"

The look of annoyance did not fade from her face, however, and it was evident that the visit was ill-timed.

"Do I disturb you?" asked Helene.

"Not at all, not at all," answered the other. "You'll understand in a moment. We have been getting up a surprise. We are rehearsing *Caprice* to play it on one of my Wednesdays. We had selected this morning for rehearsal, thinking nobody would know of it. But you'll stay now? You will have to keep silence about it, that's all."

Then, clapping her hands and addressing herself to Madame Berthier, who was standing in the middle of the drawing-room, she began once more, without paying any further attention to Helene: "Come, come; we must get on. You don't give sufficient point to the sentence 'To make a purse unknown to one's husband would in the eyes of most people seem rather more than romantic.' Say that again."

Intensely surprised at finding her engaged in this way, Helene had sat down. The chairs and tables had been pushed against the wall, the carpet thus being left clear. Madame Berthier, a delicate blonde, repeated her soliloquy, with her eyes fixed on the ceiling in her effort to recall the words; while plump Madame de Guiraud, a beautiful brunette, who had assumed the character of Madame de Lery, reclined in an armchair awaiting her cue. The ladies, in their unpretentious morning gowns, had doffed neither bonnets nor gloves. Seated in front of them, her hair in disorder and a volume of Musset in her hand, was Juliette, in a dressing-gown of white cashmere. Her face wore the serious expression of a stage-manager tutoring his actors as to the tones they should speak in and the by-play they should introduce. The day being dull, the small curtains of embroidered tulle had been pulled aside and swung across the knobs of the window-fastenings, so that the garden could be seen, dark and damp.

"You don't display sufficient emotion," declared Juliette. "Put a little more meaning into it. Every word ought to tell. Begin again: 'I'm going to finish your toilette, my dear little purse.'"

"I shall be an awful failure," said Madame Berthier languidly. "Why don't you play the part instead of me? You would make a delicious Mathilda."

"I! Oh, no! In the first place, one needs to be fair. Besides, I'm a very good teacher, but a bad pupil. But let us get on—let us get on!"

Helene sat still in her corner. Madame Berthier, engrossed in her part, had not even turned round. Madame de Guiraud had merely honored her with a slight nod. She realized that she was in the way, and that she ought to have declined to stay. If she still remained, it was no longer through the sense of a duty to be fulfilled, but rather by reason of a strange feeling stirring vaguely in her heart's depth's—a feeling which had previously thrilled her in this selfsame spot. The unkindly greeting which Juliette had bestowed on her pained her. However, the young woman's friendships were usually capricious; she worshipped people for three months, threw herself on their necks, and seemed to live for them alone; then one morning, without affording any explanation, she appeared to lose all consciousness of being acquainted with them. Without doubt, in this, as in everything else, she was simply yielding to a fashionable craze, an inclination to love the people who were loved by her own circle. These sudden veerings of affection, however, deeply wounded Helene, for her generous and undemonstrative heart had its ideal in eternity. She often left the Deberles plunged in sadness, full of despair when she thought how fragile and unstable was the basis of human love. And on this occasion, in this crisis in her life, the thought brought her still keener pain.

"We'll skip the scene with Chavigny," said Juliette. "He won't be here this morning. Let us see Madame de Lery's entrance. Now, Madame de Guiraud, here's your cue." Then she read from her book: "'Just imagine my showing him this purse.'"

"'Oh! it's exceedingly pretty. Let me look at it,'" began Madame de Guiraud in a falsetto voice, as she rose with a silly expression on her face.

When the servant had opened the door to her, Helene had pictured a scene entirely different from this. She had imagined that she would find Juliette displaying excessive nervousness, with pallid cheeks, hesitating and yet allured, shivering at the very thought of assignation. She had pictured herself imploring her to reflect, till the young woman, choked with sobs, threw herself into her arms. Then they would have mingled their tears together, and Helene would have quitted her with the thought that Henri was henceforward lost to her, but that she had secured his happiness. However, there had been nothing of all this; she had merely fallen on this rehearsal, which was wholly unintelligible to her; and she saw Juliette before her with unruffled features, like one who has had a good night's rest, and with her mind sufficiently at ease to discuss Madame Berthier's by-play, without troubling herself in the least degree about what she would do in the afternoon. This indifference and frivolity chilled Helene, who had come to the house with passion consuming her.

A longing to speak fell on her. At a venture she inquired: "Who will play the part of Chavigny?"

"Why, Malignon, of course," answered Juliette, turning round with an air of astonishment. "He played Chavigny all last winter. It's a nuisance he can't come to the rehearsals. Listen, ladies; I'm going to read Chavigny's part. Unless that's done, we shall never get on."

Thereupon she herself began acting the man's part, her voice deepening unconsciously, whilst she assumed a cavalier air in harmony with the situation. Madame Berthier renewed her warbling tones, and Madame de Guiraud took infinite pains to be lively and witty. When Pierre came in to put some more wood on the fire he slyly glanced at the ladies, who amused him immensely.

Helene, still fixed in her resolve, despite some heart-shrinking, at-tempted however to take Juliette aside.

"Only a minute. I've something to say to you."

"Oh, impossible, my dear! You see how much I am engaged. To-morrow, if you have the time."

Helene said no more. The young woman's unconcern displeased her. She felt anger growing within her as she observed how calm and collected Juliette was, when she herself had endured such intense agony since the night before. At one moment she was on the point of rising and letting things take their course. It was exceedingly foolish of her to wish to save this woman; her nightmare began once more; her hands slipped into her pocket, and finding the letter there, clasped it in a fever-ish grasp. Why should she have any care for the happiness of others, when they had no care for her and did not suffer as she did?

"Oh! capital, capital," exclaimed Juliette of a sudden.

Madame Berthier's head was now reclining on Madame de Guiraud's shoulder, and she was declaring through her sobs: "'I am sure that he loves her; I am sure of it!'"

"Your success will be immense," said Juliette. "Say that once more: 'I am sure that he loves her; I am sure of it.' Leave your head as it is. You're divine. Now, Madame de Guiraud, your turn."

"'No, no, my child, it cannot be; it is a caprice, a fancy,'" replied the stout lady.

"Perfect! but oh, the scene is a long one, isn't it? Let us rest a little while. We must have that incident in proper working order."

Then they all three plunged into a discussion regarding the arrange-ment of the drawing-room. The dining-room door, to the left, would serve for entrances and exits; an easy-chair could be placed on the right, a couch at the farther end, and the table could be pushed close to the fireplace. Helene, who had risen, followed them about, as though she felt an interest in these scenic arrangements. She had now abandoned her idea of eliciting an explanation, and merely wished to make a last effort to prevent Juliette from going to the place of meeting.

"I intended asking you," she said to her, "if it isn't to-day that you mean to pay Madame de Chermette a visit?"

"Yes, this afternoon."

"Then, if you'll allow me, I'll go with you; it's such a long time since

I promised to go to see her."

For a moment Juliette betrayed signs of embarrassment, but speedily regained her self-possession.

"Of course, I should be very happy. Only I have so many things to look after; I must do some shopping first, and I have no idea at what time I shall be able to get to Madame de Chermette's."

"That doesn't matter," said Helene; "it will enable me to have a walk."

"Listen; I will speak to you candidly. Well, you must not press me. You would be in my way. Let it be some other Monday."

This was said without a trace of emotion, so flatly and with so quiet a smile that Helene was dumbfounded and uttered not another syllable. She was obliged to lend some assistance to Juliette, who suddenly decided to bring the table close to the fireplace. Then she drew back, and the rehearsal began once more. In a soliloquy which followed the scene, Madame de Guiraud with considerable power spoke these two sentences: "But what a treacherous gulf is the heart of man! In truth, we are worth more than they!"

And Helene, what ought she to do now? Within her breast the question raised a storm that stirred her to vague thoughts of violence. She experienced an irresistible desire to be revenged on Juliette's tranquility, as if that self-possession were an insult directed against her own fevered heart. She dreamed of facilitating her fall, that she might see whether she would always retain this unruffled demeanor. And she thought of herself scornfully as she recalled her delicacy and scruples. Twenty times already she ought to have said to Henri: "I love you; let us go away together." Could she have done so, however, without the most intense emotion? Could she have displayed the callous composure of this woman, who, three hours before her first assignation, was rehearsing a comedy in her own home? Even at this moment she trembled more than Juliette; what maddened her was the consciousness of her own passion amidst the quiet cheerfulness of this drawing-room; she was terrified lest she should burst out into some angry speech. Was she a coward, then?

But all at once a door opened, and Henri's voice reached her ear: "Do not disturb yourselves. I'm only passing."

The rehearsal was drawing to a close. Juliette, who was still reading Chavigny's part, had just caught hold of Madame de Guiraud's hand.

"Ernestine, I adore you!" she exclaimed with an outburst of passion-ate earnestness.

"Then Madame de Blainville is no longer beloved by you?" inquired Madame de Guiraud.

However, so long as her husband was present Juliette declined to proceed. There was no need of the men knowing anything about it. The doctor showed himself most polite to the ladies; he complimented them and predicted an immense success. With black gloves on his hands and his face clean-shaven he was about to begin his round of visits. On his entry he had merely greeted Helene with a slight bow. At the Come-die Francais he had seen some very great actress in the character of Madame de Lery, and he acquainted Madame de Guiraud with some of the usual by-play of the scene.

"At the moment when Chavigny is going to throw himself at your feet, you fling the purse into the fire. Dispassionately, you know, with-out any anger, like a woman who plays with love."

"All right; leave us alone," said Juliette. "We know all about it."

At last, when they had heard him close his study door, she began once more: "Ernestine, I adore you!"

Prior to his departure Henri had saluted Helene with the same slight bow. She sat dumb, as though awaiting some catastrophe. The sudden appearance of the husband had seemed to her ominous; but when he had gone, his courtesy and evident blindness made him seem to her ridiculous. So he also gave attention to this idiotic comedy! And there was no loving fire in his eye as he looked at her sitting there! The whole house had become hateful and cold to her. Here was a downfall; there was nothing to restrain her any longer, for she abhorred Henri as much as Juliette. Within her pocket she held the letter in her convulsive grasp. At last, murmuring "Good-bye for the present," she quitted the room, her head swimming and the furniture seeming to dance around her. And in her ears rang these words, uttered by Madame de Guiraud:

"Adieu. You will perhaps think badly of me to-day, but you will have some kindly feeling for me to-morrow, and, believe me, that is much better than a caprice."

When Helene had shut the house door and reached the pavement, she drew the letter with a violent, almost mechanical gesture from her pocket, and dropped it into the letter-box. Then she stood motionless for a few seconds, still dazed, her eyes glaring at the narrow brass plate which had fallen back again in its place.

"It is done," she exclaimed in a whisper.

Once more she pictured the rooms hung with pink cretonne. Malignon and Juliette were there together; but all of a sudden the wall was riven open, and the husband entered. She was conscious of no more, and a great calm fell on her. Instinctively she looked around to see if any one had observed her dropping the letter in the box. But the street was deserted. Then she turned the corner and went back home.

"Have you been good, my darling?" she asked as she kissed Jeanne.

The child, still seated on the same chair, raised a gloomy face towards her, and without answering threw both arms around her neck, and kissed her with a great gasp. Her grief indeed had been intense.

At lunch-time Rosalie seemed greatly surprised. "Madame surely went for a long walk," said she.

"Why do you think so?" asked Helene.

"Because madame is eating with such an appetite. It is long since madame ate so heartily."

It was true; she was very hungry; with her sudden relief she had felt her stomach empty. She experienced a feeling of intense peace and content. After the shocks of these last two days a stillness fell upon her spirit, her limbs relaxed and became as supple as though she had just left a bath. The only sensation that remained to her was one of heaviness somewhere, an indefinable load that weighed upon her.

When she returned to her bedroom her eyes were at once directed towards the clock, the hands of which pointed to twenty-five minutes past twelve. Juliette's assignation was for three o'clock. Two hours and a half must still elapse. She made the reckoning mechanically. Moreover, she was in no hurry; the hands of the clock were moving on, and no one in the world could stop them. She left things to their own accomplishment. A child's cap, long since begun, was lying unfinished on the table. She took it up and began to sew at the window. The room was plunged in unbroken silence. Jeanne had seated herself in her usual place, but her arms hung idly beside her.

"Mamma," she said, "I cannot work; it's no fun at all."

"Well, my darling, don't do anything. Oh, wait a minute, you can thread my needles!"

In a languid way the child silently attended to the duty assigned her. Having carefully cut some equal lengths of cotton, she spent a long

time in finding the eyes of the needles, and was only just ready with
one of them threaded when her mother had finished with the last.

"You see," said the latter gently, "this will save time. The last of my
six little caps will be finished to-night."

She turned round to glance at the clock—ten minutes past one. Still
nearly two hours. Juliette must now be beginning to dress. Henri had received the letter. Oh, he would certainly go. The instructions were precise; he would find the place without delay. But it all seemed so far off
still, and she felt no emotional fever, but went on sewing with regular
stitches as industriously as a work-girl. The minutes slipped by one by
one. At last two o'clock struck.

A ring at the bell came as a surprise.

"Who can it be, mother darling?" asked Jeanne, who had jumped on
her chair. "Oh, it's you," she continued, as Monsieur Rambaud entered
the room. "Why did you ring so loudly? You gave me quite a fright."

The worthy man was in consternation—to tell the truth, his tug at
the bell had been a little too violent.

"I am not myself to-day, I'm ill," the child resumed. "You must not
frighten me."

Monsieur Rambaud displayed the greatest solicitude. What was the
matter with his poor darling? He only sat down, relieved, when Helene
had signed to him that the child was in her dismals, as Rosalie was wont
to say. A call from him in the daytime was a rare occurrence, and so he
at once set about explaining the object of his visit. It concerned some
fellow-townsman of his, an old workman who could find no employ-
ment owing to his advanced years, and who lived with his paralytic wife
in a tiny little room. Their wretchedness could not be pictured. He himself had gone up that morning to make a personal investigation. Their
lodging was a mere hole under the tiles, with a swing window, through
whose broken panes the wind beat in. Inside, stretched on a mattress,
he had found a woman wrapped in an old curtain, while the man squat-
ted on the floor in a state of stupefaction, no longer finding sufficient
courage even to sweep the place.

"Oh, poor things, poor things!" exclaimed Helene, moved to tears.

It was not the old workman who gave Monsieur Rambaud any uneasiness. He would remove him to his own house and find him something to do. But there was the wife with palsied frame, whom the
husband dared not leave for a moment alone, and who had to be rolled

up like a bundle; where could she be put? what was to be done with her?

"I thought of you," he went on. "You must obtain her instant admission to an asylum. I should have gone straight to Monsieur Deberle, but I imagined you knew him better and would have greater influence with him. If he would be kind enough to interest himself in the matter, it could all be arranged to-morrow."

Trembling with pity, her cheeks white, Jeanne listened to the tale.

"Oh, mamma!" she murmured with clasped hands, "be kind—get the admission for the poor woman!"

"Yes, yes, of course," said Helene, whose emotion was increasing. "I will speak to the doctor as soon as I can; he will himself take every requisite step. Give me their names and the address, Monsieur Rambaud."

He scribbled a line on the table, and said as he rose: "It is thirty-five minutes past two. You would perhaps find the doctor at home now."

She had risen at the same time, and as she looked at the clock a fierce thrill swept through her frame. In truth it was already thirty-five minutes past two, and the hands were still creeping on. She stammered out that the doctor must have started on his round of visits. Her eyes were riveted on the dial. Meantime, Monsieur Rambaud remained standing hat in hand, and beginning his story once more. These poor people had sold everything, even their stove, and since the setting in of winter had spent their days and nights alike without a fire. At the close of December they had been four days without food. Helene gave vent to a cry of compassion. The hands of the clock now marked twenty minutes to three. Monsieur Rambaud devoted another two minutes to his farewell: "Well, I depend on you," he said. And stooping to kiss Jeanne, he added: "Good-bye, my darling."

"Good-bye; don't worry; mamma won't forget. I'll make her remember."

When Helene came back from the ante-room, whither she had gone in company with Monsieur Rambaud, the hands of the clock pointed to a quarter to three. Another quarter of an hour and all would be over. As she stood motionless before the fireplace, the scene which was about to be enacted flashed before her eyes: Juliette was already there; Henri entered and surprised her. She knew the room; she could see the scene in its minutest details with terrible vividness. And still affected by Monsieur Rambaud's awful story she felt a mighty shudder rise from her limbs to her face. A voice cried out within her that what she had done—the writing of that letter, that cowardly denunciation— was a crime. The truth came to her with dazzling clearness. Yes, it was a crime she had committed! She recalled to memory the gesture with which she had flung the letter into the box; she recalled it with a sense of stupor such as might come over one on seeing another commit an evil action, without thought of intervening. She was as if awaking from a dream. What was it that had happened? Why was she here, with eyes ever fixed on the hands of that dial? Two more minutes had slipped away.

"Mamma," said Jeanne, "if you like, we'll go to see the doctor to-gether to-night. It will be a walk for me. I feel stifling to-day."

Helene, however, did not hear; thirteen minutes must yet elapse. But she could not allow so horrible a thing to take place! In this stormy awakening of her rectitude she felt naught but a furious craving to prevent it. She must prevent it; otherwise she would be unable to live. In a state of frenzy she ran about her bedroom.

"Ah, you're going to take me!" exclaimed Jeanne joyously. "We're going to see the doctor at once, aren't we, mother darling?"

"No, no," Helene answered, while she hunted for her boots, stooping to look under the bed.

They were not to be found; but she shrugged her shoulders with supreme indifference when it occurred to her that she could very well run out in the flimsy house-slippers she had on her feet. She was now turning the wardrobe topsy-turvy in her search for her shawl. Jeanne crept up to her with a coaxing air: "Then you're not going to the doctor's, mother darling?"

"No."

"Say that you'll take me all the same. Oh! do take me; it will be such a pleasure!"

But Helene had at last found her shawl, and she threw it over her shoulders. Good heavens! only twelve minutes left—just time to run. She would go—she would do something, no matter what. She would decide on the way.

"Mamma dear, do please take me with you," said Jeanne in tones that grew lower and more imploring.

"I cannot take you," said Helene; "I'm going to a place where children don't go. Give me my bonnet."

Jeanne's face blanched. Her eyes grew dim, her words came with a gasp. "Where are you going?" she asked.

The mother made no reply—she was tying the strings of her bonnet.

Then the child continued: "You always go out without me now. You went out yesterday, you went out to-day, and you are going out again. Oh, I'm dreadfully grieved, I'm afraid to be here all alone. I shall die if you leave me here. Do you hear, mother darling? I shall die."

Then bursting into loud sobs, overwhelmed by a fit of grief and rage, she clung fast to Helene's skirts.

"Come, come, leave me; be good, I'm coming back," her mother repeated.

"No, no, I won't have it!" the child exclaimed through her sobs. "Oh, you don't love me any longer, or you would take me with you. Yes, yes, I am sure you love other people better. Take me with you, take me with you, or I'll stay here on the floor; you'll come back and find me on the floor."

She wound her little arms round her mother's legs; she wept with face buried in the folds of her dress; she clung to her and weighed upon her to prevent her making a step forward. And still the hands of the clock moved steadily on; it was ten minutes to three. Then Helene thought that she would never reach the house in time, and, nearly distracted, she wrenched Jeanne from her grasp, exclaiming: "What an unbearable child! This is veritable tyranny! If you sob any more, I'll have something to say to you!"

She left the room and slammed the door behind her. Jeanne had staggered back to the window, her sobs suddenly arrested by this brutal treatment, her limbs stiffened, her face quite white. She stretched her hands towards the door, and twice wailed out the words: "Mamma! mamma!" And then she remained where she had fallen on a chair, with eyes staring and features distorted by the jealous thought that her mother was deceiving her.

On reaching the street, Helene hastened her steps. The rain had ceased, but great drops fell from the housetops on to her shoulders. She had resolved that she would reflect outside and fix on some plan. But now she was only inflamed with a desire to reach the house. When she reached the Passage des Eaux, she hesitated for just one moment. The descent had become a torrent; the water of the gutters of the Rue Raynouard was rushing down it. And as the stream bounded over the steps, between the close-set walls, it broke here and there into foam, whilst the edges of the stones, washed clear by the downpour, shone out like glass. A gleam of pale light, falling from the grey sky, made the Passage look whiter between the dusky branches of the trees. Helene went down it, scarcely raising her skirts. The water came up to her ankles. She almost lost her flimsy slippers in the puddles; around her, down the whole way, she heard a gurgling sound, like the murmuring of brooklets coursing through the grass in the depths of the woods.

All at once she found herself on the stairs in front of the door. She stood there, panting in a state of torture. Then her memory came back, and she decided to knock at the kitchen.

"What, is it you?" exclaimed Mother Fetu.

There was none of the old whimper in her voice. Her little eyes were sparkling, and a complacent grin had spread over the myriad wrinkles of her face. All the old deference vanished, and she patted Helene's hands as she listened to her broken words. The young woman gave her twenty francs.

"May God requite you!" prayed Mother Fetu in her wonted style. "Whatever you please, my dear!"

CHAPTER XIX.

Leaning back in an easy-chair, with his legs stretched out before the huge, blazing fire, Malignon sat waiting. He had considered it a good idea to draw the window-curtains and light the wax candles. The outer room, in which he had seated himself, was brilliantly illuminated by a small chandelier and a pair of candelabra; whilst the other apartment was plunged in shadow, the swinging crystal lamp alone casting on the floor a twilight gleam. Malignon drew out his watch.

"The deuce," he muttered. "Is she going to keep me waiting again?"

He gave vent to a slight yawn. He had been waiting for an hour already, and it was small amusement to him. However, he rose and cast a glance over his preparations.

The arrangement of the chairs did not please him, and he rolled a couch in front of the fireplace. The cretonne hangings had a ruddy glow, as they reflected the light of the candles; the room was warm, silent, and cozy, while outside the wind came and went in sudden gusts. All at once the young man heard three hurried knocks at the door. It was the signal.

"At last!" he exclaimed aloud, his face beaming jubilantly.

He ran to open the door, and Juliette entered, her face veiled, her figure wrapped in a fur mantle. While Malignon was gently closing the door, she stood still for a moment, with the emotion that checked the words on her lips undetected.

However, before the young man had had time to take her hand, she raised her veil, and displayed a smiling face, rather pale, but quite unruffled.

"What, you have lighted up the place!" she exclaimed. "Why? I thought you hated candles in broad daylight!"

Malignon, who had been making ready to clasp her with a passionate gesture that he had been rehearsing, was put somewhat out of countenance by this remark, and hastened to explain that the day was too
wretched, and that the windows looked on to waste patches of ground.
Besides, night was his special delight.

"Well, one never knows how to take you," she retorted jestingly.
"Last spring, at my children's ball, you made such a fuss, declaring that
the place was like some cavern, some dead-house. However, let us say
that your taste has changed."

She seemed to be paying a mere visit, and affected a courage which
slightly deepened her voice. This was the only indication of her uneasiness. At times her chin twitched somewhat, as though she felt some
uneasiness in her throat. But her eyes were sparkling, and she tasted to
the full the keen pleasure born of her imprudence. She thought of
Madame de Chermette, of whom such scandalous stories were related.
Good heavens, it seemed strange all the same.

"Let us have a look round," she began.

And thereupon she began inspecting the apartment. He followed in
her footsteps, while she gazed at the furniture, examined the walls,
looked upwards, and started back, chattering all the time.

"I don't like your cretonne; it is so frightfully common!" said she.
"Where did you buy that abominable pink stuff? There's a chair that
would be nice if the wood weren't covered with gilding. Not a picture,
not a nick-nack—only your chandelier and your candelabra, which are
by no means in good style! Ah well, my dear fellow; I advise you to
continue laughing at my Japanese pavilion!"

She burst into a laugh, thus revenging herself on him for the old af-
fronts which still rankled in her breast.

"Your taste is a pretty one, and no mistake! You don't know that my
idol is worth more than the whole lot of your things! A draper's shop-
man wouldn't have selected that pink stuff. Was it your idea to fascinate
your washerwoman?"

Malignon felt very much hurt, and did not answer. He made an attempt to lead her into the inner room; but she remained on the threshold, declaring that she never entered such gloomy places. Besides, she
could see quite enough; the one room was worthy of the other. The
whole of it had come from the Saint-Antoine quarter.

But the hanging lamp was her special aversion. She attacked it with merciless raillery—what a trashy thing it was, such as some little work-girl with no furniture of her own might have dreamt of! Why, lamps in the same style could be bought at all the bazaars at seven francs fifty centimes apiece.

"I paid ninety francs for it," at last ejaculated Malignon in his impatience.

Thereupon she seemed delighted at having angered him.

On his self-possession returning, he inquired: "Won't you take off your cloak?"

"Oh, yes, I will," she answered; "it is dreadfully warm here."

She took off her bonnet as well, and this with her fur cloak he hastened to deposit in the next room. When he returned, he found her seated in front of the fire, still gazing round her. She had regained her gravity, and was disposed to display a more conciliatory demeanor.

"It's all very ugly," she said; "still, you are not amiss here. The two rooms might have been made very pretty."

"Oh, they're good enough for my purpose," he thoughtlessly replied, with a careless shrug of the shoulders.

The next moment, however, he bitterly regretted these silly words. He could not possibly have been more impertinent or clumsy. Juliette hung her head, and a sharp pang darted through her bosom. Then he sought to turn to advantage the embarrassment into which he had plunged her.

"Juliette!" he said pleadingly, as he leaned towards her.

But with a gesture she forced him to resume his seat. It was at the seaside, at Trouville, that Malignon, bored to death by the constant sight of the sea, had hit upon the happy idea of falling in love. One evening he had taken hold of Juliette's hand. She had not seemed offended; in fact, she had at first bantered him over it. Soon, though her head was empty and her heart free, she imagined that she loved him. She had, so far, done nearly everything that her friends did around her; a lover only was lacking, and curiosity and a craving to be like the others had impelled her to secure one. However, Malignon was vain enough to imagine that he might win her by force of wit, and allowed her time to accustom herself to playing the part of a coquette. So, on the first outburst, which took place one night when they stood side by side gazing at the sea like a pair of lovers in a comic opera, she had repelled him, in her astonishment and vexation that he should spoil the romance which served as an amusement to her.

On his return to Paris Malignon had vowed that he would be more skilful in his attack. He had just reacquired influence over her, during a fit of boredom which had come on with the close of a wearying winter, when the usual dissipations, dinners, balls, and first-night performances were beginning to pall on her with their dreary monotony. And at last, her curiosity aroused, allured by the seeming mystery and piquancy of an intrigue, she had responded to his entreaties by consenting to meet him. However, so wholly unruffled were her feelings, that she was as little disturbed, seated here by the side of Malignon, as when she paid visits to artists' studios to solicit pictures for her charity bazaars.

"Juliette, Juliette," murmured the young man, striving to speak in caressing tones.

"Come, be sensible," she merely replied; and taking a Chinese fan from the chimney-piece, she resumed—as much at her ease as though she had been sitting in her own drawing-room: "You know we had a rehearsal this morning. I'm afraid I have not made a very happy choice in Madame Berthier. Her 'Mathilda' is a snivelling, insufferable affair. You remember that delightful soliloquy when she addresses the purse—'Poor little thing, I kissed you a moment ago'? Well, she declaims it like a school-girl who has learnt a complimentary greeting. It's so vexatious!"

"And what about Madame de Guiraud?" he asked, as he drew his chair closer and took her hand.

"Oh, she is perfection. I've discovered in her a 'Madame de Lery,' with some sarcasm and animation."

While speaking she surrendered her hand to the young man, and he kissed it between her sentences without her seeming to notice it.

"But the worst of it all, you know," she resumed, "is your absence. In the first place, you might say something to Madame Berthier; and besides, we shall not be able to get a good *ensemble* if you never come."

He had now succeeded in passing his arm round her waist.

"But as I know my part," he murmured.

"Yes, that's all very well; but there's the arrangement of the scenes to look after. It is anything but obliging on your part to refuse to give us three or four mornings."

She was unable to continue, for he was raining a shower of kisses on her neck. At this she could feign ignorance no longer, but pushed him away, tapping him the while with the Chinese fan which she still retained in her hand. Doubtless, she had registered a vow that she would not allow any further familiarity. Her face was now flushed by the heat reflected from the fire, and her lips pouted with the very expression of an inquisitive person whom her feelings astonish. Moreover, she was really getting frightened.

"Leave me alone," she stammered, with a constrained smile. "I shall get angry."

But he imagined that he had moved her, and once more took hold of her hands. To her, however, a voice seemed to be crying out, "No!" It was she herself protesting before she had even answered her own heart.

"No, no," she said again. "Let me go; you are hurting me!" And thereupon, as he refused to release her, she twisted herself violently from his grasp. She was acting in obedience to some strange emotion; she felt angry with herself and with him. In her agitation some disjointed phrases escaped her lips. Yes, indeed, he rewarded her badly for her trust. What a brute he was! She even called him a coward. Never in her life would she see him again. But he allowed her to talk on, and ran after her with a wicked and brutal laugh. And at last she could do no more than gasp in the momentary refuge which she had sought behind a chair. They were there, gazing at one another, her face transformed by shame and his by passion, when a noise broke through the stillness. At first they did not grasp its significance. A door had opened, some steps crossed the room, and a voice called to them:

"Fly, fly! You will be caught!"

It was Helene. Astounded, they both gazed at her. So great was their stupefaction that they lost consciousness of their embarrassing situation. Juliette indeed displayed no sign of confusion.

"Fly, fly," said Helene again. "Your husband will be here in two minutes."

"My husband," stammered the young woman; "my husband!— why—for what reason?"

She was losing her wits. Her brain was in a turmoil. It seemed to her prodigious that Helene should be standing there speaking to her of her husband.

But Helene made an angry gesture.

"Oh! if you think I've time to explain," said she,—"he is on the way here. I give you warning. Disappear at once, both of you."

Then Juliette's agitation became extraordinary. She ran about the rooms like a maniac, screaming out disconnected sentences.

"My God! my God!—I thank you.—Where is my cloak?—How horrid it is, this room being so dark!—Give me my cloak.—Bring me a candle, to help me to find my cloak.—My dear, you mustn't mind if I don't stop to thank you.—I can't get my arms into the sleeves—no, I can't get them in—no, I can't!"

She was paralyzed with fear, and Helene was obliged to assist her with her cloak. She put her bonnet on awry, and did not even tie the ribbons. The worst of it, however, was that they lost quite a minute in hunting for her veil, which had fallen on the floor. Her words came with a gasp; her trembling hands moved about in bewilderment, fumbling over her person to ascertain whether she might be leaving anything behind which might compromise her.

"Oh, what a lesson! what a lesson! Thank goodness, it is well over!"

Malignon was very pale, and made a sorry appearance. His feet beat a tattoo on the ground, as he realized that he was both scorned and ridiculous. His lips could only give utterance to the wretched question:

"Then you think I ought to go away as well?"

Then, as no answer was vouchsafed him, he took up his cane, and went on talking by way of affecting perfect composure. They had plenty of time, said he. It happened that there was another staircase, a small servants' staircase, now never used, but which would yet allow of their descent. Madame Deberle's cab had remained at the door; it would convey both of them away along the quays. And again he repeated: "Now calm yourself. It will be all right. See, this way."

He threw open a door, and the three dingy, dilapidated, little rooms, which had not been repaired and were full of dirt, appeared to view. A puff of damp air entered the boudoir. Juliette, ere she stepped through all that squalor, gave final expression to her disgust.

"How could I have come here?" she exclaimed in a loud voice. "What a hole! I shall never forgive myself."

"Be quick, be quick!" urged Helene, whose anxiety was as great as her own.

She pushed Juliette forward, but the young woman threw herself sobbing on her neck. She was in the throes of a nervous reaction. She was overwhelmed with shame, and would fain have defended herself, fain have given a reason for being found in that man's company. Then instinctively she gathered up her skirts, as though she were about to cross a gutter. With the tip of his boot Malignon, who had gone on first, was clearing away the plaster which littered the back staircase. The doors were shut once more.

Meantime, Helene had remained standing in the middle of the sitting-room. Silence reigned there, a warm, close silence, only disturbed by the crackling of the burnt logs. There was a singing in her ears, and she heard nothing. But after an interval, which seemed to her interminable, the rattle of a cab suddenly resounded. It was Juliette's cab rolling away.

Then Helene sighed, and she made a gesture of mute gratitude. The thought that she would not be tortured by everlasting remorse for having acted despicably filled her with pleasant and thankful feelings. She felt relieved, deeply moved, and yet so weak, now that this awful crisis was over, that she lacked the strength to depart in her turn. In her heart she thought that Henri was coming, and that he must meet someone in this place. There was a knock at the door, and she opened it at once.

The first sensation on either side was one of bewilderment. Henri entered, his mind busy with thoughts of the letter which he had received, and his face pale and uneasy. But when he caught sight of her a cry escaped his lips.

"You! My God! It was you!"

The cry betokened more astonishment than pleasure. But soon there came a furious awakening of his love.

"You love me, you love me!" he stammered. "Ah! it was you, and I did not understand."

He stretched out his arm as he spoke; but Helene, who had greeted his entrance with a smile, now started back with wan cheeks. Truly she had waited for him; she had promised herself that they would be together for a moment, and that she would invent some fiction. Now, however, full consciousness of the situation flashed upon her; Henri believed it to be an assignation. Yet she had never for one moment desired such a thing, and her heart rebelled.

"Henri, I pray you, release me," said she.

He had grasped her by the wrists, and was drawing her slowly towards him, as though to kiss her. The love that had been surging within him for months, but which had grown less violent owing to the break in their intimacy, now burst forth more fiercely than ever.

"Release me," she resumed. "You are frightening me. I assure you, you are mistaken."

His surprise found voice once more.

"Was it not you then who wrote to me?" he asked.

She hesitated for a second. What could she say in answer?

"Yes," she whispered at last.

She could not betray Juliette after having saved her. An abyss lay before her into which she herself was slipping. Henri was now glancing round the two rooms in wonderment at finding them illumined and furnished in such gaudy style. He ventured to question her.

"Are these rooms yours?" he asked.

But she remained silent.

"Your letter upset me so," he continued. "Helene, you are hiding something from me. For mercy's sake, relieve my anxiety!"

She was not listening to him; she was reflecting that he was indeed right in considering this to be an assignation. Otherwise, what could she have been doing there? Why should she have waited for him? She could devise no plausible explanation. She was no longer certain whether she had not given him this rendezvous. A network of chance and circumstance was enveloping her yet more tightly; there was no escape from it. Each second found her less able to resist.

"You were waiting for me, you were waiting for me!" he repeated passionately, as he bent his head to kiss her. And then as his lips met hers she felt it beyond her power to struggle further; but, as though in mute acquiescence, fell, half swooning and oblivious of the world, upon his neck.

CHAPTER XX.

Jeanne, with her eyes fixed on the door, remained plunged in grief over her mother's sudden departure. She gazed around her; the room was empty and silent; but she could still hear the waning sounds of hurrying footsteps and rustling skirts, and last the slamming of the outer door. Then nothing stirred, and she was alone.

All alone, all alone. Over the bed hung her mother's dressing-gown, flung there at random, the skirt bulging out and a sleeve lying across the bolster, so that the garment looked like some person who had fallen down overwhelmed with grief, and sobbing in misery. There was some linen scattered about, and a black neckerchief lay on the floor like a blot of mourning. The chairs were in disorder, the table had been pushed in front of the wardrobe, and amidst it all she was quite alone. She felt her tears choking her as she looked at the dressing-gown which no longer garmented her mother, but was stretched there with the ghastly semblance of death. She clasped her hands, and for the last time wailed, "Mamma! mamma!" The blue velvet hangings, however, deadened the sound. It was all over, and she was alone.

Then the time slipped away. The clock struck three. A dismal, dingy light came in through the windows. Dark clouds were sailing over the sky, which made it still gloomier. Through the panes of glass, which were covered with moisture, Paris could only be dimly seen; the watery vapor blurred it; its far-away outskirts seemed hidden by thick smoke. Thus the city even was no longer there to keep the child company, as on bright afternoons, when, on leaning out a little, it seemed to her as though she could touch each district with her hand.

What was she to do? Her little arms tightened in despair against her bosom. This desertion seemed to her mournful, passing all bounds, characterized by an injustice and wickedness that enraged her. She had never known anything so hateful; it struck her that everything was going to vanish; nothing of the old life would ever come back again. Then she caught sight of her doll seated near her on a chair, with its back against a cushion, and its legs stretched out, its eyes staring at her as though it were a human being. It was not her mechanical doll, but a large one with a pasteboard head, curly hair, and eyes of enamel, whose fixed look sometimes frightened her. What with two years' constant dressing and undressing, the paint had got rubbed off the chin and cheeks, and the limbs, of pink leather stuffed with sawdust, had become limp and wrinkled like old linen. The doll was just now in its night attire, arrayed only in a bed-gown, with its arms twisted, one in the air and the other hanging downwards. When Jeanne realized that there was still some-one with her, she felt for an instant less unhappy. She took the doll in her arms and embraced it ardently, while its head swung back, for its neck was broken. Then she chattered away to it, telling it that it was Jeanne's best-behaved friend, that it had a good heart, for it never went out and left Jeanne alone. It was, said she, her treasure, her kitten, her dear little pet. Trembling with agitation, striving to prevent herself from weeping again, she covered it all over with kisses.

This fit of tenderness gave her some revengeful consolation, and the doll fell over her arm like a bundle of rags. She rose and looked out, with her forehead against a window-pane. The rain had ceased falling, and the clouds of the last downpour, driven before the wind, were nearing the horizon towards the heights of Pere-Lachaise, which were wrapped in gloom; and against this stormy background Paris, il-lumined by a uniform clearness, assumed a lonely, melancholy grandeur. It seemed to be uninhabited, like one of those cities seen in a night-mare—the reflex of a world of death. To Jeanne it certainly appeared anything but pretty. She was now idly dreaming of those she had loved since her birth. Her oldest sweetheart, the one of her early days at Mar-seilles, had been a huge cat, which was very heavy; she would clasp it with her little arms, and carry it from one chair to another without pro-voking its anger in the least; but it had disappeared, and that was the first misfortune she remembered. She had next had a sparrow, but it died; she had picked it up one morning from the bottom of its cage. That made two. She never reckoned the toys which got broken just to grieve her, all kinds of wrongs which had caused her much suffering be-

cause she was so sensitive. One doll in particular, no higher than one's
hand, had driven her to despair by getting its head smashed; she had
cherished it to a such a degree that she had buried it by stealth in a corner of the yard; and some time afterwards, overcome by a craving to
look on it once more, she had disinterred it, and made herself sick with
terror whilst gazing on its blackened and repulsive features.

However, it was always the others who were the first to fail in their
love. They got broken; they disappeared. The separation, at all events,
was invariably their fault. Why was it? She herself never changed. When
she loved any one, her love lasted all her life. Her mind could not grasp
the idea of neglect and desertion; such things seemed to her mon-
strously wicked, and never occurred to her little heart without giving it
a deadly pang. She shivered as a host of vague ideas slowly awoke within
her. So people parted one day; each went his own way, never to meet
or love each other again. With her eyes fixed on the limitless and dreary
expanse of Paris, she sat chilled by all that her childish passion could divine of life's hard blows.

Meantime her breath was fast dimming the glass. With her hands
she rubbed away the vapor that prevented her from looking out. Several monuments in the distance, wet with the rain, glittered like browny
ice. There were lines of houses, regular and distinct, which, with their
fronts standing out pale amidst the surrounding roofs, looked like outstretched linen—some tremendous washing spread to dry on fields of
ruddy grass. The sky was clearing, and athwart the tail of the cloud
which still cloaked the city in gloom the milky rays of the sun were beginning to stream. A brightness seemed to be hesitating over some of
the districts; in certain places the sky would soon begin to smile. Jeanne
gazed below, over the quay and the slopes of the Trocadero; the street
traffic was about to begin afresh after that violent downpour. The cabs
again passed by at a jolting crawl, while the omnibuses rattled along the
still lonely streets with a louder noise than usual. Umbrellas were being
shut up, and wayfarers, who had taken shelter beneath the trees, ventured from one foot pavement to another through muddy streams
which were rushing into the gutters.

Jeanne noticed with special interest a lady and a little girl, both of
them fashionably dressed, who were standing beneath the awning of a
toy-shop near the bridge. Doubtless they had been caught in the
shower, and had taken refuge there. The child would fain have carried

away the whole shop, and had pestered her mother to buy her a hoop. Both were now leaving, however, and the child was running along full of glee, driving the hoop before her. At this Jeanne's melancholy returned with intensified force; her doll became hideous. She longed to have a hoop and to be down yonder and run along, while her mother slowly walked behind her and cautioned her not to go too far. Then, however, everything became dim again. At each minute she had to rub the glass clear. She had been enjoined never to open the window; but she was full of rebellious thoughts; she surely might gaze out of the window, if she were not to be taken for a walk. So she opened it, and leaned out like a grown-up person—in imitation of her mother when she ensconced herself there and lapsed into silence.

The air was mild, and moist in its mildness, which seemed to her delightful. A darkness slowly rising over the horizon induced her to lift her head. To her imagination it seemed as if some gigantic bird with outstretched wings were hovering on high. At first she saw nothing; the sky was clear; but at last, at the angle of the roof, a gloomy cloud made its appearance, sailing on and speedily enveloping the whole heaven. Another squall was rising before a roaring west wind. The daylight was quickly dying away, and the city grew dark, amidst a livid shimmer, which imparted to the house-fronts a rusty tinge.

Almost immediately afterwards the rain fell. The streets were swept by it; the umbrellas were again opened; and the passers-by, fleeing in every direction, vanished like chaff. One old lady gripped her skirts with both hands, while the torrent beat down on her bonnet as though it were falling from a spout. And the rain travelled on; the cloud kept pace with the water ragefully falling upon Paris; the big drops enfiladed the avenues of the quays, with a gallop like that of a runaway horse, raising a white dust which rolled along the ground at a prodigious speed. They also descended the Champs-Elysees, plunged into the long narrow streets of the Saint-Germain district, and at a bound filled up all the open spaces and deserted squares. In a few seconds, behind this veil which grew thicker and thicker, the city paled and seemed to melt away. It was as though a curtain were being drawn obliquely from heaven to earth. Masses of vapor arose too; and the vast, splashing pit-a-pat was as deafening as any rattle of old iron.

Jeanne, giddy with the noise, started back. A leaden wall seemed to have been built up before her. But she was fond of rain; so she returned, leaned out again, and stretched out her arms to feel the big, cold rain-drops splashing on her hands. This gave her some amusement, and she got wet to the sleeves. Her doll must, of course, like herself, have a headache, and she therefore hastened to put it astride the window-rail, with its back against the side wall. She thought, as she saw the drops pelting down upon it, that they were doing it some good. Stiffly erect, its little teeth displayed in a never-fading smile, the doll sat there, with one shoulder streaming with water, while every gust of wind lifted up its night-dress. Its poor body, which had lost some of its sawdust stuffing, seemed to be shivering.

What was the reason that had prevented her mother from taking her with her? wondered Jeanne. The rain that beat down on her hands seemed a fresh inducement to be out. It must be very nice, she argued, in the street. Once more there flashed on her mind's eye the little girl driving her hoop along the pavement. Nobody could deny that she had gone out with her mamma. Both of them had even seemed to be exceedingly well pleased. This was sufficient proof that little girls were taken out when it rained.

But, then, willingness on her mother's part was requisite. Why had she been unwilling? Then Jeanne again thought of her big cat which had gone away over the houses opposite with its tail in the air, and of the poor little sparrow which she had tempted with food when it was dead, and which had pretended that it did not understand. That kind of thing always happened to her; nobody's love for her was enduring enough. Oh! she would have been ready in a couple of minutes; when she chose she dressed quickly enough; it was only a question of her boots, which Rosalie buttoned, her jacket, her hat, and it was done. Her mother might easily have waited two minutes for her. When she left home to see her friends, she did not turn her things all topsy-turvy as she had done that afternoon; when she went to the Bois de Boulogne, she led her gently by the hand, and stopped with her outside every shop in the Rue de Passy.

Jeanne could not get to the bottom of it; her black eyebrows frowned, and her delicate features put on a stern, jealous expression which made her resemble some wicked old maid. She felt in a vague way that her mother had gone to some place where children never go. She had not been taken out because something was to be hidden from her. This thought filled her with unutterable sadness, and her heart throbbed with pain.

The rain was becoming finer, and through the curtain which veiled Paris glimpses of buildings were occasionally afforded. The dome of the Invalides, airy and quivering, was the first to reappear through the glittering vibration of the downpour. Next, some of the districts emerged into sight as the torrent slackened; the city seemed to rise from a deluge that had overwhelmed it, its roofs all streaming, and every street filled with a river of water from which vapor still ascended. But suddenly there was a burst of light; a ray of sunshine fell athwart the shower. For a moment it was like a smile breaking through tears.

The rain had now ceased to fall over the Champs-Elysees district; but it was sabring the left bank, the Cite, and the far-away suburbs; in the sunshine the drops could be seen flashing down like innumerable slender shafts of steel. On the right a rainbow gleamed forth. As the gush of light streamed across the sky, touches of pink and blue appeared on the horizon, a medley of color, suggestive of a childish attempt at water-color painting. Then there was a sudden blaze—a fall of golden snow, as it were, over a city of crystal. But the light died away, a cloud rolled up, and the smile faded amidst tears; Paris dripped and dripped, with a prolonged sobbing noise, beneath the leaden-hued sky.

Jeanne, with her sleeves soaked, was seized with a fit of coughing. But she was unconscious of the chill that was penetrating her; she was now absorbed in the thought that her mother had gone into Paris. She had come at last to know three buildings—the Invalides, the Pantheon, and the Tower of St.-Jacques. She now slowly went over their names, and pointed them out with her finger without attempting to think what they might be like were she nearer to them. Without doubt, however, her mother was down there; and she settled in her mind that she was in the Pantheon, because it astonished her the most, huge as it was, towering up through the air, like the city's head-piece. Then she began to question herself. Paris was still to her the place where children never go; she was never taken there. She would have liked to know it, however, that she might have quietly said to herself: "Mamma is there; she is doing such and such a thing." But it all seemed to her too immense; it was impossible to find any one there. Then her glance travelled towards the other end of the plain. Might her mother not rather be in one of that cluster of houses on the hill to the left? or nearer in, beneath those huge trees, whose bare branches seemed as dead as firewood? Oh! if she could only have lifted up the roofs! What could that gloomy edifice be? What was that street along which something of enormous bulk seemed to be running? And what could that district be at sight of which she always felt frightened, convinced as she was that people fought one another there? She could not see it distinctly, but, to tell the truth, its aspects stirred one; it was very ugly, and must not be looked at by little girls.

A host of indefinable ideas and suppositions, which brought her to the verge of weeping, awoke trouble in Jeanne's ignorant, childish mind. From the unknown world of Paris, with its smoke, its endless noises, its powerful, surging life, an odor of wretchedness, filth, and crime seemed to be wafted to her through the mild, humid atmosphere, and she was forced to avert her head, as though she had been leaning over one of those pestilential pits which breathe forth suffocation from their unseen horrors. The Invalides, the Pantheon, the Tower of Saint-Jacques—these she named and counted; but she knew nothing of anything else, and she sat there, terrified and ashamed, with the all-absorbing thought that her mother was among those wicked places, at some spot which she was unable to identify in the depths yonder.

Suddenly Jeanne turned round. She could have sworn that some-body had walked into the bedroom, that a light hand had even touched her shoulder. But the room was empty, still in the same disorder as when Helene had left. The dressing-gown, flung across the pillow, still lay in the same mournful, weeping attitude. Then Jeanne, with pallid cheeks, cast a glance around, and her heart nearly burst within her. She was alone! she was alone! And, O Heaven, her mother, in forsaking her, had pushed her with such force that she might have fallen to the floor. The thought came back to her with anguish; she again seemed to feel the pain of that outrage on her wrists and shoulders. Why had she been struck? She had been good, and had nothing to reproach herself with. She was usually spoken to with such gentleness that the punishment she had received awoke feelings of indignation within her. She was thrilled by a sensation of childish fear, as in the old times when she was threatened with the approach of the wolf, and looked for it and saw it not: it was lingering in some shady corner, with many other things that were going to overwhelm her. However, she was full of suspicion; her face paled and swelled with jealous fury. Of a sudden, the thought that her mother must love those whom she had gone to see far more than she loved her came upon her with such crushing force that her little hands clutched her bosom. She knew it now; yes, her mother was false to her.

Over Paris a great sorrow seemed to be brooding, pending the arrival of a fresh squall. A murmur travelled through the darkened air, and heavy clouds were hovering overhead. Jeanne, still at the window, was convulsed by another fit of coughing; but in the chill she experienced she felt herself revenged; she would willingly have had her illness return. With her hands pressed against her bosom, she grew conscious of some pain growing more intense within her. It was an agony to which her body abandoned itself. She trembled with fear, and did not again venture to turn round; she felt quite cold at the idea of glancing into the room any more. To be little means to be without strength. What could this new complaint be which filled her with mingled shame and bitter pleasure? With stiffened body, she sat there as if waiting —every one of her pure and innocent limbs in an agony of revulsion. From the innermost recesses of her being all her woman's feelings were aroused, and there darted through her a pang, as though she had received a blow from a distance. Then with failing heart she cried out chokingly: "Mamma! mamma!" No one could have known whether she called to her mother for aid, or whether she accused her of having inflicted on her the pain which seemed to be killing her.

At that moment the tempest burst. Through the deep and ominous stillness the wind howled over the city, which was shrouded in darkness; and afterwards there came a long-continued crashing —window-shutters beating to and fro, slates flying, chimney-tops and gutter-pipes rattling on to the pavements. For a few seconds a calm ensued; then there blew another gust, which swept along with such mighty strength that the ocean of roofs seemed convulsed, tossing about in waves, and then disappearing in a whirlpool. For a moment chaos reigned. Some enormous clouds, like huge blots of ink, swept through a host of smaller ones, which were scattered and floated like shreds of rag which the wind tore to pieces and carried off thread by thread. A second later two clouds rushed upon one another, and rent one another with crashing reports, which seemed to sprinkle the coppery expanse with wreckage; and every time the hurricane thus veered, blowing from every point of the compass, the thunder of opposing navies resounded in the atmosphere, and an awful rending and sinking followed, the hanging frag-

ments of the clouds, jagged like huge bits of broken walls, threatening
Paris with imminent destruction. The rain was not yet falling. But suddenly a cloud burst above the central quarters, and a water-spout ascended the Seine. The river's green ribbon, riddled and stirred to its
depths by the splashing drops, became transformed into a stream of
mud; and one by one, behind the downpour, the bridges appeared to
view again, slender and delicately outlined in the mist; while, right and
left, the trees edging the grey pavements of the deserted quays were
shaken furiously by the wind. Away in the background, over Notre-
Dame, the cloud divided and poured down such a torrent of water that
the island of La Cite seemed submerged. Far above the drenched
houses the cathedral towers alone rose up against a patch of clear sky,
like floating waifs.

On every side the water now rushed down from the heavens. Three
times in succession did the right bank appear to be engulfed. The first
fall inundated the distant suburbs, gradually extending its area, and beating on the turrets of Saint-Vincent-de-Paul and Saint-Jacques, which
glistened in the rain. Then two other downpours, following in hot haste
one upon the other, streamed over Montmartre and the Champs-Elysees. At times a glimpse could be obtained of the glass roof of the
Palace of Industry, steaming, as it were, under the splashing water; of
Saint-Augustin, whose cupola swam in a kind of fog like a clouded
moon; of the Madeleine, which spread out its flat roof, looking like
some ancient court whose flagstones had been freshly scoured; while,
in the rear, the huge mass of the Opera House made one think of a dis-
masted vessel, which with its hull caught between two rocks, was re-
sisting the assaults of the tempest.

On the left bank of the Seine, also hidden by a watery veil, you perceived the dome of the Invalides, the spires of Sainte-Clotilde, and the
towers of Saint-Sulpice, apparently melting away in the moist atmosphere. Another cloud spread out, and from the colonnade of the Pantheon sheets of water streamed down, threatening to inundate what lay
below. And from that moment the rain fell upon the city in all directions; one might have imagined that the heavens were precipitating
themselves on the earth; streets vanished, sank into the depths, and
men reappeared, drifting on the surface, amidst shocks whose violence
seemed to foretell the end of the city. A prolonged roar ascended—
the roar of all the water rushing along the gutters and falling into the

drains. And at last, above muddy-looking Paris, which had assumed with the showers a dingy-yellow hue, the livid clouds spread themselves out in uniform fashion, without stain or rift. The rain was becoming finer, and was falling sharply and vertically; but whenever the wind again rose, the grey hatching was curved into mighty waves, and the raindrops, driven almost horizontally, could be heard lashing the walls with a hissing sound, till, with the fall of the wind, they again fell vertically, peppering the soil with a quiet obstinacy, from the heights of Passy away to the level plain of Charenton. Then the vast city, as though overwhelmed and lifeless after some awful convulsion, seemed but an expanse of stony ruins under the invisible heavens.

Jeanne, who had sunk down by the window, had wailed out once more, "Mamma! mamma!" A terrible weariness deprived her limbs of their strength as she lingered there, face to face with the engulfing of Paris. Amidst her exhaustion, whilst the breeze played with her tresses, and her face remained wet with rain, she preserved some taste of the bitter pleasure which had made her shiver, while within her heart there was a consciousness of some irretrievable woe. Everything seemed to her to have come to an end; she realized that she was getting very old. The hours might pass away, but now she did not even cast a glance into the room. It was all the same to her to be forgotten and alone. Such despair possessed the child's heart that all around her seemed black. If she were scolded, as of old, when she was ill, it would surely be very wrong. She was burning with fever; something like a sick headache was weighing on her. Surely too, but a moment ago, something had snapped within her. She could not prevent it; she must inevitably submit to whatever might be her fate. Besides, weariness was prostrating her. She had joined her hands over the window-bar, on which she rested her head, and, though at times she opened her eyes to gaze at the rain, drowsiness was stealing over her.

And still and ever the rain kept beating down; the livid sky seemed dissolving in water. A final blast of wind had passed by; a monotonous roar could be heard. Amidst a solemn quiescence the sovereign rain poured unceasingly upon the silent, deserted city it had conquered; and behind this sheet of streaked crystal Paris showed like some phantom place, with quivering outlines, which seemed to be melting away. To Jeanne the scene now brought nothing beyond sleepiness and horrid dreams, as though all the mystery and unknown evil were rising up in vapor to pierce her through and make her cough. Every time she opened her eyes she was seized with a fit of coughing, and would remain for a few seconds looking at the scene; which as her head fell back once more, clung to her mind, and seemed to spread over her and crush her.

The rain was still falling. What hour might it be now? Jeanne could not have told. Perhaps the clock had ceased going. It seemed to her too great a fatigue to turn round. It was surely at least a week since her mother had quitted her. She had abandoned all expectation of her return; she was resigned to the prospect of never seeing her again. Then she became oblivious of everything—the wrongs which had been done her, the pain which she had just experienced, even the loneliness in which she was suffered to remain. A weight, chilly like stone, fell upon her. This only was certain: she was very unhappy—ah! as unhappy as the poor little waifs to whom she gave alms as they huddled together in gateways. Ah! Heaven! how coughing racked one, and how penetrating was the cold when there was no nobody to love one! She closed her heavy eyelids, succumbing to a feverish stupor; and the last of her thoughts was a vague memory of childhood, of a visit to a mill, full of yellow wheat, and of tiny grains slipping under millstones as huge as houses.

Hours and hours passed away; each minute was a century. The rain beat down without ceasing, with ever the same tranquil flow, as though all time and eternity were allowed it to deluge the plain. Jeanne had fallen asleep. Close by, her doll still sat astride the iron window-bar; and, with its legs in the room and its head outside, its nightdress clinging to its rosy skin, its eyes glaring, and its hair streaming with water, it looked not unlike a drowned child; and so emaciated did it appear in its comical yet distressing posture of death, that it almost brought tears of pity to the eyes. Jeanne coughed in her sleep; but now she never once opened her eyes. Her head swayed to and fro on her crossed arms, and the cough spent itself in a wheeze without awakening her. Nothing more existed for her. She slept in the darkness. She did not even withdraw her hand, from whose cold, red fingers bright raindrops were trickling one by one into the vast expanse which lay beneath the window. This went on for hours and hours. Paris was slowly waning on the horizon, like some phantom city; heaven and earth mingled together in an indistinguishable jumble; and still and ever with unflagging persistency did the grey rain fall.

CHAPTER XXI.

Night had long gathered in when Helene returned. From her umbrella the water dripped on step after step, whilst clinging to the balusters she ascended the staircase. She stood for a few seconds outside her door to regain her breath; the deafening rush of the rain still sounded in her ears; she still seemed to feel the jostling of hurrying foot-passengers, and to see the reflections from the street-lamps dancing in the puddles. She was walking in a dream, filled with the surprise of the kisses that had been showered upon her; and as she fumbled for her key she believed that her bosom felt neither remorse nor joy. Circumstances had compassed it all; she could have done naught to prevent it. But the key was not to be found; it was doubtless inside, in the pocket of her other gown. At this discovery her vexation was intense; it seemed as though she were denied admission to her own home. It became necessary that she should ring the bell.

"Oh! it's madame!" exclaimed Rosalie as she opened the door. "I was beginning to feel uneasy."

She took the umbrella, intending to place it in the kitchen sink, and then rattled on:

"Good gracious! what torrents! Zephyrin, who has just come, was drenched to the skin. I took the liberty, madame, of keeping him to dinner. He has leave till ten o'clock."

Helene followed her mechanically. She felt a desire to look once more on everything in her home before removing her bonnet.

"You have done quite right, my girl," she answered.

For a moment she lingered on the kitchen threshold, gazing at the bright fire. Then she instinctively opened the door of a cupboard, and promptly shut it again. Everything was in its place, chairs and tables alike; she found them all again, and their presence gave her pleasure.

Zephyrin had, in the meantime, struggled respectfully to his feet. She nodded to him, smiling.

"I didn't know whether to put the roast on," began the maid.

"Why, what time is it?" asked Helene.

"Oh, it's close on seven o'clock, madame."

"What! seven o'clock!"

Astonishment riveted her to the floor; she had lost all consciousness of time, and seemed to awaken from a dream.

"And where's Jeanne?" she asked.

"Oh! she has been very good, madame. I even think she must have fallen asleep, for I haven't heard her for some time."

"Haven't you given her a light?"

Embarrassment closed Rosalie's lips; she was unwilling to relate that Zephyrin had brought her some pictures which had engrossed her attention. Mademoiselle had never made the least stir, so she could scarcely have wanted anything. Helene, however, paid no further heed to her, but ran into the room, where a dreadful chill fell upon her.

"Jeanne! Jeanne!" she called.

No answer broke the stillness. She stumbled against an arm-chair. From the dining-room, the door of which she had left ajar, some light streamed across a corner of the carpet. She felt a shiver come over her, and she could have declared that the rain was falling in the room, with its moist breath and continuous streaming. Then, on turning her head, she at once saw the pale square formed by the open window and the gloomy grey of the sky.

"Who can have opened this window?" she cried. "Jeanne! Jeanne!"

Still no answering word. A mortal terror fell on Helene's heart. She must look out of this window; but as she felt her way towards it, her hands lighted on a head of hair—it was Jeanne's. And then, as Rosalie entered with a lamp, the child appeared with blanched face, sleeping with her cheek upon her crossed arms, while the big raindrops from the roof splashed upon her. Her breathing was scarcely perceptible, so overcome she was with despair and fatigue. Among the lashes of her large, bluey eyelids there were still two heavy tears.

"The unhappy child!" stammered Helene. "Oh, heavens! she's icy cold! To fall asleep there, at such a time, when she had been expressly forbidden to touch the window! Jeanne, Jeanne, speak to me; wake up, Jeanne!"

Rosalie had prudently vanished. The child, on being raised in her mother's embrace, let her head drop as though she were unable to shake off the leaden slumber that had seized upon her. At last, however, she raised her eyelids; but the glare of the lamp dazzled her, and she remained benumbed and stupid.

"Jeanne, it's I! What's wrong with you? See, I've just come back," said Helene.

But the child seemingly failed to understand her; in her stupefaction she could only murmur: "Oh! Ah!"

She gazed inquiringly at her mother, as though she failed to recognize her. And suddenly she shivered, growing conscious of the cold air of the room. Her memory was awakening, and the tears rolled from her eyelids to her cheeks. Then she commenced to struggle, in the evident desire to be left alone.

"It's you, it's you! Oh, leave me; you hold me too tight! I was so comfortable."

She slipped from her mother's arms with affright in her face. Her uneasy looks wandered from Helene's hands to her shoulders; one of those hands was ungloved, and she started back from the touch of the moist palm and warm fingers with a fierce resentment, as though fleeing from some stranger's caress. The old perfume of vervain had died away; Helene's fingers had surely become greatly attenuated, and her hand was unusually soft. This skin was no longer hers, and its touch exasperated Jeanne.

"Come, I'm not angry with you," pleaded Helene. "But, indeed, have you behaved well? Come and kiss me."

Jeanne, however, still recoiled from her. She had no remembrance of having seen her mother dressed in that gown or cloak. Besides, she looked so wet and muddy. Where had she come from dressed in that dowdy style.

"Kiss me, Jeanne," repeated Helene.

But her voice also seemed strange; in Jeanne's ears it sounded louder. Her old heartache came upon her once more, as when an injury had been done her; and unnerved by the presence of what was unknown and horrible to her, divining, however, that she was breathing an atmosphere of falsehood, she burst into sobs.

"No, no, I entreat you! You left me all alone; and oh! I've been so miserable!"

"But I'm back again, my darling. Don't weep any more; I've come home!"

"Oh no, no! it's all over now! I don't wish for you any more! Oh, I waited and waited, and have been so wretched!"

Helene took hold of the child again, and gently sought to draw her to her bosom; but she resisted stubbornly, plaintively exclaiming:

"No, no; it will never be the same! You are not the same!"

"What! What are you talking of, child?"

"I don't know; you are not the same."

"Do you mean to say that I don't love you any more?"

"I don't know; you are no longer the same! Don't say no. You don't feel the same! It's all over, over, over. I wish to die!"

With blanching face Helene again clasped her in her arms. Did her looks, then, reveal her secret? She kissed her, but a shudder ran through the child's frame, and an expression of such misery crept into her face that Helene forbore to print a second kiss upon her brow. She still kept hold of her, but neither of them uttered a word. Jeanne's sobbing fell to a whisper, a nervous revolt stiffening her limbs the while. Helene's first thought was that much notice ought not to be paid to a child's whims; but to her heart there stole a feeling of secret shame, and the weight of her daughter's body on her shoulder brought a blush to her cheeks. She hastened to put Jeanne down, and each felt relieved.

"Now, be good, and wipe your eyes," said Helene. "We'll make everything all right."

The child acquiesced in all gentleness, but seemed somewhat afraid and glanced covertly at her mother. All at once her frame was shaken by a fit of coughing.

"Good heavens! why, you've made yourself ill now! I cannot stay away from you a moment. Did you feel cold?

"Yes, mamma; in the back."

"See here; put on this shawl. The dining-room stove is lighted, and you'll soon feel warm. Are you hungry?"

Jeanne hesitated. It was on the tip of her tongue to speak the truth and say no; but she darted a side glance at her mother, and, recoiling, answered in a whisper: "Yes, mamma."

"Ah, well, it will be all right," exclaimed Helene, desirous of tranquillizing herself. "Only, I entreat you, you naughty child, don't frighten me like this again."

On Rosalie re-entering the room to announce that dinner was ready, Helene severely scolded her. The little maid's head drooped; she stammered out that it was all very true, for she ought to have looked better after mademoiselle. Then, hoping to mollify her mistress, she busied herself in helping her to change her clothes. "Good gracious! madame was in a fine state!" she remarked, as she assisted in removing each mud-stained garment, at which Jeanne glared suspiciously, still racked by torturing thoughts.

"Madame ought to feel comfortable now," exclaimed Rosalie when it was all over. "It's awfully nice to get into dry clothes after a drenching."

Helene, on finding herself once more in her blue dressing-gown, gave vent to a slight sigh, as though a new happiness had welled up within her. She again regained her old cheerfulness; she had rid herself of a burden in throwing off those bedraggled garments. She washed her face and hands; and while she stood there, still glistening with moisture, her dressing-gown buttoned up to her chin, she was slowly approached by Jeanne, who took one of her hands and kissed it.

At table, however, not a word passed between mother and daughter. The fire flared with a merry roar, and there was a look of happiness about the little dining-room, with its bright mahogany and gleaming china. But the old stupor which drove away all thought seemed to have again fallen on Helene; she ate mechanically, though with an appearance of appetite. Jeanne sat facing her, and quietly watched her over her glass, noting each of her movements. But all at once the child again coughed, and her mother, who had become unconscious of her presence, immediately displayed lively concern.

"Why, you're coughing again! Aren't you getting warm?"

"Oh, yes, mamma; I'm very warm."

Helene leaned towards her to feel her hand and ascertain whether she was speaking the truth. Only then did she perceive that her plate was still full.

"Why, you said you were hungry. Don't you like what you have there?"

"Oh, yes, mamma; I'm eating away."

With an effort Jeanne swallowed a mouthful. Helene looked at her for a time, but soon again began dreaming of the fatal room which she had come from. It did not escape the child that her mother took little interest in her now. As the dinner came to an end, her poor wearied frame sank down on the chair, and she sat there like some bent, aged woman, with the dim eyes of one of those old maids for whom love is past and gone.

"Won't mademoiselle have any jam?" asked Rosalie. "If not, can I remove the cloth?"

Helene still sat there with far-away looks.

"Mamma, I'm sleepy," exclaimed Jeanne in a changed voice. "Will you let me go to bed? I shall feel better in bed."

Once more her mother seemed to awake with a start to consciousness of her surroundings.

"You are suffering, my darling! where do you feel the pain? Tell me."

"No, no; I told you I'm all right! I'm sleepy, and it's already time for me to go to bed."

She left her chair and stood up, as though to prove that there was no illness threatening her: but her benumbed feet tottered over the floor on her way to the bedroom. She leaned against the furniture, and her hardihood was such that not a tear came from her, despite the feverish fire darting through her frame. Her mother followed to assist her to bed; but the child had displayed such haste in undressing herself that she only arrived in time to tie up her hair for the night. Without need of any helping hand Jeanne slipped between the sheets, and quickly closed her eyes.

"Are you comfortable?" asked Helene, as she drew up the bed-clothes and carefully tucked her in.

"Yes, quite comfortable. Leave me alone, and don't disturb me. Take away the lamp."

Her only yearning was to be alone in the darkness, that she might reopen her eyes and chew the cud of her sorrows, with no one near to watch her. When the light had been carried away, her eyes opened quite wide.

Nearby, in the meantime, Helene was pacing up and down her room. She was seized with a wondrous longing to be up and moving about; the idea of going to bed seemed to her insufferable. She glanced at the clock —twenty minutes to nine; what was she to do? she rummaged about in a drawer, but forgot what she was seeking for. Then she wandered to her bookshelves, glancing aimlessly over the books; but the very reading of the titles wearied her. A buzzing sprang up in her ears with the room's stillness; the loneliness, the heavy atmosphere, were as an agony to her. She would fain have had some bustle going on around her, have had someone there to speak to—something, in short, to draw her from herself. She twice listened at the door of Jeanne's little room, from which, however, not even a sound of breathing came. Everything was quiet; so she turned back once more, and amused herself by taking up and replacing whatever came to her hand. Then suddenly the thought flashed across her mind that Zephyrin must still be with Rosalie. It was a relief to her; she was delighted at the idea of not being alone, and stepped in her slippers towards the kitchen.

She was already in the ante-room, and was opening the glass door of the inner passage, when she detected the re-echoing clap of a swinging box on the ears, and the next moment Rosalie could be heard exclaiming:

"Ha, ha! you think you'll nip me again, do you? Take your paws off!"

"Oh! that's nothing, my charmer!" exclaimed Zephyrin in his husky, guttural voice. "That's to show how I love you—in this style, you know—"

But at that moment the door creaked, and Helene, entering, discovered the diminutive soldier and the servant maid seated very quietly at table, with their noses bent over their plates. They had assumed an air of complete indifference; their innocence was certain. Yet their faces were red with blushes, and their eyes aflame, and they wriggled restlessly on their straw-bottomed chairs. Rosalie started up and hurried forward.

"Madame wants something?"

Helene had no pretext ready to her tongue. She had come to see them, to chat with them, and have their company. However, she felt a sudden shame, and dared not say that she required nothing.

"Have you any hot water?" she asked, after a silence.

"No, madame; and my fire is nearly out. Oh, but it doesn't matter; I'll give you some in five minutes. It boils in no time."

She threw on some charcoal, and then set the kettle in place; but seeing that her mistress still lingered in the doorway, she said:

"I'll bring the water to you in five minutes, madame."

Helene responded with a wave of the hand.

"I'm not in a hurry for it; I'll wait. Don't disturb yourself, my girl; eat away, eat away. There's a lad who'll have to go back to barracks."

Rosalie thereupon sat down again. Zephyrin, who had also been standing, made a military salute, and returned to the cutting of his meat, with his elbows projecting as though to show that he knew how to conduct himself at table. Thus eating together, after madame had finished dinner, they did not even draw the table into the middle of the kitchen, but contented themselves with sitting side by side, with their noses turned towards the wall. A glorious prospect of stewpans was before them. A bunch of laurel and thyme hung near, and a spice-box exhaled a piquant perfume. Around them—the kitchen was not yet tidied—was all the litter of the things cleared away from the dining-room; however, the spot seemed a charming one to these hungry sweethearts, and especially to Zephyrin, who here feasted on such things as were never seen within the walls of his barracks. The predominant odor was one of roast meat, seasoned with a dash of vinegar—the vinegar of the salad. In the copper pans and iron pots the reflected light from the gas was dancing; and as the heat of the fire was beyond endurance, they had set the window ajar, and a cool breeze blew in from the garden, stirring the blue cotton curtain.

"Must you be in by ten o'clock exactly?" asked Helene.

"I must, madame, with all deference to you," answered Zephyrin.

"Well, it's along way off. Do you take the "bus'?"

"Oh, yes, madame, sometimes. But you see a good swinging walk is much the best."

She had taken a step into the kitchen, and leaning against the dresser, her arms dangling and her hands clasped over her dressing-gown, she began gossiping away about the wretched weather they had had that day, about the food which was rationed out in barracks, and the high price of eggs. As soon, however, as she had asked a question and their answer had been given the conversation abruptly fell. They experienced some discomfort with her standing thus behind their backs. They did not turn round, but spoke into their plates, their shoulders bent beneath her gaze, while, to conform to propriety, each mouthful they swallowed was as small as possible. On the other hand, Helene had now regained her tranquility, and felt quite happy there.

"Don't fret, madame," said Rosalie; "the kettle is singing already. I wish the fire would only burn up a little better!"

She wanted to see to it, but Helene would not allow her to disturb herself. It would be all right by-and-by. An intense weariness now pervaded the young woman's limbs. Almost mechanically she crossed the kitchen and approached the window, where she observed the third chair, which was very high, and when turned over became a stepladder. However, she did not sit down on it at once, for she had caught sight of a number of pictures heaped up on a corner of the table.

"Dear me!" she exclaimed, as she took them in her hand, inspired with the wish of gratifying Zephyrin.

The little soldier gaped with a silent chuckle. His face beamed with smiles, and his eyes followed each picture, his head wagging whenever something especially lovely was being examined by madame.

"That one there," he suddenly remarked, "I found in the Rue du Temple. She's a beautiful woman, with flowers in her basket."

Helene sat down and inspected the beautiful woman who decorated the gilt and varnished lid of a box of lozenges, every stain on which had been carefully wiped off by Zephyrin. On the chair a dishcloth was hanging, and she could not well lean back. She flung it aside, however, and once more lapsed into her dreaming. Then the two sweethearts remarked madame's good nature, and their restraint vanished— in the end, indeed, her very presence was forgotten by them. One by one the pictures had dropped from her hands on to her knees, and, with a vague smile playing on her face, she examined the sweethearts and listened to their talk.

"I say, my dear," whispered the girl, "won't you have some more mutton?"

He answered neither yes nor no, but swung backwards and forwards on his chair as though he had been tickled, then contentedly stretched himself, while she placed a thick slice on his plate. His red epaulets moved up and down, and his bullet-shaped head, with its huge projecting ears, swayed to and fro over his yellow collar as though it were the head of some Chinese idol. His laughter ran all over him, and he was almost bursting inside his tunic, which he did not unbutton, however, out of respect for madame.

"This is far better than old Rouvet's radishes!" he exclaimed at last, with his mouth full.

This was a reminiscence of their country home; and at thought of it they both burst into immoderate laughter. Rosalie even had to hold on to the table to prevent herself from falling. One day, before their first communion, it seemed, Zephyrin had filched three black radishes from old Rouvet. They were very tough radishes indeed—tough enough to break one's teeth; but Rosalie all the same had crunched her share of the spoil at the back of the schoolhouse. Hence it was that every time they chanced to be taking a meal together Zephyrin never omitted to ejaculate: "Yes; this is better than old Rouvet's radishes!"

And then Rosalie's laughter would become so violent that nine times out of ten her petticoat-string would give way with an audible crack.

"Hello! has it parted?" asked the little soldier, with triumph in his tone.

But Rosalie responded with a good slap.

"It's disgusting to make me break the string like this!" said she. "I put a fresh one on every week."

However, he came nearer to her, intent on some joke or other, by way of revenging the blow; but with a furious glance she reminded him that her mistress was looking on. This seemed to trouble him but little, for he replied with a rakish wink, as much as to say that no woman, not even a lady, disliked a little fun. To be sure, when folks are sweethearting, other people always like to be looking on.

"You have still five years to serve, haven't you?" asked Helene, leaning back on the high wooden-seated chair, and yielding to a feeling of tenderness.

"Yes, madame; perhaps only four if they don't need me any longer."

It occurred to Rosalie that her mistress was thinking of her marriage, and with assumed anger, she broke in:

"Oh! madame, he can stick in the army for another ten years if he likes! I sha'n't trouble myself to ask the Government for him. He is becoming too much of a rake; yes, I believe he's going to the dogs. Oh! it's useless for you to laugh—that won't take with me. When we go before the mayor to get married, we'll see on whose side the laugh is!"

At this he chuckled all the more, in order that he might show himself a lady-killer before madame, and the maid's annoyance then became real.

"Oh!" said she, "we know all about that! You know, madame, he's still a booby at heart. You've no idea how stupid that uniform makes them all! That's the way he goes on with his comrades; but if I turned him out, you would hear him sobbing on the stairs. Oh, I don't care a fig for you, my lad! Why, whenever I please, won't you always be there to do as I tell you?"

She bent forward to observe him closely; but, on seeing that his good-natured, freckled face was beginning to cloud over, she was suddenly moved, and prattled on, without any seeming transition:

"Ah! I didn't tell you that I've received a letter from auntie. The Guignard lot want to sell their house—aye, and almost for nothing too. We might perhaps be able to take it later on."

"By God!" exclaimed Zephyrin, brightening, "we should be quite at home there. There's room enough for two cows."

With this idea they lapsed into silence. They were now having some dessert. The little soldier licked the jam on his bread with a child's greedy satisfaction, while the servant girl carefully pared an apple with a maternal air.

"Madame!" all at once exclaimed Rosalie, "there's the water boiling now."

Helene, however, never stirred. She felt herself enveloped by an atmosphere of happiness. She gave a continuance to their dreams, and pictured them living in the country in the Guignards' house and possessed of two cows. A smile came to her face as she saw Zephyrin sitting there to all appearance so serious, though in reality he was patting Rosalie's knee under the table, whilst she remained very stiff, affecting an innocent demeanor. Then everything became blurred. Helene lost all definite sense of her surroundings, of the place where she was, and of what had brought her there. The copper pans were flashing on the walls; feelings of tenderness riveted her to the spot; her eyes had a faraway look. She was not affected in any way by the disorderly state of the kitchen; she had no consciousness of having demeaned herself by coming there; all she felt was a deep pleasure, as when a longing has been satisfied. Meantime the heat from the fire was bedewing her pale brow with beads of perspiration, and behind her the wind, coming in through the half-open window, quivered delightfully on her neck.

"Madame, your water is boiling," again said Rosalie. "There will be soon none left in the kettle."

She held the kettle before her, and Helene, for the moment astonished, was forced to rise. "Oh, yes! thank you!"

She no longer had an excuse to remain, and went away slowly and regretfully. When she reached her room she was at a loss what to do with the kettle. Then suddenly within her there came a burst of passionate love. The torpor which had held her in a state of semi-unconsciousness gave way to a wave of glowing feeling, the rush of which thrilled her as with fire. She quivered, and memories returned to her—memories of her passion and of Henri.

While she was taking off her dressing-gown and gazing at her bare arms, a noise broke on her anxious ear. She thought she had heard Jeanne coughing. Taking up the lamp she went into the closet, but found the child with eyelids closed, seemingly fast asleep. However, the moment the mother, satisfied with her examination, had turned her back, Jeanne's eyes again opened widely to watch her as she returned to her room. There was indeed no sleep for Jeanne, nor had she any desire to sleep. A second fit of coughing racked her bosom, but she buried her head beneath the coverlet and stifled every sound. She might go away for ever now; her mother would never miss her. Her eyes were still wide open in the darkness; she knew everything as though knowledge had come with thought, and she was dying of it all, but dying without a murmur.

CHAPTER XXII.

Next day all sorts of practical ideas took possession of Helene's mind. She awoke impressed by the necessity of keeping watch over her happiness, and shuddering with fear lest by some imprudent step she might lose Henri. At this chilly morning hour, when the room still seemed asleep, she felt that she idolized him, loved him with a transport which pervaded her whole being. Never had she experienced such an anxiety to be diplomatic. Her first thought was that she must go to see Juliette that very morning, and thus obviate the need of any tedious explanations or inquiries which might result in ruining everything.

On calling upon Madame Deberle at about nine o'clock she found her already up, with pallid cheeks and red eyes like the heroine of a tragedy. As soon as the poor woman caught sight of her, she threw herself sobbing upon her neck exclaiming that she was her good angel. She didn't love Malignon, not in the least, she swore it! Gracious heavens! what a foolish affair! It would have killed her—there was no doubt of that! She did not now feel herself to be in the least degree qualified for ruses, lies, and agonies, and the tyranny of a sentiment that never varied. Oh, how delightful did it seem to her to find herself free again! She laughed contentedly; but immediately afterwards there was another outburst of tears as she besought her friend not to despise her. Beneath her feverish unrest a fear lingered; she imagined that her husband knew everything. He had come home the night before trembling with agitation. She overwhelmed Helene with questions; and Helene, with a hardihood and facility at which she herself was amazed, poured into her ears a story, every detail of which she invented offhand. She vowed to Juliette that her husband doubted her in nothing. It was she, Helene, who had become acquainted with everything, and, wishing to save her,

had devised that plan of breaking in upon their meeting. Juliette listened to her, put instant credit in the fiction, and, beaming through her
tears, grew sunny with joy. She threw herself once more on Helene's
neck. Her caresses brought no embarrassment to the latter; she now
experienced none of the honorable scruples that had at one time affected her. When she left her lover's wife after extracting a promise
from her that she would try to be calm, she laughed in her sleeve at her
own cunning; she was in a transport of delight.

Some days slipped away. Helene's whole existence had undergone
a change; and in the thoughts of every hour she no longer lived in her
own home, but with Henri. The only thing that existed for her was that
next-door house in which her heart beat. Whenever she could find an
excuse to do so she ran thither, and forgot everything in the content of
breathing the same air as her lover. In her first rapture the sight of Juliette even flooded her with tenderness; for was not Juliette one of
Henri's belongings? He had not, however, again been able to meet her
alone. She appeared loth to give him a second assignation. One evening,
when he was leading her into the hall, she even made him swear that he
would never again visit the house in the Passage des Eaux, as such an
act might compromise her.

Meantime, Jeanne was shaken by a short, dry cough, that never
ceased, but became severer towards evening every day. She would then
be slightly feverish, and she grew weak with the perspiration that bathed
her in her sleep. When her mother cross-questioned her, she answered
that she wasn't ill, that she felt no pain. Doubtless her cold was coming to an end. Helene, tranquillized by the explanation, and having no
adequate idea of what was going on around her, retained, however, in
her bosom, amidst the rapture that made up her life, a vague feeling of
sorrow, of some weight that made her heart bleed despite herself. At
times, when she was plunged in one of those causeless transports which
made her melt with tenderness, an anxious thought would come to
her—she imagined that some misfortune was hovering behind her. She
turned round, however, and then smiled. People are ever in a tremble
when they are too happy. There was nothing there. Jeanne had coughed
a moment before, but she had some *tisane* to drink; there would be no
ill effects.

However, one afternoon old Doctor Bodin, who visited them in
the character of a family friend, prolonged his stay, and stealthily, but

carefully, examined Jeanne with his little blue eyes. He questioned her
as though he were having some fun with her, and on this occasion uttered no warning word. Two days later, however, he made his appearance again; and this time, not troubling to examine Jeanne, he talked
away merrily in the fashion of a man who has seen many years and
many things, and turned the conversation on travelling. He had once
served as a military surgeon; he knew every corner of Italy. It was a
magnificent country, said he, which to be admired ought to be seen in
spring. Why didn't Madame Grandjean take her daughter there? From
this he proceeded by easy transitions to advising a trip to the land of the
sun, as he styled it. Helene's eyes were bent on him fixedly. "No, no,"
he exclaimed, "neither of you is ill! Oh, no, certainly not! Still, a change
of air would mean new strength!" Her face had blanched, a mortal chill
had come over her at the thought of leaving Paris. Gracious heavens!
to go away so far, so far! to lose Henri in a moment, their love to droop
without a morrow! Such was the agony which the thought gave her that
she bent her head towards Jeanne to hide her emotion. Did Jeanne wish
to go away? The child, with a chilly gesture, had intertwined her little
fingers. Oh! yes, she would so like to go! She would so like to go away
into the sunny land, quite alone, she and her mother, quite alone! And
over her poor attenuated face with its cheeks burning with fever, there
swept the bright hope of a new life. But Helene would listen to no
more; indignation and distrust led her to imagine that all of them—the
Abbe, Doctor Bodin, Jeanne herself—were plotting to separate her
from Henri. When the old doctor noticed the pallor of her cheeks, he
imagined that he had not spoken so cautiously as he might have done,
and hastened to declare that there was no hurry, albeit he silently resolved to return to the subject at another time.

It happened that Madame Deberle intended to stop at home that
day. As soon as the doctor had gone Helene hastened to put on her
bonnet. Jeanne, however, refused to quit the house; she felt better beside the fire; she would be very good, and would not open the window.
For some time past she had not teased her mother to be allowed to go
with her; still she gazed after her as she went out with a longing look.
Then, when she found herself alone, she shrunk into her chair and sat
for hours motionless.

"Mamma, is Italy far away?" she asked as Helene glided towards
her to kiss her.

"Oh! very far away, my pet!"

Jeanne clung round her neck, and not letting her rise again at the moment, whispered: "Well, Rosalie could take care of everything here. We should have no need of her. A small travelling-trunk would do for us, you know! Oh! it would be delightful, mother dear! Nobody but us two! I should come back quite plump—like this!"

She puffed out her cheeks and pictured how stout her arms would be. Helene's answer was that she would see; and then she ran off with a final injunction to Rosalie to take good care of mademoiselle.

The child coiled herself up in the chimney-corner, gazing at the ruddy fire and deep in reverie. From time to time she moved her hands forward mechanically to warm them. The glinting of the flames dazzled her large eyes. So absorbed was she in her dreaming that she did not hear Monsieur Rambaud enter the room. His visits had now become very frequent; he came, he would say, in the interests of the poor paralytic woman for whom Doctor Deberle had not yet been able to secure admission into the Hospital for Incurables. Finding Jeanne alone, he took a seat on the other side of the fireplace, and chatted with her as though she were a grown-up person. It was most regrettable; the poor woman had been waiting a week; however, he would go down presently to see the doctor, who might perhaps give him an answer. Meanwhile he did not stir.

"Why hasn't your mother taken you with her?" he asked.

Jeanne shrugged her shoulders with a gesture of weariness. It disturbed her to go about visiting other people. Nothing gave her any pleasure now.

"I am getting old," she added, "and I can't be always amusing myself. Mamma finds entertainment out of doors, and I within; so we are not together."

Silence ensued. The child shivered, and held her hands out towards the fire which burnt steadily with a pinky glare; and, indeed, muffled as she was in a huge shawl, with a silk handkerchief round her neck and another encircling her head, she did look like some old dame. Shrouded in all these wraps, it struck one that she was no larger than an ailing bird, panting amidst its ruffled plumage. Monsieur Rambaud, with hands clasped over his knees, was gazing at the fire. Then, turning towards Jeanne, he inquired if her mother had gone out the evening before. She answered with a nod, yes. And did she go out the evening before that and the previous day? The answer was always yes, given with a nod of the head; her mother quitted her every day.

At this the child and Monsieur Rambaud gazed at one another for a long time, their faces pale and serious, as though they shared some great sorrow. They made no reference to it—a chit like her and an old man could not talk of such a thing together; but they were well aware why they were so sad, and why it was a pleasure to them to sit like this on either side of the fireplace when they were alone in the house. It was a comfort beyond telling. They loved to be near one another that their forlornness might pain them less. A wave of tenderness poured into their hearts; they would fain have embraced and wept together.

"You are cold, my dear old friend, I'm certain of it," said Jeanne; "come nearer the fire."

"No, no, my darling; I'm not cold."

"Oh! you're telling a fib; your hands are like ice! Come nearer, or I shall get vexed."

It was now his turn to display his anxious care.

"I could lay a wager they haven't left you any drink. I'll run and make some for you; would you like it? Oh! I'm a good hand at making it. You would see, if I were your nurse, you wouldn't be without anything you wanted."

He did not allow himself any more explicit hint. Jeanne somewhat sharply declared she was disgusted with *tisane*; she was compelled to drink too much of it. However, now and then she would allow Monsieur Rambaud to flutter round her like a mother; he would slip a pillow under her shoulders, give her the medicine that she had almost forgotten, or carry her into the bedroom in his arms. These little acts of devotion thrilled both with tenderness. As Jeanne eloquently declared with her sombre eyes, whose flashes disturbed the old man so sorely, they were playing the parts of the father and the little girl while her mother was absent. Then, however, sadness would all at once fall upon them; their talk died away, and they glanced at one another stealthily with pitying looks.

That afternoon, after a lengthy silence, the child asked the question which she had already put to her mother: "Is Italy far away?"

"Oh! I should think so," replied Monsieur Rambaud. "It's away over yonder, on the other side of Marseilles, a deuce of a distance! Why do you ask me such a question?"

"Oh! because—" she began gravely. But she burst into loud complaints at her ignorance. She was always ill, and she had never been sent to school. Then they both became silent again, lulled into forgetfulness by the intense heat of the fire.

In the meantime Helene had found Madame Deberle and her sister Pauline in the Japanese pavilion where they so frequently whiled away the afternoon. Inside it was very warm, a heating apparatus filled it with a stifling atmosphere.

The large windows were shut, and a full view could be had of the little garden, which, in its winter guise, looked like some large sepia drawing, finished with exquisite delicacy, the little black branches of the trees showing clear against the brown earth. The two sisters were carrying on a sharp controversy.

"Now, be quiet, do!" exclaimed Juliette; "it is evidently our interest to support Turkey."

"Oh! I've had a talk about it with a Russian," replied Pauline, who was equally excited. "We are much liked at St. Petersburg, and it is only there that we can find our proper allies."

Juliette's face assumed a serious look, and, crossing her arms, she exclaimed: "Well, and what will you do with the balance of power in Europe?"

The Eastern crisis was the absorbing topic in Paris at that moment; it was the stock subject of conversation, and no woman who pretended to any position could speak with propriety of anything else. Thus, for two days past, Madame Deberle had with passionate fervor devoted herself to foreign politics. Her ideas were very pronounced on the various eventualities which might arise; and Pauline greatly annoyed her by her eccentricity in advocating Russia's cause in opposition to the clear interests of France. Juliette's first desire was to convince her of her folly, but she soon lost her temper.

"Pooh! hold your tongue; you are talking foolishly! Now, if you had only studied the matter carefully with me—"

But she broke off to greet Helene, who entered at this moment.

"Good-day, my dear! It is very kind of you to call. I don't suppose you have any news. This morning's paper talked of an ultimatum. There has been a very exciting debate in the English House of Commons!"

"No, I don't know anything," answered Helene, who was astounded by the question. "I go out so little!"

However, Juliette had not waited for her reply, but was busy explaining to Pauline why it was necessary to neutralize the Black Sea; and her talk bristled with references to English and Russian generals, whose names she mentioned in a familiar way and with faultless pronunciation. However, Henri now made his appearance with several newspapers in his hand. Helene at once realized that he had come there for her sake; for their eyes had sought one another and exchanged a long, meaning glance. And when their hands met it was in a prolonged and silent clasp that told how the personality of each was lost in the other.

"Is there anything in the papers?" asked Juliette feverishly.

"In the papers, my dear?" repeated the doctor; "no there's never anything."

For a time the Eastern Question dropped into the background. There were frequent allusions to someone whom they were expecting, but who did not make his appearance. Pauline remarked that it would soon be three o'clock. Oh he would come, declared Madame Deberle; he had given such a definite promise; but she never hinted at any name. Helene listened without understanding; things which had no connection with Henri did not in the least interest her. She no longer brought her work when she now came down into the garden; and though her visits would last a couple of hours, she would take no part in the conversation, for her mind was ever filled with the same childish dream wherein all others miraculously vanished, and she was left alone with him. However, she managed to reply to Juliette's questions, while Henri's eyes, riveted on her own, thrilled her with a delicious languor. At last he stepped behind her with the intention of pulling up one of the blinds, and she fully divined that he had come to ask another meeting, for she noticed the tremor that seized him when he brushed against her hair.

"There's a ring at the bell; that must be he!" suddenly exclaimed Pauline.

Then the faces of the two sisters assumed an air of indifference. It was Malignon who made his appearance, dressed with greater care than ever, and having a somewhat serious look. He shook hands; but eschewed his customary jocularity, thus returning, in a ceremonious manner, to this house where for some time he had not shown his face.

While the doctor and Pauline were expostulating with him on the rarity of his visits, Juliette bent down and whispered to Helene, who, despite her supreme indifference, was overcome with astonishment:

"Ah! you are surprised? Dear me! I am not angry with him at all! he's such a good fellow at heart that nobody could long be angry with him! Just fancy! he has unearthed a husband for Pauline. It's splendid, isn't it?"

"Oh! no doubt," answered Helene complaisantly.

"Yes, one of his friends, immensely rich, who did not think of getting married, but whom he has sworn to bring here! We were waiting for him to-day to have some definite reply. So, as you will understand, I had to pass over a lot of things. Oh! there's no danger now; we know one another thoroughly."

Her face beamed with a pretty smile, and she blushed slightly at the memories she conjured up; but she soon turned round and took possession of Malignon. Helene likewise smiled. These accommodating circumstances in life seemed to her sufficient excuse for her own delinquencies. It was absurd to think of tragic melodramas; no, everything wound up with universal happiness. However, while she had thus been indulging in the cowardly, but pleasing, thought that nothing was absolutely indefensible, Juliette and Pauline had opened the door of the pavilion, and were now dragging Malignon in their train into the garden. And, all at once, Helene heard Henri speaking to her in a low and passionate voice:

"I beseech you, Helene! Oh! I beseech you—"

She started to her feet, and gazed around her with sudden anxiety. They were quite alone; she could see the three others walking slowly along one of the walks. Henri was bold enough to lay his hand on her shoulder, and she trembled as she felt its pressure.

"As you wish," she stammered, knowing full well what question it was that he desired to ask.

Then, hurriedly, they exchanged a few words.

"At the house in the Passage des Eaux," said he.

"No, it is impossible—I have explained to you, and you swore to me—"

"Well, wherever you like, so that I may see you! In your own house—this evening. Shall I call?"

The idea was repellant to her. But she could only refuse with a sign, for fear again came upon her as she observed the two ladies and Malignon returning. Madame Deberle had taken the young man away under pretext of showing him some clumps of violets which were in full blossom notwithstanding the cold weather. Hastening her steps, she entered the pavilion before the others, her face illumined by a smile.

"It's all arranged," she exclaimed.

"What's all arranged?" asked Helene, who was still trembling with excitement and had forgotten everything.

"Oh, that marriage! What a riddance! Pauline was getting a bit of a nuisance. However, the young man has seen her and thinks her charming! To-morrow we're all going to dine with papa. I could have embraced Malignon for his good news!"

With the utmost self-possession Henri had contrived to put some distance between Helene and himself. He also expressed his sense of Malignon's favor, and seemed to share his wife's delight at the prospect of seeing their little sister settled at last. Then he turned to Helene, and informed her that she was dropping one of her gloves. She thanked him. They could hear Pauline laughing and joking in the garden. She was leaning towards Malignon, murmuring broken sentences in his ear, and bursting into loud laughter as he gave her whispered answers. No doubt he was chatting to her confidentially about her future husband. Standing near the open door of the pavilion, Helene meanwhile inhaled the cold air with delight.

It was at this moment that in the bedroom up above a silence fell on Jeanne and Monsieur Rambaud, whom the intense heat of the fire filled with languor. The child woke up from the long-continued pause with a sudden suggestion which seemed to be the outcome of her dreamy fit:

"Would you like to go into the kitchen? We'll see if we can get a glimpse of mamma!"

"Very well; let us go," replied Monsieur Rambaud.

Jeanne felt stronger that day, and reaching the kitchen without any assistance pressed her face against a windowpane. Monsieur Rambaud also gazed into the garden. The trees were bare of foliage, and through the large transparent windows of the Japanese pavilion they could make out every detail inside. Rosalie, who was busy attending to the soup, reproached mademoiselle with being inquisitive. But the child had caught sight of her mother's dress; and pointed her out, whilst flattening her face against the glass to obtain a better view. Pauline meanwhile looked up, and nodded vigorously. Then Helene also made her appearance, and signed to the child to come down.

"They have seen you, mademoiselle," said the servant girl. "They want you to go down."

Monsieur Rambaud opened the window, and every one called to him to carry Jeanne downstairs. Jeanne, however, vanished into her room, and vehemently refused to go, accusing her worthy friend of having purposely tapped on the window. It was a great pleasure to her to look at her mother, but she stubbornly declared she would not go near that house; and to all Monsieur Rambaud's questions and entreaties she would only return a stern "Because!" which was meant to explain everything.

"It is not you who ought to force me," she said at last, with a gloomy look.

But he told her that she would grieve her mother very much, and that it was not right to insult other people. He would muffle her up well, she would not catch cold; and, so saying, he wound the shawl round her body, and taking the silk handkerchief from her head, set a knitted hood in its place. Even when she was ready, however, she still protested her unwillingness; and when in the end she allowed him to carry her down, it was with the express proviso that he would take her up again the moment she might feel poorly. The porter opened the door by which the two houses communicated, and when they entered the garden they were hailed with exclamations of joy. Madame Deberle, in particular, displayed a vast amount of affection for Jeanne; she ensconced her in a chair near the stove, and desired that the windows might be closed, for the air she declared was rather sharp for the dear child. Malignon had now left. As Helene began smoothing the child's dishevelled hair, somewhat ashamed to see her in company muffled up in a shawl and a hood, Juliette burst out in protest:

"Leave her alone! Aren't we all at home here? Poor Jeanne! we are glad to have her!"

She rang the bell, and asked if Miss Smithson and Lucien had returned from their daily walk. No, they had not yet returned. It was just as well, she declared; Lucien was getting beyond control, and only the night before had made the five Levasseur girls sob with grief.

"Would you like to play at *pigeon vole*?" asked Pauline, who seemed to have lost her head with the thought of her impending marriage. "That wouldn't tire you."

But Jeanne shook her head in refusal. Beneath their drooping lids her eyes wandered over the persons who surrounded her. The doctor had just informed Monsieur Rambaud that admission to the Hospital for Incurables had been secured for his *protegee*, and in a burst of emotion the worthy man clasped his hands as though some great personal favor had been conferred on him. They were all lounging on their chairs, and the conversation became delightfully friendly. Less effort was shown in following up remarks, and there were at times intervals of silence. While Madame Deberle and her sister were busily engaged in discussion, Helene said to the two men:

"Doctor Bodin has advised us to go to Italy."

"Ah! that is why Jeanne was questioning me!" exclaimed Monsieur Rambaud. "Would it give you any pleasure to go away there?"

Without vouchsafing any answer, the child clasped her little hands upon her bosom, while her pale face flushed with joy. Then, stealthily, and with some fear, she looked towards the doctor; it was he, she understood it, whom her mother was consulting. He started slightly, but retained all his composure. Suddenly, however, Juliette joined in the conversation, wishing, as usual, to have her finger in every pie.

"What's that? Are you talking about Italy? Didn't you say you had an idea of going to Italy? Well, it's a droll coincidence! Why, this very morning, I was teasing Henri to take me to Naples! Just fancy, for ten years now I have been dreaming of seeing Naples! Every spring he promises to take me there, but he never keeps his word!"

"I didn't tell you that I would not go," murmured the doctor.

"What! you didn't tell me? Why, you refused flatly, with the excuse that you could not leave your patients!"

Jeanne was listening eagerly. A deep wrinkle now furrowed her pale brow, and she began twisting her fingers mechanically one after the other.

"Oh! I could entrust my patients for a few weeks to the care of a brother-physician," explained the doctor. "That's to say, if I thought it would give you so much pleasure—"

"Doctor," interrupted Helene, "are you also of opinion that such a journey would benefit Jeanne?"

"It would be the very thing; it would thoroughly restore her to health. Children are always the better for a change."

"Oh! then," exclaimed Juliette, "we can take Lucien, and we can all go together. That will be pleasant, won't it?"

"Yes, indeed; I'll do whatever you wish," he answered, smiling.

Jeanne lowered her face, wiped two big tears of passionate anger and grief from her eyes, and fell back in her chair as though she would fain hear and see no more; while Madame Deberle, filled with ecstasy by the idea of such unexpected pleasure, began chattering noisily. Oh! how kind her husband was! She kissed him for his self-sacrifice. Then, without the loss of a moment, she busied herself with sketching the necessary preparations. They would start the very next week. Goodness gracious! she would never have time to get everything ready! Next she wanted to draw out a plan of their tour; they would need to visit this and that town certainly; they could stay a week at Rome; they must stop at a little country place that Madame de Guiraud had mentioned to her; and she wound up by engaging in a lively discussion with Pauline, who was eager that they should postpone their departure till such time as she could accompany them with her husband.

"Not a bit of it!" exclaimed Juliette; "the wedding can take place when we come back."

Jeanne's presence had been wholly forgotten. Her eyes were riveted on her mother and the doctor. The proposed journey, indeed, now offered inducements to Helene, as it must necessarily keep Henri near her. In fact, a keen delight filled her heart at the thought of journeying together through the land of the sun, living side by side, and profiting by the hours of freedom. Round her lips wreathed a smile of happy relief; she had so greatly feared that she might lose him; and deemed herself fortunate in the thought that she would carry her love along with her. While Juliette was discoursing of the scenes they would travel through, both Helene and Henri, indeed, indulged in the dream that they were already strolling through a fairy land of perennial spring, and each told the other with a look that their passion would reign there, aye, wheresoever they might breathe the same air.

In the meantime, Monsieur Rambaud, who with unconscious sadness had slowly lapsed into silence, observed Jeanne's evident discomfort.

"Aren't you well, my darling?" he asked in a whisper.

"No! I'm quite ill! Carry me up again, I implore you."

"But we must tell your mamma."

"Oh, no, no! mamma is busy; she hasn't any time to give to us. Carry me up, oh! carry me up again."

He took her in his arms, and told Helene that the child felt tired. In answer she requested him to wait for her in her rooms; she would hasten after them. The little one, though light as a feather, seemed to slip from his grasp, and he was forced to come to a standstill on the second landing. She had leaned her head against his shoulder, and each gazed into the other's face with a look of grievous pain. Not a sound broke upon the chill silence of the staircase. Then in a low whisper he asked her:

"You're pleased, aren't you, to go to Italy?"

But she thereupon burst into sobs, declaring in broken words that she no longer had any craving to go, and would rather die in her own room. Oh! she would not go, she would fall ill, she knew it well. She would go nowhere—nowhere. They could give her little shoes to the poor. Then amidst tears she whispered to him:

"Do you remember what you asked me one night?"

"What was it, my pet?"

"To stay with mamma always—always—always! Well, if you wish so still, I wish so too!"

The tears welled into Monsieur Rambaud's eyes. He kissed her lovingly, while she added in a still lower tone:

"You are perhaps vexed by my getting so angry over it. I didn't understand, you know. But it's you whom I want! Oh! say that it will be soon. Won't you say that it will be soon? I love you more than the other one."

Below in the pavilion, Helene had begun to dream once more. The proposed journey was still the topic of conversation; and she now experienced an unconquerable yearning to relieve her overflowing heart, and acquaint Henri with all the happiness which was stifling her. So, while Juliette and Pauline were wrangling over the number of dresses that ought to be taken, she leaned towards him and gave him the assignation which she had refused but an hour before.

"Come to-night; I shall expect you."

But as she at last ascended to her own rooms, she met Rosalie flying terror-stricken down the stairs. The moment she saw her mistress, the girl shrieked out:

"Madame! madame! Oh! make haste, do! Mademoiselle is very ill! She's spitting blood!"

CHAPTER XXIII.

On rising from the dinner-table the doctor spoke to his wife of a confinement case, in close attendance on which he would doubtless have to pass the night. He quitted the house at nine o'clock, walked down to the riverside, and paced along the deserted quays in the dense nocturnal darkness. A slight moist wind was blowing, and the swollen Seine rolled on in inky waves. As soon as eleven o'clock chimed, he walked up the slopes of the Trocadero, and began to prowl round the house, the huge square pile of which seemed but a deepening of the gloom. Lights could still be seen streaming through the dining-room windows of Helene's lodging. Walking round, he noted that the kitchen was also brilliantly lighted up. And at this sight he stopped short in astonishment, which slowly developed into uneasiness. Shadows traversed the blinds; there seemed to be considerable bustle and stir up there. Perhaps Monsieur Rambaud had stayed to dine? But the worthy man never left later than ten o'clock. He, Henri, dared not go up; for what would he say should Rosalie open the door? At last, as it was nearing midnight, mad with impatience and throwing prudence to the winds, he rang the bell, and walked swiftly past the porter's room without giving his name. At the top of the stairs Rosalie received him.

"It's you, sir! Come in. I will go and announce you. Madame must be expecting you."

She gave no sign of surprise on seeing him at this hour. As he entered the dining-room without uttering a word, she resumed distractedly: "Oh! mademoiselle is very ill, sir. What a night! My legs are sinking under me!" Thereupon she left the room, and the doctor mechanically took a seat. He was oblivious of the fact that he was a medical man. Pacing along the quay he had conjured up a vision of a very different reception. And now he was there, as though he were paying a visit, waiting with his hat on his knees. A grievous coughing in the next room alone broke upon the intense silence.

At last Rosalie made her appearance once more, and hurrying across the dining-room with a basin in her hand, merely remarked: "Madame says you are not to go in."

He sat on, powerless to depart. Was their meeting to be postponed till another day, then? He was dazed, as though such a thing had seemed to him impossible. Then the thought came to him that poor Jeanne had very bad health; children only brought on sorrow and vexation. The door, however, opened once more, and Doctor Bodin entered, with a thousand apologies falling from his lips. For some time he chattered away: he had been sent for, but he would always be exceedingly pleased to enter into consultation with his renowned fellow-practitioner.

"Oh! no doubt, no doubt," stammered Doctor Deberle, whose ears were buzzing.

The elder man, his mind set at rest with regard to all questions of professional etiquette, then began to affect a puzzled manner, and expressed his doubts of the meaning of the symptoms. He spoke in a whisper, and described them in technical phraseology, frequently pausing and winking significantly. There was coughing without expectoration, very pronounced weakness, and intense fever. Perhaps it might prove a case of typhoid fever. But in the meantime he gave no decided opinion, as the anaemic nervous affection, for which the patient had been treated so long, made him fear unforeseen complications.

"What do you think?" he asked, after delivering himself of each remark.

Doctor Deberle answered with evasive questions. While the other was speaking, he felt ashamed at finding himself in that room. Why had he come up?

"I have applied two blisters," continued the old doctor. "I'm waiting the result. But, of course, you'll see her. You will then give me your opinion."

So saying he led him into the bedroom. Henri entered it with a shudder creeping through his frame. It was but faintly lighted by a lamp. There thronged into his mind the memories of other nights, when there had been the same warm perfume, the same close, calm atmosphere, the same deepening shadows shrouding the furniture and hangings. But there was no one now to come to him with outstretched hands as in those olden days. Monsieur Rambaud lay back in an arm-chair exhausted, seemingly asleep. Helene was standing in front of the bed, robed in a white dressing-gown, but did not turn her head; and her figure, in its death-like pallor, appeared to him extremely tall. Then for a moment's space he gazed on Jeanne. Her weakness was so great that she could not open her eyes without fatigue. Bathed in sweat, she lay in a stupor, her face ghastly, save that a burning flush colored each cheek.

"It's galloping consumption," he exclaimed at last, speaking aloud in spite of himself, and giving no sign of astonishment, as though he had long foreseen what would happen.

Helene heard him and looked at him. She seemed to be of ice, her eyes were dry, and she was terribly calm.

"You think so, do you?" rejoined Doctor Bodin, giving an approving nod in the style of a man who had not cared to be the first to express this opinion.

He sounded the child once more. Jeanne, her limbs quite lifeless, yielded to the examination without seemingly knowing why she was being disturbed. A few rapid sentences were exchanged between the two physicians. The old doctor murmured some words about amphoric breathing, and a sound such as a cracked jar might give out. Nevertheless, he still affected some hesitation, and spoke, suggestively, of capillary bronchitis. Doctor Deberle hastened to explain that an accidental cause had brought on the illness; doubtless it was due to a cold; however, he had already noticed several times that an anaemical tendency would produce chest diseases. Helene stood waiting behind him.

"Listen to her breathing yourself," said Doctor Bodin, giving way to Henri.

He leaned over the child, and seemed about to take hold of her. She had not raised her eyelids; but lay there in self-abandonment, consumed by fever. Her open nightdress displayed her childish breast, where as yet there were but slight signs of coming womanhood; and nothing could be more chaste or yet more harrowing than the sight of this dawning maturity on which the Angel of Death had already laid his hand. She had displayed no aversion when the old doctor had touched her. But the moment Henri's fingers glanced against her body she started as if she had received a shock. In a transport of shame she awoke from the coma in which she had been plunged, and, like a maiden in alarm, clasped her poor puny little arms over her bosom, exclaiming the while in quavering tones: "Mamma! mamma!"

Then she opened her eyes, and on recognizing the man who was bending over her, she was seized with terror. Sobbing with shame, she drew the bed-cover over her bosom. It seemed as though she had grown older by ten years during her short agony, and on the brink of death had attained sufficient womanhood to understand that this man, above all others, must not lay hands on her. She wailed out again in piteous entreaty: "Mamma! mamma! I beseech you!"

Helene, who had hitherto not opened her lips, came close to Henri. Her eyes were bent on him fixedly; her face was of marble. She touched him, and merely said in a husky voice: "Go away!"

Doctor Bodin strove to appease Jeanne, who now shook with a fresh fit of coughing. He assured her that nobody would annoy her again, that every one would go away, to prevent her being disturbed.

"Go away," repeated Helene, in a deep whisper in her lover's ear. "You see very well that we have killed her!"

Then, unable to find a word in reply, Henri withdrew. He lingered for a moment longer in the dining-room, awaiting he knew not what, something that might possibly take place. But seeing that Doctor Bodin did not come out, he groped his way down the stairs without even Rosalie to light him. He thought of the awful speed with which galloping consumption—a disease to which he had devoted earnest study—carried off its victims; the miliary tubercles would rapidly multiply, the stifling sensation would become more and more pronounced; Jeanne would certainly not last another three weeks.

The first of these passed by. In the mighty expanse of heaven before the window, the sun rose and set above Paris, without Helene being more than vaguely conscious of the pitiless, steady advance of time. She grasped the fact that her daughter was doomed; she lived plunged in a stupor, alive only to the terrible anguish that filled her heart. It was but waiting on in hopelessness, in certainty that death would prove merciless. She could not weep, but paced gently to and fro, tending the sufferer with slow, regulated movements. At times, yielding to fatigue, she would fall upon a chair, whence she gazed at her for hours. Jeanne grew weaker and weaker; painful vomiting was followed by exhaustion; the fever never quitted her. When Doctor Bodin called, he examined her for a little while and left some prescription; but his drooping shoulders, as he left the room, were eloquent of such powerlessness that the mother forbore to accompany him to ask even a question.

On the morning after the illness had declared itself, Abbe Jouve had made all haste to call. He and his brother now again came every evening, exchanging a mute clasp of the hand with Helene, and never venturing to ask any news. They had offered to watch by the bedside in succession, but she sent them away when ten o'clock struck; she would have no one in the bedroom during the night. One evening the Abbe, who had seemed absorbed by some idea since the previous day, took her aside.

"There is one thing I've thought of," he whispered. "Her health has put obstacles in the darling child's way; but her first communion might take place here."

His meaning at first did not seem to dawn on Helene. The thought that, despite all his indulgence, he should now allow his priestly character the ascendant and evince no concern but in spiritual matters, came on her with surprise, and even wounded her somewhat. With a careless gesture she exclaimed: "No, no; I would rather she wasn't worried. If there be a heaven, she will have no difficulty in entering its gates."

That evening, however, Jeanne experienced one of those deceptive improvements in health which fill the dying with illusions as to their condition. Her hearing, rendered more acute by illness, had enabled her to catch the Abbe's words.

"It's you, dear old friend!" said she. "You spoke about the first communion. It will be soon, won't it?"

"No doubt, my darling," he answered.

Then she wanted him to come near to speak to her. Her mother had propped her up with the pillow, and she reclined there, looking very little, with a smile on her fever-burnt lips, and the shadow of death already passing over her brilliant eyes.

"Oh! I'm getting on very well," she began. "I could get up if I wanted. But tell me: should I have a white gown and flowers? Will the church be as beautiful as it was in the Month of Mary?"

"More beautiful, my pet."

"Really? Will there be as many flowers, and will there be such sweet chants? It will be soon, soon—you promise me, won't you?"

She was wrapt in joy. She gazed on the curtains of the bed, and murmured in her transport that she was very fond of the good God, and had seen Him while she was listening to the canticles. Even now she could hear organs pealing, see lights that circled round, and flowers in great vases hovering like butterflies before her eyes. Then another fit of coughing threw her back on the pillow. However, her face was still flushed with a smile; she seemed to be unconscious of her cough, but continued:

"I shall get up to-morrow. I shall learn my catechism without a mistake, and we'll be all very happy."

A sob came from Helene as she stood at the foot of the bed. She had been powerless to weep, but a storm of tears rushed up from her bosom as Jeanne's laughter fell on her ear. Then, almost stifling, she fled into the dining-room, that she might hide her despair. The Abbe followed her. Monsieur Rambaud had at once started up to engage the child's attention.

"Oh dear! mamma cried out! Has she hurt herself?" she asked.

"Your mamma?" he answered. "No, she didn't cry out; she was laughing because you are feeling so well."

In the dining-room, her head bowed dejectedly on the table, Helene strove to stifle her sobs with her clasped hands. The Abbe hung over her, and prayed her to restrain her emotion. But she raised her face, streaming with tears, and bitterly accused herself. She declared to him that she herself had killed her daughter, and a full confession escaped from her lips in a torrent of broken words. She would never have succumbed to that man had Jeanne remained beside her. It had been fated that she should meet him in that chamber of mystery. God in Heaven! she ought to die with her child; she could live no longer. The priest, terrified, sought to calm her with the promise of absolution.

But there was a ring at the bell, and a sound of voices came from the lobby. Helene dried her tears as Rosalie made her appearance.

"Madame, it's Dr. Deberle, who—"

"I don't wish him to come in."

"He is asking after mademoiselle."

"Tell him she is dying."

The door had been left open, and Henri had heard everything. Without awaiting the return of the servant girl, he walked down the stairs. He came up every day, received the same answer, and then went away.

The visits which Helene received quite unnerved her. The few ladies whose acquaintance she had made at the Deberles' house deemed it their duty to tender her their sympathy. Madame de Chermette, Madame Levasseur, Madame de Guiraud, and others also presented themselves. They made no request to enter, but catechised Rosalie in such loud voices that they could be heard through the thin partitions. Giving way to impatience, Helene would then receive them in the dining-room, where, without sitting down, she spoke with them very briefly. She went about all day in her dressing-gown, careless of her attire, with her lovely hair merely gathered up and twisted into a knot. Her eyes often closed with weariness; her face was flushed; she had a bitter taste in her mouth; her lips were clammy, and she could scarcely articulate. When Juliette called, she could not exclude her from the bedroom, but allowed her to stay for a little while beside the bed.

"My dear," Madame Deberle said to her one day in friendly tones, "you give way too much. Keep up your spirits."

Helene was about to reply, when Juliette, wishing to turn her thoughts from her grief, began to chat about the things which were occupying the gossips of Paris: "We are certainly going to have a war. I am in a nice state about it, as I have two cousins who will have to serve."

In this style she would drop in upon them on returning from her rambles through Paris, her brain bursting with all the tittle-tattle collected in the course of the afternoon, and her long skirts whirling and rustling as she sailed through the stillness of the sick-room. It was altogether futile for her to lower her voice and assume a pitiful air; her indifference peeped through all disguise; it could be seen that she was happy, quite joyous indeed, in the possession of perfect health. Helene was very downcast in her company, her heart rent by jealous anguish.

"Madame," said Jeanne one evening, "why doesn't Lucien come to play with me?"

Juliette was embarrassed for a moment, and merely answered with a smile.

"Is he ill too?" continued the child.

"No, my darling, he isn't ill; he has gone to school."

Then, as Helene accompanied her into the ante-room, she wished to apologize for her prevarication.

"Oh! I would gladly bring him; I know that there's no infection. But children get frightened with the least thing, and Lucien is such a stupid. He would just burst out sobbing when he saw your poor angel—"

"Yes, indeed; you are quite right," interrupted Helene, her heart ready to break with the thought of this woman's gaiety, and her happiness in possessing a child who enjoyed robust health.

A second week had passed away. The disease was following its usual course, robbing Jeanne every hour of some of her vitality. Fearfully rapid though it was, however, it evinced no haste, but, in accomplishing the destruction of that delicate, lovable flesh, passed in turn through each foreseen phase, without skipping a single one of them. Thus the spitting of blood had ceased, and at intervals the cough disappeared. But such was the oppressive feeling which stifled the child that you could detect the ravages of the disease by the difficulty she experienced in breathing. Such weakness could not withstand so violent an attack; and the eyes of the Abbe and Monsieur Rambaud constantly moistened with tears as they heard her. Day and night under the shelter of the curtains the sound of oppressed breathing arose; the poor darling, whom the slightest shock seemed likely to kill, was yet unable to die, but lived on and on through the agony which bathed her in sweat. Her mother, whose strength was exhausted, and who could no longer bear to hear that rattle, went into the adjoining room and leaned her head against the wall.

Jeanne was slowly becoming oblivious to her surroundings. She no longer saw people, and her face bore an unconscious and forlorn expression, as though she had already lived all alone in some unknown sphere. When they who hovered round her wished to attract her attention, they named themselves that she might recognize them; but she would gaze at them fixedly, without a smile, then turn herself round towards the wall with a weary look. A gloominess was settling over her; she was passing away amidst the same vexation and sulkiness as she had displayed in past days of jealous outbursts. Still, at times the whims characteristic of sickness would awaken her to some consciousness. One morning she asked her mother:

"To-day is Sunday, isn't it?"

"No, my child," answered Helene; "this is only Friday. Why do you wish to know?"

Jeanne seemed to have already forgotten the question she had asked. But two days later, while Rosalie was in the room, she said to her in a whisper: "This is Sunday. Zephyrin is here; ask him to come and see me."

The maid hesitated, but Helene, who had heard, nodded to her in token of consent. The child spoke again:

"Bring him; come both of you; I shall be so pleased."

When Rosalie entered the sick-room with Zephyrin, she raised herself on her pillow. The little soldier, with bare head and hands spread out, swayed about to hide his intense emotion. He had a great love for mademoiselle, and it grieved him unutterably to see her "shouldering arms on the left," as he expressed it in the kitchen. So, in spite of the previous injunctions of Rosalie, who had instructed him to put on a bright expression, he stood speechless, with downcast face, on seeing her so pale and wasted to a skeleton. He was still as tender-hearted as ever, despite his conquering airs. He could not even think of one of those fine phrases which nowadays he usually concocted so easily. The maid behind him gave him a pinch to make him laugh. But he could only stammer out:

"I beg pardon—mademoiselle and every one here—"

Jeanne was still raising herself with the help of her tiny arms. She widely opened her large, vacant eyes; she seemed to be looking for something; her head shook with a nervous trembling. Doubtless the stream of light was blinding her as the shadows of death gathered around.

"Come closer, my friend," said Helene to the soldier. "It was mademoiselle who asked to see you."

The sunshine entered through the window in a slanting ray of golden light, in which the dust rising from the carpet could be seen circling. March had come, and the springtide was already budding out of doors. Zephyrin took one step forward, and appeared in the sunshine; his little round, freckled face had a golden hue, as of ripe corn, while the buttons on his tunic glittered, and his red trousers looked as sanguineous as a field of poppies. At last Jeanne became aware of his presence there; but her eye again betrayed uneasiness, and she glanced restlessly from one corner to another.

"What do you want, my child?" asked her mother. "We are all here." She understood, however, in a moment. "Rosalie, come nearer. Mademoiselle wishes to see you."

Then Rosalie, in her turn, stepped into the sunlight. She wore a cap, whose strings, carelessly tossed over her shoulders, flapped round her head like the wings of a butterfly. A golden powder seemed to fall on her bristly black hair and her kindly face with its flat nose and thick lips.

And for Jeanne there were only these two in the room—the little soldier and the servant girl, standing elbow to elbow under the ray of sunshine. She gazed at them.

"Well, my darling," began Helene again, "you do not say anything
to them! Here they are together."

Jeanne's eyes were still fixed on them, and her head shook with the
tremor of a very aged woman. They stood there like man and wife,
ready to take each other's arm and return to their country-side. The
spring sun threw its warmth on them, and eager to brighten mademoiselle they ended by smiling into each other's face with a look of mingled embarrassment and tenderness. The very odor of health was
exhaled from their plump round figures. Had they been alone, Zephyrin
without doubt would have caught hold of Rosalie, and would have received for his pains a hearty slap. Their eyes showed it.

"Well, my darling, have you nothing to say to them?"

Jeanne gazed at them, her breathing growing yet more oppressed.
And still she said not a word, but suddenly burst into tears. Zephyrin
and Rosalie had at once to quit the room.

"I beg pardon—mademoiselle and every one—" stammered the
little soldier, as he went away in bewilderment.

This was one of Jeanne's last whims. She lapsed into a dull stupor,
from which nothing could rouse her. She lay there in utter loneliness,
unconscious even of her mother's presence. When Helene hung over
the bed seeking her eyes, the child preserved a stolid expression, as
though only the shadow of the curtain had passed before her. Her lips
were dumb; she showed the gloomy resignation of the outcast who
knows that she is dying. Sometimes she would long remain with her
eyelids half closed, and nobody could divine what stubborn thought
was thus absorbing her. Nothing now had any existence for her save her
big doll, which lay beside her. They had given it to her one night to divert her during her insufferable anguish, and she refused to give it back,
defending it with fierce gestures the moment they attempted to take it
from her. With its pasteboard head resting on the bolster, the doll was
stretched out like an invalid, covered up to the shoulders by the coun-
terpane. There was little doubt the child was nursing it, for her burning
hands would, from time to time, feel its disjointed limbs of flesh-tinted
leather, whence all the sawdust had exuded. For hours her eyes would
never stray from those enamel ones which were always fixed, or from

those white teeth wreathed in an everlasting smile. She would suddenly grow affectionate, clasp the doll's hands against her bosom and press her cheek against its little head of hair, the caressing contact of which seemed to give her some relief. Thus she sought comfort in her affection for her big doll, always assuring herself of its presence when she awoke from a doze, seeing nothing else, chatting with it, and at times summoning to her face the shadow of a smile, as though she had heard it whispering something in her ear.

The third week was dragging to an end. One morning the old doctor came and remained. Helene understood him: her child would not live through the day. Since the previous evening she had been in a stupor that deprived her of the consciousness even of her own actions. There was no longer any struggle with death; it was but a question of hours. As the dying child was consumed by an awful thirst, the doctor had merely recommended that she should be given some opiate beverage, which would render her passing less painful; and the relinquishing of all attempts at cure reduced Helene to a state of imbecility. So long as the medicines had littered the night-table she still had entertained hopes of a miraculous recovery. But now bottles and boxes had vanished, and her last trust was gone. One instinct only inspired her now— to be near Jeanne, never leave her, gaze at her unceasingly. The doctor, wishing to distract her attention from the terrible sight, strove, by assigning some little duties to her, to keep her at a distance. But she ever and ever returned, drawn to the bedside by the physical craving to see. She waited, standing erect, her arms hanging beside her, and her face swollen by despair.

About one o'clock Abbe Jouve and Monsieur Rambaud arrived. The doctor went to meet them, and muttered a few words. Both grew pale, and stood stock-still in consternation, while their hands began to tremble. Helene had not turned round.

The weather was lovely that day; it was one of those sunny afternoons typical of early April. Jeanne was tossing in her bed. Her lips moved painfully at times with the intolerable thirst which consumed her. She had brought her poor transparent hands from under the coverlet, and waved them gently to and fro. The hidden working of the disease was accomplished, she coughed no more, and her dying voice came like a faint breath. For a moment she turned her head, and her eyes sought the light. Doctor Bodin threw the window wide open, and then Jeanne at once became tranquil, with her cheek resting on the pillow and her looks roving over Paris, while her heavy breathing grew fainter and slower.

During the three weeks of her illness she had thus many times turned towards the city that stretched away to the horizon. Her face grew grave, she was musing. At this last hour Paris was smiling under the glittering April sunshine. Warm breezes entered from without, with bursts of urchin's laughter and the chirping of sparrows. On the brink of the grave the child exerted her last strength to gaze again on the scene, and follow the flying smoke which soared from the distant suburbs. She recognized her three friends, the Invalides, the Pantheon, and the Tower of Saint-Jacques; then the unknown began, and her weary eyelids half closed at sight of the vast ocean of roofs. Perhaps she was dreaming that she was growing much lighter and lighter, and was fleeting away like a bird. Now, at last, she would soon know all; she would perch herself on the domes and steeples; seven or eight flaps of her wings would suffice, and she would be able to gaze on the forbidden mysteries that were hidden from children. But a fresh uneasiness fell upon her, and her hands groped about; she only grew calm again when she held her large doll in her little arms against her bosom. It was evidently her wish to take it with her. Her glances wandered far away amongst the chimneys glinting with the sun's ruddy light.

Four o'clock struck, and the bluish shadows of evening were already gathering. The end was at hand; there was a stifling, a slow and passive agony. The dear angel no longer had strength to offer resistance. Monsieur Rambaud, overcome, threw himself on his knees, convulsed with silent sobbing, and dragged himself behind a curtain to hide his grief. The Abbe was kneeling at the bedside, with clasped hands, repeating the prayers for the dying.

"Jeanne! Jeanne!" murmured Helene, chilled to the heart with a horror which sent an icy thrill through her very hair.

She had repulsed the doctor and thrown herself on the ground, leaning against the bed to gaze into her daughter's face. Jeanne opened her eyes, but did not look at her mother. She drew her doll—her last love—still closer. Her bosom heaved with a big sigh, followed by two fainter ones. Then her eyes paled, and her face for a moment gave signs of a fearful anguish. But speedily there came relief; her mouth remained open, she breathed no more.

"It is over," said the doctor, as he took her hand.

Jeanne's big, vacant eyes were fixed on Paris. The long, thin, lamb-like face was still further elongated, there was a sternness on its features, a grey shadow falling from its contracted brows. Thus even in death she retained the livid expression of a jealous woman. The doll, with its head flung back, and its hair dishevelled, seemed to lie dead beside her.

"It is over," again said the doctor, as he allowed the little cold hand to drop.

Helene, with a strained expression on her face, pressed her hands to her brow as if she felt her head splitting open. No tears came to her eyes; she gazed wildly in front of her. Then a rattling noise mounted in her throat; she had just espied at the foot of the bed a pair of shoes that lay forgotten there. It was all over. Jeanne would never put them on again; the little shoes could be given to the poor. And at the sight Helene's tears gushed forth; she still knelt on the floor, her face pressed against the dead child's hand, which had slipped down. Monsieur Rambaud was sobbing. The Abbe had raised his voice, and Rosalie, standing at the door of the dining-room, was biting her handkerchief to check the noise of her grief.

At this very moment Doctor Deberle rang the bell. He was unable to refrain from making inquiries.

"How is she now?" he asked.

"Oh, sir!" wailed Rosalie, "she is dead."

He stood motionless, stupefied by the announcement of the end which he had been expecting daily. At last he muttered: "O God! the poor child! what a calamity!"

He could only give utterance to those commonplace but heartrending words. The door shut once more, and he went down the stairs.

CHAPTER XXIV.

When Madame Deberle was apprised of Jeanne's death she wept, and gave way to one of those outbursts of emotion that kept her in a flutter for eight-and-forty hours. Hers was a noisy and immoderate grief. She came and threw herself into Helene's arms. Then a phrase dropped in her hearing inspired her with the idea of imparting some affecting surroundings to the child's funeral, and soon wholly absorbed her. She offered her services, and declared her willingness to undertake every detail. The mother, worn out with weeping, sat overwhelmed in her chair; Monsieur Rambaud, who was acting in her name, was losing his head. So he accepted the offer with profuse expressions of gratitude. Helene merely roused herself for a moment to express the wish that there should be some flowers—an abundance of flowers.

Without losing a minute, Madame Deberle set about her task. She spent the whole of the next day in running from one lady friend to another, bearing the woeful tidings. It was her idea to have a following of little girls all dressed in white. She needed at least thirty, and did not return till she had secured the full number. She had gone in person to the Funeral Administration, discussed the various styles, and chosen the necessary drapery. She would have the garden railings hung with white, and the body might be laid out under the lilac trees, whose twigs were already tipped with green. It would be charming.

"If only it's a fine day to-morrow!" she giddily remarked in the evening when her scurrying to and fro had come to an end.

The morning proved lovely; there was a blue sky and a flood of sunshine, the air was pure and invigorating as only the air of spring can be. The funeral was to take place at ten o'clock. By nine the drapery had been hung up. Juliette ran down to give the workmen her ideas of what should be done. She did not wish the trees to be altogether covered. The white cloth, fringed with silver, formed a kind of porch at the garden gate, which was thrown back against the lilac trees. However, Juliette soon returned to her drawing-room to receive her lady guests. They were to assemble there to prevent Madame Grandjean's two rooms from being filled to overflowing. Still she was greatly annoyed at her husband having had to go that morning to Versailles—for some consultation or other, he explained, which he could not well neglect. Thus she was left alone, and felt she would never be able to get through with it all. Madame Berthier was the first arrival, bringing her two daughters with her.

"What do you think!" exclaimed Madame Deberle; "Henri has deserted me! Well, Lucien, why don't you say good-day?"

Lucien was already dressed for the funeral, with his hands in black gloves. He seemed astonished to see Sophie and Blanche dressed as though they were about to take part in some church procession. A silk sash encircled the muslin gown of each, and their veils, which swept down to the floor, hid their little caps of transparent tulle. While the two mothers were busy chatting, the three children gazed at one another, bearing themselves somewhat stiffly in their new attire. At last Lucien broke the silence by saying: "Jeanne is dead."

His heart was full, and yet his face wore a smile—a smile born of amazement. He had been very quiet since the evening before, dwelling on the thought that Jeanne was dead. As his mother was up to her ears in business, and took no notice of him, he had plied the servants with questions. Was it a fact, he wanted to know, that it was impossible to move when one was dead?"

"She is dead, she is dead!" echoed the two sisters, who looked like rosebuds under their white veils. "Are we going to see her?"

Lucien pondered for a time, and then, with dreamy eyes and opened mouth, seemingly striving to divine the nature of this problem which lay beyond his ken, he answered in a low tone:

"We shall never see her again."

However, several other little girls now entered the room. On a sign from his mother Lucien advanced to meet them. Marguerite Tissot, her muslin dress enveloping her like a cloud, seemed a child-Virgin; her fair hair, escaping from underneath her little cap, looked, through the snowy veil, like a tippet figured with gold. A quiet smile crept into every face when the five Levasseurs made their appearance; they were all dressed alike, and trooped along in boarding-school fashion, the eldest first, the youngest last; and their skirts stood out to such an extent that they quite filled one corner of the room. But on little Mademoiselle Guiraud's entry the whispering voices rose to a higher key; the others laughed and crowded round to see her and kiss her. She was like some white turtle-dove with its downy feathers ruffled. Wrapped in rustling gauze, she looked as round as a barrel, but still no heavier than a bird. Her mother even could not find her hands. By degrees the drawing-room seemed to be filling with a cloud of snowballs. Several boys, in their black coats, were like dark spots amidst the universal white. Lucien, now that his little wife was dead, desired to choose another. However, he displayed the greatest hesitation. He would have preferred a wife like Jeanne, taller than himself; but at last he settled on Marguerite, whose hair fascinated him, and to whom he attached himself for the day.

"The corpse hasn't been brought down yet," Pauline muttered at this moment in Juliette's ear.

Pauline was as flurried as though the preliminaries of a ball were in hand. It was with the greatest difficulty that her sister had prevented her from donning a white dress for the ceremony.

"Good gracious!" exclaimed Juliette; "what are they dreaming about? I must run up. Stay with these ladies."

She hastily left the room, where the mothers in their mourning at-tire sat chatting in whispers, while the children dared not make the least movement lest they should rumple their dresses. When she had reached the top of the staircase and entered the chamber where the body lay, Juliette's blood was chilled by the intense cold. Jeanne still lay on the bed, with clasped hands; and, like Marguerite and the Levasseur girls, she was arrayed in a white dress, white cap, and white shoes. A wreath of white roses crowned the cap, as though she were a little queen about to be honored by the crowd of guests who were waiting below. In front of the window, on two chairs, was the oak coffin lined with satin, look-ing like some huge jewel casket. The furniture was all in order; a wax taper was burning; the room seemed close and gloomy, with the damp smell and stillness of a vault which has been walled up for many years. Thus Juliette, fresh from the sunshine and smiling life of the outer world, came to a sudden halt, stricken dumb, without the courage to ex-plain that they must needs hurry.

"A great many people have come," she stammered at last. And then, as no answer was forthcoming, she added, just for the sake of saying something: "Henri has been forced to attend a consultation at Versailles; you will excuse him."

Helene, who sat in front of the bed, gazed at her with vacant eyes. They were wholly unable to drag her from that room. For six-and-thirty hours she had lingered there, despite the prayers of Monsieur Rambaud and the Abbe Jouve, who kept watch with her. During the last two nights she had been weighed to the earth by immeasurable agony. Besides, she had accomplished the grievous task of dressing her daughter for the last time, of putting on those white silk shoes, for she would allow no other to touch the feet of the little angel who lay dead. And now she sat motionless, as though her strength were spent, and the intensity of her grief had lulled her into forgetfulness.

"Have you got some flowers?" she exclaimed after an effort, her eyes still fixed on Madame Deberle.

"Yes, yes, my dear," answered the latter. "Don't trouble yourself about that."

Since her daughter had breathed her last, Helene had been consumed with one idea—there must be flowers, flowers, an overwhelming profusion of flowers. Each time she saw anybody, she grew uneasy, seemingly afraid that sufficient flowers would never be obtained.

"Are there any roses?" she began again after a pause.

"Yes. I assure you that you will be well pleased."

She shook her head, and once more fell back into her stupor. In the meantime the undertaker's men were waiting on the landing. It must be got over now without delay. Monsieur Rambaud, who was himself affected to such a degree that he staggered like a drunken man, signed to Juliette to assist him in leading the poor woman from the room. Each slipped an arm gently beneath hers, and they raised her up and led her towards the dining-room. But the moment she divined their intention, she shook them from her in a last despairing outburst. The scene was heartrending. She threw herself on her knees at the bedside and clung passionately to the sheets, while the room re-echoed with her piteous shrieks. But still Jeanne lay there with her face of stone, stiff and icy-cold, wrapped round by the silence of eternity. She seemed to be frowning; there was a sour pursing of the lips, eloquent of a revengeful nature; and it was this gloomy, pitiless look, springing from jealousy and transforming her face, which drove Helene so frantic. During the preceding thirty-six hours she had not failed to notice how the old spiteful expression had grown more and more intense upon her daughter's face, how more and more sullen she looked the nearer she approached the grave. Oh, what a comfort it would have been if Jeanne could only have smiled on her for the last time!

"No, no!" she shrieked. "I pray you, leave her for a moment. You cannot take her from me. I want to embrace her. Oh, only a moment, only a moment!"

With trembling arms she clasped her child to her bosom, eager to dispute possession with the men who stood in the ante-room, with their backs turned towards her and impatient frowns on their faces. But her lips were powerless to breathe any warmth on the cold countenance; she became conscious that Jeanne's obstinacy was not to be overcome, that she refused forgiveness. And then she allowed herself to be dragged away, and fell upon a chair in the dining-room, with the one mournful cry, again and again repeated: "My God! My God!"

Monsieur Rambaud and Madame Deberle were overcome by emotion. There was an interval of silence, but when the latter opened the door halfway it was all over. There had been no noise—scarcely a stir. The screws, oiled beforehand, now closed the lid for ever. The chamber was left empty, and a white sheet was thrown over the coffin.

The bedroom door remained open, and no further restraint was put upon Helene. On re-entering the room she cast a dazed look on the furniture and round the walls. The men had borne away the corpse. Rosalie had drawn the coverlet over the bed to efface the slight hollow made by the form of the little one whom they had lost. Then opening her arms with a distracted gesture and stretching out her hands, Helene rushed towards the staircase. She wanted to go down, but Monsieur Rambaud held her back, while Madame Deberle explained to her that it was not the thing to do. But she vowed she would behave rationally, that she would not follow the funeral procession. Surely they could allow her to look on; she would remain quiet in the garden pavilion. Both wept as they heard her pleading. However, she had to be dressed. Juliette threw a black shawl round her to conceal her morning wrap. There was no bonnet to be found; but at last they came across one from which they tore a bunch of red vervain flowers. Monsieur Rambaud, who was chief mourner, took hold of Helene's arm.

"Do not leave her," whispered Madame Deberle as they reached the garden. "I have so many things to look after!"

And thereupon she hastened away. Helene meanwhile walked with difficulty, her eyes ever seeking something. As soon as she had found herself out of doors she had drawn a long sigh. Ah! what a lovely morning! Then she looked towards the iron gate, and caught sight of the little coffin under the white drapery. Monsieur Rambaud allowed her to take but two or three steps forward.

"Now, be brave," he said to her, while a shudder ran through his own frame.

They gazed on the scene. The narrow coffin was bathed in sunshine. At the foot of it, on a lace cushion, was a silver crucifix. To the left the holy-water sprinkler lay in its font. The tall wax tapers were burning with almost invisible flames. Beneath the hangings, the branches of the trees with their purple shoots formed a kind of bower. It was a nook full of the beauty of spring, and over it streamed the golden sunshine irradiating the blossoms with which the coffin was covered. It seemed as if flowers had been raining down; there were clusters of white roses, white camellias, white lilac, white carnations, heaped in a snowy mass of petals; the coffin was hidden from sight, and from the pall some of the white blossoms were falling, the ground being strewn with periwinkles and hyacinths. The few persons passing along the Rue Vineuse paused with a smile of tender emotion before this sunny garden where the little body lay at peace amongst the flowers. There seemed to be a music stealing up from the snowy surroundings; in the glare of light the purity of the blossoms grew dazzling, and the sun flushed hangings, nosegays, and wreaths of flowers, with a very semblance of life. Over the roses a bee flew humming.

"Oh, the flowers! the flowers!" murmured Helene, powerless to say another word.

She pressed her handkerchief to her lips, and her eyes filled with tears. Jeanne must be warm, she thought, and with this idea a wave of emotion rose in her bosom; she felt very grateful to those who had enveloped her child in flowers. She wished to go forward, and Monsieur Rambaud made no effort to hold her back. How sweet was the scene beneath the cloud of drapery! Perfumes were wafted upwards; the air was warm and still. Helene stooped down and chose one rose only, that she might place it in her bosom. But suddenly she commenced to tremble, and Monsieur Rambaud became uneasy.

"Don't stay here," he said, as he drew her away. "You promised not to make yourself unwell."

He was attempting to lead her into the pavilion when the door of the drawing-room was thrown open. Pauline was the first to appear. She had undertaken the duty of arranging the funeral procession. One by one, the little girls stepped into the garden. Their coming seemed like some sudden outburst of bloom, a miraculous flowering of May. In the open air the white skirts expanded, streaked moire-like by the sunshine with shades of the utmost delicacy. An apple-tree above was raining down its blossoms; gossamer-threads were floating to and fro; the dresses were instinct with all the purity of spring. And their number still increased; they already surrounded the lawn; they yet lightly descended the steps, sailing on like downy balls suddenly expanding beneath the open sky.

The garden was now a snowy mass, and as Helene gazed on the crowd of little girls, a memory awoke within her. She remembered another joyous season, with its ball and the gay twinkling of tiny feet. She once more saw Marguerite in her milk-girl costume, with her can hanging from her waist; and Sophie, dressed as a waiting-maid, and revolving on the arm of her sister Blanche, whose trappings as Folly gave out a merry tinkle of bells. She thought, too, of the five Levasseur girls, and of the Red Riding-Hoods, whose number had seemed endless, with their ever-recurring cloaks of poppy-colored satin edged with black velvet; while little Mademoiselle Guiraud, with her Alsatian butterfly bow in her hair, danced as if demented opposite a Harlequin twice as tall as herself. To-day they were all arrayed in white. Jeanne, too, was in white, her head laid amongst white flowers on the white satin pillow. The delicate-faced Japanese maiden, with hair transfixed by long pins, and purple tunic embroidered with birds, was leaving them for ever in a gown of snowy white.

"How tall they have all grown!" exclaimed Helene, as she burst into tears.

They were all there but her daughter; she alone was missing. Monsieur Rambaud led her to the pavilion; but she remained on the threshold, anxious to see the funeral procession start. Several of the ladies bowed to her quietly. The children looked at her, with some astonishment in their blue eyes. Meanwhile Pauline was hovering round, giving orders. She lowered her voice for the occasion, but at times forgot herself.

"Now, be good children! Look, you little stupid, you are dirty already! I'll come for you in a minute; don't stir."

The hearse drove up; it was time to start, but Madame Deberle appeared, exclaiming: "The bouquets have been forgotten! Quick, Pauline, the bouquets!"

Some little confusion ensued. A bouquet of white roses had been prepared for each little girl; and these bouquets now had to be distributed. The children, in an ecstasy of delight, held the great clusters of flowers in front of them as though they had been wax tapers; Lucien, still at Marguerite's side, daintily inhaled the perfume of her blossoms as she held them to his face. All these little maidens, their hands filled with flowers, looked radiant with happiness in the golden light; but suddenly their faces grew grave as they perceived the men placing the coffin on the hearse.

"Is she inside that thing?" asked Sophie in a whisper.

Her sister Blanche nodded assent. Then, in her turn, she said: "For men it's as big as this!"

She was referring to the coffin, and stretched out her arms to their widest extent. However, little Marguerite, whose nose was buried amongst her roses, was seized with a fit of laughter; it was the flowers, said she, which tickled her. Then the others in turn buried their noses in their bouquets to find out if it were so; but they were remonstrated with, and they all became grave once more.

The funeral procession was now filing into the street. At the corner of the Rue Vineuse a woman without a cap, and with tattered shoes on her feet, wept and wiped her cheeks with the corner of her apron. People stood at many windows, and exclamations of pity ascended through the stillness of the street. Hung with white silver-fringed drapery the hearse rolled on without a sound; nothing fell on the ear save the measured tread of the two white horses, deadened by the solid earthen roadway. The bouquets and wreaths, borne on the funeral car, formed a very harvest of flowers; the coffin was hidden by them; every jolt tossed the heaped-up mass, and the hearse slowly sprinkled the street with lilac blossom. From each of the four corners streamed a long ribbon of white watered silk, held by four little girls—Sophie and Marguerite, one of the Levasseur family, and little Mademoiselle

Guiraud, who was so small and so uncertain on her legs that her mother
walked beside her. The others, in a close body, surrounded the hearse,
each bearing her bouquet of roses. They walked slowly, their veils
waved, and the wheels rolled on amidst all this muslin, as though borne
along on a cloud, from which smiled the tender faces of cherubs. Then
behind, following Monsieur Rambaud, who bowed his pale face, came
several ladies and little boys, Rosalie, Zephyrin, and the servants of
Madame Deberle. To these succeeded five empty mourning carriages.
And as the hearse passed along the sunny street like a car symbolical of
springtide, a number of white pigeons wheeled over the mourners'
heads.

"Good heavens! how annoying!" exclaimed Madame Deberle when
she saw the procession start off. "If only Henri had postponed that
consultation! I told him how it would be!"

She did not know what to do with Helene, who remained prostrate
on a seat in the pavilion. Henri might have stayed with her and afforded
her some consolation. His absence was a horrible nuisance. Luckily,
Mademoiselle Aurelie was glad to offer her services; she had no liking
for such solemn scenes, and while watching over Helene would be able
to attend to the luncheon which had to be prepared ere the children's
return. So Juliette hastened after the funeral, which was proceeding towards the church by way of the Rue de Passy.

The garden was now deserted; a few workmen only were folding up
the hangings. All that remained on the gravelled path over which Jeanne
had been carried were the scattered petals of a camellia. And Helene,
suddenly lapsing into loneliness and stillness, was thrilled once more
with the anguish of this eternal separation. Once again—only once
again!—to be at her darling's side! The never-fading thought that Jeanne
was leaving her in anger, with a face that spoke solely of gloomy hatred,
seared her heart like a red-hot iron. She well divined that Mademoiselle
Aurelie was there to watch her, and cast about for some opportunity to
escape and hasten to the cemetery.

"Yes, it's a dreadful loss," began the old maid, comfortably seated
in an easy-chair. "I myself should have worshipped children, and little
girls in particular. Ah, well! when I think of it I am pleased that I never
married. It saves a lot of grief!"

It was thus she thought to divert the mother. She chatted away
about one of her friends who had had six children; they were now all

dead. Another lady had been left a widow with a big lad who struck her; he might die, and there would be no difficulty in comforting her. Helene appeared to be listening to all this; she did not stir, but her whole frame quivered with impatience.

"You are calmer now," said Mademoiselle Aurelie, after a time. "Well, in the end we always have to get the better of our feelings."

The dining-room communicated with the Japanese pavilion, and, rising up, the old maid opened the door and peered into the room. The table, she saw, was covered with pastry and cakes. Meantime, in an instant Helene sped through the garden; the gate was still open, the workmen were just carrying away their ladder.

On the left the Rue Vineuse turns into the Rue des Reservoirs, from which the cemetery of Passy can be entered. On the Boulevard de la Muette a huge retaining wall has been reared, and the cemetery stretches like an immense terrace commanding the heights, the Trocadero, the avenues, and the whole expanse of Paris. In twenty steps Helene had reached the yawning gateway, and saw before her the lonely expanse of white gravestones and black crosses. She entered. At the corners of the first walk two large lilac trees were budding. There were but few burials here; weeds grew thickly, and a few cypress trees threw solemn shadows across the green. Helene hurried straight on; a troop of frightened sparrows flew off, and a grave-digger raised his head towards her after flinging aside a shovelful of earth. The procession had probably not yet arrived from the church; the cemetery seemed empty to her. She turned to the right, and advanced almost to the edge of the terrace parapet; but, on looking round, she saw behind a cluster of acacias the little girls in white upon their knees before the temporary vault into which Jeanne's remains had a moment before been lowered. Abbe Jouve, with outstretched hand, was giving the farewell benediction. She heard nothing but the dull thud with which the stone slab of the vault fell back into its place. All was over.

Meanwhile, however, Pauline had observed her and pointed her out to Madame Deberle, who almost gave way to anger. "What!" she exclaimed; "she has come. But it isn't at all proper; it's very bad taste!"

So saying she stepped forward, showing Helene by the expression of her face that she disapproved of her presence. Some other ladies also followed with inquisitive looks. Monsieur Rambaud, however, had already rejoined the bereaved mother, and stood silent by her side. She was leaning against one of the acacias, feeling faint, and weary with the sight of all those mourners. She nodded her head in recognition of their sympathetic words, but all the while she was stifling with the thought that she had come too late; for she had heard the noise of the stone falling back into its place. Her eyes ever turned towards the vault, the step of which a cemetery keeper was sweeping.

"Pauline, see to the children," said Madame Deberle.

The little girls rose from their knees looking like a flock of white sparrows. A few of the tinier ones, lost among their petticoats, had seated themselves on the ground, and had to be picked up. While Jeanne was being lowered down, the older girls had leaned forward to see the bottom of the cavity. It was so dark they had shuddered and turned pale. Sophie assured her companions in a whisper that one remained there for years and years. "At nighttime too?" asked one of the little Levasseur girls. "Of course—at night too—always!" Oh, the night! Blanche was nearly dead with the idea. And they all looked at one another with dilated eyes, as if they had just heard some story about robbers. However, when they had regained their feet, and stood grouped around the vault, released from their mourning duties, their cheeks became pink again; it must all be untrue, those stories could only have been told for fun. The spot seemed pleasant, so pretty with its long grass; what capital games they might have had at hide-and-seek behind all the tombstones! Their little feet were already itching to dance away, and their white dresses fluttered like wings. Amidst the graveyard stillness the warm sunshine lazily streamed down, flushing their faces. Lucien had thrust his hand beneath Marguerite's veil, and was feeling her hair and asking if she put anything on it, to make it so yellow. The little one drew herself up, and he told her that they would marry each other some day. To this Marguerite had no objection, but she was afraid that he might pull her hair. His hands were still wandering over it; it seemed to him as soft as highly-glazed letter-paper.

"Don't go so far away," called Pauline.

"Well, we'll leave now," said Madame Deberle. "There's nothing more to be done, and the children must be hungry."

The little girls, who had scattered like some boarding-school at play, had to be marshalled together once more. They were counted, and baby Guiraud was missing; but she was at last seen in the distance, gravely toddling along a path with her mother's parasol. The ladies then turned towards the gateway, driving the stream of white dresses before them. Madame Berthier congratulated Pauline on her marriage, which was to take place during the following month. Madame Deberle informed them that she was setting out in three days' time for Naples, with her husband and Lucien. The crowd now quickly disappeared; Zephyrin and Rosalie were the last to remain. Then in their turn they went off, linked together, arm-in-arm, delighted with their outing, although their hearts were heavy with grief. Their pace was slow, and for a moment longer they could be seen at the end of the path, with the sunshine dancing over them.

"Come," murmured Monsieur Rambaud to Helene.

With a gesture she entreated him to wait. She was alone, and to her it seemed as though a page had been torn from the book of her life. As soon as the last of the mourners had disappeared, she knelt before the tomb with a painful effort. Abbe Jouve, robed in his surplice, had not yet risen to his feet. Both prayed for a long time. Then, without speaking, but with a glowing glance of loving-kindness and pardon, the priest assisted her to rise.

"Give her your arm," he said to Monsieur Rambaud.

Towards the horizon stretched Paris, all golden in the radiance of that spring morning. In the cemetery a chaffinch was singing.

CHAPTER XXV.

Two years were past and gone. One morning in December the little cemetery lay slumbering in the intense cold. Since the evening before snow had been falling, a fine snow, which a north wind blew before it. From the paling sky the flakes now fell at rarer intervals, light and buoyant, like feathers. The snow was already hardening, and a thick trimming of seeming swan's-down edged the parapet of the terrace. Beyond this white line lay Paris, against the gloomy grey on the horizon.

Madame Rambaud was still praying on her knees in the snow before the grave of Jeanne. Her husband had but a moment before risen silently to his feet. Helene and her old lover had been married in November at Marseilles. Monsieur Rambaud had disposed of his business near the Central Markets, and had come to Paris for three days, in order to conclude the transaction. The carriage now awaiting them in the Rue des Reservoirs was to take them back to their hotel, and thence with their travelling-trunks to the railway station. Helene had made the journey with the one thought of kneeling here. She remained motionless, with drooping head, as if dreaming, and unconscious of the cold ground that chilled her knees.

Meanwhile the wind was falling. Monsieur Rambaud had stepped to the terrace, leaving her to the mute anguish which memory evoked. A haze was stealing over the outlying districts of Paris, whose immensity faded away in this pale, vague mist. Round the Trocadero the city was of a leaden hue and lifeless, while the last snowflakes slowly fluttered down in pale specks against the gloomy background. Beyond the chimneys of the Army Bakehouse, the brick towers of which had a coppery tint, these white dots descended more thickly; a gauze seemed to be floating in the air, falling to earth thread by thread. Not a breath stirred as the dream-like shower sleepily and rhythmically descended from the atmosphere. As they neared the roofs the flakes seemed to falter in their flight; in myriads they ceaselessly pillowed themselves on one another, in such intense silence that even blossoms shedding their petals make more noise; and from this moving mass, whose descent through space was inaudible, there sprang a sense of such intense peacefulness that earth and life were forgotten. A milky whiteness spread more and more over the whole heavens though they were still darkened here and there by wreaths of smoke. Little by little, bright clusters of houses became plainly visible; a bird's-eye view was obtained of the whole city, inter-sected by streets and squares, which with their shadowy depths de-scribed the framework of the several districts.

Helene had slowly risen. On the snow remained the imprint of her knees. Wrapped in a large, dark mantle trimmed with fur, she seemed amidst the surrounding white very tall and broad-shouldered. The bor-der of her bonnet, a twisted band of black velvet, looked like a diadem throwing a shadow on her forehead. She had regained her beautiful, placid face with grey eyes and pearly teeth. Her chin was full and rounded, as in the olden days, giving her an air of sturdy sense and de-termination. As she turned her head, her profile once more assumed statuesque severity and purity. Beneath the untroubled paleness of her cheeks her blood coursed calmly; everything showed that honor was again ruling her life. Two tears had rolled from under her eyelids; her present tranquility came from her past sorrow. And she stood before the grave on which was reared a simple pillar inscribed with Jeanne's name and two dates, within which the dead child's brief existence was compassed.

Around Helene stretched the cemetery, enveloped in its snowy pall, through which rose rusty monuments and iron crosses, like arms thrown up in agony. There was only one path visible in this lonely cor-ner, and that had been made by the footmarks of Helene and Mon-sieur Rambaud. It was a spotless solitude where the dead lay sleeping. The walks were outlined by the shadowy, phantom-like trees. Ever and anon some snow fell noiselessly from a branch that had been too heav-ily burdened. But nothing else stirred. At the far end, some little while ago, a black tramping had passed by; someone was being buried be-neath this snowy winding-sheet. And now another funeral train ap-peared on the left. Hearses and mourners went their way in silence, like shadows thrown upon a spotless linen cloth.

Helene was awaking from her dream when she observed a beggar-woman crawling along near her. It was Mother Fetu, the snow deadening the sound of her huge man's boots, which were burst and bound round with bits of string. Never had Helene seen her weighed down by such intense misery, or covered with filthier rags, though she was fatter than ever, and wore a stupid look. In the foulest weather, despite hard frosts or drenching rain, the old woman now followed funerals in order to speculate on the pity of the charitable. She well knew that amongst the gravestones the fear of death makes people generous; and so she prowled from tomb to tomb, approaching the kneeling mourners at the moment they burst into tears, for she understood that they were then powerless to refuse her. She had entered with the last funeral train, and a moment previously had espied Helene. But she had not recognized her benefactress, and with gasps and sobs began to relate how she had two children at home who were dying of hunger. Helene listened to her, struck dumb by this apparition. The children were without fire to warm them; the elder was going off in a decline. But all at once Mother Fetu's words came to an end. Her brain was evidently working beneath the myriad wrinkles of her face, and her little eyes began to blink. Good gracious! it was her benefactress! Heaven, then, had hearkened to her prayers! And without seeking to explain the story about the children, she plunged into a whining tale, with a ceaseless rush of words. Several of her teeth were missing, and she could be understood with difficulty. The gracious God had sent every affliction on her head, she declared. The gentleman lodger had gone away, and she had only just been enabled to rise after lying for three months in bed; yes, the old pain still remained, it now gripped her everywhere; a neighbor had told her that a spider must have got in through her mouth while she was asleep. If she had only had a little fire, she could have warmed her stomach; that was the only thing that could relieve her now. But nothing could be had for nothing—not even a match. Perhaps she was right in thinking that madame had been travelling? That was her own concern, of course. At all events, she looked very well, and fresh, and beautiful. God would requite her for all her kindness. Then, as Helene began to draw out her purse, Mother Fetu drew breath, leaning against the railing that encircled Jeanne's grave.

The funeral processions had vanished from sight. Somewhere in a grave close at hand a digger, whom they could not see, was wielding his pickaxe with regular strokes.

Meanwhile the old woman had regained her breath, and her eyes were riveted on the purse. Then, anxious to extort as large a sum as possible, she displayed considerable cunning, and spoke of the other lady. Nobody could say that she was not a charitable lady; still, she did not know what to do with her money—it never did one much good. Warily did she glance at Helene as she spoke. And next she ventured to mention the doctor's name. Oh! he was good. Last summer he had again gone on a journey with his wife. Their boy was thriving; he was a fine child. But just then Helene's fingers, as she opened the purse, began to tremble, and Mother Fetu immediately changed her tone. In her stupidity and bewilderment she had only now realized that the good lady was standing beside her daughter's grave. She stammered, gasped, and tried to bring tears to her eyes. Jeanne, said she, had been so dainty a darling, with such loves of little hands; she could still see her giving her silver in charity. What long hair she had! and how her large eyes filled with tears when she gazed on the poor! Ah! there was no replacing such an angel; there were no more to be found like her, were they even to search the whole of Passy. And when the fine days came, said Mother Fetu, she would gather some daisies in the moat of the fortifications and place them on her tomb. Then, however, she lapsed into silence frightened by the gesture with which Helene cut her short. Was it possible, she thought, that she could no longer find the right thing to say? Her good lady did not weep, and only gave her a twenty-sou piece.

Monsieur Rambaud, meanwhile, had walked towards them from the parapet of the terrace. Helene hastened to rejoin him. At the sight of the gentleman Mother Fetu's eyes began to sparkle. He was unknown to her; he must be a new-comer. Dragging her feet along, she followed Helene, invoking every blessing of Heaven on her head; and when she had crept close to Monsieur Rambaud, she again spoke of the doctor. Ah! his would be a magnificent funeral when he died, were the poor people whom he had attended for nothing to follow his corpse! He was rather fickle in his loves—nobody could deny that. There were ladies in Passy who knew him well. But all that didn't prevent him from worshipping his wife—such a pretty lady, who, had she wished, might have easily gone wrong, but had given up such ideas long ago. Their home was quite a turtle-doves' nest now. Had madame paid them a visit yet? They were certain to be at home; she had but a few moments previously observed that the shutters were open in the Rue Vineuse. They had formerly had such regard for madame that surely they would be delighted to receive her with open arms!

The old hag leered at Monsieur Rambaud as she thus mumbled away. He listened to her with the composure of a brave man. The memories that were being called up before him brought no shadow to his unruffled face. Only it occurred to him that the pertinacity of the old beggar was annoying Helene, and so he hastened to fumble in his pocket, in his turn giving her some alms, and at the same time waving her away. The moment her eyes rested on another silver coin Mother Fetu burst into loud thanks. She would buy some wood at once; she would be able to warm her afflicted body—that was the only thing now to give her stomach any relief. Yes, the doctor's home was quite a nest of turtle-doves, and the proof was that the lady had only last winter given birth to a second child—a beautiful little daughter, rosy-cheeked and fat, who must now be nearly fourteen months old. On the day of the baptism the doctor had put a hundred sous into her hand at the door of the church. Ah! good hearts came together. Madame had brought her good luck. Pray God that madame might never have a sorrow, but every good fortune! yes, might that come to pass in the name of the Father, the Son, and the Holy Ghost!

Helene stood upright gazing on Paris, while Mother Fetu vanished among the tombs, muttering three *Paters* and three *Aves*. The snow had ceased falling; the last of the flakes had fluttered slowly and wearily on to the roofs; and through the dissolving mist the golden sun could be seen tinging the pearly-grey expanse of heaven with a pink glow. Over Montmartre a belt of blue fringed the horizon; but it was so faint and delicate that it seemed but a shadow such as white satin might throw. Paris was gradually detaching itself from amidst the smoke, spreading out more broadly with its snowy expanses the frigid cloak which held it in death-like quiescence. There were now no longer any fleeting specks of white making the city shudder, and quivering in pale waves over the dull-brown house-fronts. Amidst the masses of snow that girt them round the dwellings stood out black and gloomy, as though mouldy with centuries of damp. Entire streets appeared to be in ruins, as if undermined by some gunpowder explosion, with roofs ready to give way and windows already driven in. But gradually, as the belt of blue broadened in the direction of Montmartre, there came a stream of light, pure and cool as the waters of a spring; and Paris once more shone out as under a glass, which lent even to the outlying districts the distinctness of a Japanese picture.

Wrapped in her fur mantle, with her hands clinging idly to the cuffs of the sleeves, Helene was musing. With the persistency of an echo one thought unceasingly pursued her—a child, a fat, rosy daughter, had been born to them. In her imagination she could picture her at the love-compelling age when Jeanne had commenced to prattle. Baby girls are such darlings when fourteen months old! She counted the months—fourteen: that made two years when she took the remaining period into consideration—exactly the time within a fortnight. Then her brain conjured up a sunny picture of Italy, a realm of dreamland, with golden fruits where lovers wandered through the perfumed nights, with arms round one another's waists. Henri and Juliette were pacing before her eyes beneath the light of the moon. They loved as husband and wife do when passion is once more awakened within them. To think of it—a tiny girl, rosy and fat, its bare body flushed by the warm sunshine, while it strives to stammer words which its mother arrests with kisses! And Helene thought of all this without any anger; her heart was mute, yet seemingly derived yet greater quietude from the sadness of her spirit. The land of the sun had vanished from her vision; her eyes wandered slowly over Paris, on whose huge frame winter had laid his freezing hand. Above the Pantheon another patch of blue was now spreading in the heavens.

Meanwhile memory was recalling the past to life. At Marseilles she had spent her days in a state of coma. One morning as she went along the Rue des Petites-Maries, she had burst out sobbing in front of the home of her childhood. That was the last occasion on which she had wept. Monsieur Rambaud was her frequent visitor; she felt his presence near her to be a protection. Towards autumn she had one evening seen him enter, with red eyes and in the agony of a great sorrow; his brother, Abbe Jouve, was dead. In her turn she comforted him. What followed she could not recall with any exactitude of detail. The Abbe ever seemed to stand behind them, and influenced by thought of him she succumbed resignedly. When M. Rambaud once more hinted at his wish, she had nothing to say in refusal. It seemed to her that what he asked was but sensible. Of her own accord, as her period of mourning was drawing to an end, she calmly arranged all the details with him. His hands trembled in a transport of tenderness. It should be as she pleased; he had waited for months; a sign sufficed him. They were married in mourning garb. On the wedding night he, like her first husband, kissed her bare feet—feet fair as though fashioned out of marble. And thus life began once more.

While the belt of blue was broadening on the horizon, this awakening of memory came with an astounding effect on Helene. Had she lived through a year of madness, then? To-day, as she pictured the woman who had lived for nearly three years in that room in the Rue Vineuse, she imagined that she was passing judgment on some stranger, whose conduct revolted and surprised her. How fearfully foolish had been her act! how abominably wicked! Yet she had not sought it. She had been living peacefully, hidden in her nook, absorbed in the love of her daughter. Untroubled by any curious thoughts, by any desire, she had seen the road of life lying before her. But a breath had swept by, and she had fallen. Even at this moment she was unable to explain it; she had evidently ceased to be herself; another mind and heart had controlled her actions. Was it possible? She had done those things? Then an icy chill ran through her; she saw Jeanne borne away beneath roses. But in the torpor begotten of her grief she grew very calm again, once more without a longing or curiosity, once more proceeding along the path of duty that lay so straight before her. Life had again begun for her, fraught with austere peacefulness and pride of honesty.

Monsieur Rambaud now moved near her to lead her from this place of sadness. But Helene silently signed to him her wish to linger a little longer. Approaching the parapet she gazed below into the Avenue de la Muette, where a long line of old cabs in the last stage of decay stretched beside the footpath. The hoods and wheels looked blanched, the rusty horses seemed to have been rotting there since the dark ages. Some cabmen sat motionless, freezing within their frozen cloaks. Over the snow other vehicles were crawling along, one after the other, with the utmost difficulty. The animals were losing their foothold, and stretching out their necks, while their drivers with many oaths descended from their seats and held them by the bridle; and through the windows you could see the faces of the patient "fares," reclining against the cushions, and resigning themselves to the stern necessity of taking three-quarters of an hour to cover a distance which in other weather would have been accomplished in ten minutes. The rumbling of the wheels was deadened by the snow; only the voices vibrated upward, sounding shrill and distinct amidst the silence of the streets; there were loud calls, the laughing exclamations of people slipping on the icy paths, the angry whip-cracking of carters, and the snorting of terrified horses. In the distance, to the right, the lofty trees on the quay seemed to be spun of glass, like huge Venetian chandeliers, whose flower-decked arms the designer had whimsically twisted. The icy north wind had transformed the trunks into columns, over which waved downy boughs and feathery tufts, an exquisite tracery of black twigs edged with white trimmings. It was freezing, and not a breath stirred in the pure air.

Then Helene told her heart that she had known nothing of Henri. For a year she had seen him almost every day; he had lingered for hours and hours near her, to speak to her and gaze into her eyes. Yet she knew nothing of him. Whence had he come? how had he crept into her intimacy? what manner of man was he that she had yielded to him—she who would rather have perished than yield to another? She knew nothing of him; it had all sprung from some sudden tottering of her reason. He had been a stranger to her on the last as on the first day. In vain did she patch together little scattered things and circumstances—his words, his acts, everything that her memory recalled concerning him. He loved his wife and his child; he smiled with delicate grace; he outwardly appeared a well-bred man. Then she saw him again with inflamed visage, and trembling with passion. But weeks passed, and he vanished from her sight. At this moment she could not have said where she had spoken to him for the last time. He had passed away, and his shadow had gone with him. Their story had no other ending. She knew him not.

Over the city the sky had now become blue, and every cloud had vanished. Wearied with her memories, and rejoicing in the purity before her, Helene raised her head. The blue of the heavens was exquisitely clear, but still very pale in the light of the sun, which hung low on the horizon, and glittered like a silver lamp. In that icy temperature its rays shed no heat on the glittering snow. Below stretched the expanses of roofs—the tiles of the Army Bakehouse, and the slates of the houses on the quay—like sheets of white cloth fringed with black. On the other bank of the river, the square stretch of the Champ-de-Mars seemed a steppe, the black dots of the straggling vehicles making one think of sledges skimming along with tinkling bells; while the elms on the Quai d'Orsay, dwarfed by the distance, looked like crystal flowers bristling with sharp points. Through all the snow-white sea the Seine rolled its muddy waters edged by the ermine of its banks; since the evening before ice had been floating down, and you could clearly see the masses crushing against the piers of the Pont des Invalides, and vanishing swiftly beneath the arches. The bridges, growing more and more delicate with the distance, seemed like the steps of a ladder of white lace reaching as far as the sparkling walls of the Cite, above which the towers of Notre-Dame reared their snow-white crests. On the left the level plain was broken up by other peaks. The Church of Saint-Augustin, the Opera House, the Tower of Saint-Jacques, looked like mountains clad with eternal snow. Nearer at hand the pavilions of the Tuileries and the Louvre, joined together by newly erected buildings, resembled a ridge of hills with spotless summits. On the right, too, were the white tops of the Invalides, of Saint-Sulpice, and the Pantheon, the last in the dim distance, outlining against the sky a palace of fairyland with dressings of bluish marble. Not a sound broke the stillness. Grey-looking hollows revealed the presence of the streets; the public squares were like yawning crevasses. Whole lines of houses had vanished. The fronts of the neighboring dwellings alone showed distinctly with the thousand streaks of light reflected from their windows. Beyond, the expanse of snow intermingled and merged into a seeming lake, whose blue shadows blended with the blue of the sky. Huge and clear in the bright, frosty atmosphere, Paris glittered in the light of the silver sun.

Then Helene for the last time let her glance sweep over the unpitying city which also remained unknown to her. She saw it once more, tranquil and with immortal beauty amidst the snow, the same as when she had left it, the same as it had been every day for three long years. Paris to her was full of her past life. In its presence she had loved, in its presence Jeanne had died. But this companion of her every-day existence retained on its mighty face a wondrous serenity, unruffled by any emotion, as though it were but a mute witness of the laughter and the tears which the Seine seemed to roll in its flood. She had, according to her mood, endowed it with monstrous cruelty or almighty goodness. To-day she felt that she would be ever ignorant of it, in its indifference and immensity. It spread before her; it was life.

However, Monsieur Rambaud now laid a light hand on her arm to lead her away. His kindly face was troubled, and he whispered:

"Do not give yourself pain."

He divined her every thought, and this was all he could say. Madame Rambaud looked at him, and her sorrow became appeased. Her cheeks were flushed by the cold; her eyes sparkled. Her memories were already far away. Life was beginning again.

"I'm not quite certain whether I shut the big trunk properly," she exclaimed.

Monsieur Rambaud promised that he would make sure. Their train started at noon, and they had plenty of time. Some gravel was being scattered on the streets; their cab would not take an hour. But, all at once, he raised his voice:

"I believe you've forgotten the fishing-rods!" said he.

"Oh, yes; quite!" she answered, surprised and vexed at her forgetfulness. "We ought to have bought them yesterday!"

The rods in question were very handy ones, the like of which could not be purchased at Marseilles. They there owned near the sea a small country house, where they purposed spending the summer. Monsieur Rambaud looked at his watch. On their way to the railway station they would still be able to buy the rods, and could tie them up with the umbrellas. Then he led her from the place, tramping along, and taking short cuts between the graves. The cemetery was empty; only the imprint of their feet now remained on the snow. Jeanne, dead, lay alone, facing Paris, for ever and for ever.

AFTERWARD

There can be no doubt in the mind of the judicial critic that in the pages of "A Love Episode" the reader finds more of the poetical, more of the delicately artistic, more of the subtle emanation of creative and analytical genius, than in any other of Zola's works, with perhaps one exception. The masterly series of which this book is a part furnishes a well-stocked gallery of pictures by which posterity will receive vivid and adequate impressions of life in France during a certain period. There was a strain of Greek blood in Zola's veins. It would almost seem that down through the ages with this blood there had come to him a touch of that old Greek fatalism, or belief in destiny or necessity. The Greek tragedies are pervaded and permeated, steeped and dyed with this idea of relentless fate. It is called heredity, in these modern days. Heredity plus environment,—in these we find the keynote of the great productions of the leader of the "naturalistic" school of fiction.

It has been said that art, in itself, should have no moral. It has been further charged that the tendencies of some of Zola's works are hurtful. But, in the books of this master, the aberrations of vice are nowhere made attractive, or insidiously alluring. The shadow of expiation, remorse, punishment, retribution is ever present, like a death's-head at a feast. The day of reckoning comes, and bitterly do the culprits realize that the tortuous game of vice is not worth the candle. Casuistical theologians may attempt to explain away the notions of punishment in the life to come, of retribution beyond the grave. But the shallowest thinker will not deny the realities of remorse. To how many confessions, to how many suicides has it led? Of how many reformed lives has it been the mainspring? The great lecturer, John B. Gough, used to tell a story of a railway employee whose mind was overthrown by his disastrous error in misplacing a switch, and who spent his days in the mad-house repeating the phrase: "If I only had, if I only had." His was not an intentional or wilful dereliction. But in the hearts of how many repentant sinners does there not echo through life a similar mournful refrain. This lesson has been taught by Zola in more than one of his romances.

In "A Love Episode" how poignant is this expiation! In all literature there is nothing like the portrayal of the punishment of Helene Grandjean. Helene and little Jeanne are reversions of type. The old "neurosis," seen in earlier branches of the family, reappears in these characters. Readers of the series will know where it began. Poor little Jeanne, most pathetic of creations, is a study in abnormal jealousy, a jealousy which seems to be clairvoyant, full of supernatural intuitions, turning everything to suspicion, a jealousy which blights and kills. Could the memory of those weeks of anguish fade from Helene's soul? This dying of a broken heart is not merely the figment of a poet's fancy. It has happened in real life. The coming of death, save in the case of the very aged, seems, nearly always, brutally cruel, at least to those friends who survive. Parents know what it is to sit with bated breath and despairing heart beside the bed of a sinking child. Seconds seem hours, and hours weeks. The impotency to succour, the powerlessness to save, the dumb despair, the overwhelming grief, all these are sorrowful realities. How vividly are they pictured by Zola. And, added to this keenness of grief in the case of Helene Grandjean, was the sense that her fault had contributed to the illness of her daughter. Each sigh of pain was a reproach. The pallid and ever-paling cheek was a whip of scorpions, lashing the mother's naked soul. Will ethical teachers say that there is no salutary moral lesson in this vivid picture? To many it seems better than a cart-load of dull tracts or somnolent homilies. Poor, pathetic little Jeanne, lying there in the cemetery of Passy—where later was erected the real tomb of Marie Bashkirtseff, though dead she yet spoke a lesson of contrition to her mother. And though the second marriage of Helene has been styled an anti-climax, yet it is true enough to life. It does not remove the logical and artistic inference that the memory of Jeanne's sufferings lingered with ever recurring poignancy in the mother's heart.

In a few bold lines Zola sketches a living character. Take the picture of old Mere Fetu. One really feels her disagreeable presence, and is annoyed with her whining, leering, fawning, sycophancy. One almost resents her introduction into the pages of the book. There is something palpably odious about her personality. A pleasing contrast is formed by the pendant portraits of the awkward little soldier and his kitchen-sweetheart. This homely and wholesome couple one may meet any afternoon in Paris, on leave-of-absence days. Their portraits, and the delicious description of the children's party, are evidently studies from life. With such vivid verisimilitude is the latter presented that one imagines, the day after reading the book, that he has been present at the pleasant function, and has admired the fluffy darlings, in their dainty costumes, with their chubby cavaliers.

It is barely fair to an author to give him the credit of knowing something about the proper relative proportions of his characters. And so, although Dr. Deberle is somewhat shadowy, he certainly serves the author's purpose, and—well, Dr. Deberle is not the hero of "An Episode of Love." Rambaud and the good Abbe Jouve are certainly strong enough. There seems to be a touch of Dickens about them.

Cities sometimes seem to be great organisms. Each has an individuality, a specific identity, so marked, and peculiarities so especially characteristic of itself, that one might almost allow it a soul. Down through the centuries has fair Lutetia come, growing in the artistic graces, until now she stands the playground of princes and the capital of the world, even as mighty Rome among the ancients. And shall we object, because a few pages of "A Love Episode" are devoted to descriptions of Paris? Rather let us be thankful for them. These descriptions of the wonderful old city form a glorious pentatych. They are invaluable to two classes of readers, those who have visited Paris and those who have not. To the former they recall the days in which the spirit of the French metropolis seemed to possess their being and to take them under its wondrous spell. To the latter they supply hints of the majesty and attractiveness of Paris, and give some inkling of its power to please. And Zola loved his Paris as a sailor loves the sea.

www.ingramcontent.com/pod-product-compliance
Lightning Source LLC
Chambersburg PA
CBHW020843020726
47497CB00005B/1233